SHORT
STORIES
FOR
INSIGHT

SHORT STORIES FOR INSIGHT

Edited by

TERESA FERSTER GLAZIER

COLLEGE OF SAN MATEO

Harcourt, Brace & World, Inc.

NEW YORK / CHICAGO / SAN FRANCISCO / ATLANTA

ISBN: 0-15-580990-3

Library of Congress Catalog Card Number: 67-16823

Printed in the United States of America

ACKNOWLEDGMENTS

The author thanks the following publishers and copyright holders for their permission to use the selections reprinted in this book.

BRANDT & BRANDT. For "Freedom's a Hard-bought Thing" by Stephen Vincent Benét. From *Selected Works of Stephen Vincent Benét,* Holt, Rinehart and Winston, Inc. Copyright, 1940, by Stephen Vincent Benét. Reprinted by permission of Brandt & Brandt. For "Butcher Bird" by Wallace Stegner. First published in *Harper's Magazine.* Copyright, 1941, by Wallace Stegner. Reprinted by permission of Brandt & Brandt.

CHATTO & WINDUS LTD. For "The Darling." From *The Darling and Other Stories,* by Anton Chekhov, translated by Constance Garnett. By permission of Mr. David Garnett and Chatto & Windus Ltd.

DOUBLEDAY & COMPANY, INC. For "The Forks," copyright 1947 by J. F. Powers from *Prince of Darkness and Other Stories,* by J. F. Powers. Reprinted by permission of Doubleday & Company, Inc. For "The Elephant's Child" from *Just So Stories* by Rudyard Kipling. Reprinted by permission of Doubleday & Company, Inc.

E. P. DUTTON & Co., INC. For "War." From the book *The Medals and Other Stories* by Luigi Pirandello. Copyright, 1939, by E. P. Dutton & Co., Inc. Reprinted by permission of the publishers.

HARCOURT, BRACE & WORLD, INC. For "Rope." From *Flowering Judas and Other Stories*, copyright, 1930, 1935, renewed, 1958, 1963, by Katherine Anne Porter. Reprinted by permission of Harcourt, Brace & World, Inc. For "A Worn Path." Copyright, 1941, by Eudora Welty. Reprinted from her volume, A *Curtain of Green*, by permission of Harcourt, Brace & World, Inc. For "Mr. Cornelius, I Love You." Copyright, 1952, by Jessamyn West. Reprinted from her volume, *Cress Delahanty*, by permission of Harcourt, Brace & World, Inc.

HOLT, RINEHART AND WINSTON, INC. For "The Heyday of the Blood." From *Hillsboro People* by Dorothy Canfield. Copyright 1915 by Holt, Rinehart and Winston, Inc. Copyright 1943 by Dorothy Canfield Fisher. Reprinted by permission of Holt, Rinehart and Winston, Inc.

ALFRED A. KNOPF, INC. For "The Other Side of the Hedge." From *The Collected Tales of E. M. Forster*. Published 1947 by Alfred A. Knopf, Inc. Reprinted by permission.

MCINTOSH AND OTIS, INC. For "How Mr. Hogan Robbed a Bank." Copyright © 1956 by John Steinbeck. Appeared originally in *The Atlantic Monthly*. Reprinted by permission of McIntosh and Otis, Inc.

THE MACMILLAN COMPANY. For "The Darling." Reprinted by permission of the publisher from *The Darling and Other Stories*, by Anton Chekhov, translated by Constance Garnett. Copyright 1916 by The Macmillan Company, copyright renewed 1944 by Constance Garnett.

JAMES MCCONKEY. For "Houlihan's Surrender." © 1948 by James McConkey. Reprinted with permission.

HAROLD MATSON COMPANY, INC. For "How Beautiful with Shoes." Copyright 1932, and 1959 by Wilbur Daniel Steele. Reprinted by permission of the Harold Matson Company, Inc.

THE NEW YORKER. For "Then We'll Set It Right" by Robert Gorham Davis. Reprinted by permission; Copr. © 1943 by The New Yorker Magazine, Inc. For "The Code" by Richard T. Gill. Reprinted by permission; Copr. © 1957 The New Yorker Magazine, Inc.

LOUISA NEWLIN. For "Our Last Day in Venice." Copyright © 1965 by The Atlantic Monthly Company, Boston, Massachusetts. Reprinted with permission.

HAROLD OBER ASSOCIATES INCORPORATED. For "I Want to Know Why" by Sherwood Anderson. Reprinted by permission of Harold Ober Associates Incorporated. Copyright 1919 by Eleanor Anderson, copyright renewed.

CHARLES SCRIBNER'S SONS. "The Killers" (Copyright 1927 Charles Scribner's Sons; renewal copyright © 1955) is reprinted with the permission of Charles Scribner's Sons from *Men Without Women* by Ernest Hemingway. "A Mother in Mannville" (Copyright 1936 The Curtis Publishing Company; renewal copyright © 1964 Norton Baskin) is reprinted with the permission of Charles Scribner's Sons from *When the Whippoorwill——* by Marjorie Kinnan Rawlings.

SIDGWICK & JACKSON LTD. For "The Other Side of the Hedge." From *The Collected Tales of E. M. Forster*.

HELEN THURBER. For "The Catbird Seat." Copr. © 1945 James Thurber. From *The Thurber Carnival*, published by Harper & Row, Publishers, Inc. Originally printed in *The New Yorker*. For "The Secret Life of Walter Mitty." Copr. © 1942 James Thurber. From *My World—And Welcome to It*, published by Harcourt, Brace & World, Inc.

THE VIKING PRESS. For "Eveline." From *Dubliners* by James Joyce. Originally published by B. W. Huebsch, Inc. in 1916. All rights reserved. Reprinted by permission of The Viking Press, Inc.

A. P. WATT & SON. For "The Elephant's Child." From *Just So Stories* by Rudyard Kipling. Reprinted by permission of Mrs. George Bambridge and The Macmillan Company of Canada Ltd.

PREFACE

This book is based on the belief that a student can, with guidance, teach himself to analyze short stories. By keeping in mind the various elements to look for in a short story, he can develop a method of critical analysis that he can apply not only to other short stories but to all imaginative literature.

The stories—chosen for their appeal to students as well as for their literary excellence—are paired thematically and are followed by specific questions that teach the student what to look for and help him re-examine the details of a story to search out its final meaning. For the questions following the first story of each pair there are suggested answers at the back of the book so that the student may check his thinking as he studies rather than having to wait until class time to find out whether his approach is valid. The second story of each pair —with questions but no answers—leads the student to analyze independently, making use of the critical methods learned from working with previous stories.

This approach should have value for both student and instructor. The student will gradually come to have confidence in his ability to analyze a story and will find that a careful analysis, far from being burdensome, leads to understanding and enjoyment. The instructor will be freed from some of the detailed teaching of the elements of the short story and will be able to devote more class time to discussing debatable questions and to exploring the broader implications of a story's theme.

Since critical analysis is of value only as it illuminates meaning, it is hoped that the student will find these stories have something to say to him and that his study will give him insight not only into the art of the short story but into some of the complexities of life as well.

PREFACE

CONTENTS

WHAT TO LOOK FOR IN A SHORT STORY   3

EIGHT ELEMENTS OF THE SHORT STORY   4

THE YOUNGER GENERATION REBELS
The Elephant's Child   RUDYARD KIPLING   13
Our Last Day in Venice   LOUISA NEWLIN   21

LONELINESS
The Lament   ANTON CHEKHOV   31
The Darling   ANTON CHEKHOV   37

LOVE CREATES A NEW AWARENESS
How Beautiful with Shoes   WILBUR DANIEL STEELE   53
Mr. Cornelius, I Love You   JESSAMYN WEST   77

DISILLUSIONMENT
The Killers   ERNEST HEMINGWAY   95
I Want to Know Why   SHERWOOD ANDERSON   106

THE MOTIVATION IS LOVE
A Worn Path   EUDORA WELTY   119
A Mother in Mannville   MARJORIE KINNAN RAWLINGS   129

THE FAILURE TO COMMUNICATE
Butcher Bird   WALLACE STEGNER   141
Rope   KATHERINE ANNE PORTER   154

SOME ESCAPE, SOME FIGHT BACK
    The Secret Life of Walter Mitty JAMES THURBER   165
    The Catbird Seat JAMES THURBER   171

SURRENDERING TO REALITY
    The Code RICHARD T. GILL   183
    Houlihan's Surrender JAMES MC CONKEY   196

ATTITUDES TOWARD WAR
    Then We'll Set It Right ROBERT GORHAM DAVIS   213
    War LUIGI PIRANDELLO   223

HOW HONEST MUST ONE BE?
    How Mr. Hogan Robbed a Bank JOHN STEINBECK   231
    The Forks J. F. POWERS   241

A QUESTION OF VALUES
    The Other Side of the Hedge E. M. FORSTER   259
    The Heyday of the Blood DOROTHY CANFIELD FISHER   267

THE STRUGGLE FOR FREEDOM
    Eveline JAMES JOYCE   281
    Freedom's a Hard-bought Thing STEPHEN VINCENT BENÉT   288

REVIEW QUESTIONS   303

SUGGESTED ANSWERS TO QUESTIONS   305

BIOGRAPHICAL NOTES   331

ALTERNATE TABLE OF

CONTENTS

ACCORDING TO THE ELEMENTS
OF THE SHORT STORY

CONFLICT

RUDYARD KIPLING   *The Elephant's Child*   13
LOUISA NEWLIN   *Our Last Day in Venice*   21
JAMES THURBER   *The Catbird Seat*   171

POINT OF VIEW

SHERWOOD ANDERSON   *I Want to Know Why*   106
KATHERINE ANNE PORTER   *Rope*   154
DOROTHY CANFIELD FISHER   *The Heyday of the Blood*   267

SETTING

JESSAMYN WEST   *Mr. Cornelius, I Love You*   77
WALLACE STEGNER   *Butcher Bird*   141
JAMES JOYCE   *Eveline*   281

CHARACTER

ANTON CHEKHOV   *The Darling*   37
WILBUR DANIEL STEELE   *How Beautiful with Shoes*   53
MARJORIE KINNAN RAWLINGS   *A Mother in Mannville*   129

THEME

ANTON CHEKHOV   *The Lament*   31
RICHARD T. GILL   *The Code*   183
ROBERT GORHAM DAVIS   *Then We'll Set It Right*   213

STYLE

ERNEST HEMINGWAY   *The Killers*   95

EUDORA WELTY   *A Worn Path*   119

JAMES THURBER   *The Secret Life of Walter Mitty*   165

IRONY

JAMES MC CONKEY   *Houlihan's Surrender*   196

LUIGI PIRANDELLO   *War*   223

JOHN STEINBECK   *How Mr. Hogan Robbed a Bank*   231

SYMBOLISM

J. F. POWERS   *The Forks*   241

E. M. FORSTER   *The Other Side of the Hedge*   259

STEPHEN VINCENT BENÉT   *Freedom's a Hard-bought Thing*   288

SHORT STORIES FOR INSIGHT

WHAT TO LOOK FOR IN A SHORT STORY

Most short stories give pleasure in the reading. But some stories do more than that. Besides giving pleasure, they give the reader a moment of insight into some aspect of life or human nature. They make him pause, ponder, evaluate—not only the story but perhaps his own life as well. Instead of encouraging him to run away from life—as escape stories do—they help him to delve deeper into its meaning.

Such stories of insight are thus obviously not for speed reading. In fact, the better the story the more it is enhanced by thoughtful reading and rereading. One test of the excellence of a short story is whether it can be read a second or even a third time with enjoyment.

A story of insight is a small work of art and, like a painting by Picasso or a symphony by Beethoven, deserves more than casual consideration. Appreciation of a painting is heightened by an awareness of its composition, its color scheme, its technique; the pleasure of listening to a symphony grows with an understanding of its form, its instrumentation, its motifs; similarly the enjoyment of a short story increases with the discovery of its conflict, its theme, its irony, its symbols.

A first reading will not reveal—even to the experienced reader—all the elements that combine to make the story a work of art. When you read the last word of a story you have really just *begun* your reading. You must pause, reflect, reread—until you see more than just "what happens," until you comprehend some of the subtle meanings and discover what the author is saying, for each story was written because the author had something to say, some observation to make, that he felt he could express best in a short story.

Frequently a student says, "When I read a story by myself, I just don't get it. Then when it's discussed in class, it becomes perfectly clear, and I wonder why I didn't get the meaning in the first place."

This book is designed to help you "get the meaning in the first place."

In each pair of stories, the first one is followed by questions to help you learn what to look for and, in the back of the book, suggested answers so that you may check your thinking. You may not even need to refer to the answers, but if you do, remember that as in mathematics the important thing is not the answer but learning how to find the answer. In short, the purpose of this book is to help you learn to analyze stories for yourself. Therefore the second story of each pair has questions only, so that you may work out your answers without help.

Even in the stories with suggested answers, there is still much room for discussion. You will probably not agree with all the answers, and you will find that, far from exhausting the meaning of a story, they merely *begin* to interpret it. After you have discovered what the author is saying, you will then want to relate his theme to life and argue its validity.

Learning to get the most out of these twenty-four stories should help you develop a technique of reading that will enable you to read other stories—and in fact *all* imaginative literature—more perceptively.

EIGHT ELEMENTS OF THE SHORT STORY

*B*efore starting to read the stories, you should become familiar with the following eight basic elements. They are not the only elements that will be found in short stories, nor will all of them be found in every story, but they are good ones to begin with.

1. CONFLICT

Conflict is an essential element in almost every short story. When life goes along smoothly there is little material for a story, but the moment a conflict arises there is something to write about. The conflict may be the struggle of man against man, man against society, man against his environment, or man against himself. It may be a physical conflict, or it may be a conflict entirely within a character's mind, but it is always a struggle between the central character and some opposing force. For example, a boy may be in conflict with his parents, with the code of morals in his town, with hostile surroundings, or with his conscience. He may have a physical conflict with a bully or a mental conflict caused by a feeling of inferiority. To identify the conflict, the reader should ask, "What is the main character struggling against?"

Whatever the conflict, it produces the action of the story. Unlike action in life, action in a story is selective. The author carefully chooses and arranges events in a way that will most effectively express what he wishes to say. Whereas the reader might fail to see a meaning in the myriad events of real life, he is led to do so when particular events are selected and arranged in a story.

The solution of the conflict—whether the central character overcomes the opposing force or submits to it—is of great significance. But the mature reader evaluates the ending of a story not by whether it is happy or unhappy but by whether it is convincing, whether it seems to be the only credible ending for this particular situation and these particular characters.

2. POINT OF VIEW

It is often important to be aware of the point of view from which a story is told, that is, who is telling it and how much he knows about it. Although many variations are possible, there are four basic points of view. The author may write the story as if it is being told by:

An *all-knowing narrator*, who is like a god looking down from above. He knows everything about all the characters, even their thoughts, and he may also make judgments about them. The narrator of "Our Last Day in Venice," for example, reports not only the action of the story but the thoughts of both the mother and the daughter.

A *limited all-knowing narrator*, who is all-knowing about one character only. He reports everything through the eyes and thoughts of that one character. In "Butcher Bird," for example, all the characters and events are described as they appear to the little boy; and "Eveline" is almost entirely an account of what goes on in Eveline's mind.

A *character* in the story, who tells his own story or one he has participated in. (This point of view uses "I" whereas the *limited all-knowing narrator* uses "he" or "she.") This method has the advantage of making the story seem authentic but also the disadvantage of allowing no direct description of the storyteller. In "I Want to Know Why," for example, the author cannot describe the sensitivity and thoughtfulness of the boy except through the boy's own words.

An *observer*, who tells the story as if he were seeing it on a stage. He reports what he sees and hears but nothing more; he cannot look within the minds of the characters or make judgments about them. "The Killers," for example, is told in three scenes almost like a play.

In telling a particular story, the author chooses the point of view that will allow him to tell his story most effectively.

3. SETTING

The setting of a story is where and when it takes place—the locale, the social environment, the period. Even the atmosphere, which creates the mood of the story, may be considered part of the setting.

The setting may be important to the development of the story, influencing the characters and determining the action. "Eveline," for example, though it deals with a universal problem, could not take place anywhere but in Dublin. Elsewhere it would be a different story. Similarly "A Worn Path" depends heavily on the Mississippi countryside for its effect.

On the other hand, the setting may be unimportant and may have no particular effect upon the characters or the action. "The Secret Life of Walter Mitty" could take place in California or in Canada as well as in Connecticut. And "Rope" has no more specific setting than "the country," implying that it could take place anywhere.

4. CHARACTER

Unlike a novel, which has many characters, a short story usually centers chiefly on one character. He may be a *type character* with little to distinguish him from the rest of his group and may, in fact, stand for his group. The Elephant's Child stands for curious children in general. Or he may be an *individual character*, as complex and contradictory as a person in real life. The husband in "Butcher Bird" is a hard-working, capable farmer who is kind to his family upon occasion but is generally negative and resentful.

Sometimes an author chooses a type character to suggest that the character is universal—the middleclass good provider Mr. Hogan, for example—but whether the character is a type or an individual there is always something of the universal about him. The reader may say of any well-drawn character, "I know someone just like that."

A character may remain the same at the end of the story as he was at the beginning, or he may, and more often does, change or achieve a new insight as a result of the conflict he has experienced.

Often it is easier to understand short story characters than it is to understand real people because the author is able to choose certain characteristics to emphasize, just as he chooses and arranges events. Actually, after analyzing a number of characters in short stories, the reader may find it easier to understand people in real life.

5. THEME

When an author writes a story it is because he has something to say, some observation to make about life or human nature.[1] He may want to express such an idea as "Curiosity is a good thing" or "The older and younger generations clash" or "Man lives a lonely life" or "Modern man has lost his sense of right and wrong" or any other idea that he feels is important. By writing about a specific character and situation he can present an idea that will apply to many people and many situations. That is, through his story he makes a generalization—a statement he regards as generally true in life—and this generalization, called the theme, gives the story its meaning.

While the theme is seldom stated directly, the thoughtful reader should be able to discover it and to express it in a single sentence. It

[1] Some stories, such as Westerns, mysteries, and many popular magazine stories, are written purely for entertainment, but they do not require more than casual reading and are not considered here.

is, of course, possible to state the theme in more than one way, and occasionally there are minor themes as well as the major one; but in general the central theme of a well-written short story should be fairly obvious. Noting how the author resolves the conflict will usually lead to a discovery of the theme.

Once he has discovered the theme, the reader will notice aspects of the story he may have missed before, and he will see how each incident adds to the total meaning, how each element makes the theme vivid and memorable. In short, the discovery of the theme will illuminate the entire story.

If the theme has been effectively brought out, the reader should have gained, as he finishes the story, a new awareness of some phase of life or an insight into some aspect of human nature—and perhaps an insight into his own life also. He will be inclined to think, "How true that is. That's just the way life goes." Thus the theme will hold true not only for the characters in the story but for many readers as well. It will have what is called universal appeal.

6. STYLE

Style is an author's characteristic way of expressing himself in language. Style is *how* he says what he has to say. It includes the choice of words, the sound of words, the structure and rhythm of sentences, the use of figures of speech.

The most frequently used figure of speech, the metaphor, should be noted particularly because it adds much to the picturesque quality of language. (The simile, even though there is a slight distinction, is here classed as a metaphor.) The metaphor compares two unlike things: ". . . the moss hung as white as lace from every limb" or ". . . the door to the office blew open with the suddenness of a gas-main explosion" or ". . . Cue's mammy and daddy were gone like last year's crop." Sometimes a metaphor is merely implied: "Monsignor . . . had broken wild curates before, plenty of them, and . . . he would ride again." The author here is comparing the priest to a cowboy breaking horses.

Frequently the style of writing—how the story is told—is quite as important as what is told. In "A Worn Path" the precise metaphors and the simple turns of speech add to the characterization of old Phoenix, and in "The Killers" the blunt, spare style underscores the action. A careful consideration of the distinctive qualities of an author's style will add to the reader's understanding and appreciation of a story.

7. IRONY

Irony is frequently an important element in a short story—either *verbal irony*, in which the speaker means the opposite of what he says, or the *irony of situation*, in which the situation or action is the opposite of what one would expect. *Verbal irony* is used in "Rope" when the wife, annoyed by her husband's buying a coil of rope, says, "Undoubtedly it would be useful, twenty-four yards of rope. . . ." She obviously means exactly the opposite. The *irony of situation* is found in "Houlihan's Surrender" when, just as Houlihan has achieved his lifelong desire for independence, fate makes him completely dependent again.

An understanding of the irony within a story may aid in discovering the theme since the ironic contrast often brings out the author's meaning.

8. SYMBOLISM

Authors often use symbols to make their writing more meaningful. A symbol is something that stands for something else: a flag for a country, a cross for Christianity, a dollar sign for money, Uncle Sam for the United States. Such symbols are recognized by everyone.

In literature, however, symbols are not always so easy to recognize because an author may choose to let something stand for something else in just one particular story. For example, a traveler on a narrow, dusty road may stand for mankind journeying through life; an odor of dusty cretonne may stand for a dull, stifling existence; a boiling pot may stand for the boiling unrest of the slaves. A symbol is both itself and something deeper than itself; it is the repeated use of some word, object, place, or person that has special significance. Symbols are used extensively in "The Other Side of the Hedge," "Eveline," and "Freedom's a Hard-bought Thing." The perceptive reader will watch for symbols and for the greater depth of meaning that they suggest.

The various elements of the short story are, of course, interdependent, and it is really necessary for the reader to be aware of all of them at the same time. The first story in this collection, "The Elephant's Child," contains seven of these elements in very simple form, thus providing examples of what to look for in the more complex stories that follow.

THE YOUNGER GENERATION REBELS

THE ELEPHANT'S CHILD
RUDYARD KIPLING

In the High and Far-Off Times the Elephant, O Best Beloved had no trunk. He had only a blackish, bulgy nose, as big as a boot, that he could wriggle about from side to side; but he couldn't pick up things with it. But there was one Elephant—a new Elephant—an Elephant's Child—who was full of 'satiable curtiosity, and that means he asked ever so many questions. *And* he lived in Africa, and he filled all Africa with his 'satiable curtiosities. He asked his tall aunt, the Ostrich, why her tail-feathers grew just so, and his tall aunt, the Ostrich, spanked him with her hard, hard claw. He asked his tall uncle, the Giraffe, what made his skin spotty, and his tall uncle, the Giraffe, spanked him with his hard, hard hoof. And still he was full of 'satiable curtiosity! He asked his broad aunt, the Hippopotamus, why her eyes were red, and his broad aunt, the Hippopotamus, spanked him with her broad, broad hoof; and he asked his hairy uncle, the Baboon, why melons tasted just so, and his hairy uncle, the Baboon, spanked him with his hairy, hairy paw. And *still* he was full of 'satiable curtiosity! He asked questions about everything that he saw, or heard, or felt, or smelt, or touched, and all his uncles and his aunts spanked him. And still he was full of 'satiable curtiosity!

One fine morning in the middle of the Precession of the Equinoxes this 'satiable Elephant's Child asked a new fine question that he had never asked before. He asked, "What does the Crocodile have for dinner?" Then everybody said, "Hush!" in a loud and dretful tone, and they spanked him immediately and directly, without stopping, for a long time.

By and by, when that was finished, he came upon Kolokolo Bird sitting in the middle of a wait-a-bit thorn-bush, and he said, "My father has spanked me, and my mother has spanked me; all my aunts and uncles have spanked me for my 'satiable curtiosity; and *still* I want to know what the Crocodile has for dinner!"

Then Kolokolo Bird said, with a mournful cry, "Go to the banks of the great grey-green greasy Limpopo River, all set about with fever-trees, and find out."

That very next morning, when there was nothing left of the Equinoxes, because the Precession had preceded according to precedent, this 'satiable Elephant's Child took a hundred pounds of bananas (the little short red kind), and a hundred pounds of sugar-cane (the long purple kind), and seventeen melons (the greeny-crackly kind), and said to all his dear families, "Good-bye. I am going to the great grey-green, greasy Limpopo River, all set about with fever-trees, to find out what the Crocodile has for dinner." And they all spanked him once more for luck, though he asked them most politely to stop.

Then he went away, a little warm, but not at all astonished, eating melons, and throwing the rind about, because he could not pick it up.

He went from Graham's Town to Kimberley, and from Kimberley to Khama's Country, and from Khama's Country he went east by north, eating melons all the time, till at last he came to the banks of the great grey-green, greasy Limpopo River, all set about with fever-trees, precisely as Kolokolo Bird had said.

Now you must know and understand, O Best Beloved, that till that very week, and day, and hour, and minute, this 'satiable Elephant's Child had never seen a Crocodile, and did not know what one was like. It was all his 'satiable curtiosity.

The first thing that he found was a Bi-Coloured-Python-Rock-Snake curled round a rock.

" 'Scuse me," said the Elephant's Child most politely, "but have you seen such a thing as a Crocodile in these promiscuous parts?"

"*Have* I seen a Crocodile?" said the Bi-Coloured-Python-Rock-Snake, in a voice of dretful scorn. "What will you ask me next?"

" 'Scuse me," said the Elephant's Child, "but could you kindly tell me what he has for dinner?"

Then the Bi-Coloured-Python-Rock-Snake uncoiled himself very quickly from the rock, and spanked the Elephant's Child with his scalesome, flailsome tail.

"That is odd," said the Elephant's Child, "because my father and my mother, and my uncle and my aunt, not to mention my other aunt, the Hippopotamus, and my other uncle, the Baboon, have all spanked me for my 'satiable curtiosity—and I suppose this is the same thing."

So he said good-bye very politely to the Bi-Coloured-Python-Rock-Snake, and helped to coil him up on the rock again, and went on, a little warm, but not at all astonished, eating melons, and throwing the rind about, because he could not pick it up, till he trod on what he thought was a log of wood at the very edge of the great grey-green, greasy Limpopo River, all set about with fever-trees.

But it was really the Crocodile, O Best Beloved, and the Crocodile winked one eye—like this!

" 'Scuse me," said the Elephant's Child most politely, "but do you happen to have seen a Crocodile in these promiscuous parts?"

Then the Crocodile winked the other eye, and lifted half his tail out of the mud; and the Elephant's Child stepped back most politely, beeause he did not wish to be spanked again.

"Come hither, Little One," said the Crocodile. "Why do you ask such things?"

" 'Scuse me," said the Elephant's Child most politely, "but my father has spanked me, my mother has spanked me, not to mention my tall aunt, the Ostrich, and my tall uncle, the Giraffe, who can kick ever so hard, as well as my broad aunt, the Hippopotamus, and my hairy uncle, the Baboon, *and* including the Bi-Coloured-Python-Rock-Snake, with the scalesome, flailsome tail, just up the bank, who spanks harder than any of them; and *so*, if it's quite all the same to you, I don't want to be spanked any more."

"Come hither, Little One," said the Crocodile, "for I am the Crocodile," and he wept crocodile-tears to show it was quite true.

Then the Elephant's Child grew all breathless, and panted, and kneeled down on the bank and said, "You are the very person I have been looking for all these long days. Will you please tell me what you have for dinner?"

"Come hither, Little One," said the Crocodile, "and I'll whisper."

Then the Elephant's Child put his head down close to the Crocodile's musky, tusky mouth, and the Crocodile caught him by his little nose, which up to that very week, day, hour, and minute, had been no bigger than a boot, though much more useful.

"I think," said the Crocodile—and he said it between his teeth, like this—"I think to-day I will begin with Elephant's Child!"

At this, O Best Beloved, the Elephant's Child was much annoyed, and he said, speaking through his nose, like this, "Led go! You are hurtig be!"

Then the Bi-Coloured-Python-Rock-Snake scuffled down from the bank and said, "My young friend, if you do not now, immediately and instantly, pull as hard as ever you can, it is my opinion that your acquaintance in the large-pattern leather ulster" (and by this he meant the Crocodile) "will jerk you into yonder limpid stream before you can say Jack Robinson."

This is the way Bi-Coloured-Python-Rock-Snakes always talk.

Then the Elephant's Child sat back on his little haunches, and pulled, and pulled, and pulled, and his nose began to stretch. And the Crocodile floundered into the water, making it all creamy with great sweeps of his tale, and *he* pulled, and pulled, and pulled.

And the Elephant's Child's nose kept on stretching; and the Elephant's Child spread all his little four legs and pulled, and pulled, and pulled, and his nose kept on stretching; and the Crocodile threshed his tail like an oar, and *he* pulled, and pulled, and pulled, and at each pull the Elephant's Child's nose grew longer and longer —and it hurt him hijjus!

Then the Elephant's Child felt his legs slipping, and he said through his nose, which was now nearly five feet long, "This is too butch for be!"

Then the Bi-Coloured-Python-Rock-Snake came down from the bank, and knotted himself in a double-clove-hitch round the Elephant's Child's hind legs, and said, "Rash and inexperienced traveller, we will now seriously devote ourselves to a little high tension, because if we do not, it is my impression that yonder self-propelling man-of-war with the armour-plated upper deck" (and by this, O Best Beloved, he meant the Crocodile) "will permanently vitiate your future career."

That is the way all Bi-Coloured-Python-Rock-Snakes always talk.

So he pulled, and the Elephant's Child pulled, and the Crocodile pulled; but the Elephant's Child and the Bi-Coloured-Python-Rock-Snake pulled hardest; and at last the Crocodile let go of the Elephant's

Child's nose with a plop that you could hear all up and down the Limpopo.

Then the Elephant's Child sat down most hard and sudden; but first he was careful to say "Thank you" to the Bi-Coloured-Python-Rock-Snake; and next he was kind to his poor pulled nose, and wrapped it all up in cool banana leaves, and hung it in the great grey-green, greasy Limpopo to cool.

"What are you doing that for?" said the Bi-Coloured-Python-Rock-Snake.

" 'Scuse me," said the Elephant's Child, "but my nose is badly out of shape, and I am waiting for it to shrink."

"Then you will have to wait a long time," said the Bi-Coloured-Python-Rock-Snake. "Some people do not know what is good for them."

The Elephant's Child sat there for three days waiting for his nose to shrink. But it never grew any shorter, and, besides, it made him squint. For, O Best Beloved, you will see and understand that the Crocodile had pulled it out into a really truly trunk same as all Elephants have to-day.

At the end of the third day a fly came and stung him on the shoulder, and before he knew what he was doing he lifted up his trunk and hit that fly dead with the end of it.

" 'Vantage number one!" said the Bi-Coloured-Python-Rock-Snake. "You couldn't have done that with a mere-smear nose. Try and eat a little now."

Before he thought what he was doing the Elephant's Child put out his trunk and plucked a large bundle of grass, dusted it clean against his fore legs, and stuffed it into his own mouth.

" 'Vantage number two!" said the Bi-Coloured-Python-Rock-Snake. "You couldn't have done that with a mere-smear nose. Don't you think the sun is very hot here?"

"It is," said the Elephant's Child, and before he thought what he was doing he schlooped up a schloop of mud from the banks of the great grey-green, greasy Limpopo, and slapped it on his head, where it made a cool schloopy-sloshy mud-cap all trickly behind his ears.

" 'Vantage number three!" said the Bi-Coloured-Python-Rock-Snake. "You couldn't have done that with a mere-smear nose. Now how do you feel about being spanked again?"

" 'Scuse me," said the Elephant's Child, "but I should not like it at all."

"How would you like to spank somebody?" said the Bi-Coloured-Python-Rock-Snake.

"I should like it very much indeed," said the Elephant's Child.

"Well," said the Bi-Coloured-Python-Rock-Snake, "you will find that new nose of yours very useful to spank people with."

"Thank you," said the Elephant's Child, "I'll remember that; and now I think I'll go home to all my dear families and try."

So the Elephant's Child went home across Africa frisking and whisking his trunk. When he wanted fruit to eat he pulled fruit down from a tree, instead of waiting for it to fall as he used to do. When he wanted grass he plucked grass up from the ground, instead of going on his knees as he used to do. When the flies bit him he broke off the branch of a tree and used it as a fly-whisk; and he made himself a new, cool, slushy-squshy mud-cap whenever the sun was hot. When he felt lonely walking through Africa he sang to himself down his trunk, and the noise was louder than several brass bands. He went especially out of his way to find a broad Hippopotamus (she was no relation of his), and he spanked her very hard, to make sure that the Bi-Coloured-Python-Rock-Snake had spoken the truth about his new trunk. The rest of the time he picked up the melon rinds that he had dropped on his way to the Limpopo—for he was a Tidy Pachyderm.

One dark evening he came back to all his dear families, and he coiled up his trunk and said, "How do you do?" They were very glad to see him, and immediately said, "Come here and be spanked for your 'satiable curiosity."

"Pooh," said the Elephant's Child. "I don't think you peoples know anything about spanking; but I do, and I'll show you."

Then he uncurled his trunk and knocked two of his dear brothers head over heels.

"O Bananas!" said they, "where did you learn that trick, and what have you done to your nose?"

"I got a new one from the Crocodile on the banks of the great grey-green, greasy Limpopo River," said the Elephant's Child. "I asked him what he had for dinner, and he gave me this to keep."

"It looks very ugly," said his hairy uncle, the Baboon.

"It does," said the Elephant's Child. "But it's very useful," and he picked up his hairy uncle, the Baboon, by one hairy leg, and hove him into a hornet's nest.

Then that bad Elephant's Child spanked all his dear families for a long time, till they were very warm and greatly astonished. He pulled out his tall Ostrich aunt's tail-feathers; and he caught his tall uncle, the Giraffe, by the hind leg, and dragged him through a thorn-bush; and he shouted at his broad aunt, the Hippopotamus, and blew bubbles into her ear when she was sleeping in the water after meals; but he never let anyone touch Kolokolo Bird.

At last things grew so exciting that his dear families went off one by one in a hurry to the banks of the great grey-green, greasy Limpopo River, all set about with fever-trees, to borrow new noses from the Crocodile. When they came back nobody spanked anybody any more; and ever since that day, O Best Beloved, all the Elephants you will ever see, besides all those that you won't, have trunks precisely like the trunk of the 'satiable Elephant's Child.

QUESTIONS

"The Elephant's Child" is a story which, like *Alice in Wonderland* and *Winnie-the-Pooh*, was written originally for children but has been enjoyed quite as much by adults. It is placed first in this collection because it illustrates in the simplest possible form seven elements of the short story.

1. Look again at the section on *Conflict* (p. 4) and then define the simple conflict in this story, a conflict which divides the characters into two sides—essentially the "good guys" and the "bad guys."

2. Who is telling the story and to whom? (See *Point of View*, p. 5.) Is the listener important?

3. Is the setting essential to the story? (See *Setting*, p. 6.)

4. Are the characters types or individuals? (See *Character*, p. 6.)

5. Look again at the section on *Theme* (p. 7) and formulate the theme of this story. What is Kipling saying about children and grownups? About nonconformists and conservatives?

6. What irony is found in the ending? (See *Irony*, p. 9.)

7. Since the conflict is so very simple, it must then be the way the story is told, the style, which makes it interesting to adults. What are the stylistic devices which make this distinctly Kipling's writing rather than just any author's writing? (See *Style*, p. 8.)

8. This is one of two short stories in this collection (the other is "Freedom's a Hard-Bought Thing") that will be more fully enjoyed if read aloud. Try reading it aloud—preferably to a small child —to get the full effect of the rhythm, the word choice, the humor.

OUR LAST DAY IN VENICE
LOUISA NEWLIN

Mrs. Brownell and her daughter, Felicity, were sitting at a table outside the expensive café in the Piazza San Marco, waiting for Felicity's husband to come back from the Giorgione exhibition. They did not look at all alike, nor did they even seem acquainted until they began to talk; they had the air of strangers sitting in the last two chairs, in accidental and uncomfortable juxtaposition.

"Look at this light," Mrs. Brownell said breathlessly. "Is it like this in Rome in the evenings?"

"M*m*," said Felicity. "Well, it's gold like this, anyhow. But it's softer, somehow—here you have all the glittering of the water. Peter could describe it better than I. I guess it's really quite different."

Mrs. Brownell sighed. "I wish we could go to Florence, and to Rome, and maybe even to Naples. I wanted to come to Rome and see your room, and meet your friends, so that I'd be able to picture you, but your father said Venice was the farthest south he'd go in August." Mr. Brownell was back at the hotel taking a nap after a late lunch on a sunny terrace. "There are things in Florence I've wanted to see since I was fifteen and took history of art at boarding school." She sat up straight, drew a deep breath, and smiled; she was determined that this trip was going to be fun. "But this is lovely, lovely," she said. "Look at San Marco, Felicity—just look at it! Have you ever seen anything like it?"

Felicity turned her head and looked obligingly at San Marco. Some bad moments had come dangerously close during the three days her parents had been here, and she wanted this last day to go well. "No," she said truthfully, "I never have. There *is* nothing like it."

Mrs. Brownell seized on this. "I really feel, Felicity, that you and I have something I never had with my mother—a real intellectual companionship." Mrs. Brownell made this statement often, and always as though she were saying it for the first time.

Felicity smiled politely and shifted uneasily in her chair. "Yes," she said.

"A daughter's a daughter the rest of her life," Mrs. Brownell said hopefully, as though she did not really believe it but thought that saying it might make it true. To state things in a positive way was safer than to pose questions.

Felicity smiled politely again and patted her mother's hand. "I'd like a gelati," she said. "A gelati with chocolate sauce. Do you mind? Would you like one too?"

"Of course I don't mind, darling," said Mrs. Brownell. "I really couldn't, not after the pastry at lunch. But you go right ahead—you're still too thin, missy."

"Too thin for what?" Felicity could not help feeling annoyed. She had been told too often by her mother and grandmother that she was too thin, and that her hair was too long.

"Oh, now, Felicity," her mother said hastily, "don't be so prickly. I just think you'd feel so much better if you weighed five or ten pounds more." Mrs. Brownell remembered saying confidently just before Felicity's wedding that she was sure the girl would put on weight once she was married; she would blossom like a rose, she had told her daughter joyously.

"I feel fine," Felicity said, getting up. "I'm going to get my gelati —we'll never get that waiter back."

Mrs. Brownell watched her as she moved between the tables, as quickly as though she were following a path. She wished Felicity would not wear those brown thong sandals all the time. She knew Venice was informal—she herself was not wearing a hat—and she did not mind so much Felicity's pale lips—Peter did not like lipstick—or that awful black jersey blouse she seemed to be so fond of, but she did mind dusty feet and dirty toenails. However, she had tried very hard not to criticize and to be grateful that at least the young couple had consented to stay with them at the Gritti Palace, at Mr. Brownell's expense.

Felicity came back, carrying the dish of gelati in one hand and a new cup of coffee in the other. "Oh, dear—" said Mrs. Brownell, and then decided not to finish.

"What's the matter?" Felicity asked. "I bet it's the coffee."

Her mother nodded. "Look, Mother," said Felicity, "I'm twenty-two years old, and it's up to me to decide how much coffee and how many cigarettes are good for me. Do I *look* sick?"

Mrs. Brownell had to admit that she did not. In fact, Felicity had become so brown during the last year that her skin was beginning to look almost leathery, but this was somethng else Mrs. Brownell had decided not to mention. "I guess one never stops trying to bring up one's children," she said.

"I guess not." Felicity drank some of her coffee. "What time is it getting to be? Peter ought to be back pretty soon."

Mrs. Brownell looked at her watch. "It's only four thirty," she said. "He won't be back until at least five, do you think?" She had looked forward to this afternoon alone with her daughter; when Peter was with them, Felicity seemed to withdraw from her completely to join her husband in his moody silences. "If he goes to get a haircut, he'll be even later," she added, then immediately wished she had left that alone; she knew perfectly well that this was not at all likely.

Felicity laughed. "Dear Mother, I doubt it very much. But admit he's been good—he's worn a white shirt and a tie to dinner every single night."

Mrs. Brownell, with a great effort, restrained herself from remarking that it had been the *same* white shirt. "It's a complete mystery to me why a boy who went to Exeter wouldn't *want* to wear a tie," she said.

Felicity shrugged her shoulders. "When in Rome."

Mrs. Brownell tried to smile understandingly. She changed the subject. "I can't wait till you're in your own little house with all your nice things around you," she said.

Felicity looked startled. "What little house?" she asked suspiciously.

"Oh, just a little house, any little house. Your first home. I don't mean in Willow Grove, necessarily; it's good for young people to start out someplace new."

"But we are in our first home," said Felicity. "Our room in the *pensione* is home."

"Oh, not really your first home," Mrs. Brownell said. "You don't have any of your wedding presents with you, or your grandmother's furniture, or anything."

"Good heavens," said Felicity. "Our wedding presents. My God —excuse me, Mother—my gosh, I'd forgotten all about them. They're still in the attic, aren't they?" She almost wondered aloud if they could be sold, but stopped herself in time.

"Of course they're in the attic. Of course you haven't forgotten them," Mrs. Brownell said crossly. "You've got some perfectly lovely things. I only wish Peter hadn't made you take so many of them back."

"We'll use up the credit someday," Felicity said, and thought that, after all, they could probably use the credit to send wedding presents to other people. As for the ones they had kept, she dimly remembered row upon row of glasses—monogrammed highball glasses, glasses with ducks on them, oldfashioned glasses decorated with the Exeter emblem—and stacks of plates depicting scenes of Old New York, Audubon bird plates, square plates, freeform plates, casserole dishes, martini pitchers, water pitchers, milk pitchers, candy dishes, compotes, silver serving spoons. . . .

"Most of those stores like you to use up credit within a year," Mrs. Brownell said, and then as casually as she could, "When are you coming back, by the way? Your father and I were hoping that maybe by Christmas——"

"I doubt we'll be back for Christmas, Mother," said Felicity, trying to be gentle. "I hate to disappoint you. I suppose it's possible, but it really depends on how Peter's work is going. He's just beginning to feel he's actually putting on canvas what he wants to put there."

Mrs. Brownell sighed. Felicity knew that her parents were unable to consider painting as work, and she braced herself in case her mother should ask again, "But what does Peter plan to *do*?"

"You do realize," Mrs. Brownell started, squinting at a flock of pigeons which had risen abruptly into the air without apparent motivation, "you do realize that Peter's best chance for a good job is back where he has roots. Oh, I know you're going to say roots don't mean anything anymore, but as far as getting started goes, they do, believe me."

Felicity did not know what, if anything, she ought to say at this point. She and her brother, Harry, had discovered quite early that the easiest way to get along with their mother was to speak as little as possible. She remained silent.

Mrs. Brownell stopped pretending to watch the pigeons and leaned closer. "Felicity, do you mind if I ask you something?"

Felicity looked up at the campanile. She tilted her head way back, and by half focusing on moving clouds, indulged in the optical illusion that the building was falling, a game she and Harry had played as children. "Not at all," she said. "Go right ahead."

"Look at me when I'm talking to you, Felicity," her mother said sharply.

Felicity jerked her head forward obediently, blinking at the purple dots she saw swimming before her. Mrs. Brownell dropped her voice to a significant whisper: "How are things?"

Felicity squirmed. "I'm not pregnant, if that's what you mean."

"I don't really mean that, though you ought to realize what a wonderful cementer children are. What I mean is, are things all right? Is Peter a good husband?"

"Of course he's a good husband," said Felicity, blushing. "We don't need any cement."

"I don't understand why you won't be frank with me," said her mother. "I've always tried so hard to be frank with you about things and discussed things with you openly." Felicity's face was still pink, and Mrs. Brownell changed her tack; perhaps the reason her daughter would not respond was that there *was* some trouble. "I want you to know that you can confide in me," she said eagerly. "I never felt I could confide in my mother."

"Everything is just fine, Mother," Felicity said impatiently, and thought to herself, finer than you'll ever know. "It's just that there are certain things too private to hash over with anyone. And if you're worried about children—well, we just don't want any right now. I promise you we'll have some someday."

"Harry was born eleven months after we were married," Mrs. Brownell said. "But things are different these days, I suppose." Her voice was getting louder. "I may not have any close friends who are artists, but I know several musicians, and I know all about that sort of people. They may be very interesting and creative, but they don't make very good husbands and wives, believe me."

"Peter–is–a–wonderful–husband," Felicity said, enunciating each word firmly.

Mrs. Brownell went on talking as though she had not heard. "I knew we shouldn't have let you go away to that college. It was too far away. I knew it was too far away. My parents wouldn't even let me go to the Curtis Institute of Music, right in the same city, and I wanted to so badly, but it was good for me. It's good for people to have to make sacrifices to please other people." She paused, but Felicity did not look up. "I tried to keep up with you when you went away to college. I tried so hard to read Wallace Stevens and those other people you kept talking about when you came back." Her voice was quivering, and some people at nearby tables turned to look dispassionately at her. She tried to bring her voice into control. "You must think of your father's feelings, too," she said. "Your father's feelings are hurt that after everything he's done for us, you don't seem to respect what he's done in his business, or appreciate the nice things he's given you. What's wrong with you and Peter that you can't accept nice things?"

Felicity, who had hoped desperately that they were not in for a real scene, now prayed that at least the tears standing ready in her mother's eyes would not spill out. "Mother," she said helplessly, "we don't *want* nice things."

"What do you want then?" Mrs. Brownell cried shrilly.

Felicity put her face in her hands. "I don't know what we want," she said, trying to be patient. "It hasn't anything to do with hurting you. Right now we just don't know what we want. Maybe if we get rid of everything we don't want, we'll be able to see what we do want. Do you see what I mean at all?"

"No," said Mrs. Brownell flatly. "I suppose you're trying to say that you might not be coming back at all." She waited tensely for the answer, overcome by her own courage in asking it.

"That's right," said Felicity, driven there finally.

"Why did you have to do this to me on our last day in Venice?" her mother cried. "Your brother Harry's my only sane child, and even he's living in Denver."

Felicity refrained from commenting that one sane one out of two was, after all, doing pretty well. "Here comes your father," Mrs. Brownell said.

Mr. Brownell, freshly shaved and smiling contentedly, was walking toward them across the Piazza San Marco. He was not a particularly fat man, and Felicity knew from old photographs that he had once been as thin as Peter. Could Peter, even in twenty years, ever look as serene and well fed? Mr. Brownell came up to the table and put one hand on his wife's shoulder, the other hand on his daughter's. "How're my girls?" he asked cheerfully. "Have a nice afternoon? Do any shopping?"

Mrs. Brownell could not bear to burden him right then. "Very nice, darling," she said. "We haven't done much of anything."

Felicity smiled back affectionately at her father but did not dare say anything. She looked beyond him and saw her husband working his way through the thicket of tables, a chair in each hand. "Here's Peter," she said with relief. "How was the exhibition?"

"I'll take you back to it tomorrow," he said, putting down the chairs. He wiped his perspiring face on his shirt sleeve. "Please sit down, sir," he said pleasantly to Mr. Brownell, acknowledging his mother-in-law with a nod. Since none of them had ever invented satisfactory nicknames for him to call his in-laws, Peter usually avoided addressing either of them directly.

Mrs. Brownell looked at him sitting beside her daughter. She had to admit that he would be attractive if he weren't quite so unkempt; after a year here, he looked almost Italian. She turned to her own husband and reached for his hand. "Look at them, darling," she said. "Aren't you a little envious of twenty-two and twenty-five, going off and studying painting in Rome?"

Mr. Brownell shook his head and laughed. "No, I'm afraid not. I can truthfully say that I'm not."

Deprived of a companion in longing, Mrs. Brownell suddenly felt entirely deserted. The sun had gone, though the sky was still light, and a few lamps were being turned on around the piazza. "Do you think we could stay just one more day here in Venice?" Mrs. Brownell pleaded.

Her husband looked surprised. "Oh, I don't think so," he said, not noticing her desperation. "We have plane reservations for Geneva tomorrow, and hotel reservations there, and the Gritti Palace probably has people moving into our rooms tomorrow—do you mind? We've had a nice little visit with Felicity, and I've had enough of Venice for one trip."

"I don't mind at all," said Mrs. Brownell bravely. She was determined that the rest of the trip would be fun.

QUESTIONS

1. Is the conflict in this story at all similar to that in "The Elephant's Child"? How does it differ?

2. All the petty differences that come out in the story might be attributed to differing sets of values. What are these values?

3. Would this difference in values be enough to cause the deep discord between mother and daughter, or is there something more basically wrong?

4. What indication is given early in the story that there will be no solution to the conflict, that no communication will be established?

5. In "The Elephant's Child" the reader is completely on the side of the Elephant's Child. In this story is the reader sympathetic with Felicity only, or is something to be said for Mrs. Brownell too?

6. From what point of view is the story told and why?

7. Why does the author list all the wedding presents?

8. What attitude toward Felicity is indicated by Mrs. Brownell's question, "Why did you have to do this to me on our last day in Venice?"

9. Why would Mrs. Brownell like to stay "just one more day here in Venice"?

10. Are the characters the same at the end of the story as at the beginning?

11. What is the theme of the story?

ONELINESS

THE LAMENT
ANTON CHEKHOV

*I*t is twilight. A thick wet snow is twirling around the newly
lighted street lamps, and lying in soft thin layers on roofs, on horses'
backs, on people's shoulders and hats. The cabdriver Iona Potapov is
quite white, and looks like a phantom; he is bent double as far as a
human body can bend double; he is seated on his box; he never makes
a move. If a whole snowdrift fell on him, it seems as if he would not
find it necessary to shake it off. His little horse is also quite white, and
remains motionless; its immobility, its angularity, and its straight
wooden-looking legs, even close by, give it the appearance of a ginger-
bread horse worth a *kopek*. It is, no doubt, plunged in deep thought.
If you were snatched from the plow, from your usual gray surroundings, and were thrown into this slough full of monstrous lights, un-
ceasing noise, and hurrying people, you too would find it difficult not
to think.

Iona and his little horse have not moved from their place for a
long while. They left their yard before dinner, and up to now, not a
fare. The evening mist is descending over the town, the white lights
of the lamps replacing brighter rays, and the hubbub of the street
getting louder. "Cabby for Viborg way!" suddenly hears Iona.
"Cabby!"

Iona jumps, and through his snow-covered eyelashes sees an officer
in a greatcoat, with his hood over his head.

"Viborg way!" the officer repeats. "Are you asleep, eh? Viborg
way!"

With a nod of assent Iona picks up the reins, in consequence of
which layers of snow slip off the horse's back and neck. The officer
seats himself in the sleigh, the cabdriver smacks his lips to encourage
his horse, stretches out his neck like a swan, sits up, and, more from
habit than necessity, brandishes his whip. The little horse also

stretches its neck, bends its wooden-looking legs, and makes a move undecidedly.

"What are you doing, werewolf!" is the exclamation Iona hears from the dark mass moving to and fro, as soon as they have started.

"Where the devil are you going? To the r-r-right!"

"You do not know how to drive. Keep to the right!" calls the officer angrily.

A coachman from a private carriage swears at him; a passerby, who has run across the road and rubbed his shoulder against the horse's nose, looks at him furiously as he sweeps the snow from his sleeve. Iona shifts about on his seat as if he were on needles, moves his elbows as if he were trying to keep his equilibrium, and gapes about like someone suffocating, who does not understand why and wherefore he is there.

"What scoundrels they all are!" jokes the officer; "one would think they had all entered into an agreement to jostle you or fall under your horse."

Iona looks round at the officer, and moves his lips. He evidently wants to say something, but the only sound that issues is a snuffle.

"What?" asks the officer.

Iona twists his mouth into a smile, and with an effort says hoarsely:

"My son, *barin*, died this week."

"Hm! What did he die of?"

Iona turns with his whole body toward his fare, and says:

"And who knows! They say high fever. He was three days in the hospital, and then died. . . . God's will be done."

"Turn round! The devil!" sounds from the darkness. "Have you popped off, old doggie, eh? Use your eyes!"

"Go on, go on," says the officer, "otherwise we shall not get there by tomorrow. Hurry up a bit!"

The cabdriver again stretches his neck, sits up, and, with a bad grace, brandishes his whip. Several times again he turns to look at his fare, but the latter has closed his eyes, and apparently is not disposed to listen. Having deposited the officer in the Viborg, he stops by the tavern, doubles himself up on his seat, and again remains motionless, while the snow once more begins to cover him and his horse. An hour, and another. . . . Then, along the footpath, with a squeak of galoshes, and quarreling, come three young men, two of them tall and lanky, the third one short and humpbacked.

"Cabby, to the Police Bridge!" in a cracked voice calls the humpback. "The three of us for two *griveniks!*"

Iona picks up his reins, and smacks his lips. Two *griveniks* is not a fair price, but he does not mind whether it is a *rouble* or five *kopeks* —to him it is all the same now, so long as they are fares. The young men, jostling each other and using bad language, approach the sleigh, and all three at once try to get onto the seat; then begins a discussion as to which two shall sit and who shall be the one to stand. After wrangling, abusing each other, and much petulance, it is at last decided that the humpback shall stand, as he is the smallest.

"Now then, hurry up!" says the humpback in a twanging voice, as he takes his place and breathes in Iona's neck. "Old furry! Here, mate, what a cap you have! There is not a worse one to be found in all Petersburg! . . ."

"He-he!—he-he!" giggles Iona. "Such a . . . ."

"Now you, 'such a,' hurry up, are you going the whole way at this pace? Are you? . . . Do you want it in the neck?"

"My head feels like bursting," says one of the lanky ones. "Last night at the Donkmasovs, Vaska and I drank the whole of four bottles of cognac."

"I don't understand what you lie for," says the other lanky one angrily; "you lie like a brute."

"God strike me, it's the truth!"

"It's as much the truth as that a louse coughs!"

"He, he," grins Iona, "what gay young gentlemen!"

"Pshaw, go to the devil!" says the humpback indignantly.

"Are you going to get on or not, you old pest? Is that the way to drive? Use the whip a bit! Go on, devil, go on, give it to him well!"

Iona feels at his back the little man wriggling, and the tremble in his voice. He listens to the insults hurled at him, sees the people, and little by little the feeling of loneliness leaves him. The humpback goes on swearing until he gets mixed up in some elaborate six-foot oath, or chokes with coughing. The lankies begin to talk about a certain Nadejda Petrovna. Iona looks round at them several times; he waits for a temporary silence, then, turning round again, he murmurs:

"My son . . . died this week."

"We must all die," sighs the humpback, wiping his lips after an attack of coughing. "Now, hurry up, hurry up! Gentlemen, I really cannot go any farther like this! When will he get us there?"

"Well, just you stimulate him a little in the neck!"

"You old pest, do you hear, I'll bone your neck for you! If one treated the like of you with ceremony one would have to go on foot! Do you hear, old serpent Gorinytch! Or do you not care a spit?"

Iona hears rather than feels the blows they deal him.

"He, he," he laughs. "They are gay young gentlemen, God bless 'em!"

"Cabby, are you married?" asks a lanky one.

"I? He, he, gay young gentlemen! Now I have only a wife and the moist ground. . . . He, ho, ho . . . that is to say, the grave. My son has died, and I am alive. . . . A wonderful thing, death mistook the door . . . instead of coming to me, it went to my son. . . ."

Iona turns round to tell them how his son died, but at this moment, the humpback, giving a little sigh, announces, "Thank God, we have at last reached our destination," and Iona watches them disappear through the dark entrance. Once more he is alone, and again surrounded by silence. . . . His grief, which has abated for a short while, returns and rends his heart with greater force. With an anxious and hurried look, he searches among the crowds passing on either side of the street to find whether there may be just one person who will listen to him. But the crowds hurry by without noticing him or his trouble. Yet it is such an immense, illimitable grief. Should his heart break and the grief pour out, it would flow over the whole earth, so it seems, and yet no one sees it. It has managed to conceal itself in such an insignificant shell that no one can see it even by day and with a light.

Iona sees a hall porter with some sacking, and decides to talk to him.

"Friend, what sort of time is it?" he asks.

"Past nine. What are you standing here for? Move on."

Iona moves on a few steps, doubles himself up, and abandons himself to his grief. He sees it is useless to turn to people for help. In less than five minutes he straightens himself, holds up his head as if he felt some sharp pain, and gives a tug at the reins; he can bear it no longer. "The stables," he thinks, and the little horse, as if it understood, starts off at a trot.

About an hour and a half later Iona is seated by a large dirty stove. Around the stove, on the floor, on the benches, people are snoring; the air is thick and suffocatingly hot. Iona looks at the sleepers, scratches himself, and regrets having returned so early.

"I have not even earned my fodder," he thinks. "That's what's my trouble. A man who knows his job, who has had enough to eat, and his horse too, can always sleep peacefully."

A young cabdriver in one of the corners half gets up, grunts sleepily, and stretches towards a bucket of water.

"Do you want a drink?" Iona asks him.

"Don't I want a drink!"

"That's so? Your good health! But listen, mate—you know, my son is dead. . . . Did you hear? This week, in the hospital. . . . It's a long story."

Iona looks to see what effect his words have, but sees none—the young man has hidden his face and is fast asleep again. The old man sighs, and scratches his head. Just as much as the young one wants to drink, the old man wants to talk. It will soon be a week since his son died, and he has not been able to speak about it properly to anyone. One must tell it slowly and carefully; how his son fell ill, how he suffered, what he said before he died, how he died. One must describe every detail of the funeral, and the journey to the hospital to fetch the dead son's clothes. His daughter Anissia has remained in the village—one must talk about her too. Is it nothing he has to tell? Surely the listener would gasp and sigh, and sympathize with him? It is better, too, to talk to women; although they are stupid, two words are enough to make them sob.

"I'll go and look after my horse," thinks Iona; "there's always time to sleep. No fear of that!"

He puts on his coat, and goes to the stables to his horse; he thinks of the corn, the hay, the weather. When he is alone, he dares not think of his son; he can speak about him to anyone, but to think of him, and picture him to himself, is unbearably painful.

"Are you tucking in?" Iona asks his horse, looking at its bright eyes; "go on, tuck in, though we've not earned our corn, we can eat

hay. Yes! I am too old to drive—my son could have, not I. He was a
first-rate cabdriver. If only he had lived!"

Iona is silent for a moment, then continues:

"That's how it is, my old horse. There's no more Kuzma Ionitch.
He has left us to live, and he went off pop. Now let's say, you had a
foal, you were the foal's mother, and suddenly, let's say, that foal went
and left you to live after him. It would be sad, wouldn't it?"

The little horse munches, listens, and breathes over its master's
hand. . . .

Iona's feelings are too much for him, and he tells the little horse
the whole story.

QUESTIONS

1. How in the first paragraph does the author create a mood of
isolation and loneliness?

2. Why, if Iona is so burdened with grief, does he laugh with the
three young men?

3. Iona tries four times to get someone to listen to him. Why is
each failure more disappointing than the last?

4. Why does the author portray Iona as an incompetent driver,
keeping to the left instead of to the right, causing another coachman
to swear at him, and turning around to talk instead of watching his
driving?

5. What is the meaning on p. 34 of "Once more he is alone,
and again surrounded by silence. . . . His grief, which has abated for
a short while, returns and rends his heart with greater force"?

6. What is the conflict and how is it resolved?

7. This story could easily have become too sentimental. How
does the author avoid it?

8. What is the theme of the story?

THE DARLING
ANTON CHEKHOV

Olenka, the daughter of the retired collegiate assessor, Plemyannia-kov, was sitting in her back porch, lost in thought. It was hot, the flies were persistent and teasing, and it was pleasant to reflect that it would soon be evening. Dark rainclouds were gathering from the east, and bringing from time to time a breath of moisture in the air.

Kukin, who was the manager of an open-air theatre called the Tivoli, and who lived in the lodge, was standing in the middle of the garden looking at the sky.

"Again!" he observed despairingly. "It's going to rain again! Rain every day, as though to spite me. I might as well hang myself! It's ruin! Fearful losses every day."

He flung up his hands, and went on, addressing Olenka:

"There! that's the life we lead, Olga Semyonovna. It's enough to make one cry. One works and does one's utmost; one wears oneself out, getting no sleep at night, and racks one's brain what to do for the best. And then what happens? To begin with, one's public is ignorant, boorish. I give them the very best operetta, a dainty masque, first rate music-hall artists. But do you suppose that's what they want! They don't understand anything of that sort. They want a clown; what they ask for is vulgarity. And then look at the weather! Almost every evening it rains. It started on the tenth of May, and it's kept it up all May and June. It's simply awful! The public doesn't come, but I've to pay the rent just the same, and pay the artists."

The next evening the clouds would gather again, and Kukin would say with an hysterical laugh:

"Well, rain away, then! Flood the garden, drown me! Damn my luck in this world and the next! Let the artists have me up! Send me to prison!—to Siberia!—the scaffold! Ha, ha, ha!"

And next day the same thing.

Olenka listened to Kukin with silent gravity, and sometimes tears came into her eyes. In the end his misfortunes touched her; she grew to love him. He was a small thin man, with a yellow face, and curls combed forward on his forehead. He spoke in a thin tenor; as he talked his mouth worked on one side, and there was always an expression of despair on his face; yet he aroused a deep and genuine affection in her. She was always fond of some one, and could not exist without loving. In earlier days she had loved her papa, who now sat in a darkened room, breathing with difficulty; she had loved her aunt who used to come every other year from Bryansk; and before that, when she was at school, she had loved her French master. She was a gentle, softhearted, compassionate girl, with mild, tender eyes and very good health. At the sight of her full rosy cheeks, her soft white neck with a little dark mole on it, and the kind, naïve smile, which came into her face when she listened to anything pleasant, men thought, "Yes, not half bad," and smiled too, while lady visitors could not refrain from seizing her hand in the middle of a conversation, exclaiming in a gush of delight, "You darling!"

The house in which she had lived from her birth upwards, and which was left her in her father's will, was at the extreme end of the town, not far from the Tivoli. In the evenings and at night she could hear the band playing, and the crackling and banging of fireworks, and it seemed to her that it was Kukin struggling with his destiny, storming the entrenchments of his chief foe, the indifferent public; there was a sweet thrill at her heart, she had no desire to sleep, and when he returned home at daybreak, she tapped softly at her bedroom window, and showing him only her face and one shoulder through the curtain, she gave him a friendly smile. . . .

He proposed to her, and they were married. And when he had a closer view of her neck and her plump, fine shoulders, he threw up his hands, and said:

"You darling!"

He was happy, but as it rained on the day and night of his wedding, his face still retained an expression of despair.

They got on very well together. She used to sit in his office, to look after things in the Tivoli, to put down the accounts and pay the wages. And her rosy cheeks, her sweet, naïve, radiant smile, were to be seen now at the office window, now in the refreshment bar or behind the scenes of the theatre. And already she used to say to her acquaintances that the theatre was the chief and most important thing in life, and that it was only through the drama that one could derive true enjoyment and become cultivated and humane.

"But do you suppose the public understands that?" she used to say. "What they want is a clown. Yesterday we gave 'Faust Inside Out,' and almost all the boxes were empty; but if Vanitchka and I had been producing some vulgar thing, I assure you the theatre would have been packed. Tomorrow Vanitchka and I are doing 'Orpheus in Hell.' Do come."

And what Kukin said about the theatre and the actors she repeated. Like him she despised the public for their ignorance and their indifference to art; she took part in the rehearsals, she corrected the actors, she kept an eye on the behavior of the musicians, and when there was an unfavourable notice in the local paper, she shed tears, and then went to the editor's office to set things right.

The actors were fond of her and used to call her "Vanitchka and I," and "the darling"; she was sorry for them and used to lend them small sums of money, and if they deceived her, she used to shed a few tears in private, but did not complain to her husband.

They got on well in the winter too. They took the theatre in the town for the whole winter, and let it for short terms to a Little Russian company, or to a conjurer, or to a local dramatic society. Olenka grew stouter, and was always beaming with satisfaction, while Kukin grew thinner and yellower, and continually complained of their terrible losses, although he had not done badly all the winter. He used to cough at night, and she used to give him hot raspberry tea or lime-flower water, to rub him with eau-de-Cologne and to wrap him in her warm shawls.

"You're such a sweet pet!" she used to say with perfect sincerity, stroking his hair. "You're such a pretty dear!"

Towards Lent he went to Moscow to collect a new troupe, and without him she could not sleep, but sat all night at her window, looking at the stars, and she compared herself with the hens, who are awake all night and uneasy when the cock is not in the hen-house. Kukin was detained in Moscow, and wrote that he would be back at Easter, adding some instructions about the Tivoli. But on the Sunday before Easter, late in the evening, came a sudden ominous knock at the gate; some one was hammering on the gate as though on a barrel—boom, boom, boom! The drowsy cook went flopping with her bare feet through the puddles, as she ran to open the gate.

"Please open," said some one outside in a thick bass. "There is a telegram for you."

Olenka had received telegrams from her husband before, but this time for some reason she felt numb with terror. With shaking hands she opened the telegram and read as follows:

"Ivan Petrovitch died suddenly to-day. Awaiting immate instructions fufuneral Tuesday."

That was how it was written in the telegram—"fufuneral," and the utterly incomprehensible word "immate." It was signed by the stage manager of the operatic company.

"My darling!" sobbed Olenka. "Vanitchka, my precious, my darling! Why did I ever meet you! Why did I know you and love you! Your poor heart-broken Olenka is all alone without you!"

Kukin's funeral took place on Tuesday in Moscow, Olenka returned home on Wednesday, and as soon as she got indoors she threw herself on her bed and sobbed so loudly that it could be heard next door, and in the street.

"Poor darling!" the neighbours said, as they crossed themselves. "Olga Semyonovna, poor darling! How she does take on!"

Three months later Olenka was coming home from mass, melancholy and in deep mourning. It happened that one of her neighbours, Vassily Andreitch Pustovalov, returning home from church, walked back beside her. He was the manager at Babakayev's, the timber merchant's. He wore a straw hat, a white waistcoat, and a gold watch-chain, and looked more like a country gentleman than a man in trade.

"Everything happens as it is ordained, Olga Semyonovna," he said gravely, with a sympathetic note in his voice; "and if any of our dear ones die, it must be because it is the will of God, so we ought to have fortitude and bear it submissively."

After seeing Olenka to her gate, he said good-bye and went on. All day afterwards she heard his sedately dignified voice, and whenever she shut her eyes she saw his dark beard. She liked him very much. And apparently she had made an impression on him too, for not long afterwards an elderly lady, with whom she was only slightly acquainted, came to drink coffee with her, and as soon as she was seated at table began to talk about Pustovalov, saying that he was an excellent man whom one could thoroughly depend upon, and that any girl would be glad to marry him. Three days later Pustovalov came himself. He did not stay long, only about ten minutes, and he did not say much, but when he left, Olenka loved him—loved him so much that she lay awake all night in a perfect fever, and in the morning she sent for the elderly lady. The match was quickly arranged, and then came the wedding.

Pustovalov and Olenka got on very well together when they were married.

Usually he sat in the office till dinner-time, then he went out on business, while Olenka took his place, and sat in the office till evening, making up accounts and booking orders.

"Timber gets dearer every year; the price rises twenty per cent," she would say to her customers and friends. "Only fancy we used to sell local timber, and now Vassitchka always has to go for wood to the Mogilev district. And the freight!" she would add, covering her cheeks with her hands in horror. "The freight!"

It seemed to her that she had been in the timber trade for ages and ages, and that the most important and necessary thing in life was timber; and there was something intimate and touching to her in the very sound of words such as "baulk," "post," "beam," "pole," "scantling," "batten," "lath," "plank," etc.

At night when she was asleep she dreamed of perfect mountains of planks and boards, and long strings of wagons, carting timber somewhere far away. She dreamed that a whole regiment of six-inch beams forty feet high, standing on end, was marching upon the timber-yard; that logs, beams, and boards knocked together with the resounding crash of dry wood, kept falling and getting up again, piling themselves on each other. Olenka cried out in her sleep, and Pustovalov said to her tenderly: "Olenka, what's the matter, darling? Cross yourself!"

Her husband's ideas were hers. If he thought the room was too hot, or that business was slack, she thought the same. Her husband did not care for entertainments, and on holidays he stayed at home. She did likewise.

"You are always at home or in the office," her friends said to her. "You should go to the theatre, darling, or to the circus."

"Vassitchka and I have no time to go to theatres," she would answer sedately. "We have no time for nonsense. What's the use of these theatres?"

On Saturdays Pustovalov and she used to go to the evening service; on holidays to early mass, and they walked side by side with softened faces as they came home from church. There was a pleasant fragrance about them both, and her silk dress rustled agreeably. At home they drank tea, with fancy bread and jams of various kinds, and afterwards they ate pie. Every day at twelve o'clock there was a savoury smell of beet-root soup and of mutton or duck in their yard, and on fast-days of fish, and no one could pass the gate without feeling hungry. In the office the samovar was always boiling, and customers were regaled with tea and cracknels. Once a week the couple went to the baths and returned side by side, both red in the face.

"Yes, we have nothing to complain of, thank God," Olenka used to say to her acquaintances. "I wish every one were as well off as Vassitchka and I."

When Pustovalov went away to buy wood in the Mogilev district, she missed him dreadfully, lay awake and cried. A young veterinary surgeon in the army, called Smirnin, to whom they had let their lodge, used sometimes to come in in the evening. He used to talk to her and play cards with her, and this entertained her in her husband's absence. She was particularly interested in what he told her of his home life. He was married and had a little boy, but was separated from his wife because she had been unfaithful to him, and now he hated her and used to send her forty roubles a month for the maintenance of their son. And hearing of all this, Olenka sighed and shook her head. She was sorry for him.

"Well, God keep you," she used to say to him at parting, as she lighted him down the stairs with a candle. "Thank you for coming to cheer me up, and may the Mother of God give you health."

And she always expressed herself with the same sedateness and dignity, the same reasonableness, in imitation of her husband. As the veterinary surgeon was disappearing behind the door below, she would say:

"You know, Vladimir Platonitch, you'd better make it up with your wife. You should forgive her for the sake of your son. You may be sure the little fellow understands."

And when Pustovalov came back, she told him in a low voice about the veterinary surgeon and his unhappy home life, and both sighed and shook their heads and talked about the boy, who, no doubt, missed his father, and by some strange connection of ideas, they went up to the holy ikons, bowed to the ground before them and prayed that God would give them children.

And so the Pustovalovs lived for six years quietly and peaceably in love and complete harmony.

But behold! one winter day after drinking hot tea in the office, Vassily Andreitch went out into the yard without his cap on to see about sending off some timber, caught cold and was taken ill. He had the best doctors, but he grew worse and died after four months' illness. And Olenka was a widow once more.

"I've nobody, now you've left me, my darling," she sobbed, after her husband's funeral. "How can I live without you, in wretchedness and misery! Pity me, good people, all alone in the world!"

She went about dressed in black with long "weepers," and gave up wearing hat and gloves for good. She hardly ever went out, except to church, or to her husband's grave, and led the life of a nun. It was not till six months later that she took off the weepers and opened the shutters of the windows. She was sometimes seen in the mornings, going with her cook to market for provisions, but what went on in her house and how she lived now could only be surmised. People guessed, from seeing her drinking tea in her garden with the veterinary surgeon, who read the newspaper aloud to her, and from the fact that, meeting a lady she knew at the post-office, she said to her:

"There is no proper veterinary inspection in our town, and that's the cause of all sorts of epidemics. One is always hearing of people's getting infection from the milk supply, or catching diseases from horses and cows. The health of domestic animals ought to be as well cared for as the health of human beings."

She repeated the veterinary surgeon's words, and was of the same opinion as he about everything. It was evident that she could not live a year without some attachment, and had found new happiness in the lodge. In any one else this would have been censured, but no one could think ill of Olenka; everything she did was so natural. Neither she nor the veterinary surgeon said anything to other people of the change in their relations, and tried, indeed, to conceal it, but without success, for Olenka could not keep a secret. When he had visitors, men serving in his regiment, and she poured out tea or served the supper, she would begin talking of the cattle plague, of the foot and mouth disease, and of the municipal slaughter-houses. He was dreadfully embarrassed, and when the guests had gone, he would seize her by the hand and hiss angrily:

"I've asked you before not to talk about what you don't understand. When we veterinary surgeons are talking among ourselves, please don't put your word in. It's really annoying."

And she would look at him with astonishment and dismay, and ask him in alarm: "But, Voloditchka, what *am* I to talk about?"

And with tears in her eyes she would embrace him, begging him not to be angry, and they were both happy.

But this happiness did not last long. The veterinary surgeon departed, departed for ever with his regiment, when it was transferred to a distant place—to Siberia, it may be. And Olenka was left alone.

Now she was absolutely alone. Her father had long been dead, and his armchair lay in the attic, covered with dust and lame of one leg. She got thinner and plainer, and when people met her in the street they did not look at her as they used to, and did not smile to her; evidently her best years were over and left behind, and now a new sort of life had begun for her, which did not bear thinking about. In the evening Olenka sat in the porch, and heard the band playing and the fireworks popping in the Tivoli, but now the sound stirred no response. She looked into her yard without interest, thought of nothing, wished for nothing, and afterwards, when night came on she went to bed and dreamed of her empty yard. She ate and drank as it were unwillingly.

And what was worst of all, she had no opinions of any sort. She saw the objects about her and understood what she saw, but could not form any opinion about them, and did not know what to talk about. And how awful it is not to have any opinions! One sees a bottle, for instance, or the rain, or a peasant driving in his cart, but what the bottle is for, or the rain, or the peasant, and what is the meaning of it, one can't say, and could not even for a thousand roubles. When she had Kukin, or Pustovalov, or the veterinary surgeon, Olenka could explain everything, and give her opinion about anything you like, but now there was the same emptiness in her brain and in her heart as there was in her yard outside. And it was as harsh and as bitter as wormwood in the mouth.

Little by little the town grew in all directions. The road became a street, and where the Tivoli and the timber-yard had been, there were new turnings and houses. How rapidly time passes! Olenka's house grew dingy, the roof got rusty, the shed sank on one side, and the whole yard was overgrown with docks and stinging-nettles. Olenka herself had grown plain and elderly; in summer she sat in the porch, and her soul, as before, was empty and dreary and full of bitterness. In winter she sat at her window and looked at the snow. When she caught the scent of spring, or heard the chime of the church bells, a sudden rush of memories from the past came over her, there was a tender ache in her heart, and her eyes brimmed over with tears; but this was only for a minute, and then came emptiness again and the sense of the futility of life. The black kitten, Briska, rubbed against her and purred softly, but Olenka was not touched by these feline caresses. That was not what she needed. She wanted a love that would absorb her whole being, her whole soul and reason—that would give her ideas and an object in life, and would warm her old blood. And she would shake the kitten off her skirt and say with vexation:

"Get along; I don't want you!"

And so it was, day after day and year after year, and no joy, and no opinions. Whatever Mavra, the cook, said she accepted.

One hot July day, towards evening, just as the cattle were being driven away, and the whole yard was full of dust, some one suddenly knocked at the gate. Olenka went to open it herself and was dumbfounded when she looked out: she saw Smirnin, the veterinary surgeon, grey-headed, and dressed as a civilian. She suddenly remembered everything. She could not help crying and letting her head fall on his breast without uttering a word, and in the violence of her feeling she did not notice how they both walked into the house and sat down to tea.

"My dear Vladimir Platonitch! What fate has brought you?" she muttered, trembling with joy.

"I want to settle here for good, Olga Semyonovna," he told her. "I have resigned my post, and have come to settle down and try my luck on my own account. Besides, it's time for my boy to go to school. He's a big boy. I am reconciled with my wife, you know."

"Where is she?" asked Olenka.

"She's at the hotel with the boy, and I'm looking for lodgings."

"Good gracious, my dear soul! Lodgings? Why not have my house? Why shouldn't that suit you? Why, my goodness, I wouldn't take any rent!" cried Olenka in a flutter, beginning to cry again. "You live here, and the lodge will do nicely for me. Oh dear! how glad I am!"

Next day the roof was painted and the walls were whitewashed, and Olenka, with her arms akimbo, walked about the yard giving directions. Her face was beaming with her old smile, and she was brisk and alert as though she had waked from a long sleep. The veterinary's wife arrived—a thin, plain lady, with short hair and a peevish expression. With her was her little Sasha, a boy of ten, small for his age, blue-eyed, chubby, with dimples in his cheeks. And scarcely had the boy walked into the yard when he ran after the cat, and at once there was the sound of his gay, joyous laugh.

"Is that your puss, auntie?" he asked Olenka. "When she has little ones, do give us a kitten. Mamma is awfully afraid of mice."

Olenka talked to him, and gave him tea. Her heart warmed and there was a sweet ache in her bosom, as though the boy had been her own child. And when he sat at the table in the evening, going over his lessons, she looked at him with deep tenderness and pity as she murmured to herself:

"You pretty pet! . . . my precious! . . . Such a fair little thing, and so clever."

" 'An island is a piece of land which is entirely surrounded by water,' " he read aloud.

"An island is a piece of land," she repeated, and this was the first opinion to which she gave utterance with positive conviction after so many years of silence and dearth of ideas.

Now she had opinions of her own, and at supper she talked to Sasha's parents, saying how difficult the lessons were at the high schools, but that yet the high-school was better than a commercial one, since with a high-school education all careers were open to one, such as being a doctor or an engineer.

Sasha began going to the high school. His mother departed to

Harkov to her sister's and did not return; his father used to go off every day to inspect cattle, and would often be away from home for three days together, and it seemed to Olenka as though Sasha was entirely abandoned, that he was not wanted at home, that he was being starved, and she carried him off to her lodge and gave him a little room there.

And for six months Sasha had lived in the lodge with her. Every morning Olenka came into his bedroom and found him fast asleep, sleeping noiselessly with his hand under his cheek. She was sorry to wake him.

"Sashenka," she would say mournfully, "get up, darling. It's time for school."

He would get up, dress and say his prayers, and then sit down to breakfast, drink three glasses of tea, and eat two large cracknels and half a buttered roll. All this time he was hardly awake and a little ill-humoured in consequence.

"You don't quite know your fable, Sashenka," Olenka would say, looking at him as though he were about to set off on a long journey. "What a lot of trouble I have with you! You must work and do your best, darling, and obey your teachers."

"Oh, do leave me alone!" Sasha would say.

Then he would go down the street to school, a little figure, wearing a big cap and carrying a satchel on his shoulder. Olenka would follow him noiselessly.

"Sashenka!" she would call after him, and she would pop into his hand a date or a caramel. When he reached the street where the school was, he would feel ashamed of being followed by a tall, stout woman; he would turn round and say:

"You'd better go home, auntie. I can go the rest of the way alone."

She would stand still and look after him fixedly till he had disappeared at the school-gate.

Ah, how she loved him! Of her former attachments not one had been so deep; never had her soul surrendered to any feeling so spontaneously, so disinterestedly, and so joyously as now that her maternal instincts were aroused. For this little boy with the dimple in his cheek and the big school cap, she would have given her whole life, she would have given it with joy and tears of tenderness. Why? Who can tell why?

When she had seen the last of Sasha, she returned home, contented and serene, brimming over with love; her face, which had grown younger during the last six months, smiled and beamed; people meeting her looked at her with pleasure.

"Good-morning, Olga Semyonovna, darling. How are you, darling?"

"The lessons at the high school are very difficult now," she would relate at the market. "It's too much; in the first class yesterday they gave him a fable to learn by heart, and a Latin translation and a problem. You know it's too much for a little chap."

And she would begin talking about the teachers, the lessons, and the school books, saying just what Sasha said.

At three o'clock they had dinner together: in the evening they learned their lessons together and cried. When she put him to bed, she would stay a long time making the Cross over him and murmuring a prayer; then she would go to bed and dream of that far-away misty future when Sasha would finish his studies and become a doctor or an engineer, would have a big house of his own with horses and a carriage, would get married and have children. . . . She would fall asleep still thinking of the same thing, and tears would run down her cheeks from her closed eyes, while the black cat lay purring beside her: "Mrr, mrr, mrr."

Suddenly there would come a loud knock at the gate.

Olenka would wake up breathless with alarm, her heart throbbing. Half a minute later would come another knock.

"It must be a telegram from Harkov," she would think, beginning to tremble from head to foot. "Sasha's mother is sending for him from Harkov. . . . Oh, mercy on us!"

She was in despair. Her head, her hands, and her feet would turn chill, and she would feel that she was the most unhappy woman in the world. But another minute would pass, voices would be heard: it would turn out to be the veterinary surgeon coming home from the club.

"Well, thank God!" she would think.

And gradually the load in her heart would pass off, and she would feel at ease. She would go back to bed thinking of Sasha, who lay sound asleep in the next room, sometimes crying out in his sleep:

"I'll give it you! Get away! Shut up!"

QUESTIONS

The five people in this character study are sometimes called by the last name, sometimes by the first two names, and sometimes by the diminutive of the first name. The following list may be helpful:

> Olga Semyonovna Plemyanniakov (Olenka)
> Ivan Petrovitch Kukin (Vanitchka)
> Vassily Andreitch Pustovalov (Vassitchka)
> Vladimir Platonitch Smirnin (Voloditchka)
> Sasha (Sashenka)

1. How does the setting reflect the moods of Olenka?

2. What are the characteristics of Olenka's love? Do her attachments last long? Is her love related to pity?

3. As in many of his stories, Chekhov is here concerned with the loneliness and isolation of the individual. Olenka must have someone to love, someone upon whom she can lavish her affection, or she feels alone and desolate. Do any of the other characters exhibit a feeling of isolation?

4. The action is divided into four episodes—Olenka's life with her two husbands, with the veterinary surgeon, and with Sasha—all separated by periods of emptiness and dreariness. What part does chance play in each episode?

5. Critics disagree about Chekhov's attitude toward Olenka. Is he making fun of her as a woman with no mind of her own and no inner resources, a woman who must depend entirely on others for all her ideas? Or is he sympathetic toward her in her great capacity for devotion?

Some light is thrown on the question by a Russian contemporary of Chekhov, Leo Tolstoy, who writes:

> The author evidently means to mock at the pitiful creature—as he judges her with his intellect, but not with his heart—the Darling, who after first sharing Kukin's anxiety about his theatre, then throwing herself into the interests of the timber trade, then under the influence of the veterinary surgeon regarding the campaign against the foot and mouth disease as the most important matter in the world, is finally engrossed in

the grammatical questions and the interests of the little schoolboy in the big cap. Kukin's surname is absurd, even his illness and the telegram announcing his death, the timber merchant with his respectability, the veterinary surgeon, even the boy—all are absurd, but the soul of The Darling, with her faculty of devoting herself with her whole being to any one she loves, is not absurd, but marvellous and holy.

I believe that while he was writing "The Darling," the author had in his mind, though not in his heart, a vague image of a new woman; of her equality with man; of a woman mentally developed, learned, working independently for the good of society as well as, if not better than, a man; of the woman who has raised and upholds the woman question; and in writing "The Darling" he wanted to show what woman ought not to be. . . . but when he began to speak, the poet blessed what he had come to curse. In spite of its exquisite gay humour, I at least cannot read without tears some passages of this wonderful story. I am touched by the description of her complete devotion and love for Kukin and all that he cares for, and for the timber merchant and for the veterinary surgeon, and even more of her sufferings when she is left alone and has no one to love; and finally the account of how with all the strength of womanly, motherly feelings (of which she has no experience in her own life) she devotes herself with boundless love to the future man, the schoolboy in the big cap.

The author makes her love the absurd Kukin, the insignificant timber merchant, and the unpleasant veterinary surgeon, but love is no less sacred whether its object is a Kukin or a Spinoza, a Pascal, or a Schiller, and whether the objects of it change as rapidly as with the Darling, or whether the object of it remains the same throughout the whole life.

. . .

He . . . intended to curse, but the god of poetry forbade him, and commanded him to bless. And he did bless, and unconsciously clothes this sweet creature in such an exquisite radiance that she will always remain a type of what a woman can be in order to be happy herself, and to make the happiness of those with whom destiny throws her.

What makes the story so excellent is that the effect is unintentional.

6. What is the conflict and how is it resolved?
7. How does the resolution of the conflict bring out the theme?

LOVE CREATES A NEW AWARENESS

HOW BEAUTIFUL WITH SHOES
WILBUR DANIEL STEELE

By the time the milking was finished, the sow, which had far-
rowed the past week, was making such a row that the girl spilled a
pint of the warm milk down the trough-lead to quiet the animal before taking the pail to the well-house. Then in the quiet she heard a
sound of hoofs on the bridge, where the road crossed the creek a
hundred yards below the house, and she set the pail down on the
ground beside her bare, barn-soiled feet. She picked it up again. She
set it down. It was as if she calculated its weight.

That was what she was doing, as a matter of fact, setting off
against its pull toward the well-house the pull of that wagon team in
the road, with little more of personal will or wish in the matter than
has a wooden weathervane between two currents in the wind. And as
with the vane, so with the wooden girl—the added behest of a whip-
lash cracking in the distance was enough; leaving the pail at the barn
door, she set off in a deliberate, docile beeline through the cow-yard,
over the fence, and down in a diagonal across the farm's one tilled
field toward the willow brake that walled the road at the dip. And
once under way, though her mother came to the kitchen door and
called in her high, flat voice, "Amarantha, where you goin', Amarantha?", the girl went on apparently unmoved, as though she had
been as deaf as the woman in the doorway; indeed, if there was emotion in her it was the purely sensuous one of feeling the clods of the
furrows breaking softly between her toes. It was springtime in
the mountains.

"Amarantha, why don't you answer me, Amarantha?"

For moments after the girl had disappeared beyond the willows
the widow continued to call, unaware through long habit of how absurd it sounded, the name which that strange man her husband had
put upon their daughter in one of his moods. Mrs. Doggett had been

deaf so long she did not realize that nobody else ever thought of it for the broad-fleshed, slow-minded girl, but called her Mary or, even more simply, Mare.

Ruby Herter had stopped his team this side of the bridge, the mules' heads turned into the lane to his father's farm beyond the road. A big-barreled, heavy-limbed fellow with a square, sallow, not unhandsome face, he took out youth in ponderous gestures of masterfulness; it was like him to have cracked his whip above his animals' ears the moment before he pulled them to a halt. When he saw the girl getting over the fence under the willows he tongued the wad of tobacco out of his mouth into his palm, threw it away beyond the road, and drew a sleeve of his jumper across his lips.

"Don't run yourself out o' breath, Mare; I got all night."

"I was comin'." It sounded sullen only because it was matter of fact.

"Well, keep a-comin' and give us a smack." Hunched on the wagon seat, he remained motionless for some time after she had arrived at the hub, and when he stirred it was but to cut a fresh bit of tobacco, as if already he had forgotten why he threw the old one away. Having satisfied his humor, he unbent, climbed down, kissed her passive mouth, and hugged her up to him, roughly and loosely, his hands careless of contours. It was not out of the way; they were used to handling animals both of them; and it was spring. A slow warmth pervaded the girl, formless, nameless, almost impersonal.

Her betrothed pulled her head back by the braid of her yellow hair. He studied her face, his brows gathered and his chin out.

"Listen, Mare, you wouldn't leave nobody else hug and kiss you, dang you!"

She shook her head, without vehemence or anxiety.

"Who's that?" She hearkened up the road. "Pull your team out," she added, as a Ford came in sight around the bend above the house, driven at speed. "Geddap!" she said to the mules herself.

But the car came to a halt near them, and one of the five men crowded in it called, "Come on, Ruby, climb in. They's a loony loose out o' Dayville Asylum, and they got him trailed over somewheres on Split Ridge, and Judge North phoned up to Slosson's store for ever'body come help circle him—come on, hop the runnin'-board!"

Ruby hesitated, an eye on his team.

"Scared, Ruby?" The driver raced his engine. "They say this boy's a killer."

"Mare, take the team in and tell pa." The car was already moving when Ruby jumped it. A moment after it had sounded on the bridge it was out of sight.

"Amarantha, Amarantha, why don't you come, Amarantha?"

Returning from her errand, fifteen minutes later, Mare heard the plaint lifted in the twilight. The sun had dipped behind the back ridge, and though the sky was still bright with day, the dusk began to smoke up out of the plowed field like a ground-fog. The girl had returned through it, got the milk, and started toward the well-house before the widow saw her.

"Daughter, seems to me you might!" she expostulated without change of key. "Here's some young man friend o' yourn stopped to say howdy, and I been rackin' my lungs out after you. . . . Put that milk in the cool and come!"

Some young man friend? But there was no good to be got from puzzling. Mare poured the milk in the pan in the dark of the low house over the well, and as she came out, stooping, she saw a figure waiting for her, black in silhouette against the yellowing sky.

"Who are you?" she asked, a native timidity making her sound sulky.

" 'Amarantha!' " the fellow mused. "That's poetry." And she knew then that she did not know him.

She walked past, her arms straight down and her eyes front. Strangers always affected her with a kind of muscular terror simply by being strangers. So she gained the kitchen steps, aware by his tread that he followed. There, taking courage at sight of her mother in the doorway, she turned on him, her eyes down at the level of his knees.

"Who are you and what d' y' want?"

He still mused. "Amarantha! Amarantha in Carolina! That makes me happy!"

Mare hazarded one upward look. She saw that he had red hair, brown eyes, and hollows under his cheek-bones, and though the green sweater he wore on top of a gray overall was plainly not meant for him, sizes too large as far as girth went, yet he was built so long of limb that his wrists came inches out of the sleeves and made his big hands look even bigger.

Mrs. Doggett complained. "Why don't you introduce us, daughter?"

The girl opened her mouth and closed it again. Her mother, unaware that no sound had come out of it, smiled and nodded, evidently taking to the tall, homely fellow and tickled by the way he could not seem to get his eyes off her daughter. But the daughter saw none of it, all her attention centered upon the stranger's hands.

Restless, hard-fleshed, and chap-bitten, they were like a countryman's hands; but the fingers were longer than the ordinary, and slightly spatulate at their ends, and these ends were slowly and continuously at play among themselves.

The girl could not have explained how it came to her to be frightened and at the same time to be calm, for she was inept with words. It was simply that in an animal way she knew animals, knew them in health and ailing, and when they were ailing she knew by instinct, as her father had known, how to move so as not to fret them.

Her mother had gone in to light up; from beside the lamp-shelf she called back, "If he's aimin' to stay to supper you should've told me, Amarantha, though I guess there's plenty of the side-meat to go 'round, if you'll bring me in a few more turnips and potatoes, though it is late."

At the words the man's cheeks moved in and out. "I'm very hungry," he said.

Mare nodded deliberately. Deliberately, as if her mother could hear her, she said over her shoulder, "I'll go get the potatoes and turnips, ma." While she spoke she was moving, slowly, softly, at first, toward the right of the yard, where the fence gave over into the field. Unluckily her mother spied her through the window.

"Amarantha, where *are* you goin'?"

"I'm goin' to get the potatoes and turnips." She neither raised her voice nor glanced back, but lengthened her stride. "He won't hurt her," she said to herself. "He won't hurt her; it's me, not her," she kept repeating, while she got over the fence and down into the shadow that lay more than ever like a fog on the field.

The desire to believe that it actually did hide her, the temptation to break from her rapid but orderly walk grew till she could no longer fight it. She saw the road willows only a dash ahead of her. She ran, her feet floundering among the furrows.

She neither heard nor saw him, but when she realized he was with her she knew he had been with her all the while. She stopped, and he stopped, and so they stood, with the dark open of the field all around. Glancing sidewise presently, she saw he was no longer looking at her with those strangely importunate brown eyes of his, but had raised them to the crest of the wooded ridge behind her.

By and by, "What does it make you think of?" he asked. And when she made no move to see, "Turn around and look!" he said, and though it was low and almost tender in its tone, she knew enough to turn.

A ray of the sunset hidden in the west struck through the tops of the topmost trees, far and small up there, a thin, bright hem.

"What does it make you think of, Amarantha? . . . Answer!"

"Fire," she made herself say.

"Or blood."

"Or blood, yeh. That's right, or blood." She had heard a Ford going up the road beyond the willows, and her attention was not on what she said.

The man soliloquized. "Fire and blood, both; spare one or the other, and where is beauty, the way the world is? It's an awful thing to have to carry, but Christ had it. Christ came with a sword. I love beauty, Amarantha. . . . I say, I love beauty!"

"Yeh, that's right, I hear." What she heard was the car stopping at the house.

"Not prettiness. Prettiness'll have to go with ugliness, because it's only ugliness trigged up. But beauty!" Now again he was looking at her. "Do you know how beautiful you are, Amarantha, 'Amarantha sweet and fair'?" Of a sudden, reaching behind her, he began to unravel the meshes of her hair-braid, the long, flat-tipped fingers at once impatient and infinitely gentle. " 'Braid no more that shining hair!' "

Flat-faced Mare Doggett tried to see around those glowing eyes so near to hers, but wise in her instinct, did not try too hard. "Yeh," she temporized. "I mean, no, I mean."

"Amarantha, I've come a long, long way for you. Will you come away with me now?"

"Yeh—that is—in a minute I will, mister—yeh. . . ."

"Because you want to, Amarantha? Because you love me as I love you? Answer!"

"Yeh—sure—uh . . . *Ruby!*"

The man tried to run, but there were six against him, coming up out of the dark that lay in the plowed ground. Mare stood where she was while they knocked him down and got a rope around him; after that she walked back toward the house with Ruby and Older Haskins, her father's cousin.

Ruby wiped his brow and felt of his muscles. "Gees, you're lucky we come, Mare. We're no more'n past the town, when they come hollerin' he'd broke over this way."

When they came to the fence the girl sat on the rail for a moment and rebraided her hair before she went into the house, where they were making her mother smell ammonia.

Lots of cars were coming. Judge North was coming, somebody said. When Mare heard this she went into her bedroom off the kitchen and got her shoes and put them on. They were brand new two-dollar shoes with cloth tops, and she had only begun to break them in last Sunday; she wished afterwards she had put her stockings on too, for they would have eased the seams. Or else that she had put on the old button pair, even though the soles were worn through.

Judge North arrived. He thought first of taking the loony straight through to Dayville that night, but then decided to keep him in the lock-up at the courthouse till morning and make the drive by day. Older Haskins stayed in, gentling Mrs. Doggett, while Ruby went out to help get the man into the Judge's sedan. Now that she had them on, Mare didn't like to take the shoes off till Older went; it might make him feel small, she thought.

Older Haskins had a lot of facts about the loony.

"His name's Humble Jewett," he told them. "They belong back in Breed County, all them Jewetts, and I don't reckon there's none on 'em that's not a mite unbalanced. He went to college though, worked his way, and he taught somethin' 'rother in some academy-school a spell, till he went off his head all of a sudden and took after folks with an axe. I remember it in the paper at the time. They give out one while how the Principal wasn't goin' to live, and there was others—there was a girl he tried to strangle. That was four-five year back."

Ruby came in guffawing. "Know the only thing they can get 'im

to say, Mare? Only God thing he'll say is, 'Amarantha, she's goin'
with me.' . . . Mare!"

"Yeh, I know."

The cover of the kettle the girl was handling slid off on the stove
with a clatter. A sudden sick wave passed over her. She went out to
the back, out into the air. It was not till now she knew how frightened
she had been.

Ruby went home, but Older Haskins stayed to supper with them,
and helped Mare do the dishes afterward; it was nearly nine when he
left. The mother was already in bed, and Mare was about to sit down
to get those shoes off her wretched feet at last, when she heard the
cow carrying on up at the barn, lowing and kicking, and next minute
the sow was in it with a horning note. It might be a fox passing by to
get at the henhouse, or a weasel. Mare forgot her feet, took a broom-
handle they used in boiling clothes, opened the back door, and stepped
out. Blinking the lamplight from her eyes, she peered up toward the
outbuildings, and saw the gable end of the barn standing like a red
arrow in the dark, and the top of a butternut tree beyond it drawn in
skeleton traceries, and just then a cock crowed.

She went to the right corner of the house and saw where the light
came from, ruddy above the woods down the valley. Returning into
the house, she bent close to her mother's ear and shouted, "Somethin's a-fire down to the town, looks like," then went out again and up
to the barn. "Soh! Soh!" she called in to the animals. She climbed
up and stood on the top rail of the cow-pen fence, only to find she
could not locate the flame even there.

Ten rods behind the buildings a mass of rock mounted higher
than their ridgepoles, a chopped-off buttress of the back ridge, covered with oak scrub and wild grapes and blackberries, whose thorny
ropes the girl beat away from her skirt with the broom-handle as she
scrambled up in the wine-colored dark. Once at the top, and the brush
held aside, she could see the tongue-tip of the conflagration half a mile
away at the town. And she knew by the bearing of the two church
steeples that it was the building where the lock-up was that was burning.

There is a horror in knowing animals trapped in a fire, no matter what the animals.

"Oh, my God!" Mare said.

A car went down the road. Then there was a horse galloping. That would be Older Haskins probably. People were out at Ruby's father's farm; she could hear their voices raised. There must have been another car up from the other way, for lights wheeled and shouts were exchanged in the neighborhood of the bridge. Next thing she knew, Ruby was at the house below, looking for her probably.

He was telling her mother. Mrs. Doggett was not used to him, so he had to shout even louder than Mare had to.

"What y' reckon he done, the hellion! he broke the door and killed Lew Fyke and set the courthouse afire! . . . Where's Mare?"

Her mother would not know. Mare called. "Here, up the rock here."

She had better go down. Ruby would likely break his bones if he tried to climb the rock in the dark, not knowing the way. But the sight of the fire fascinated her simple spirit, the fearful element, more fearful than ever now, with the news. "Yes, I'm comin'," she called sulkily, hearing feet in the brush. "You wait; I'm comin'."

When she turned and saw it was Humble Jewett, right behind her among the branches, she opened her mouth to screech. She was not quick enough. Before a sound came out he got one hand over her face and the other arm around her body.

Mare had always thought she was strong, and the loony looked gangling, yet she was so easy for him that he need not hurt her. He made no haste and little noise as he carried her deeper into the undergrowth. Where the hill began to mount it was harder though. Presently he set her on her feet. He let the hand that had been over her mouth slip down to her throat, where the broad-tipped fingers wound, tender as yearning, weightless as caress.

"I was afraid you'd scream before you knew who 'twas, Amarantha. But I didn't want to hurt your lips, dear heart, your lovely, quiet lips."

It was so dark under the trees she could hardly see him, but she felt his breath on her mouth, near to. But then, instead of kissing her, he said, "No! No!" took from her throat for an instant the hand that had held her mouth, kissed its palm, and put it back softly against her skin.

"Now, my love, let's go before they come."

She stood stock still. Her mother's voice was to be heard in the distance, strident and meaningless. More cars were on the road. Nearer, around the rock, there were sounds of tramping and thrashing. Ruby fussed and cursed. He shouted, "Mare, dang you, where are you, Mare?", his voice harsh with uneasy anger. Now, if she aimed to do anything, was the time to do it. But there was neither breath nor power in her windpipe. It was as if those yearning fingers had paralyzed the muscles.

"Come!" The arm he put around her shivered against her shoulder blades. It was anger. "I hate killing. It's a dirty, ugly thing. It makes me sick." He gagged, judging by the sound. But then he ground his teeth. "Come away, my love!"

She found herself moving. Once when she broke a branch underfoot with an instinctive awkwardness he chided her. "Quiet, my heart, else they'll hear!" She made herself heavy. He thought she grew tired and bore more of her weight till he was breathing hard.

Men came up the hill. There must have been a dozen spread out, by the angle of their voices as they kept touch. Always Humble Jewett kept caressing Mare's throat with one hand; all she could do was hang back.

"You're tired and you're frightened," he said at last. "Get down here."

There were twigs in the dark, the overhang of a thicket of some sort. He thrust her in under this, and lay beside her on the bed of groundpine. The hand that was not in love with her throat reached across her; she felt the weight of its forearm on her shoulder and its fingers among the strands of her hair, eagerly, but tenderly, busy. Not once did he stop speaking, no louder than breathing, his lips to her ear.

"'Amarantha sweet and fair—Ah, braid no more that shining hair. . . .'"

Mare had never heard of Lovelace, the poet; she thought the loony was just going on, hardly listened, got little sense. But the cadence of it added to the lethargy of all her flesh.

"'Like a clew of golden thread—Most excellently ravellèd. . . .'"

Voices loudened; feet came tramping; a pair went past not two rods away.

" '. . . Do not then wind up the light—In ribbands, and o'er-cloud in night. . . .' "

The search went on up the woods, men shouting to one another and beating the brush.

" '. . . But shake your head and scatter day!' I've never loved, Amarantha. They've tried me with prettiness, but prettiness is too cheap, yes, it's too cheap."

Mare was cold, and the coldness made her lazy. All she knew was that he talked on.

"But dogwood blowing in the spring isn't cheap. The earth of a field isn't cheap. Lots of times I've lain down and kissed the earth of a field, Amarantha. That's beauty, and a kiss for beauty." His breath moved up her cheek. He trembled violently. "No, no, not yet!" He got to his knees and pulled her by an arm. "We can go now."

They went back down the slope, but at an angle, so that when they came to the level they passed two hundred yards to the north of the house, and crossed the road there. More and more her walking was like sleepwalking, the feet numb in their shoes. Even where he had to let go of her, crossing the creek on stones, she stepped where he stepped with an obtuse docility. The voices of the searchers on the back ridge were small in distance when they began to climb the face of Coward Hill, on the opposite side of the valley.

There is an old farm on top of Coward Hill, big hayfields as flat as tables. It had been half-past nine when Mare stood on the rock above the barn; it was toward midnight when Humble Jewett put aside the last branches of the woods and led her out on the height, and half a moon had risen. And a wind blew there, tossing the withered tops of last year's grasses, and mists ran with the wind, and ragged shadows with the mists, and mares'-tails of clear moonlight among the shadows, so that now the boles of birches on the forest's edge beyond the fences were but opal blurs and now cut alabaster. It struck so cold against the girl's cold flesh, this wind, that another wind of shivers blew through her, and she put her hands over her face and eyes. But the madman stood with his eyes wide open and his mouth open, drinking the moonlight and the wet wind.

His voice, when he spoke at last, was thick in his throat.

"Get down on your knees." He got down on his and pulled her after. "And pray!"

Once in England a poet sang four lines. Four hundred years have forgotten his name, but they have remembered his lines. The daft man knelt upright, his face raised to the wild scud, his long wrists hanging to the dead grass. He began simply:

> "O western wind, when wilt thou blow
> That the small rain down can rain?"

The Adam's-apple was big in his bent throat. As simply he finished.

> "Christ, that my love were in my arms
> And I in my bed again!"

Mare got up and ran. She ran without aim or feeling in the power of the wind. She told herself again that the mists would hide her from him, as she had done at dusk. And again, seeing that he ran at her shoulder, she knew he had been there all the while, making a race of it, flailing the air with his long arms for joy of play in the cloud of spring, throwing his knees high, leaping the moon-blue waves of the brown grass, shaking his bright hair; and her own hair was a weight behind her, lying level on the wind. Once a shape went bounding ahead of them for instants; she did not realize it was a fox till it was gone.

She never thought of stopping; she never thought anything, except once, "Oh, my God, I wish I had my shoes off!" And what would have been the good in stopping or in turning another way, when it was only play? The man's ecstasy magnified his strength. When a snake-fence came at them he took the top rail in flight, like a college hurdler and, seeing the girl hesitate and half turn as if to flee, he would have releaped it without touching a hand. But then she got a loom of buildings, climbed over quickly, before he should jump, and ran along the lane that ran with the fence.

Mare had never been up there, but she knew that the farm and the house belonged to a man named Wyker, a kind of cousin of Ruby Herter's, a violent, bearded old fellow who lived by himself. She could not believe her luck. When she had run half the distance and Jewett had not grabbed her, doubt grabbed her instead. "Oh, my God, go careful!" she told herself. "Go slow!" she implored herself, and stopped running, to walk.

Here was a misgiving the deeper in that it touched her special knowledge. She had never known an animal so far gone that its instincts failed it; a starving rat will scent the trap sooner than a fed one. Yet, after one glance at the house they approached, Jewett paid it no further attention, but walked with his eyes to the right, where the cloud had blown away, and wooded ridges, like black waves rimed with silver, ran down away toward the Valley of Virginia.

"I've never lived!" In his single cry there were two things, beatitude and pain.

Between the bigness of the falling world and his eyes the flag of her hair blew. He reached out and let it whip between his fingers. Mare was afraid it would break the spell then, and he would stop looking away and look at the house again. So she did something almost incredible; she spoke.

"It's a pretty—I mean—a beautiful view down that-a-way."

"God Almighty beautiful, to take your breath away. I knew I'd never loved, Belovéd—" He caught a foot under the long end of one of the boards that covered the well and went down heavily on his hands and knees. It seemed to make no difference. "But I never knew I'd never lived," he finished in the same tone of strong rapture, quadruped in the grass, while Mare ran for the door and grabbed the latch.

When the latch would not give, she lost what little sense she had. She pounded with her fists. She cried with all her might: "Oh—hey—in there—hey—in there!" Then Jewett came and took her gently between his hands and drew her away, and then, though she was free, she stood in something like an awful embarrassment while he tried shouting.

"Hey! Friend! whoever you are, wake up and let my love and me come in!"

"No!" wailed the girl.

He grew peremptory. "Hey, wake up!" He tried the latch. He passed to full fury in a wink's time; he cursed, he kicked, he beat the door till Mare thought he would break his hands. Withdrawing, he ran at it with his shoulder; it burst at the latch, went slamming in, and left a black emptiness. His anger dissolved in a big laugh. Turning in time to catch her by a wrist, he cried joyously, "Come, my Sweet One!"

"No! No! Please—aw—listen. There ain't nobody there. He ain't to home. It wouldn't be right to go in anybody's house if they weren't to home, you know that."

His laugh was blither than ever. He caught her high in his arms. "I'd do the same by his love and him if 'twas my house, I would." At the threshold he paused and thought, "That is, if she was the true love of his heart forever."

The room was the parlor. Moonlight slanted in at the door, and another shaft came through a window and fell across a sofa, its covering dilapidated, showing its wadding in places. The air was sour, but both of them were farm-bred.

"Don't, Amarantha!" His words were pleading in her ear. "Don't be so frightened."

He set her down on the sofa. As his hands let go of her they were shaking.

"But look, I'm frightened too." He knelt on the floor before her, reached out his hands, withdrew them. "See, I'm afraid to touch you." He mused, his eyes rounded. "Of all the ugly things there are, fear is the ugliest. And yet, see, it can be the very beautifulest. That's a strange queer thing."

The wind blew in and out of the room, bringing the thin, little bitter sweetness of new April at night. The moonlight that came across Mare's shoulders fell full upon his face, but hers it left dark, ringed by the aureole of her disordered hair.

"Why do you wear a halo, Love?" He thought about it. "Because you're an angel, is that why?" The swift, untempered logic of the mad led him to dismay. His hands came flying to hers, to make sure they were of earth; and he touched her breast, her shoulders, and her hair. Peace returned to his eyes as his fingers twined among the strands.

" 'Thy hair is as a flock of goats that appear from Gilead. . . .' " He spoke like a man dreaming. " 'Thy temples are like a piece of pomegranate within thy locks.' "

Mare never knew that he could not see her for the moonlight.

"Do you remember, Love?"

She dared not shake her head under his hand. "Yeh, I reckon," she temporized.

"You remember how I sat at your feet, long ago, like this, and made up a song? And all the poets in all the world have never made one to touch it, have they, Love?"

"Ugh-ugh—never."

" 'How beautiful are thy feet with shoes. . . .' Remember?"

"Oh, my God, what's he sayin' now?" she wailed to herself.

How beautiful are thy feet with shoes, O prince's daughter! the joints of thy thighs are like jewels, the work of the hands of a cunning workman.

Thy navel is like a round goblet, which wanteth not liquor; thy belly is like an heap of wheat set about with lilies.

Thy two breasts are like two young roes that are twins."

Mare had not been to church since she was a little girl, when her mother's black dress wore out. "No, no!" she wailed under her breath. "You're awful to say such awful things." She might have shouted it; nothing could have shaken the man now, rapt in the immortal, passionate periods of Solomon's song.

". . . now also thy breasts shall be as clusters of the vine, and the smell of thy nose like apples."

Hotness touched Mare's face for the first time. "Aw, no, don't talk so!"

"And the roof of thy mouth like the best wine for my belovéd . . . causing the lips of them that are asleep to speak."

He had ended. His expression changed. Ecstasy gave place to anger, love to hate. And Mare felt the change in the weight of the fingers in her hair.

"What do you mean, I mustn't say it like that?" But it was not to her his fury spoke, for he answered himself straightway. "Like poetry, Mr. Jewett; I won't have blasphemy around my school."

"Poetry! My God! if that isn't poetry—if that isn't music——"
. . . "It's Bible, Jewett. What you're paid to teach here is *literature.*"

"Doctor Ryeworth, you're the blasphemer and you're an ignorant man." . . . "And your Principal. And I won't have you going around reading sacred allegory like earthly love."

"Ryeworth, you're an old man, a dull man, a dirty man, and you'd be better dead."

Jewett's hands had slid down from Mare's head. "Then I went to put my fingers around his throat, so. But my stomach turned, and I didn't do it. I went to my room. I laughed all the way to my room. I sat in my room at my table and I laughed. I laughed all afternoon and long after dark came. And then, about ten, somebody came and stood beside me in my room."

" 'Wherefore dost thou laugh, son?'

"Then I knew who He was, He was Christ.

" 'I was laughing about that dirty, ignorant, crazy old fool, Lord.'

" 'Wherefore dost thou laugh?'

"I didn't laugh any more. He didn't say any more. I kneeled down, bowed my head.

" 'Thy will be done! Where is he, Lord?'

" 'Over at the girls' dormitory, waiting for Blossom Sinckley.'

"Brassy Blossom, dirty Blossom. . . ."

It had come so suddenly it was nearly too late. Mare tore at his hands with hers, tried with all her strength to pull her neck away.

"Filthy Blossom! and him an old filthy man, Blossom! and you'll find him in Hell when you reach there, Blossom. . . ."

It was more the nearness of his face than the hurt of his hands that gave her power of fright to choke out three words.

"*I—ain't—Blossom!*"

Light ran in crooked veins. Through the veins she saw his face bewildered. His hands loosened. One fell down and hung; the other he lifted and put over his eyes, took it away again and looked at her.

"Amarantha!" His remorse was fearful to see. "What have I done!" His hands returned to hover over the hurts, ravening with pity, grief and tenderness. Tears fell down his cheeks. And with that, dammed desire broke its dam.

"Amarantha, my love, my dove, my beautiful love—"

"*And I ain't Amarantha neither, I'm Mary! Mary, that's my name!*"

She had no notion what she had done. He was like a crystal crucible that a chemist watches, changing hue in a wink with one adeptly added drop; but hers was not the chemist's eye. All she knew was that she felt light and free of him; all she could see of his face as he stood away above the moonlight were the whites of his eyes.

"Mary!" he muttered. A slight paroxysm shook his frame. So in the transparent crucible desire changed its hue. He retreated farther, stood in the dark by some tall piece of furniture. And still she could see the whites of his eyes.

"Mary! Mary Adorable!" A wonder was in him. "Mother of God!"

Mare held her breath. She eyed the door, but it was too far. And already he came back to go on his knees before her, his shoulders so bowed and his face so lifted that it must have cracked his neck, she thought; all she could see on the face was pain.

"Mary Mother, I'm sick to my death. I'm so tired."

She had seen a dog like that, one she had loosed from a trap after it had been there three days, its caught leg half gnawed free. Something about the eyes.

"Mary Mother, take me in your arms. . . ."

Once again her muscles tightened. But he made no move.

". . . and give me sleep."

No, they were worse than the dog's eyes.

"Sleep, sleep! why won't they let me sleep? Haven't I done it all yet, Mother? Haven't I washed them yet of all their sins? I've drunk the cup that was given me; is there another? They've mocked me and reviled me, broken my brow with thorns and my hands with nails, and I've forgiven them, for they knew not what they did. Can't I go to sleep now, Mother?"

Mare could not have said why, but now she was more frightened than she had ever been. Her hands lay heavy on her knees, side by side, and she could not take them away when he bowed his head and rested his face upon them.

After a moment he said one thing more. "Take me down gently when you take me from the Tree."

Gradually the weight of his body came against her shins, and he slept.

The moon streak that entered by the eastern window crept north across the floor, thinner and thinner; the one that fell through the southern doorway traveled east and grew fat. For a while Mare's feet pained her terribly and her legs too. She dared not move them, though, and by and by they did not hurt so much.

A dozen times, moving her head slowly on her neck, she canvassed the shadows of the room for a weapon. Each time her eyes came back to a heavy earthenware pitcher on a stand some feet to the left of the sofa. It would have had flowers in it when Wyker's wife was alive; probably it had not been moved from its dust-ring since she died. It would be a long grab, perhaps too long; still, it might be done if she had her hands.

To get her hands from under the sleeper's head was the task she set herself. She pulled first one, then the other, infinitesimally. She waited. Again she tugged a very, very little. The order of his breathing was not disturbed. But at the third trial he stirred.

"Gently! gently!" His own muttering waked him more. With some drowsy instinct of possession he threw one hand across her wrists, pinning them together between thumb and fingers. She kept dead quiet, shut her eyes, lengthened her breathing, as if she too slept.

There came a time when what was pretense grew a peril; strange as it was, she had to fight to keep her eyes open. She never knew whether or not she really napped. But something changed in the air, and she was wide awake again. The moonlight was fading on the doorsill, and the light that runs before dawn waxed in the window behind her head.

And then she heard a voice in the distance, lifted in maundering song. It was old man Wyker coming home after a night, and it was plain he had had some whiskey.

Now a new terror laid hold of Mare.

"Shut up, you fool you!" she wanted to shout. "Come quiet, quiet!" She might have chanced it now to throw the sleeper away from her and scramble and run, had his powers of strength and quickness not taken her simple imagination utterly in thrall.

Happily the singing stopped. What had occurred was that the farmer had espied the open door and, even befuddled as he was, wanted to know more about it quietly. He was so quiet that Mare began to fear he had gone away. He had the squirrel-hunter's foot, and the first she knew of him was when she looked and saw his head in the doorway, his hard, soiled, whiskery face half up-side-down with craning.

He had been to the town. Between drinks he had wandered in and out of the night's excitement; had even gone a short distance with one search party himself. Now he took in the situation in the room. He used his forefinger. First he held it to his lips. Next he pointed it with a jabbing motion at the sleeper. Then he tapped his own forehead and described wheels. Lastly, with his whole hand, he made pushing gestures, for Mare to wait. Then he vanished as silently as he had appeared.

The minutes dragged. The light in the east strengthened and turned rosy. Once she thought she heard a board creaking in another part of the house, and looked down sharply to see if the loony stirred. All she could see of his face was a temple with freckles on it and the sharp ridge of a cheekbone, but even from so little she knew how deeply and peacefully he slept. The door darkened. Wyker was there again. In one hand he carried something heavy; with the other he beckoned.

"Come jumpin'!" he said out loud.

Mare went jumping, but her cramped legs threw her down half way to the sill; the rest of the distance she rolled and crawled. Just as she tumbled through the door it seemed as if the world had come to an end above her; two barrels of a shotgun discharged into a room make a noise. Afterwards all she could hear in there was something twisting and bumping on the floor-boards. She got up and ran.

Mare's mother had gone to pieces; neighbor women put her to bed when Mare came home. They wanted to put Mare to bed, but she would not let them. She sat on the edge of her bed in her lean-to bedroom off the kitchen, just as she was, her hair down all over her shoulders and her shoes on, and stared away from them, at a place in the wallpaper.

"Yeh, I'll go myself. Lea' me be!"

The women exchanged quick glances, thinned their lips, and left her be. "God knows," was all they would answer to the questionings of those that had not gone in, "but she's gettin' herself to bed."

When the doctor came though he found her sitting just as she had been, still dressed, her hair down on her shoulders and her shoes on.

"What d' y' want?" she muttered and stared at the place in the wallpaper.

How could Doc Paradise say, when he did not know himself?

"I didn't know if you might be—might be feeling very smart, Mary."

"I'm all right. Lea' me be."

It was a heavy responsibility. Doc shouldered it. "No, it's all right," he said to the men in the road. Ruby Herter stood a little apart, chewing sullenly and looking another way. Doc raised his voice to make certain it carried. "Nope, nothing."

Ruby's ears got red, and he clamped his jaws. He knew he ought to go in and see Mare, but he was not going to do it while everybody hung around waiting to see if he would. A mule tied near him reached out and mouthed his sleeve in idle innocence; he wheeled and banged a fist against the side of the animal's head.

"Well, what d' y' aim to do 'bout it?" he challenged its owner.

He looked at the sun then. It was ten in the morning. "Hell, I got work!" he flared, and set off down the road for home. Doc looked at Judge North, and the Judge started after Ruby. But Ruby shook his head angrily. "Lea' me be!" He went on, and the Judge came back.

It got to be eleven and then noon. People began to say, "Like enough she'd be as thankful if the whole neighborhood wasn't camped here." But none went away.

As a matter of fact they were no bother to the girl. She never saw them. The only move she made was to bend her ankles over and rest her feet on edge; her shoes hurt terribly and her feet knew it, though she did not. She sat all the while staring at that one figure in the wallpaper, and she never saw the figure.

Strange as the night had been, this day was stranger. Fright and physical pain are perishable things once they are gone. But while pain merely dulls and telescopes in memory and remains diluted pain, terror looked back upon has nothing of terror left. A gambling chance taken, at no matter what odds, and won was a sure thing since the world's beginning; perils come through safely were never perilous. But what fright does do in retrospect is this—it heightens each sensuous recollection, like a hard, clear lacquer laid on wood, bringing out the color and grain of it vividly.

Last night Mare had lain stupid with fear on groundpine beneath a bush, loud foot-falls and light whispers confused in her ear. Only now, in her room, did she smell the groundpine.

Only now did the conscious part of her brain begin to make words of the whispering.

"Amarantha," she remembered, "Amarantha sweet and fair." That was as far as she could go for the moment, except that the rhyme with "fair" was "hair." But then a puzzle, held in abeyance, brought other words. She wondered what "ravel Ed" could mean. "*Most excellently ravelléd.*" It was left to her mother to bring the end.

They gave up trying to keep her mother out at last. The poor woman's prostration took the form of fussiness.

"Good gracious, daughter, you look a sight. Them new shoes, half ruined; ain't your feet *dead?* And look at your hair, all tangled like a wild one!"

She got a comb.

"Be quiet, daughter; what's ailin' you. Don't shake your head!"

" '*But shake your head and scatter day.*' "

"What you say, Amarantha?" Mrs. Doggett held an ear down.

"Go 'way! Lea' me be!"

Her mother was hurt and left. And Mare ran, as she stared at the wallpaper.

"*Christ, that my love were in my arms. . . .*"

Mare ran. She ran through a wind white with moonlight and wet with "the small rain." And the wind she ran through, it ran through her, and made her shiver as she ran. And the man beside her leaped high over the waves of the dead grasses and gathered the wind in his arms, and her hair was heavy and his was tossing, and a little fox ran before them across the top of the world. And the world spread down around in waves of black and silver, more immense than she had ever known the world could be, and more beautiful.

"*God Almighty beautiful, to take your breath away!*"

Mare wondered, and she was not used to wondering. "Is it only crazy folks ever run like that and talk that way?"

She no longer ran; she walked; for her breath was gone. And there was some other reason, some other reason. Oh, yes, it was because her feet were hurting her. So, at last, and roundabout, her shoes had made contact with her brain.

Bending over the side of the bed, she loosened one of them mechanically. She pulled it half off. But then she looked down at it sharply, and she pulled it on again.

"*How beautiful. . . .*"

Color overspread her face in a slow wave.

"*How beautiful are thy feet with shoes. . . .*"

"Is it only crazy folks ever say such things?"

"*O prince's daughter!*"

"Or call you that?"

By and by there was a knock at the door. It opened, and Ruby Herter came in.

"Hello, Mare old girl!" His face was red. He scowled and kicked at the floor. "I'd 'a' been over sooner, except we got a mule down sick." He looked at his dumb betrothed. "Come on, cheer up, forget it! He won't scare you no more, not that boy, not what's left o' him. What you lookin' at, sourface? Ain't you glad to see me?"

Mare quit looking at the wallpaper and looked at the floor.

"Yeh," she said.

"That's more like it, babe." He came and sat beside her; reached down behind her and gave her a spank. "Come on, give us a kiss, babe!" He wiped his mouth on his jumper sleeve, a good farmer's sleeve, spotted with milking. He put his hands on her; he was used to handling animals. "Hey, you, warm up a little; reckon I'm goin' to do all the lovin'?"

"Ruby, lea' me be!"

"What!"

She was up, twisting. He was up, purple.

"What's ailin' of you, Mare? What you bawlin' about?"

"Nothin'—only go 'way!"

She pushed him to the door and through it with all her strength, and closed it in his face, and stood with her weight against it, crying, "Go 'way! Go 'way! Lea' me be!"

QUESTIONS

1. In the description of Mare, the "broad-fleshed, slow-minded" farm girl, what detail is mentioned which is of great importance later in the story?

2. The young man waiting at Mare's home answers her simple question "Who are you?" by saying "Amarantha! That's poetry." Why does his answer make Mare sure that she does not know him?

3. How does Mare come to realize that this is the man who has escaped from the Asylum?

4. After they have stopped running, the young man says,

"Amarantha sweet and fair . . . Braid no more that shining hair!"
He is quoting from a poem by a seventeenth century English poet,
Richard Lovelace. As was the custom then, the poet was praising
extravagantly his lady's beauty:

To Amarantha, That She Would Dishevel Her Hair

Amarantha sweet and fair,
Ah, braid no more that shining hair!
As my curious hand or eye,
Hovering round thee, let it fly.

. . .

Ev'ry tress must be confessed
But neatly tangled at the best,
Like a clue of golden thread,
Most excellently raveled.

Do not then wind up that light
In ribands, and o'ercloud in night;
Like the sun in's early ray,
But shake your head and scatter day.

. . .

What two facts about the girl make the young man think of this
particular poem?

5. After Jewett is caught and Mare is back at home, Older
Haskins tells what he knows about Jewett. Which fact explains why
Jewett happens to know a seventeenth-century poem?

6. When Jewett cannot make anyone in Wyker's house open the
door, he passes "to full fury in a wink's time." What future events
does this instability of mood prepare the reader for?

7. Once inside the house, Jewett touches Mare's hair and is reminded of a line in another poem, "The Song of Solomon" in the
Bible. Immediately he imagines he is the poet composing the "Song"
and quotes at length from the following verses of it:

Chapter 4
1. Behold, thou art fair, my love; behold, thou art fair; thou hast
doves' eyes within thy locks: thy hair is as a flock of goats, that appear
from mount Gilead.
2. Thy teeth are like a flock of sheep that are even shorn, which

came up from the washing; whereof every one bear twins, and none is barren among them.

3. Thy lips are like a thread of scarlet, and thy speech is comely: thy temples are like a piece of a pomegranate within thy locks.

. . .

Chapter 7

1. How beautiful are thy feet with shoes, O prince's daughter! the joints of thy thighs are like jewels, the work of the hands of a cunning workman.

2. Thy navel is like a round goblet, which wanteth not liquor: thy belly is like an heap of wheat set about with lilies.

3. Thy two breasts are like two young roes that are twins.

. . .

8. I said, I will go up to the palm tree, I will take hold of the boughs thereof: now also thy breasts shall be as clusters of the vine, and the smell of thy nose like apples;

9. And the roof of thy mouth like the best wine for my beloved, that goeth down sweetly, causing the lips of those that are asleep to speak.

What words of Mare's cause Jewett's ecstasy to turn suddenly to anger and lead him to reenact the scene in which his intolerant principal, Doctor Ryeworth, once said that he must not read this poem to his classes?

8. Jewett's mind flits rapidly from one scene to another in his past, and now he imagines that Mare is Blossom, until her words *"I— ain't—Blossom!"* bring him back again to the world of reality. Her next words, however, send him off into another delusion. Who does he now think that Mare is, and who is he?

9. The first part of the story is an account of Mare's experience; the second part is Mare's reflection on that experience and her reaction to it. Why would the story be less effective if it had ended with the death of Jewett?

10. What is meant by the statement on p. 71, "But what fright does do in retrospect is this—it heightens each sensuous recollection, like a hard, clear lacquer laid on wood, bringing out the color and grain of it vividly"?

11. Mare, now in her own room, remembers many of the details she had hardly been conscious of during her frightening experience. Compare the paragraph on p. 63 beginning "Mare got up and ran" (a description of the actual flight) with the paragraph on p. 72 be-

ginning "Mare ran" (Mare's recollection of the flight). How do the two paragraphs differ? As Mare goes over in her mind all the details of that race through the fields, she becomes aware of something that she had not been aware of at the time, something that her experience with a literate and sensitive person has given her a glimpse of. What is it?

12. As she recalls some of the lines of poetry that Jewett had repeated, she wonders, "Is it only crazy folks ever run like that and talk that way?" Would she have any way of knowing?

13. As she loosens one of her shoes mechanically, she remembers the line of poetry, "How beautiful are thy feet with shoes," and she pulls the shoe back on, somehow thinking that Jewett had been talking about *her* feet and *her* shoes. What are her shoes a symbol of to her now? (See *Symbolism*, p. 9.)

14. Is there anything ironic about Jewett's being the person to awaken Mare to the beauty in life and love?

15. What is the conflict? Is it something more than Mare's conflict with a madman?

16. Is Mare the same person she was at the beginning of the story? Will she ever be? As in many good stories the reader is left to imagine the final outcome. What is going to happen to Mare?

17. What is the theme of the story?

MR. CORNELIUS, I LOVE YOU
JESSAMYN WEST

Mr. and Mrs. Delahanty, Cress, and Cress's friends, Jo Grogan and Bernadine Deevers, sat down to the Delahanty dinner table on Wednesday evening. The table was round with a white cloth that dipped at its four corners to the floor, so that in the dusk of the dining room the cloth seemed actually to be supporting the table. Mrs. Delahanty, who hadn't even expected Cress home for dinner, let alone Jo and Bernadine, felt apologetic about the food which, besides being rather uninviting, was skimpy in amount: a small salmon loaf, Harvard beets, mashed potatoes, and for dessert a cabinet pudding which did nothing to redeem the meal that had gone before. But the girls didn't seem to know or care what they put in their mouths and she decided that strawberries and fresh asparagus would have been wasted on them.

A mockingbird was singing in the orange grove outside the opened windows and the girls listened, a spoonful of cabinet pudding lifted to their opened lips—then, as the song ceased, put the spoons down without having tasted a bite. Mr. and Mrs. Delahanty had given up trying to carry on a conversation with them and treated them as so many portraits ranged round their dining room—"Girls at Dusk," or "Reveries of Youth." They talked their own talk and let the girls dream their dreams, wrap their feet around the rungs of their chairs, and listen (mouths open, eyes closed) to the bird song.

"I saw Doc Mendenhall in town today," Mr. Delahanty said.

Mrs. Delahanty said "Yes?" waiting for whatever it was that made this fact worth reporting, but Bernadine interrupted his train of thought, if he had one, by extending her long arms toward the darkening windows and singing very softly, "Oh night of love, oh beauteous night." Bernadine was barefooted (it was the spring's great fad at high school) though she was eighteen, and wore an elaborate blue voile dress which drifted about her like a sky-stained cloud. Bernadine was to be married the day after school was out and sometimes, Mrs. Delahanty felt, overplayed her role of bride-to-be.

It was already, unbelievably, the last week of school which, in Southern California, is the second week in June, a time climatically as well as scholastically neither one thing nor another, neither spring nor summer, neither truly school nor truly vacation. Class routines had been relaxed but not abandoned. Grade-wise, the feeling among the students was that the year was already water over the dam; still they couldn't be positive; some of the teachers were still going through the motions of setting down grades in their record books. Climatically the days started spring-like, damp and gray with threat even of one more unseasonal rain; at 1 P.M. exactly the day did an aboutface, took on September inclinations. At that hour the overcast burned away and the tawny grasses, sun-bleached foothills, and smoldering flowers of full summer emerged. It was very confusing after getting up into a dripping cold which made sweaters and open fires necessary, to finish the day barefooted, hot-cheeked, and as naked as possible.

Cress and Jo both wore shorts and halters. Cress had shasta daisies tucked in the V of her halter and Jo Grogan, with those three flame-colored hibiscus in her short dark hair, might have been August itself on any calendar of girls. As the day darkened the white tablecloth grew silvery, the mockingbird retreated deeper into the orchard, and Mrs. Delahanty felt that the whole scene might be unreal, a mirage cast up into the present out of either the past or the future— that girls *had* sat in many a darkening room in years gone by and would so sit in the future; but that "now," the present minute, was unreal, only the past whisking by on its way to the future, or the future casting a long prophetic shadow to rearwards.

"Jo," she said briskly, "if you'll put some more custard on your pudding you might be able to eat it."

"I beg your pardon," said Jo. "Were you speaking to me?"

"Never mind," Mrs. Delahanty told her. "I was only urging you to eat."

"Oh food!" said Cress. "Food. Who cares about food?"

"I do," said Bernadine. "Howie adores puddings. Will you copy down this recipe for me, Mrs. Delahanty? I plan to serve Howie a different pudding every single night for thirty nights. I already have twenty-two recipes."

"Tapioca, jello, and bread," said Jo, sing-songing. "If puddings be the food of love, cook on."

The mockingbird had ceased to sing. The leaves of the bougain-villaea vine which clambered over the dining-room wall rustled faintly. Mrs. Delahanty began taking the spoons from the serving dishes.

Mr. Delahanty remarked in the voice of a man who has had the words in mind for some time, "Doc Mendenhall says that Frank Cornelius had a bad hemorrhage this morning."

Mrs. Delahanty laid the spoons down, clattering. "Oh John!" she said. "I understood he was getting better."

There was a note in her voice of condemnation, as if Mr. Cornelius had not tried hard enough, as if he were a turncoat, a traitor to his generation—and hers. When old people sickened and died, men and women in their seventies and eighties, that was to be expected. But thirty-eight! That was a direct threat to her and John.

"I don't think he's taken very good care of himself," Mr. Delahanty explained. "You can't throw off t.b. just by wishing. You've got to cooperate, rest, stay put. I've seen Cornelius about town off and on all spring. Baseball, things like that. Staggering around half-alive. I saw him yesterday, sitting along the road out by his place. Today, a hemorrhage. He was asking for . . . ."

Cress sprang to her feet, interrupting her father. "You mustn't say that. You have no right to say that." She pulled the daisies from the neck of her halter and passed them from hand to hand distractedly. "You don't have any idea what it's like to be dying. Do you?" she insisted.

Mr. Delahanty agreed instantly. "No, I don't, Crescent. The worst I ever had was a touch of shingles."

"Don't be funny," Cress said, her chin quivering. "Don't be funny about death. How can you understand how terrible it is for Mr. Cornelius to think he may die, no matter how much he takes care of himself? And that if he doesn't go out and see the sunshine and people and trees today he may never see them again. Never, never. And you were never a great athlete like Mr. Cornelius, so it's a thousand times worse for him than it would be for you to stay in bed. And you blame him. You blame him for not giving in. You blame him," she paused, trying to steady her voice. "I hate—I hate *people* who say cruel things like that." She looked at her father and Mr. Delahanty looked back. Then she dropped her daisies onto her plate amidst the uneaten salmon and beets and ran from the room.

Mrs. Delahanty, after the sound of the slammed door had stopped echoing, leaned over and began to gather up the daisies. The two girls excused themselves and left the room.

"What did I say?" Mr. Delahanty asked. "To cause all that?"

Mrs. Delahanty continued without speaking to shake bits of food from the flowers. "Gertrude, did what I said sound cruel and hateful to you?"

"No, John, not to me," she answered. "But then I'm not in love with Mr. Cornelius."

In her bedroom, Cress sat on the floor, her head on the window sill. When she felt an arm about her shoulders, Jo's by the weight and pressure, she said, "Go away, please go away and leave me alone." The arm remained where it was. Jo knew, and so did Bernadine. Not much, because there wasn't much to know, except that she had seen Mr. Cornelius three times to look at him and had spoken to him twice and that she loved him and would willingly die for him.

There was "not much to know" in what was called the outside world; but inside herself, in her dreams and imaginings there was nothing *but* Mr. Cornelius. She had decided out of her experience of loving Mr. Cornelius that the knowledge people had of one another, parents of children, anyway, was almost nothing. She could sit at the dinner table with her father and mother, answering their questions about school, but being in reality thousands of miles away in some hot dry land nursing Mr. Cornelius back to health; and her father and mother never noticed her absence in the least.

In her dreams she and Mr. Cornelius sometimes went away together, Mr. Cornelius saying, "Cress, without knowing it I have been searching for you all of my life. My sickness is no more than the sum of my disappointment, and without you I can never get well."

Sometimes in her dreams Mrs. Cornelius came to her and the gist of what she said was, "My life with Mr. Cornelius has been a failure. He has not many months to live. I do not want to stand between him and his happiness in the little time that is left. Go, with my blessing."

But for the most part Mrs. Cornelius and the Cornelius boys did not exist in her dreams; even the world, as she knew it in what was called "real life," was greatly altered; or, perhaps, simplified. Changed, anyway, so that it consisted of nothing but sunshine, a background of sand or water, and a grassy or sandy bank against which Mr. Cornelius reclined, getting well. And as he got well she waited on him, and talked to him. As a matter of fact, every thought in her mind had become part of an unending monologue directed toward the omnipresent mental image of Mr. Cornelius. Everything she saw immediately became words in a report to Mr. Cornelius; and if, by chance, some experience was so absorbing as to momentarily obscure his image, she made up for it by living the whole scene through once again just for him. Sometimes she imagined that Mr. Cornelius kissed her. She had to be careful about these imaginings however. She had never been kissed, family didn't count, of course, and since she supposed that when you were kissed by the man you loved, the sensations were near to swooning, swooning was what she nearly did whenever she had imaginings of this kind.

Most often she simply helped Mr. Cornelius as he reclined in the midst of the sunny simplified landscape, his thin beautiful face becoming tanned and fuller as his health improved; but not more beautiful. That was impossible. She doted on his hawk-nose and dark crest; she dismissed every other face she saw as pudgy and ill-shaped by comparison. In her dream she picked flowers for Mr. Cornelius, went to the library for him, read to him, smoothed his brow, sometimes kissed him and always, always gazed at him with enraptured eyes. But all the time she was imagining this life with Mr. Cornelius she suffered, because Mr. Cornelius was dying and there was nothing she could do about it; she suffered because she had feelings which she did not know how to express, suffered because she had put the core of her life outside its circumference.

She sat up, and Jo took her arm away. It was still light enough to see Bernadine on the floor leaning against the bed, and Jo by her side. The pitcher of white stock on her desk reflected what light there was, like a moon. The room was quiet and warm and full of misery.

"There is nothing you can do, Cress," Jo said. "You love him and he is dying. You can't do anything about either one. All you can do is to endure it."

"I can do something," Cress said.

"What?" Jo asked.

"I can go to Mr. Cornelius and tell him I love him."

"Oh no," Bernadine said, very shocked. "You can't do that."

"Why not?" Cress asked.

"You don't know whether he loves you or not."

"What does that have to do with it? I'm not going to him to ask him if he loves me. I'm going to tell him that I love him."

"Is that what you really want to do, Cress?" Jo asked.

"No—if you mean by want to, do I feel good about going. I feel awful about going. It makes me feel sick to my stomach to even think about it. It gives me the shakes."

Jo once again put an arm around Cress's shoulders. "It's a fact," she reported to Bernadine. "She's shaking like a leaf."

"Look, Cress," Bernadine said. "I'm almost married myself. It's just a matter of days. For all practical purposes I *am* married. You must think of Mr. Cornelius, Cress, and what he'd feel. I know if Howie was sick and maybe dying he wouldn't want some other woman coming to his sick bed and saying, 'I love you.' The first thing he'd do, I know, is say to me, 'Bernadine, throw this madwoman out.' And that's exactly what Mr. Cornelius is liable to say to you."

"I know it," Cress said bleakly.

"Well, then?" Bernadine asked, pride of reasoning in her voice. "Are you still going?"

Cress huddled silent, unanswering.

"It's probably not a very kind thing to do," Jo suggested in her deep, thoughtful voice. "Go to see him now when he's so sick."

"Oh I *know* that. If I just asked myself what was kind I would never do it. But what has kindness got to do with love? I'm not doing it to be kind to Mr. Cornelius. I'm doing it because I have to."

"Have to?" Jo reminded her, steadily. "You don't have to. Sit right here. Sit still. By morning everything will be different."

"By morning Mr. Cornelius may be dead."

"Well then," Bernadine said, "all your problems will be over. Mr. Cornelius will be dead and you'll be sad. But you won't have bothered him or made a fool of yourself."

"I don't care about making a fool of myself."

"You do care. You're still shaking. And think about Mrs. Cornelius. How's she going to feel about someone barging in on her sick husband, making passionate declarations of love?"

"It wouldn't be passionate. I would just say, very quietly, the minute I got there, 'I love you, Mr. Cornelius.' Then leave."

"Cress," Bernadine said, "what actually do you see yourself doing? You get there, the whole family is around the bed, and doctors and priests too, maybe. What are your plans? To say 'I beg your pardon but I've a little message for Mr. Cornelius'? Then push your way through them all to the bedside, drop on your knee, kiss his wasted hand and say, 'Mr. Cornelius, I love you.' Is that it?"

"Oh, don't heckle her, Bernadine," Jo said.

"What I see myself doing," said Cress, "is telling Mr. Cornelius something I have to tell him."

"How," asked Bernadine, "do you see yourself getting there?" Bernadine had Howie's car while he was in the army and she had driven the girls home from school. "Do you see yourself walking eight miles?"

"If I have to," Cress said.

"O.K.," Bernadine told her. "I'll drive you. And let's go right away and get it over with."

Mr. Cornelius was still living in the small one-room tent-house at the edge of the walnut grove in which his home stood. Here he was away from the noises of his family and was able to get the fresh air he needed. It was nine o'clock when Bernadine stopped the car in front of the Cornelius ranch. A dim light was burning inside the tent-house, but there was nothing to indicate the presence of the crowd of people she had prophesied. "Here we are," she said, turning off the engine.

Cress wished for any catastrophe, however great, which would prevent her from having to leave the car. She felt real hatred for Bernadine and Jo. Why, if they were convinced that she shouldn't come, hadn't they remained steadfast? What kind of friends were they, to give way to their better judgment so weakly? And what were her parents thinking about? Why had they permitted her to go riding off into the night? To tell a strange man she loved him? True, she hadn't told them where she was going nor that she loved a strange man. But what were parents for if not to understand without being told? She blamed them for her fright and unhappiness.

Still anything that *happened* would be better than continuing to live in a make-believe world in which she only dreamed that she told Mr. Cornelius she loved him. And she knew that if Bernadine were to start the car now she would jump out and run toward the tent-house and the declaration which would start her to living inside her dream. She opened the car door and stepped out into the night air which, after the warmth of the car, was damp and cold against her bare legs and arms.

"Cheerio," said Bernadine quite calmly as she was walking away from the car under the dark canopy of the big trees toward the dimly lighted room. Why was it so hard to do what she had set her heart on doing?

She stood at the screened door looking into the room as into a picture. Why did it seem like a picture? The small number of furnishings? Their neat arrangement, dresser balanced by table, chair by bed? The light falling from a bulb, shaded by blue paper, so that part of the room was in deep shadow? But most of all, was it picture-like because she had imagined the room and Mr. Cornelius for so long, that a frame had grown up about them in her mind? Now, would it be possible to break that frame? She opened the screen door, stepped into the room and became a part of the picture by that easy act.

Mr. Cornelius lay on a high narrow bed. He lay very straight, his head supported by three or four pillows and his hands folded across an ice pack which he held to his chest. His eyes were closed and his face, in spite of his illness, was warm with color. At the sight of him all of Cress's doubts left her. Oh Mr. Cornelius, she thought, I do truly love you and I have come at last to tell you.

Without opening his eyes Mr. Cornelius said, "Joyce, I think I'm going to be sick."

Joyce. Cress was surprised at the name. It seemed too gentle for the bus driver. "It's not Joyce, Mr. Cornelius," Cress said. "It's me."

Then Mr. Cornelius opened his eyes and Cress was enchanted all over again by the enormous blaze of being alive and searching and understanding which she saw there.

"It's Cress," he said, in a very low careful voice, "the track-meet girl." Then he closed his eyes. "I'm going to be sick," he said. "Hand me the basin."

The basin, Cress saw, was an enamel wash bowl on the night stand by the bed. She got it, put it on the bed beside Mr. Cornelius.

"Help me," Mr. Cornelius said and Cress helped him the way her mother had helped her when she was sick after her tonsils were out, by putting an arm around his shoulders and supporting him.

"Don't be scared," Mr. Cornelius whispered. "It's not a hemorrhage. I'm just going to lose my supper."

He did and afterwards he lay back against his pillows for a minute or two, then he reached up his hand and rang the bell which was suspended from the headboard of his bed.

"A glass of water," he told Cress, and Cress was holding it for him to rinse his mouth when Mrs. Cornelius arrived. Mrs. Cornelius paid no more attention to her than if she'd been some kind of device to help Mr. Cornelius—like the ice pack or the bell. She took the glass from Cress's hand, slipped her arm around her husband's shoulders and said, "Frank, Frank. Oh thank God, Frank, no more blood. Just your supper and that doesn't matter. I made you eat too much. This was to be expected. If you can swallow a bite or two later I'll fix you another. How do you feel now, honey?"

Cress had backed away from the bed. Mrs. Cornelius was wearing a housecoat or dressing gown of deep red, lightened by wreaths of tiny yellow and white flowers. What she looked like now was not a General in the Russian army but Robert Louis Stevenson's wife, "trusty, dusky, vivid and true with eyes of gold and bramble dew." Her bosom, which had spoiled the lines of her chauffeur's coat, was exactly right for pillowing an invalid's head, and her chestnut hair, curled corkscrew crisp, said "Never give up," as plain as any words, said "Fight on," said "Defy the universe." And all the time she was cradling Mr. Cornelius in her arms, and helping him rinse his mouth she was pressing her cheek to his hair and speaking comforting words through which there ran a mixture of laughing and joking.

"Take this to the bathroom and empty it," she said to Cress when Mr. Cornelius had finished rinsing his mouth. She handed the basin to Cress and nodded toward a door at the back of the room. Cress, ordinarily too squeamish to pull off her own Band-Aids, marched away with it without a word.

When she returned Mr. Cornelius was once more against his pillows and Mrs. Cornelius was wiping his face with a damp cloth.

"Where'd you come from?" she asked Cress as she took the basin from her.

"From out there," Cress said, nodding toward the road. "The girls are waiting for me. In the car," she explained.

Mrs. Cornelius paused in her washing. "What did you come *for?*" she asked.

Cress welcomed the question. It was a wonderful help, like the upward spring of the diving board against her feet when she was reluctant to take off into deep water. Though she no longer had so great a need to say what she had come to say; some change had taken place in her since she had come into the room; what had been locked inside her and had been painful, because unsaid, had somehow, without a word being spoken, gotten itself partially expressed. She was not sure how. Nevertheless she had come to speak certain words. They were the answer to Mrs. Cornelius' question. They were *why* she had come.

So, louder than was necessary, and in a voice cracking with strain she said, "I came to tell Mr. Cornelius I loved him." Then she turned, resolutely, and said the words directly to Mr. Cornelius. "Mr. Cornelius, I love you."

At that Mrs. Cornelius laughed, not jeering, not angry, not unbelieving, but in the soft delighted way of a person who has received an unexpected gift, a pleasure never dreamed of but one come in the nick of time and most acceptable.

"Oh, Frankie," she said, running her hand through Mr. Cornelius' thick black hair, "look at what we've got here."

"What *we've* got," was what she'd said as if, Cress thought, I'd said I loved them both. And then, watching Mr. Cornelius reach for his wife's hand, she saw that there was nothing she could give to Mr. Cornelius without giving it also to Mrs. Cornelius. Because they were not two separated people. They were really one, the way the Bible said. It was an astounding discovery. It was almost too much for her. It held her motionless and speculating. She felt as if her mind, by an infusion of light and warmth, was being forced to expand to accommodate this new idea. And it was an idea which, contrary to all her expectations, she liked. It was exactly what she wanted. Not Mr. Cornelius alone on a stretch of desert sand and she kissing his wasted hand—in spite of her six months' dreaming. What she wanted was Mr. and Mrs. Cornelius. She was so happy for Mrs. Cornelius' presence she almost took and kissed *her* plump brown unwasted hand.

Mrs. Cornelius, however, was continuing her laughing murmur to her husband. "Frankie," she said, "oh Frankie, you old jackanapes. You old irresistible. What's all this talk about being on your last legs? Done for? Caved in? With school girls coming with professions of love? Pretty school girls. Boy, we're not cashing in our checks just yet. Not us. What's your name, dear?" she asked Cress.

Mr. Cornelius answered in his low half-whispering voice. "She's John Delahanty's daughter, Crescent. They call her Cress at school."

"Well," said Mrs. Cornelius. "I've heard the boys mention you. Where'd you see Frank?"

"At a track meet."

"I stared at her some," Mr. Cornelius said. "Reminded me of you at her age. So alive."

"Was I ever like that?" Mrs. Cornelius asked her husband.

"That's what I thought about Mr. Cornelius," Cress said.

"Alive?" asked Mrs. Cornelius.

"Oh yes. More than anyone there. More than the boys. I thought his eyes fed on the sights," she said, daring the poetry of her thoughts.

"Fed?" Mrs. Cornelius studied the word then accepted it. "I see what you mean. Now Frank," she said, "will you lie still and take care of yourself? Unknown school girls loving you and wanting you to get well. You do, don't you?" she asked Cress.

"Oh yes," Cress said. "I was willing to die for him."

Her voice evidently convinced Mrs. Cornelius. "Oh Frank," she said, "school girls willing to die for you and you not half trying."

"Mrs. Cornelius," Cress said, wanting, since even partial confession made her feel so much better, to tell everything, "I ought to tell you something else." She stumbled for words. "I ought to tell you what else I planned."

"I bet you planned to run away with Frank and nurse him back to health."

Cress was amazed. "Yes," she said, her face burning with guilt and foolishness, "yes I did. How did you know?"

"Oh Frank, don't it bring it all back to you? No wonder you

were reminded of me. *I* was going to run away with the minister," she said turning to Cress. "Save him from his wife and family. And he *was* the most beautiful man in the world, Frank. You can't hold a candle to your father—never could."

Cress wanted to say something, but she couldn't settle on what. She had too many emotions to express. Exhilaration at being released from the isolation of her dreaming; relief to find that other girls had loved secretly too, but most of all joy to have acted, to have made for herself a single undivided world in which to live.

"Oh Mrs. Cornelius," she said, "oh Mrs. Cornelius. . . ."

"Cress," asked Mrs. Cornelius, "can you play cards? Or checkers?"

"Yes," Cress said, "I can. I like to."

"And read out loud? Of course you can do that, can't you? Why don't you come read to Frank? And play cards with him? It gets so darn lonesome for him. I work. The boys work, and besides they haven't got enough patience to sit still. And the good people come in and tell Frank how their uncles or mothers passed away with consumption and for him to be resigned. He needs somebody interested in living, not dying. Would you come?"

"Oh yes. If you want me—if he wants me. I could come every day all summer."

"O.K.," Mrs. Cornelius said, "we'll plan on it. Now you'd better run on. Frank's had a bad day. He's worn out."

Cress looked at Mr. Cornelius. His eyes were closed but he opened them at Mrs. Cornelius' words and made a good-by flicker with the lids.

"Good night," Cress said.

Mrs. Cornelius went to the door with her. "We'll count on you," she said once again and put a hand on Cress's shoulder and gave her a kind of humorous loving shake before she turned away.

Cress flew to the car propelled, it seemed, by the beat of her heart as a bird is propelled by the beat of its wings. The walnut leaves were alive and fluttering in the warm air and all about her mockingbirds were singing like nightingales. As she emerged from the grove she saw the June stars big and heavy-looking like June roses. This is the happiest hour of my life, she thought, and she yearned to do something lovely for the girls, something beautiful and memorable; but all she could think of was to ask them to go to town for milk shakes.

"I could stand some food," Bernadine said, "after all that waiting."

"He was sick," Cress explained, "and Mrs. Cornelius and I had to take care of him."

"Mrs. Cornelius? Did she come out?"

"Of course," Cress answered. "Wouldn't you, if Howie was sick?"

Bernadine had no answer to this. She started the car and after they had gone a mile or so Jo asked, "Did you tell him?"

"Of course."

"Does he love you?" Bernadine asked.

Cress felt sorry for Bernadine. "You're a fine one to be getting married," she said. "Of course he doesn't. He loves Joyce."

"Joyce? Who's Joyce?"

"Mrs. Cornelius. I remind him some of her. I adore Mrs. Cornelius. She is like Mrs. Robert Louis Stevenson and *they* are one person. Mr. and Mrs. Cornelius, I mean. They are truly married. I don't suppose you understand," she said, arrogant with new knowledge, "but what is for the one is for the other. I am going to help her take care of him this summer. Isn't that wonderful? Maybe I can really help him get well. Isn't this the most gloriously beautiful night? Oh, I think it's the most significant night of my life." The two girls were silent, but Cress was too full of her own emotions to notice.

When they went into the soda fountain, she looked at their reflection in the mirror and liked what she saw. The three of them had always been proud of one another. Bernadine had glamour, Jo character, and Cress personality; that was the division they made of themselves. "Look at Bernadine, listen to Cress, and let Jo act," someone had said. Oh, but I've broken through that, Cress thought, I can act, too. She searched for some understanding of the part Mrs. Cornelius had played in that breakthrough. If she had said, "You wicked girl," or made her feel that loving was a terrible thing? Would she have been pushed back, fearful, into the narrowness of dreaming, and into dreaming's untruths? She didn't know. She couldn't hold her mind to such abstractions.

"What we want," she said to Lester Riggins, the boy at the fountain, "is simply the most stupendous, colossal, overpowering concoction you ever served."

"This a special night?" Lester asked.

"Super-special."

"How come?"

"Bernadine's going to be married."

"Known that for six months."

"Jo's been accepted for Stanford. With special praise."

"Old stuff."

"Then there's me."

"What about you?"

"I'm alive."

"That's different," Lester said. "Why didn't you tell me in the first place? How do you like it?"

"Being alive? Fine," said Cress. "Better than shooting stars."

"O.K., O.K.," Lester said. "This obviously merits the Riggins' special. Expense any issue?"

"No issue," Cress said.

He brought them something shaped, roughly, like the Eiffel Tower, but more dramatically colored.

"Here it is, girls. Here's to being alive!"

They sank their spoons in it and ate it down, their appetites equal to the whole of it, color, size, sweetness and multiplicity of ingredients.

QUESTIONS

1. In this story Jessamyn West penetrates the mind and the daydreams of a sensitive teenage girl. From what point of view is the story told, and why is it effective?

2. Is the conflict between people or within a character's mind?

3. What details of the setting create a romantic mood?

4. How do the details of setting in the following lines symbolize adolescence? "It was . . . neither one thing nor another, neither spring nor summer, neither truly school nor truly vacation. . . . It was very confusing after getting up into a dripping cold which made

sweaters and open fires necessary, to finish the day barefooted, hot-cheeked, and as naked as possible."

5. Cress's sudden outburst against her father, out of all proportion to what he has said, is an indication of her schoolgirl crush on Mr. Cornelius. But, even though her crush indicates her immaturity, Cress is wise enough to understand her reason for wanting to declare her love. What is her reason?

6. What is the meaning on p. 81 of "she . . . suffered because she had put the core of her life outside its circumference"?

7. Although the situation in which Cress finds herself in the tent-house is hardly a romantic one, more important reasons account for her change in feeling toward Mr. Cornelius. What are they?

8. As evidenced by her daydreams and her comment about Mrs. Cornelius, what particular author has Cress been reading, and how does his life parallel that of Mr. Cornelius?

9. How does her making for herself "a single undivided world in which to live" relate to Question 6 above?

10. As she flies back to the car, the walnut leaves are "alive"; she says to the boy at the fountain, "I'm alive"; and he, as he brings their concoctions, says, "Here's to being alive!" What significance does the word *alive* have for Cress?

11. What theme comes out of the resolution of the conflict?

ISILLUSIONMENT

THE KILLERS
ERNEST HEMINGWAY

he door of Henry's lunch-room opened and two men came in. They sat down at the counter.

"What's yours?" George asked them.

"I don't know," one of the men said. "What do you want to eat, Al?"

"I don't know," said Al. "I don't know what I want to eat."

Outside it was getting dark. The street-light came on outside the window. The two men at the counter read the menu. From the other end of the counter Nick Adams watched them. He had been talking to George when they came in.

"I'll have a roast pork tenderloin with apple sauce and mashed potatoes," the first man said.

"It isn't ready yet."

"What the hell do you put it on the card for?"

"That's the dinner," George explained. "You can get that at six o'clock."

George looked at the clock on the wall behind the counter.

"It's five o'clock."

"The clock says twenty minutes past five," the second man said.

"It's twenty minutes fast."

"Oh, to hell with the clock," the first man said. "What have you got to eat?"

"I can give you any kind of sandwiches," George said. "You can have ham and eggs, bacon and eggs, liver and bacon, or a steak."

"Give me chicken croquettes with green peas and cream sauce and mashed potatoes."

"That's the dinner."

"Everything we want's the dinner, eh? That's the way you work it."

"I can give you ham and eggs, bacon and eggs, liver———"

"I'll take ham and eggs," the man called Al said. He wore a derby hat and a black overcoat buttoned across the chest. His face was small and white and he had tight lips. He wore a silk muffler and gloves.

"Give me bacon and eggs," said the other man. He was about the same size as Al. Their faces were different, but they were dressed like twins. Both wore overcoats too tight for them. They sat leaning forward, their elbows on the counter.

"Got anything to drink?" Al asked.

"Silver beer, bevo, ginger-ale," George said.

"I mean you got anything to *drink?*"

"Just those I said."

"This is a hot town," said the other. "What do they call it?"

"Summit."

"Ever hear of it?" Al asked his friend.

"No," said the friend.

"What do you do here nights?" Al asked.

"They eat the dinner," his friend said. "They all come here and eat the big dinner."

"That's right," George said.

"So you think that's right?" Al asked George.

"Sure."

"You're a pretty bright boy, aren't you?"

"Sure," said George.

"Well, you're not," said the other little man. "Is he, Al?"

"He's dumb," said Al. He turned to Nick. "What's your name?"

"Adams."

"Another bright boy," Al said. "Ain't he a bright boy, Max?"

"The town's full of bright boys," Max said.

George put the two platters, one of ham and eggs, the other of bacon and eggs, on the counter. He set down two side-dishes of fried potatoes and closed the wicket into the kitchen.

"Which is yours?" he asked Al.

"Don't you remember?"

"Ham and eggs."

"Just a bright boy," Max said. He leaned forward and took the ham and eggs. Both men ate with their gloves on. George watched them eat.

"What are *you* looking at?" Max looked at George.

"Nothing."

"The hell you were. You were looking at me."

"Maybe the boy meant it for a joke, Max," Al said.

George laughed.

"*You* don't have to laugh," Max said to him. "*You* don't have to laugh at all, see?"

"All right," said George.

"So he thinks it's all right." Max turned to Al. "He thinks it's all right. That's a good one."

"Oh, he's a thinker," Al said. They went on eating.

"What's the bright boy's name down the counter?" Al asked Max.

"Hey, bright boy," Max said to Nick. "You go around on the other side of the counter with your boy friend."

"What's the idea?" Nick asked.

"There isn't any idea."

"You better go around, bright boy," Al said. Nick went around behind the counter.

"What's the idea?" George asked.

"None of your damn business," Al said. "Who's out in the kitchen?"

"The nigger."

"What do you mean the nigger?"

"The nigger that cooks."

"Tell him to come in."

"What's the idea?"

"Tell him to come in."

"Where do you think you are?"

"We know damn well where we are," the man called Max said. "Do we look silly?"

"You talk silly," Al said to him. "What the hell do you argue with this kid for? Listen," he said to George, "tell the nigger to come out here."

"What are you going to do to him?"

"Nothing. Use your head, bright boy. What would we do to a nigger?"

George opened the slit that opened back into the kitchen. "Sam," he called. "Come in here a minute."

The door to the kitchen opened and the nigger came in. "What was it?" he asked. The two men at the counter took a look at him.

"All right, nigger. You stand right there," Al said.

Sam, the nigger, standing in his apron, looked at the two men sitting at the counter. "Yes, sir," he said. Al got down from his stool.

"I'm going back to the kitchen with the nigger and bright boy," he said. "Go on back to the kitchen, nigger. You go with him, bright boy." The little man walked after Nick and Sam, the cook, back into the kitchen. The door shut after them. The man called Max sat at the counter opposite George. He didn't look at George but looked in the mirror that ran along back of the counter. Henry's had been made over from a saloon into a lunch-counter.

"Well, bright boy," Max said, looking into the mirror, "why don't you say something?"

"What's it all about?"

"Hey, Al," Max called, "bright boy wants to know what it's all about."

"Why don't you tell him?" Al's voice came from the kitchen.

"What do you think it's all about?"

"I don't know."

"What do you think?"

Max looked into the mirror all the time he was talking.

"I wouldn't say."

"Hey, Al, bright boy says he wouldn't say what he thinks it's all about."

"I can hear you, all right," Al said from the kitchen. He had propped open the slit that dishes passed through into the kitchen with a catsup bottle. "Listen, bright boy," he said from the kitchen to George. "Stand a little further along the bar. You move a little to the left, Max." He was like a photographer arranging for a group picture.

"Talk to me, bright boy," Max said. "What do you think's going to happen?"

George did not say anything.

"I'll tell you," Max said. "We're going to kill a Swede. Do you know a big Swede named Ole Andreson?"

"Yes."

"He comes here to eat every night, don't he?"

"Sometimes he comes here."

"He comes here at six o'clock, don't he?"

"If he comes."

"We know all that, bright boy," Max said. "Talk about something else. Ever go to the movies?"

"Once in a while."

"You ought to go to the movies more. The movies are fine for a bright boy like you."

"What are you going to kill Ole Andreson for? What did he ever do to you?"

"He never had a chance to do anything to us. He never even seen us."

"And he's only going to see us once," Al said from the kitchen.

"What are you going to kill him for, then?" George asked.

"We're killing him for a friend. Just to oblige a friend, bright boy."

"Shut up," said Al from the kitchen. "You talk too goddam much."

"Well, I got to keep bright boy amused. Don't I, bright boy?"

"You talk too damn much," Al said. "The nigger and my bright boy are amused by themselves. I got them tied up like a couple of girl friends in the convent."

"I suppose you were in a convent."

"You never know."

"You were in a kosher convent. That's where you were."

George looked up at the clock.

"If anybody comes in you tell them the cook is off, and if they keep after it, you tell them you'll go back and cook yourself. Do you get that, bright boy?"

"All right," George said. "What you going to do with us afterward?"

"That'll depend," Max said. "That's one of those things you never know at the time."

George looked up at the clock. It was a quarter past six. The door from the street opened. A street-car motorman came in.

"Hello, George," he said. "Can I get supper?"

"Sam's gone out," George said. "He'll be back in about half an hour."

"I'd better go up the street," the motorman said. George looked at the clock. It was twenty minutes past six.

"That was nice, bright boy," Max said. "You're a regular little gentleman."

"He knew I'd blow his head off," Al said from the kitchen.

"No," said Max. "It ain't that. Bright boy is nice. He's a nice boy. I like him."

At six-fifty-five George said: "He's not coming."

Two other people had been in the lunch-room. Once George had gone out to the kitchen and made a ham-and-egg sandwich "to go" that a man wanted to take with him. Inside the kitchen he saw Al, his derby hat tipped back, sitting on a stool beside the wicket with the muzzle of a sawed-off shotgun resting on the ledge. Nick and the cook were back to back in the corner, a towel tied in each of their mouths. George had cooked the sandwich, wrapped it up in oiled paper, put it in a bag, brought it in, and the man had paid for it and gone out.

"Bright boy can do everything," Max said. "He can cook and everything. You'd make some girl a nice wife, bright boy."

"Yes?" George said. "Your friend, Ole Andreson, isn't going to come."

"We'll give him ten minutes," Max said.

Max watched the mirror and the clock. The hands of the clock marked seven o'clock, and then five minutes past seven.

"Come on, Al," said Max. "We better go. He's not coming."

"Better give him five minutes," Al said from the kitchen.

In the five minutes a man came in, and George explained that the cook was sick.

"Why the hell don't you get another cook?" the man asked. "Aren't you running a lunch-counter?" He went out.

"Come on, Al," Max said.

"What about the two bright boys and the nigger?"

"They're all right."

"You think so?"

"Sure. We're through with it."

"I don't like it," said Al. "It's sloppy. You talk too much."

"Oh, what the hell," said Max. "We got to keep amused, haven't we?"

"You talk too much, all the same," Al said. He came out from the kitchen. The cut-off barrels of the shotgun made a slight bulge under the waist of his too tight-fitting overcoat. He straightened his coat with his gloved hands.

"So long, bright boy," he said to George. "You got a lot of luck."

"That's the truth," Max said. "You ought to play the races, bright boy."

The two of them went out the door. George watched them, through the window, pass under the arc-light and cross the street. In their tight overcoats and derby hats they looked like a vaudeville team. George went back through the swinging-door into the kitchen and untied Nick and the cook.

"I don't want any more of that," said Sam, the cook. "I don't want any more of that."

Nick stood up. He had never had a towel in his mouth before.

"Say," he said. "What the hell?" He was trying to swagger it off.

"They were going to kill Ole Andreson," George said. "They were going to shoot him when he came in to eat."

"Ole Andreson?"

"Sure."

The cook felt the corners of his mouth with his thumbs.

"They all gone?" he asked.

"Yeah," said George. "They're gone now."

"I don't like it," said the cook. "I don't like any of it at all."

"Listen," George said to Nick. "You better go see Ole Andreson."

"All right."

"You better not have anything to do with it at all," Sam, the cook, said. "You better stay way out of it."

"Don't go if you don't want to," George said.

"Mixing up in this ain't going to get you anywhere," the cook said. "You stay out of it."

"I'll go see him," Nick said to George. "Where does he live?"

The cook turned away.

"Little boys always know what they want to do," he said.

"He lives up at Hirsch's rooming-house," George said to Nick.

"I'll go up there."

Outside the arc-light shone through the bare branches of a tree. Nick walked up the street beside the car-tracks and turned at the next arc-light down a side-street. Three houses up the street was Hirsch's rooming-house. Nick walked up the two steps and pushed the bell. A woman came to the door.

"Is Ole Andreson here?"

"Do you want to see him?"

"Yes, if he's in."

Nick followed the woman up a flight of stairs and back to the end of a corridor. She knocked on the door.

"Who is it?"

"It's somebody to see you, Mr. Andreson," the woman said.

"It's Nick Adams."

"Come in."

Nick opened the door and went into the room. Ole Andreson was lying on the bed with all his clothes on. He had been a heavyweight prizefighter and he was too long for the bed. He lay with his head on two pillows. He did not look at Nick.

"What was it?" he asked.

"I was up at Henry's," Nick said, "and two fellows came in and tied up me and the cook, and they said they were going to kill you."

It sounded silly when he said it. Ole Andreson said nothing.

"They put us out in the kitchen," Nick went on. "They were going to shoot you when you came in to supper."

Ole Andreson looked at the wall and did not say anything.

"George thought I better come and tell you about it."

"There isn't anything I can do about it," Ole Andreson said.

"I'll tell you what they were like."

"I don't want to know what they were like," Ole Andreson said. He looked at the wall. "Thanks for coming to tell me about it."

"That's all right."

Nick looked at the big man lying on the bed.

"Don't you want me to go and see the police?"

"No," Ole Andreson said. "That wouldn't do any good."

"Isn't there something I could do?"

"No. There ain't anything to do."

"Maybe it was just a bluff."

"No. It ain't just a bluff."

Ole Andreson rolled over toward the wall.

"The only thing is," he said, talking toward the wall, "I just can't make up my mind to go out. I been in here all day."

"Couldn't you get out of town?"

"No," Ole Andreson said. "I'm through with all that running around."

He looked at the wall.

"There ain't anything to do now."

"Couldn't you fix it up some way?"

"No. I got in wrong." He talked in the same flat voice. "There ain't anything to do. After a while I'll make up my mind to go out."

"I better go back and see George," Nick said.

"So long," said Ole Andreson. He did not look toward Nick. "Thanks for coming around."

Nick went out. As he shut the door he saw Ole Andreson with all his clothes on, lying on the bed looking at the wall.

"He's been in his room all day," the landlady said down-stairs. "I guess he don't feel well. I said to him: 'Mr. Andreson, you ought to go out and take a walk on a nice fall day like this,' but he didn't feel like it."

"He doesn't want to go out."

"I'm sorry he don't feel well," the woman said. "He's an awfully nice man. He was in the ring, you know."

"I know it."

"You'd never know it except from the way his face is," the woman said. They stood talking just inside the street door. "He's just as gentle."

"Well, good-night, Mrs. Hirsch," Nick said.

"I'm not Mrs. Hirsch," the woman said. "She owns the place. I just look after it for her. I'm Mrs. Bell."

"Well, good-night, Mrs. Bell," Nick said.

"Good-night," the woman said.

Nick walked up the dark street to the corner under the arc-light, and then along the car-tracks to Henry's eating-house. George was inside, back of the counter.

"Did you see Ole?"

"Yes," said Nick. "He's in his room and he won't go out."

The cook opened the door from the kitchen when he heard Nick's voice.

"I don't even listen to it," he said and shut the door.

"Did you tell him about it?" George asked.

"Sure. I told him but he knows what it's all about."

"What's he going to do?"

"Nothing."

"They'll kill him."

"I guess they will."

"He must have got mixed up in something in Chicago."

"I guess so," said Nick.

"It's a hell of a thing."

"It's an awful thing," Nick said.

They did not say anything. George reached down for a towel and wiped the counter.

"I wonder what he did?" Nick said.

"Double-crossed somebody. That's what they kill them for."

"I'm going to get out of this town," Nick said.

"Yes," said George. "That's a good thing to do."

"I can't stand to think about him waiting in the room and knowing he's going to get it. It's too damned awful."

"Well," said George, "you better not think about it."

QUESTIONS

1. Probably the first thing the reader will notice about this story is its style of writing—a style which is distinctly Hemingway's and which has been imitated by many modern writers. What characteristics of the style are obvious in the first few pages, and why is it an appropriate style for the subject matter?

2. From what point of view is the story told, and why is it effective?

3. What is the first indication that the two men are from the underworld?

4. How does the statement "Henry's had been made over from a saloon into a lunch-counter" indicate the era of the story?

5. What is the effect of having the killers eat dinner in the lunchroom?

6. How does the early conversation of the killers set the tone for what is to follow?

7. What is the effect of Max's boasting to George about the planned murder?

8. As Nick leaves the rooming house, Mrs. Bell says: "I'm not Mrs. Hirsch. She owns the place. I just look after it for her. I'm Mrs. Bell." Is this irrelevant material, or is it in any way important to the story?

9. Sam, George, and Nick all react differently to what has happened. How might each of them represent the attitude of a particular segment of society?

10. Why does the story not end when Ole turns his face to the wall? In other words, whose story is this? Does the final scene in the lunchroom add anything?

11. What is the conflict?

12. What is the theme?

I WANT TO KNOW WHY
SHERWOOD ANDERSON

We got up at four in the morning, that first day in the east. On the evening before we had climbed off a freight train at the edge of town, and with the true instinct of Kentucky boys had found our way across town and to the race track and the stables at once. Then we knew we were all right. Hanley Turner right away found a nigger we knew. It was Bildad Johnson who in the winter works at Ed Becker's livery barn in our home town, Beckersville. Bildad is a good cook as almost all our niggers are and of course he, like everyone in our part of Kentucky who is anyone at all, likes the horses. In the spring Bildad begins to scratch around. A nigger from our country can flatter and wheedle anyone into letting him do most anything he wants. Bildad wheedles the stable men and the trainers from the horse farms in our country around Lexington. The trainers come into town in the evening to stand around and talk and maybe get into a poker game. Bildad gets in with them. He is always doing little favors and telling about things to eat, chicken browned in a pan, and how is the best way to cook sweet potatoes and corn bread. It makes your mouth water to hear him.

When the racing season comes on and the horses go to the races and there is all the talk on the streets in the evenings about the new colts, and everyone says when they are going over to Lexington or to the spring meeting at Churchill Downs or to Latonia, and the horsemen that have been down to New Orleans or maybe at the winter meeting at Havana in Cuba come home to spend a week before they start out again, at such a time when everything talked about in Beckersville is just horses and nothing else and the outfits start out and horse racing is in every breath of air you breathe, Bildad shows up with a job as cook for some outfit. Often when I think about it, his always going all season to the races and working in the livery barn in the winter where horses are and where men like to come and talk about horses, I wish I was a nigger. It's a foolish thing to say, but that's the way I am about being around horses, just crazy. I can't help it.

Well, I must tell you about what we did and let you in on what I'm talking about. Four of us boys from Beckersville, all whites and sons of men who live in Beckersville regular, made up our minds we were going to the races, not just to Lexington or Louisville, I don't mean, but to the big eastern track we were always hearing our Beckersville men talk about, to Saratoga. We were all pretty young then. I was just turned fifteen and I was the oldest of the four. It was my scheme. I admit that and I talked the others into trying it. There was Hanley Turner and Henry Rieback and Tom Tumberton and myself. I had thirty-seven dollars I had earned during the winter working nights and Saturdays in Enoch Myer's grocery. Henry Rieback had eleven dollars and the others, Hanley and Tom had only a dollar or two each. We fixed it all up and laid low until the Kentucky spring meetings were over and some of our men, the sportiest ones, the ones we envied the most, had cut out—then we cut out too.

I won't tell you the trouble we had beating our way on freights and all. We went through Cleveland and Buffalo and other cities and saw Niagara Falls. We bought things there, souvenirs and spoons and cards and shells with pictures of the falls on them for our sisters and mothers, but thought we had better not send any of the things home. We didn't want to put the folks on our trail and maybe be nabbed.

We got into Saratoga as I said at night and went to the track. Bildad fed us up. He showed us a place to sleep in hay over a shed and promised to keep still. Niggers are all right about things like that. They won't squeal on you. Often a white man you might meet, when you had run away from home like that, might appear to be all right and give you a quarter or a half dollar or something, and then go right and give you away. White men will do that, but not a nigger. You can trust them. They are squarer with kids. I don't know why.

At the Saratoga meeting that year there were a lot of men from home. Dave Williams and Arthur Mulford and Jerry Myers and others. Then there was a lot from Louisville and Lexington Henry Rieback knew but I didn't. They were professional gamblers and Henry Rieback's father is one too. He is what is called a sheet writer and goes away most of the year to tracks. In the winter when he is home in Beckersville he don't stay there much but goes away to cities and deals faro. He is a nice man and generous, is always sending Henry presents, a bicycle and a gold watch and a boy scout suit of clothes and things like that.

My own father is a lawyer. He's all right, but don't make much money and can't buy me things and anyway I'm getting so old now I don't expect it. He never said nothing to me against Henry, but Hanley Turner and Tom Tumberton's fathers did. They said to their boys that money so come by is no good and they didn't want their boys brought up to hear gamblers' talk and be thinking about such things and maybe embrace them.

That's all right and I guess the men know what they are talking about, but I don't see what it's got to do with Henry or with horses either. That's what I'm writing this story about. I'm puzzled. I'm getting to be a man and want to think straight and be O.K., and there's something I saw at the race meeting at the eastern track I can't figure out.

I can't help it, I'm crazy about thoroughbred horses. I've always been that way. When I was ten years old and saw I was growing to be big and couldn't be a rider I was so sorry I nearly died. Harry Hellinfinger in Beckersville, whose father is Postmaster, is grown up and too lazy to work, but likes to stand around in the street and get up jokes on boys like sending them to a hardware store for a gimlet to bore square holes and other jokes like that. He played one on me. He told me that if I would eat a half a cigar I would be stunted and not grow any more and maybe could be a rider. I did it. When father wasn't looking I took a cigar out of his pocket and gagged it down some way. It made me awful sick and the doctor had to be sent for, and then it did no good. I kept right on growing. It was a joke. When I told what I had done and why most fathers would have whipped me but mine didn't.

Well, I didn't get stunted and didn't die. It serves Harry Hellinfinger right. Then I made up my mind I would like to be a stable boy, but had to give that up too. Mostly niggers do that work and I knew father wouldn't let me go into it. No use to ask him.

If you've never been crazy about thoroughbreds it's because you've never been around where they are much and don't know any better. They're beautiful. There isn't anything so lovely and clean and full of spunk and honest and everything as some race horses. On the big horse farms that are all around our town Beckersville there are tracks and the horses run in the early morning. More than a thousand times I've got out of bed before daylight and walked two or three miles to the tracks. Mother wouldn't of let me go but father always says, "Let him alone." So I got some bread out of the bread box and some butter and jam, gobbled it and lit out.

At the tracks you sit on the fence with men, whites and niggers, and they chew tobacco and talk, and then the colts are brought out. It's early and the grass is covered with shiny dew and in another field a man is plowing and they are frying things in a shed where the track niggers sleep, and you know how a nigger can giggle and laugh and say things that make you laugh. A white man can't do it and some niggers can't but a track nigger can every time.

And so the colts are brought out and some are just galloped by stable boys, but almost every morning on a big track owned by a rich man who lives maybe in New York, there are always, nearly every morning, a few colts and some of the old race horses and geldings and mares that are cut loose.

It brings a lump up into my throat when a horse runs. I don't mean all horses but some. I can pick them nearly every time. It's in my blood like in the blood of race track niggers and trainers. Even when they just go slop-jogging along with a little nigger on their backs I can tell a winner. If my throat hurts and it's hard for me to swallow, that's him. He'll run like Sam Hill when you let him out. If he don't win every time it'll be a wonder and because they've got him in a pocket behind another or he was pulled or got off bad at the post or something. If I wanted to be a gambler like Henry Rieback's father I could get rich. I know I could and Henry says so too. All I would have to do is to wait 'til that hurt comes when I see a horse and then bet every cent. That's what I would do if I wanted to be a gambler, but I don't.

When you're at the tracks in the morning—not the race tracks but the training tracks around Beckersville—you don't see a horse, the kind I've been talking about, very often, but it's nice anyway. Any thoroughbred, that is sired right and out of a good mare and trained by a man that knows how, can run. If he couldn't what would he be there for and not pulling a plow?

Well, out of the stables they come and the boys are on their backs and it's lovely to be there. You hunch down on top of the fence and itch inside you. Over in the sheds the niggers giggle and sing. Bacon is being fried and coffee made. Everything smells lovely. Nothing smells better than coffee and manure and horses and niggers and bacon frying and pipes being smoked out of doors on a morning like that. It just gets you, that's what it does.

But about Saratoga. We was there six days and not a soul from home seen us and everything came off just as we wanted it to, fine weather and horses and races and all. We beat our way home and Bildad gave us a basket with fried chicken and bread and other eatables in, and I had eighteen dollars when we got back to Beckersville. Mother jawed and cried but Pop didn't say much. I told everything we done except one thing. I did and saw that alone. That's what I'm writing about. It got me upset. I think about it at night. Here it is.

At Saratoga we laid up nights in the hay in the shed Bildad had showed us and ate with the niggers early and at night when the race people had all gone away. The men from home stayed mostly in the grandstand and betting field, and didn't come out around the places where the horses are kept except to the paddocks just before a race when the horses are saddled. At Saratoga they don't have paddocks under an open shed as at Lexington and Churchill Downs and other tracks down in our country, but saddle the horses right out in an open place under trees on a lawn as smooth and nice as Banker Bohon's front yard here in Beckersville. It's lovely. The horses are sweaty and nervous and shine and the men come out and smoke cigars and look at them and the trainers are there and the owners, and your heart thumps so you can hardly breathe.

Then the bugle blows for post and the boys that ride come running out with their silk clothes on and you run to get a place by the fence with the niggers.

I always am wanting to be a trainer or owner, and at the risk of being seen and caught and sent home I went to the paddocks before every race. The other boys didn't but I did.

We got to Saratoga on a Friday and on Wednesday the next week the big Mullford Handicap was to be run. Middlestride was in it and Sunstreak. The weather was fine and the track fast. I couldn't sleep the night before.

What had happened was that both these horses are the kind it makes my throat hurt to see. Middlestride is long and looks awkward and is a gelding. He belongs to Joe Thompson, a little owner from home who only has a half dozen horses. The Mullford Handicap is for a mile and Middlestride can't untrack fast. He goes away slow and is always way back at the half, then he begins to run and if the race is a mile and a quarter he'll just eat up everything and get there.

Sunstreak is different. He is a stallion and nervous and belongs on the biggest farm we've got in our country, the Van Riddle place that belongs to Mr. Van Riddle of New York. Sunstreak is like a girl you think about sometimes but never see. He is hard all over and lovely too. When you look at his head you want to kiss him. He is trained by Jerry Tillford who knows me and has been good to me lots of times, lets me walk into a horse's stall to look at him close and other things. There isn't anything as sweet as that horse. He stands at the post quiet and not letting on, but he is just burning up inside. Then when the barrier goes up he is off like his name, Sunstreak. It makes you ache to see him. It hurts you. He just lays down and runs like a bird dog. There can't anything I ever see run like him except Middlestride when he gets untracked and stretches himself.

Gee! I ached to see that race and those two horses run, ached and dreaded it too. I didn't want to see either of our horses beaten. We had never sent a pair like that to the races before. Old men in Beckersville said so and the niggers said so. It was a fact.

Before the race I went over to the paddocks to see. I looked a last look at Middlestride, who isn't such a much standing in a paddock that way, then I went to see Sunstreak.

It was his day. I knew when I see him. I forgot all about being seen myself and walked right up. All the men from Beckersville were there and no one noticed me except Jerry Tillford. He saw me and something happened. I'll tell you about that.

I was standing looking at that horse and aching. In some way, I can't tell how, I knew just how Sunstreak felt inside. He was quiet and letting the niggers rub his legs and Mr. Van Riddle himself put the saddle on, but he was just a raging torrent inside. He was like the water in the river at Niagara Falls just before it goes plunk down. That horse wasn't thinking about running. He don't have to think about that. He was just thinking about holding himself back 'til the time for the running came. I knew that. I could just in a way see right inside him. He was going to do some awful running and I knew it. He wasn't bragging or letting on much or prancing or making a fuss, but just waiting. I knew it and Jerry Tillford his trainer knew. I looked up and then that man and I looked into each other's eyes. Something happened to me. I guess I loved the man as much as I did the horse because he knew what I knew. Seemed to me there wasn't anything in the world but that man and the horse and me. I cried and Jerry Tillford had a shine in his eyes. Then I came away to the fence to wait for the race. The horse was better than me, more steadier, and now I know better than Jerry. He was the quietest and he had to do the running.

Sunstreak ran first of course and he busted the world's record for a mile. I've seen that if I never see anything more. Everything came out just as I expected. Middlestride got left at the post and was way back and closed up to be second, just as I knew he would. He'll get a world's record too some day. They can't skin the Beckersville country on horses.

I watched the race calm because I knew what would happen. I was sure. Hanley Turner and Henry Rieback and Tom Tumberton were all more excited than me.

A funny thing had happened to me. I was thinking about Jerry Tillford the trainer and how happy he was all through the race. I liked him that afternoon even more than I ever liked my own father. I almost forgot the horses thinking that way about him. It was because of what I had seen in his eyes as he stood in the paddocks beside Sunstreak before the race started. I knew he had been watching and working with Sunstreak since the horse was a baby colt, had taught him to run and be patient and when to let himself out and not to quit, never. I knew that for him it was like a mother seeing her child do something brave or wonderful. It was the first time I ever felt for a man like that.

After the race that night I cut out from Tom and Hanley and Henry. I wanted to be by myself and I wanted to be near Jerry Tillford if I could work it. Here is what happened.

The track in Saratoga is near the edge of town. It is all polished up and trees around, the evergreen kind, and grass and everything painted and nice. If you go past the track you get to a hard road made of asphalt for automobiles, and if you go along this for a few miles there is a road turns off to a little rummy-looking farm house set in a yard.

That night after the race I went along that road because I had seen Jerry and some other men go that way in an automobile. I didn't expect to find them. I walked for a ways and then sat down by a fence to think. It was the direction they went in. I wanted to be as near Jerry as I could. I felt close to him. Pretty soon I went up the side road—I don't know why—and came to the rummy farm house. I was just lonesome to see Jerry, like wanting to see your father at night when you are a young kid. Just then an automobile came along and turned in. Jerry was in it and Henry Rieback's father, and Arthur Bedford from home, and Dave Williams and two other men I didn't know. They got out of the car and went into the house, all but Henry Rieback's father who quarreled with them and said he wouldn't go. It was only about nine o'clock, but they were all drunk and the rummy looking farm house was a place for bad women to stay in. That's what it was. I crept up along a fence and looked through a window and saw.

It's what give me the fantods. I can't make it out. The women in the house were all ugly mean-looking women, not nice to look at or be near. They were homely too, except one who was tall and looked a little like the gelding Middlestride, but not clean like him, but with a hard ugly mouth. She had red hair. I saw everything plain. I got up by an old rose bush by an open window and looked. The women had on loose dresses and sat around in chairs. The men came in and some sat on the women's laps. The place smelled rotten and there was rotten talk, the kind a kid hears around a livery stable in a town like Beckersville in the winter but don't ever expect to hear talked when there are women around. It was rotten. A nigger wouldn't go into such a place.

I looked at Jerry Tillford. I've told you how I had been feeling about him on account of his knowing what was going on inside of Sunstreak in the minute before he went to the post for the race in which he made a world's record.

Jerry bragged in that bad woman house as I know Sunstreak wouldn't never have bragged. He said that he made that horse, that it was him that won the race and made the record. He lied and bragged like a fool. I never heard such silly talk.

And then, what do you suppose he did! He looked at the woman in there, the one that was lean and hard-mouthed and looked a little like the gelding Middlestride, but not clean like him, and his eyes began to shine just as they did when he looked at me and at Sunstreak in the paddocks at the track in the afternoon. I stood there by the window—gee!—but I wished I hadn't gone away from the tracks, but had stayed with the boys and the niggers and the horses. The tall rotten looking woman was between us just as Sunstreak was in the paddocks in the afternoon.

Then, all of a sudden, I began to hate that man. I wanted to scream and rush in the room and kill him. I never had such a feeling before. I was so mad clean through that I cried and my fists were doubled up so my finger nails cut my hands.

And Jerry's eyes kept shining and he waved back and forth, and then he went and kissed that woman and I crept away and went back to the tracks and to bed and didn't sleep hardly any, and then next day I got the other kids to start home with me and never told them anything I seen.

I been thinking about it ever since. I can't make it out. Spring has come again and I'm nearly sixteen and go to the tracks mornings same as always, and I see Sunstreak and Middlestride and a new colt named Strident I'll bet will lay them all out, but no one thinks so but me and two or three niggers.

But things are different. At the tracks the air don't taste as good or smell as good. It's because a man like Jerry Tillford, who knows what he does, could see a horse like Sunstreak run, and kiss a woman like that the same day. I can't make it out. Darn him, what did he want to do like that for? I keep thinking about it and it spoils looking at horses and smelling things and hearing niggers laugh and everything. Sometimes I'm so mad about it I want to fight someone. It gives me the fantods. What did he do it for? I want to know why.

QUESTIONS

1. The boy says that he wants to tell about something he "did and saw" at the Saratoga race, and yet telling that incident occupies only the last fifth of the story. Why is so much preparation necessary before the actual incident is described?

2. Since the boy tells his own story, his character must become clear to the reader simply from what he says. What characteristics become evident as he tells his story?

3. In many ways the boy is like Mark Twain's Huckleberry Finn. Both boys love something in nature and turn to it for their inspiration —Huck to the Mississippi River and this boy to race horses. Thus they both find satisfaction in nature as opposed to the artificial values of civilization. They both like people for what they are rather than for what society says about them—Huck taking the Negro Jim on the raft with him down the Mississippi and this boy finding Negroes more trustworthy than whites. Both boys also question accepted values. Huck knows that by all recognized standards he should turn Jim in as a runaway slave, but he obeys his own natural moral instincts and does not do so. What accepted values does the boy in this story question?

4. Horses have all the qualities the boy admires, qualities that would be desirable in a person: "There isn't anything so lovely and clean and full of spunk and honest and everything as some race horses." How does he compare people with horses?

5. How important is the setting?

6. When the boy says about Jerry Tillford after the race, "I liked him that afternoon even more than I ever liked my own father," does he mean that he does not like his own father?

7. Just before the race the boy feels that he has an almost mystic understanding of the way Sunstreak feels, and as he and Jerry Tillford look into each other's eyes something happens. The boy transfers his idealization of the horse to the trainer because the trainer too—or so the boy thinks—knows what is going on inside Sunstreak. The boy says, "I guess I loved the man as much as I did the horse because he knew what I knew."

This little incident in the paddocks with the boy and Jerry facing each other is exactly parallel with the incident later in the evening at the "rummy farm house" when the boy and Jerry are again facing each other. Compare the two scenes as to setting, characters, conversation, action, and emotional impact. Why did the author make them parallel?

8. What is the conflict?

9. In this story, as in "The Killers," the main character is

shocked and disillusioned by something that happens. In each story the shock is not so much the discovery of evil in the world—both boys had been aware of evil before—but the discovery of the way evil is related to adults. In "The Killers" Nick Adams is shocked that adults accept evil in such a matter-of-fact way, and in this story the boy is shocked that good and evil exist together in the same adult. Aside from shock, how is this boy's reaction to his discovery similar to that of Nick in "The Killers"?

10. What is the meaning of the boy's final question "I want to know why"?

11. What is the theme of the story?

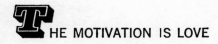

THE MOTIVATION IS LOVE

A WORN PATH
EUDORA WELTY

It was December—a bright frozen day in the early morning. Far out in the country there was an old Negro woman with her head tied in a red rag, coming along a path through the pinewoods. Her name was Phoenix Jackson. She was very old and small and she walked slowly in the dark pine shadows, moving a little from side to side in her steps, with the balanced heaviness and lightness of a pendulum in a grandfather clock. She carried a thin, small cane made from an umbrella, and with this she kept tapping the frozen earth in front of her. This made a grave and persistent noise in the still air, that seemed meditative like the chirping of a solitary little bird.

She wore a dark striped dress reaching down to her shoe tops, and an equally long apron of bleached sugar sacks, with a full pocket: all neat and tidy, but every time she took a step she might have fallen over her shoelaces, which dragged from her unlaced shoes. She looked straight ahead. Her eyes were blue with age. Her skin had a pattern all its own of numberless branching wrinkles and as though a whole little tree stood in the middle of her forehead, but a golden color ran underneath, and the two knobs of her cheeks were illumined by a yellow burning under the dark. Under the red rag her hair came down on her neck in the frailest of ringlets, still black, and with an odor like copper.

Now and then there was a quivering in the thicket. Old Phoenix said, "Out of my way, all you foxes, owls, beetles, jack rabbits, coons and wild animals! . . . Keep out from under these feet, little bob-whites. . . . Keep the big wild hogs out of my path. Don't let none of those come running my direction. I got a long way." Under her small black-freckled hand her cane, limber as a buggy whip, would switch at the brush as if to rouse up any hiding things.

On she went. The woods were deep and still. The sun made the pine needles almost too bright to look at, up where the wind rocked. The cones dropped as light as feathers. Down in the hollow was the mourning dove—it was not too late for him.

The path ran up a hill. "Seem like there is chains about my feet, time I get this far," she said, in the voice of argument old people keep to use with themselves. "Something always take a hold of me on this hill—pleads I should stay."

After she got to the top she turned and gave a full, severe look behind her where she had come. "Up through pines," she said at length. "Now down through oaks."

Her eyes opened their widest, and she started down gently. But before she got to the bottom of the hill a bush caught her dress.

Her fingers were busy and intent, but her skirts were full and long, so that before she could pull them free in one place they were caught in another. It was not possible to allow the dress to tear. "I in the thorny bush," she said. "Thorns, you doing your appointed work. Never want to let folks pass, no sir. Old eyes thought you was a pretty little *green* bush."

Finally, trembling all over, she stood free, and after a moment dared to stoop for her cane.

"Sun so high!" she cried, leaning back and looking, while the thick tears went over her eyes. "The time getting all gone here."

At the foot of this hill was a place where a log was laid across the creek.

"Now comes the trial," said Phoenix.

Putting her right foot out, she mounted the log and shut her eyes. Lifting her skirt, leveling her cane fiercely before her, like a festival figure in some parade, she began to march across. Then she opened her eyes and she was safe on the other side.

"I wasn't as old as I thought," she said.

But she sat down to rest. She spread her skirts on the bank around her and folded her hands over her knees. Up above her was a tree in a pearly cloud of mistletoe. She did not dare to close her eyes, and when a little boy brought her a plate with a slice of marble-cake on it she spoke to him. "That would be acceptable," she said. But when she went to take it there was just her own hand in the air.

So she left that tree, and had to go through a barbed-wire fence. There she had to creep and crawl, spreading her knees and stretching her fingers like a baby trying to climb the steps. But she talked loudly to herself: she could not let her dress be torn now, so late in the day, and she could not pay for having her arm or her leg sawed off if she got caught fast where she was.

At last she was safe through the fence and risen up out in the clearing. Big dead trees, like black men with one arm, were standing in the purple stalks of the withered cotton field. There sat a buzzard.

"Who you watching?"

In the furrow she made her way along.

"Glad this not the season for bulls," she said, looking sideways, "and the good Lord made his snakes to curl up and sleep in the winter. A pleasure I don't see no two-headed snake coming around that tree, where it come once. It took a while to get by him, back in the summer."

She passed through the old cotton and went into a field of dead corn. It whispered and shook and was taller than her head. "Through the maze now," she said, for there was no path.

Then there was something tall, black, and skinny there, moving before her.

At first she took it for a man. It could have been a man dancing in the field. But she stood still and listened, and it did not make a sound. It was as silent as a ghost.

"Ghost," she said sharply, "who be you the ghost of? For I have heard of nary death close by."

But there was no answer—only the ragged dancing in the wind.

She shut her eyes, reached out her hand, and touched a sleeve. She found a coat and inside that an emptiness, cold as ice.

"You scarecrow," she said. Her face lighted. "I ought to be shut up for good," she said with laughter. "My senses is gone. I too old. I the oldest people I ever know. Dance, old scarecrow," she said, "while I dancing with you."

She kicked her foot over the furrow, and with mouth drawn down, shook her head once or twice in a little strutting way. Some husks blew down and whirled in streamers about her skirts.

Then she went on, parting her way from side to side with the cane, through the whispering field. At last she came to the end, to a wagon track where the silver grass blew between the red ruts. The quail were walking around like pullets, seeming all dainty and unseen.

"Walk pretty," she said. "This the easy place. This the easy going."

She followed the track, swaying through the quiet bare fields, through the little strings of trees silver in their dead leaves, past cabins silver from weather, with the doors and windows boarded shut, all like old women under a spell sitting there. "I walking in their sleep," she said, nodding her head vigorously.

In a ravine she went where a spring was silently flowing through a hollow log. Old Phoenix bent and drank. "Sweet-gum makes the water sweet," she said, and drank more. "Nobody know who made this well, for it was here when I was born."

The track crossed a swampy part where the moss hung as white as lace from every limb. "Sleep on, alligators, and blow your bubbles." Then the track went into the road.

Deep, deep the road went down between the high green-colored banks. Overhead the live-oaks met, and it was as dark as a cave.

A black dog with a lolling tongue came up out of the weeds by the ditch. She was meditating, and not ready, and when he came at her she only hit him a little with her cane. Over she went in the ditch, like a little puff of milkweed.

Down there, her senses drifted away. A dream visited her, and she reached her hand up, but nothing reached down and gave her a pull. So she lay there and presently went to talking. "Old woman," she said to herself, "that black dog come up out of the weeds to stall your off, and now there he sitting on his fine tail, smiling at you."

A white man finally came along and found her—a hunter, a young man, with his dog on a chain.

"Well, Granny!" he laughed. "What are you doing there?"

"Lying on my back like a June-bug waiting to be turned over, mister," she said, reaching up her hand.

He lifted her up, gave her a swing in the air, and set her down. "Anything broken, Granny?"

"No sir, them old dead weeds is springy enough," said Phoenix, when she had got her breath. "I thank you for your trouble."

"Where do you live, Granny?" he asked, while the two dogs were growling at each other.

"Away back yonder, sir, behind the ridge. You can't even see it from here."

"On your way home?"

"No sir, I going to town."

"Why, that's too far! That's as far as I walk when I come out myself, and I get something for my trouble." He patted the stuffed bag he carried, and there hung down a little closed claw. It was one of the bob-whites, with its beak hooked bitterly to show it was dead. "Now you go on home, Granny!"

"I bound to go to town, mister," said Phoenix. "The time come around."

He gave another laugh, filling the whole landscape. "I know you old colored people! Wouldn't miss going to town to see Santa Claus!"

But something held old Phoenix very still. The deep lines in her face went into a fierce and different radiation. Without warning, she had seen with her own eyes a flashing nickel fall out of the man's pocket onto the ground.

"How old are you, Granny?" he was saying.

"There is no telling, mister," she said, "no telling."

Then she gave a little cry and clapped her hands and said, "Git on away from here, dog! Look! Look at that dog!" She laughed as if in admiration. "He ain't scared of nobody. He a big black dog." She whispered, "Sic him!"

"Watch me get rid of that cur," said the man. "Sic him, Pete! Sic him!"

Phoenix heard the dogs fighting, and heard the man running and throwing sticks. She even heard a gunshot. But she was slowly bending forward by that time, further and further forward, the lids stretched down over her eyes, as if she were doing this in her sleep. Her chin was lowered almost to her knees. The yellow palm of her hand came out from the fold of her apron. Her fingers slid down and along the ground under the piece of money with the grace and care they would have in lifting an egg from under a setting hen. Then she slowly straightened up, she stood erect, and the nickel was in her apron pocket. A bird flew by. Her lips moved. "God watching me the whole time. I come to stealing."

The man came back, and his own dog panted about them. "Well,

I scared him off that time," he said, and then he laughed and lifted his gun and pointed it at Phoenix.

She stood straight and faced him.

"Doesn't the gun scare you?" he said, still pointing it.

"No, sir, I seen plenty go off closer by, in my day, and for less than what I done," she said, holding utterly still.

He smiled, and shouldered the gun. "Well, Granny," he said, "you must be a hundred years old, and scared of nothing. I'd give you a dime if I had any money with me. But you take my advice and stay home, and nothing will happen to you."

"I bound to go on my way, mister," said Phoenix. She inclined her head in the red rag. Then they went in different directions, but she could hear the gun shooting again and again over the hill.

She walked on. The shadows hung from the oak trees to the road like curtains. Then she smelled wood-smoke, and smelled the river, and she saw a steeple and the cabins on their steep steps. Dozens of little black children whirled around her. There ahead was Natchez shining. Bells were ringing. She walked on.

In the paved city it was Christmas time. There were red and green electric lights strung and crisscrossed everywhere, and all turned on in the daytime. Old Phoenix would have been lost if she had not distrusted her eyesight and depended on her feet to know where to take her.

She paused quietly on the sidewalk where people were passing by. A lady came along in the crowd, carrying an armful of red-, green- and silver-wrapped presents; she gave off perfume like the red roses in hot summer, and Phoenix stopped her.

"Please, missy, will you lace up my shoe?" She held up her foot.

"What do you want, Grandma?"

"See my shoe," said Phoenix. "Do all right for out in the country, but wouldn't look right to go in a big building."

"Stand still then, Grandma," said the lady. She put her packages down on the sidewalk beside her and laced and tied both shoes tightly.

"Can't lace 'em with a cane," said Phoenix. "Thank you, missy. I doesn't mind asking a nice lady to tie up my shoe, when I gets out on the street."

Moving slowly and from side to side, she went into the big building, and into a tower of steps, where she walked up and around and around until her feet knew to stop.

She entered a door, and there she saw nailed up on the wall the document that had been stamped with the gold seal and framed in the gold frame, which matched the dream that was hung up in her head.

"Here I be," she said. There was a fixed and ceremonial stiffness over her body.

"A charity case, I suppose," said an attendant who sat at the desk before her.

But Phoenix only looked above her head. There was sweat on her face, the wrinkles in her skin shone like a bright net.

"Speak up, Grandma," the woman said. "What's your name? We must have your history, you know. Have you been here before? What seems to be the trouble with you?"

Old Phoenix only gave a twitch to her face as if a fly were bothering her.

"Are you deaf?" cried the attendant.

But then the nurse came in.

"Oh, that's just old Aunt Phoenix," she said. "She doesn't come for herself—she has a little grandson. She makes these trips just as regular as clockwork. She lives away back off the Old Natchez Trace." She bent down. "Well, Aunt Phoenix, why don't you just take a seat? We won't keep you standing after your long trip." She pointed.

The old woman sat down, bolt upright in the chair.

"Now, how is the boy?" asked the nurse.

Old Phoenix did not speak.

"I said, how is the boy?"

But Phoenix only waited and stared straight ahead, her face very solemn and withdrawn into rigidity.

"Is his throat any better?" asked the nurse. "Aunt Phoenix, don't you hear me? Is your grandson's throat any better since the last time you came for the medicine?"

With her hands on her knees, the old woman waited, silent, erect and motionless, just as if she were in armor.

"You mustn't take up our time this way, Aunt Phoenix," the nurse said. "Tell us quickly about your grandson, and get it over. He isn't dead, is he?"

At last there came a flicker and then a flame of comprehension across her face, and she spoke.

"My grandson. It was my memory had left me. There I sat and forgot why I made my long trip."

"Forgot?" The nurse frowned. "After you came so far?"

Then Phoenix was like an old woman begging a dignified forgiveness for waking up frightened in the night. "I never did go to school, I was too old at the Surrender," she said in a soft voice. "I'm an old woman without an education. It was my memory fail me. My little grandson, he is just the same, and I forgot it in the coming."

"Throat never heals, does it?" said the nurse, speaking in a loud, sure voice to old Phoenix. By now she had a card with something written on it, a little list. "Yes. Swallowed lye. When was it?—January—two-three years ago—"

Phoenix spoke unasked now. "No, missy, he not dead, he just the same. Every little while his throat begin to close up again, and he not able to swallow. He not get his breath. He not able to help himself. So the time come around, and I go on another trip for the soothing medicine."

"All right. The doctor said as long as you came to get it, you could have it," said the nurse. "But it's an obstinate case."

"My little grandson, he sit up there in the house all wrapped up, waiting by himself," Phoenix went on. "We is the only two left in the world. He suffer and it don't seem to put him back at all. He got a sweet look. He going to last. He wear a little patch quilt and peep out holding his mouth open like a little bird. I remembers so plain now. I not going to forget him again, no, the whole enduring time. I could tell him from all the others in creation."

"All right." The nurse was trying to hush her now. She brought her a bottle of medicine. "Charity," she said, making a check mark in a book.

Old Phoenix held the bottle close to her eyes, and then carefully put it into her pocket.

"I thank you," she said.

"It's Christmas time, Grandma," said the attendant. "Could I give you a few pennies out of my purse?"

"Five pennies is a nickel," said Phoenix stiffly.

"Here's a nickel," said the attendant.

Phoenix rose carefully and held out her hand. She received the nickel and then fished the other nickel out of her pocket and laid it beside the new one. She stared at her palm closely, with her head on one side.

Then she gave a tap with her cane on the floor.

"This is what come to me to do," she said. "I going to the store and buy my child a little windmill they sells, made out of paper. He going to find it hard to believe there such a thing in the world. I'll march myself back where he waiting, holding it straight up in this hand."

She lifted her free hand, gave a little nod, turned around, and walked out of the doctor's office. Then her slow step began on the stairs, going down.

QUESTIONS

1. In this story about someone who is entirely good, wholly at peace with the world, and completely filled with love, is there any conflict?

2. According to legend, the phoenix—symbol of the sun—was a bird of gold and red plumage that came back to Heliopolis—city of the sun in Egypt—every five hundred years. There it would consume itself by fire and rise again in youthful freshness from its own ashes, thus becoming a symbol of immortality. How might Old Phoenix be related to this legend?

3. Eudora Welty was originally interested in painting as well as writing, and the artist's eye is evident in her descriptions of the scenery and atmosphere along the rural path in Mississippi. How important is the setting?

4. Eudora Welty once said concerning writing, "Where does beauty come from, in the short story? Beauty . . . often comes from carefulness, lack of confusion, elimination of waste. . . ." Certainly there is no waste in this story; every detail is important. For example, the incidents on the journey may seem at first glance to be merely random happenings, but actually each is a carefully designed little scene to bring out one characteristic of Old Phoenix. How does each incident add to her portrait?

5. Along with the painter's eye for the picturesque locale, Eudora Welty has a musician's ear for turns of speech and the rhythm of language—as will be evident if the story is read aloud. She says she writes "by ear," and certainly she is adept at recording speech exactly as it falls from the lips. Point out some of the metaphors that enrich her language.

6. Is it mainly setting, style of writing, or character that makes this story moving? Or is it a combination of all three?

7. This subject could easily have become too sentimental, too full of pathos. How does the author avoid it?

8. What is the theme of the story?

A MOTHER IN MANNVILLE
MARJORIE KINNAN RAWLINGS

The orphanage is high in the Carolina mountains. Sometimes in winter the snowdrifts are so deep that the institution is cut off from the village below, from all the world. Fog hides the mountain peaks, the snow swirls down the valleys, and a wind blows so bitterly that the orphanage boys who take the milk twice daily to the baby cottage reach the door with fingers stiff in an agony of numbness.

"Or when we carry trays from the cookhouse for the ones that are sick," Jerry said, "we get our faces frostbit, because we can't put our hands over them. I have gloves," he added. "Some of the boys don't have any."

He liked the late spring, he said. The rhododendron was in bloom, a carpet of color, across the mountainsides, soft as the May winds that stirred the hemlocks. He called it laurel.

"It's pretty when the laurel blooms," he said. "Some of it's pink and some of it's white."

I was there in the autumn. I wanted quiet, isolation, to do some troublesome writing. I wanted mountain air to blow out the malaria from too long a time in the subtropics. I was homesick, too, for the flaming of maples in October, and for corn shocks and pumpkins and black-walnut trees and the lift of hills. I found them all, living in a cabin that belonged to the orphanage, half a mile beyond the orphanage farm. When I took the cabin, I asked for a boy or man to come and chop wood for the fireplace. The first few days were warm, I found what wood I needed about the cabin, no one came, and I forgot the order.

I looked up from my typewriter one late afternoon, a little startled. A boy stood at the door, and my pointer dog, my companion, was at his side and had not barked to warn me. The boy was probably twelve years old, but undersized. He wore overalls and a torn shirt, and was barefooted.

He said, "I can chop some wood today."

I said, "But I have a boy coming from the orphanage."

"I'm the boy."

"You? But you're small."

"Size don't matter, chopping wood," he said. "Some of the big boys don't chop good. I've been chopping wood at the orphanage a long time."

I visualized mangled and inadequate branches for my fires. I was well into my work and not inclined to conversation. I was a little blunt.

"Very well. There's the ax. Go ahead and see what you can do."

I went back to work, closing the door. At first the sound of the boy dragging brush annoyed me. Then he began to chop. The blows were rhythmic and steady, and shortly I had forgotten him, the sound no more of an interruption than a consistent rain. I suppose an hour and a half passed, for when I stopped and stretched, and heard the boy's steps on the cabin stoop, the sun was dropping behind the farthest mountain, and the valleys were purple with something deeper than the asters.

The boy said, "I have to go to supper now. I can come again tomorrow evening."

I said, "I'll pay you now for what you've done," thinking I should probably have to insist on an older boy. "Ten cents an hour?"

"Anything is all right."

We went together back of the cabin. An astonishing amount of solid wood had been cut. There were cherry logs and heavy roots of rhododendron, and blocks from the waste pine and oak left from the building of the cabin.

"But you've done as much as a man," I said. "This is a splendid pile."

I looked at him, actually, for the first time. His hair was the color of the corn shocks and his eyes, very direct, were like the mountain sky when rain is pending—gray, with a shadowing of that miraculous blue. As I spoke, a light came over him, as though the setting sun had touched him with the same suffused glory with which it touched the mountains. I gave him a quarter.

"You may come tomorrow," I said, "and thank you very much."

He looked at me, and at the coin, and seemed to want to speak, but could not, and turned away.

"I'll split kindling tomorrow," he said over his thin ragged shoulder. "You'll need kindling and medium wood and logs and backlogs."

At daylight I was half wakened by the sound of chopping. Again it was so even in texture that I went back to sleep. When I left my bed in the cool morning, the boy had come and gone, and a stack of kindling was neat against the cabin wall. He came again after school in the afternoon and worked until time to return to the orphanage. His name was Jerry; he was twelve years old, and he had been at the orphanage since he was four. I could picture him at four, with the same grave gray-blue eyes and the same—independence? No, the word that comes to me is "integrity."

The word means something very special to me, and the quality for which I use it is a rare one. My father had it—there is another of whom I am almost sure—but almost no man of my acquaintance possesses it with the clarity, the purity, the simplicity of a mountain stream. But the boy Jerry had it. It is bedded on courage, but it is more than brave. It is honest, but it is more than honesty. The ax handle broke one day. Jerry said the woodshop at the orphanage would repair it. I brought money to pay for the job and he refused it.

"I'll pay for it," he said. "I broke it. I brought the ax down careless."

"But no one hits accurately every time," I told him. "The fault was in the wood of the handle. I'll see the man from whom I bought it."

It was only then that he would take the money. He was standing back of his own carelessness. He was a free-will agent and he chose to do careful work, and if he failed, he took the responsibility without subterfuge.

And he did for me the unnecessary thing, the gracious thing, that we find done only by the great of heart. Things no training can teach, for they are done on the instant, with no predicated experience. He found a cubbyhole beside the fireplace that I had not noticed. There, of his own accord, he put kindling and "medium" wood, so that I might always have dry fire material ready in case of sudden wet weather. A stone was loose in the rough walk to the cabin. He dug a deeper hole and steadied it, although he came, himself, by a short cut over the bank. I found that when I tried to return his thoughtfulness with such things as candy and apples, he was wordless. "Thank you" was, perhaps, an expression for which he had had no use, for his courtesy was instinctive. He only looked at the gift and at me, and a curtain lifted, so that I saw deep into the clear well of his eyes, and gratitude was there, and affection, soft over the firm granite of his character.

He made simple excuses to come and sit with me. I could no more have turned him away than if he had been physically hungry. I suggested once that the best time for us to visit was just before supper, when I left off my writing. After that, he waited always until my typewriter had been some time quiet. One day I worked until nearly dark. I went outside the cabin, having forgotten him. I saw him going up over the hill in the twilight toward the orphanage. When I sat down on my stoop, a place was warm from his body where he had been sitting.

He became intimate, of course, with my pointer, Pat. There is a strange communion between a boy and a dog. Perhaps they possess the same singleness of spirit, the same kind of wisdom. It is difficult to explain, but it exists. When I went across the state for a week end, I left the dog in Jerry's charge. I gave him the dog whistle and the key to the cabin, and left sufficient food. He was to come two or three times a day and let out the dog, and feed and exercise him. I should return Sunday night, and Jerry would take out the dog for the last time Sunday afternoon and then leave the key under an agreed hiding place.

My return was belated and fog filled the mountain passes so treacherously that I dared not drive at night. The fog held the next morning, and it was Monday noon before I reached the cabin. The dog had been fed and cared for that morning. Jerry came early in the afternoon, anxious.

"The superintendent said nobody would drive in the fog," he said. "I came just before bedtime last night and you hadn't come. So I brought Pat some of my breakfast this morning. I wouldn't have let anything happen to him."

"I was sure of that. I didn't worry."

"When I heard about the fog, I thought you'd know."

He was needed for work at the orphanage and he had to return at once. I gave him a dollar in payment, and he looked at it and went away. But that night he came in the darkness and knocked at the door.

"Come in, Jerry," I said, "if you're allowed to be away this late."

"I told maybe a story," he said. "I told them I thought you would want to see me."

"That's true," I assured him, and I saw his relief. "I want to hear about how you managed with the dog."

He sat by the fire with me, with no other light, and told me of their two days together. The dog lay close to him, and found a comfort there that I did not have for him. And it seemed to me that being with my dog, and caring for him, had brought the boy and me, too, together, so that he felt that he belonged to me as well as to the animal.

"He stayed right with me," he told me, "except when he ran in the laurel. He likes the laurel. I took him up over the hill and we both ran fast. There was a place where the grass was high and I lay down in it and hid. I could hear Pat hunting for me. He found my trail and he barked. When he found me, he acted crazy, and he ran around and around me, in circles."

We watched the flames.

"That's an apple log," he said. "It burns the prettiest of any wood."

We were very close.

He was suddenly impelled to speak of things he had not spoken of before, nor had I cared to ask him.

"You look a little bit like my mother," he said. "Especially in the dark, by the fire."

"But you were only four, Jerry, when you came here. You have remembered how she looked, all these years?"

"My mother lives in Mannville," he said.

For a moment, finding that he had a mother shocked me as greatly as anything in my life has ever done, and I did not know why it disturbed me. Then I understood my distress. I was filled with a passionate resentment that any woman should go away and leave her son. A fresh anger added itself. A son like this one—— The orphanage was a wholesome place, the executives were kind, good people, the food was more than adequate, the boys were healthy, a ragged shirt was no hardship, nor the doing of clean labor. Granted, perhaps, that the boy felt no lack, what blood fed the bowels of a woman who did not yearn over this child's lean body that had come in parturition out of her own? At four he would have looked the same as now. Nothing, I thought, nothing in life could change those eyes. His quality must be apparent to an idiot, a fool. I burned with questions I could not ask. In any, I was afraid, there would be pain.

"Have you seen her, Jerry—lately?"

"I see her every summer. She sends for me."

I wanted to cry out, "Why are you not with her? How can she let you go away again?"

He said, "She comes up here from Mannville whenever she can. She doesn't have a job now."

His face shone in the firelight.

"She wanted to give me a puppy, but they can't let any one boy keep a puppy. You remember the suit I had on last Sunday?" He was plainly proud. "She sent me that for Christmas. The Christmas before that"—he drew a long breath, savoring the memory—"she sent me a pair of skates."

"Roller skates?"

My mind was busy, making pictures of her, trying to understand her. She had not, then, entirely deserted or forgotten him. But why, then—— I thought, "I must not condemn her without knowing."

"Roller skates. I let the other boys use them. They're always borrowing them. But they're careful of them."

What circumstance other than poverty——

"I'm going to take the dollar you gave me for taking care of Pat," he said, "and buy her a pair of gloves."

I could only say, "That will be nice. Do you know her size?"

"I think it's 8½," he said.

He looked at my hands.

"Do you wear 8½?" he asked.

"No. I wear a smaller size, a 6."

"Oh! Then I guess her hands are bigger than yours."

I hated her. Poverty or no, there was other food than bread, and the soul could starve as quickly as the body. He was taking his dollar to buy gloves for her big stupid hands, and she lived away from him, in Mannville, and contented herself with sending him skates.

"She likes white gloves," he said. "Do you think I can get them for a dollar?"

"I think so," I said.

I decided that I should not leave the mountains without seeing her and knowing for myself why she had done this thing.

The human mind scatters its interests as though made of thistle-down, and every wind stirs and moves it. I finished my work. It did not please me, and I gave my thoughts to another field. I should need some Mexican material.

I made arrangements to close my Florida place. Mexico immediately, and doing the writing there, if conditions were favorable. Then, Alaska with my brother. After that, heaven knew what or where.

I did not take time to go to Mannville to see Jerry's mother, nor even to talk with the orphanage officials about her. I was a trifle abstracted about the boy, because of my work and plans. And after my first fury at her—we did not speak of her again—his having a mother, any sort at all, not far away, in Mannville, relieved me of the ache I had had about him. He did not question the anomalous relation. He was not lonely. It was none of my concern.

He came every day and cut my wood and did small helpful favors and stayed to talk. The days had become cold, and often I let him come inside the cabin. He would lie on the floor in front of the fire, with one arm across the pointer, and they would both doze and wait quietly for me. Other days they ran with a common ecstasy through the laurel, and since the asters were now gone, he brought me back vermilion maple leaves, and chestnut boughs dripping with imperial yellow. I was ready to go.

I said to him, "You have been my good friend, Jerry. I shall often think of you and miss you. Pat will miss you too. I am leaving tomorrow."

He did not answer. When he went away, I remember that a new moon hung over the mountains, and I watched him go in silence up the hill. I expected him the next day, but he did not come. The details of packing my personal belongings, loading my car, arranging the bed over the seat, where the dog would ride, occupied me until late in the day. I closed the cabin and started the car, noticing that the sun was in the west and I should do well to be out of the mountains by nightfall. I stopped by the orphanage and left the cabin key and money for my light bill with Miss Clark.

"And will you call Jerry for me to say good-by to him?"

"I don't know where he is," she said. "I'm afraid he's not well. He didn't eat his dinner this noon. One of the other boys saw him going over the hill into the laurel. He was supposed to fire the boiler this afternoon. It's not like him; he's unusually reliable."

I was almost relieved, for I knew I should never see him again, and it would be easier not to say good-by to him.

I said, "I wanted to talk with you about his mother—why he's here—but I'm in more of a hurry than I expected to be. It's out of the question for me to see her now too. But here's some money I'd like to leave with you to buy things for him at Christmas and on his birthday. It will be better than for me to try to send him things. I could so easily duplicate—skates, for instance."

She blinked her honest spinster's eyes.

"There's not much use for skates here," she said.

Her stupidity annoyed me.

"What I mean," I said, "is that I don't want to duplicate things his mother sends him. I might have chosen skates if I didn't know she had already given them to him."

She stared at me.

"I don't understand," she said. "He has no mother. He has no skates."

QUESTIONS

1. From what point of view is the story told, and why is it effective?

2. The writer thinks that she has found a single word to sum up Jerry's character—*integrity*. What special meaning does the word have for her?

3. What incidents indicate Jerry's integrity?

4. When Jerry says, "You look a little bit like my mother. Especially in the dark, by the fire," what does he really mean?

5. How might each of the statements that Jerry makes about his "mother" apply to the writer?

6. What is the irony in the ending of the story?

7. Just as very young children create fantasies and sometimes make up dream playmates, so Jerry, out of his tremendous emotional need, has created a dream mother, patterned after the writer. Can his misrepresentation to the writer be justified?

8. What is the conflict and how is it resolved?

9. Do the characters change or remain the same?

10. What is the theme?

THE FAILURE TO COMMUNICATE

BUTCHER BIRD
WALLACE STEGNER

That summer the boy was alone on the farm except for his parents. His brother was working at Orullian's Grocery in town, and there was no one to run the trap line with or swim with in the dark, weed-smelling reservoir where garter snakes made straight rapid lines in the water and the skaters rowed close to shore. So every excursion was an adventure, even if it was only a trip across the three miles of prairie to Larsen's to get mail or groceries. He was excited at the visit to Garfield's as he was excited by everything unusual. The hot midsummer afternoon was still and breathless, the air harder to breathe than usual. He knew there was a change in weather coming because the gingersnaps in their tall cardboard box were soft and bendable when he snitched two to stick in his pocket. He could tell too by his father's grumpiness accumulated through two weeks of drought, his habit of looking off into the southwest, from which either rain or hot winds might come, that something was brewing. If it was rain everything would be fine, his father would hum under his breath getting breakfast, maybe let him drive the stoneboat or ride the mare down to Larsen's for mail. If it was hot wind they'd have to walk soft and speak softer, and it wouldn't be any fun.

They didn't know the Garfields, who had moved in only the fall before; but people said they had a good big house and a bigger barn and that Mr. Garfield was an Englishman and a little funny talking about scientific farming and making the desert blossom like the rose. The boy's father hadn't wanted to go, but his mother thought it was unneighborly not to call at least once in a whole year when people lived only four miles away. She was, the boy knew, as anxious for a change, as eager to get out of that atmosphere of waiting to see what the weather would do—that tense and teeth-gritting expectancy—as he was.

He found more than he looked for at Garfield's. Mr. Garfield was tall and bald with a big nose, and talked very softly and politely. The boy's father was determined not to like him right from the start.

When Mr. Garfield said, "Dear, I think we might have a glass of lemonade, don't you?" the boy saw his parents look at each other, saw the beginning of a contemptuous smile on his father's face, saw his mother purse her lips and shake her head ever so little. And when Mrs. Garfield, prim and spectacled, with a habit of tucking her head back and to one side while she listened to anyone talk, brought in the lemonade, the boy saw his father taste his and make a little face behind the glass. He hated any summer drink without ice in it, and had spent two whole weeks digging a dugout icehouse just so that he could have ice water and cold beer when the hot weather came.

But Mr. and Mrs. Garfield were nice people. They sat down in their new parlor and showed the boy's mother the rug and the gramophone. When the boy came up curiously to inspect the little box with the petunia-shaped horn and the little china dog with "His Master's Voice" on it, and the Garfields found that he had never seen or heard a gramophone, they put on a cylinder like a big spool of tightly wound black thread and lowered a needle on it, and out came a man's voice singing in Scotch brogue, and his mother smiled and nodded and said, "My land, Harry Lauder! I heard him once a long time ago. Isn't it wonderful, Sonny?"

It was wonderful all right. He inspected it, reached out his fingers to touch things, wiggled the big horn to see if it was loose or screwed in. His father warned him sharply to keep his hands off, but then Mr. Garfield smiled and said, "Oh, he can't hurt it. Let's play something else," and found a record about the saucy little bird on Nelly's hat that had them all laughing. They let him wind the machine and play the record over again, all by himself, and he was very careful. It was a fine machine. He wished he had one.

About the time he had finished playing his sixth or seventh record, and George M. Cohan was singing "She's a grand old rag, she's a high-flying flag, and forever in peace may she wave," he glanced at his father and discovered that he was grouchy about something. He wasn't taking any part in the conversation but was sitting with his chin in his hand staring out of the window. Mr. Garfield was looking at him a little helplessly. His eyes met the boy's and he motioned him over.

"What do you find to do all summer? Only child, are you?"

"No, sir. My brother's in Whitemud. He's twelve. He's got a job."

"So you come out on the farm to help," said Mr. Garfield. He had his hand on the boy's shoulder and his voice was so kind that the boy lost his shyness and felt no embarrassment at all in being out there in the middle of the parlor with all of them watching.

"I don't help much," he said. "I'm too little to do anything but drive the stoneboat, Pa says. When I'm twelve he's going to get me a gun and then I can go hunting."

"Hunting?" Mr. Garfield said. "What do you hunt?"

"Oh, gophers and weasels. I got a pet weasel. His name's Lucifer."

"Well," said Mr. Garfield. "You seem to be a pretty manly little chap. What do you feed your weasel?"

"Gophers." The boy thought it best not to say that the gophers were live ones he threw into the weasel's cage. He thought probably Mr. Garfield would be a little shocked at that.

Mr. Garfield straightened up and looked round at the grown folks. "Isn't it a shame," he said, "that there are so many predatory animals and pests in this country that we have to spend our time destroying them? I hate killing things."

"I hate weasels," the boy said. "I'm just saving this one till he turns into an ermine, and then I'm going to skin him. Once I speared a weasel with the pitchfork in the chicken coop and he dropped right off the tine and ran up my leg and bit me after he was speared clean through."

He finished breathlessly, and his mother smiled at him, motioning him not to talk so much. But Mr. Garfield was still looking at him kindly. "So you want to make war on the cruel things, the weasels and the hawks," he said.

"Yes, sir," the boy said. He looked at his mother and it was all right. He hadn't spoiled anything by telling about the weasels.

"Now that reminds me," Mr. Garfield said, rising. "Maybe I've got something you'd find useful."

He went into another room and came back with a .22 in his hand. "Could you use this?"

"I . . . yes, *sir!*" the boy said. He had almost, in his excitement, said "I hope to whisk in your piskers," because that was what his father always said when he meant anything real hard.

"If your parents want you to have it," Mr. Garfield said and raised his eyebrows at the boy's mother. He didn't look at the father, but the boy did.

"Can I, Pa?"

"I guess so," his father said. "Sure."

"Thank Mr. Garfield nicely," said his mother.

"Gee," the boy breathed. "Thanks, Mr. Garfield, ever so much."

"There's a promise goes with it," Mr. Garfield said. "I'd like you to promise never to shoot anything with it but the bloodthirsty animals—the cruel ones like weasels and hawks. Never anything like birds or prairie dogs."

"How about butcher birds?"

"Butcher birds?" Mr. Garfield said.

"Shrikes," said the boy's mother. "We've got some over by our place. They kill all sorts of things, snakes and gophers and other birds. They're worse than the hawks because they just kill for the fun of it."

"By all means," said Mr. Garfield. "Shoot all the shrikes you see. A thing that kills for the fun of it . . ." He shook his head and his voice got solemn, almost like the voice of Mr. McGregor, the Sunday School Superintendent in town, when he was asking the benediction. "There's something about the way the war drags on, or maybe just this country," he said, "that makes me hate killing. I just can't bear to shoot anything any more, even a weasel."

The boy's father turned cold eyes away from Mr. Garfield and looked out of the window. One big brown hand, a little dirty from the wheel of the car, rubbed against the day-old bristles on his jaws. Then he stood up and stretched. "Well, we got to be going," he said.

"Oh, stay a little while," Mr. Garfield said. "You just came. I wanted to show you my trees."

The boy's mother stared at him. "Trees?"

He smiled. "Sounds a bit odd out here, doesn't it? But I think trees will grow. I've made some plantings down below."

"I'd love to see them," she said. "Sometimes I'd give almost anything to get into a good deep shady woods. Just to smell it, and feel how cool . . ."

"There's a little story connected with these," Mr. Garfield said. He spoke to the mother alone, warmly. "When we first decided to come out here I said to Martha that if trees wouldn't grow we shouldn't stick it. That's just what I said, 'If trees won't grow we shan't stick it.' Trees are almost the breath of life to me."

The boy's father was shaken by a sudden spell of coughing, and the mother shot a quick look at him and looked back at Mr. Garfield with a light flush on her cheekbones. "I'd love to see them," she said. "I was raised in Minnesota, and I never will get used to a place as barren as this."

"When I think of the beeches back home in England," Mr. Garfield said, and shook his head with a puckering smile round his eyes.

The father lifted himself heavily out of his chair and followed the rest of them out to the coulee edge. Below them willows grew profusely along the almost-dry creek, and farther back from the water there was a grove of perhaps twenty trees about a dozen feet high.

"I'm trying cottonwoods first because they can stand dry weather," Mr. Garfield said.

The mother was looking down with all her longings suddenly plain and naked in her eyes. "It's wonderful," she said. "I'd give almost anything to have some on our place."

"I found the willows close by here," said Mr. Garfield. "Just at the south end of the hills they call Old-Man-on-His-Back, where the stream comes down."

"Stream?" the boy's father said. "You mean that trickle?"

"It's not much of a stream," Mr. Garfield said apologetically. "But . . ."

"Are there any more there?" the mother said.

"Oh, yes. You could get some. Cut them diagonally and push them into any damp ground. They'll grow."

"They'll grow about six feet high," the father said.

"Yes," said Mr. Garfield. "They're not, properly speaking, trees. Still . . ."

"It's getting pretty smothery," the father said rather loudly. "We better be getting on."

This time Mr. Garfield didn't object, and they went back to the car exchanging promises of visits. The father jerked the crank and climbed into the Ford, where the boy was sighting along his gun. "Put that down," his father said. "Don't you know any better than to point a gun around people?"

"It isn't loaded."

"They never are," his father said. "Put it down now."

The Garfields were standing with their arms round each other's waists, waiting to wave good-bye. Mr. Garfield reached over and picked something from his wife's dress.

"What was it, Alfred?" she said peering.

"Nothing. Just a bit of fluff."

The boy's father coughed violently and the car started with a jerk. With his head down almost to the wheel, still coughing, he waved, and the mother and the boy waved as they went down along the badly set cedar posts of the pasture fence. They were almost a quarter of a mile away before the boy, with a last wave of the gun, turned round again and saw that his father was purple with laughter. He rocked the car with his joy, and when his wife said, "Oh, Harry, you big fool," he pointed helplessly to his shoulder. "Would you mind," he said. "Would you mind brushing that bit o' fluff off me showldah?" He roared again, pounding the wheel. "I shawn't stick it," he said. "I bloody well shawn't stick it, you knaow!"

"It isn't fair to laugh at him," she said. "He can't help being English."

"He can't help being a sanctimonious old mudhen either, braying about his luv-ly luv-ly trees. They'll freeze out the first winter."

"How do you know? Maybe it's like he says—if they get a start they'll grow here as well as anywhere."

"Maybe there's a gold mine in our back yard too, but I'm not gonna dig to see. I couldn't stick it."

"Oh, you're just being stubborn," she said. "Just because you didn't like Mr. Garfield . . ."

He turned on her in heavy amazement. "Well, my God! Did you?"

"I thought he was very nice," she said, and sat straighter in the back seat, speaking loudly above the creak of the springs and cough of the motor. "They're trying to make a home, not just a wheat crop. I liked them."

"Uh, huh." He was not laughing any more now. Sitting beside him, the boy could see that his face had hardened and the cold look had come into his eye again. "So I should start talking like I had a mouthful of bran, and planting trees around the house that'll look like clothesline poles in two months."

"I didn't say that."

"You thought it though." He looked irritably at the sky, misted with the same delusive film of cloud that had fooled him for three days, and spat at the roadside. "You thought it all the time we were there. 'Why aren't you more like Mr. Garfield, he's such a nice man.'" With mincing savagery he swung round and mocked her. "Shall I make it a walnut grove? Or a big maple sugar bush? Or maybe you'd like an orange orchard."

The boy was looking down at his gun, trying not to hear them quarrel, but he knew what his mother's face would be like—hurt and a little flushed, her chin trembling into stubbornness. "I don't suppose you could bear to have a rug on the floor, or a gramophone?" she said.

He smacked the wheel hard. "Of course I could bear it if we could afford it. But I sure as hell would rather do without than be like that old sandhill crane."

"I don't suppose you'd like to take me over to the Old-Man-on-His-Back some day to get some willow slips either."

"What for?"

"To plant down in the coulee, by the dam."

"That dam dries up every August. Your willows wouldn't live till snow flies."

"Well, would it do any harm to try?"

"Oh, shut up!" he said. "Just thinking about that guy and his fluff and his trees gives me the pleefer."

The topless Ford lurched, one wheel at a time, through the deep burnout by their pasture corner, and the boy clambered out with his gun in his hand to slip the loop from the three-strand gate. It was then that he saw the snake, a striped limp ribbon, dangling on the fence, and a moment later the sparrow, neatly butchered and hung by the throat from the barbed wire. He pointed the gun at them. "Lookit!" he said. "Lookit what the butcher bird's been doing."

His father's violent hand waved at him from the seat. "Come on! Get the wire out of the way!"

The boy dragged the gate through the dust, and the Ford went through and up behind the house, perched on the bare edge of the coulee in the midst of its baked yard and framed by the dark fireguard overgrown with Russian thistle. Walking across that yard a few minutes later, the boy felt its hard heat under his sneakers. There was hardly a spear of grass within the fireguard. It was one of his father's prides that the dooryard should be like cement. "Pour your wash water out long enough," he said, "and you'll have a surface so hard it won't even make mud." Religiously he threw his water out three times a day, carrying it sometimes a dozen steps to dump it on a dusty or grassy spot.

The mother had objected at first, asking why they had to live in the middle of an alkali flat, and why they couldn't let grass grow up to the door. But he snorted her down. Everything round the house ought to be bare as a bone. Get a good prairie fire going and it'd jump that guard like nothing, and if they had grass to the door where'd they be? She said why not plow a wider fireguard then, one a fire couldn't jump, but he said he had other things to do besides plowing fifty-foot fireguards.

They were arguing inside when the boy came up on the step to sit down and aim his empty .22 at a fence post. Apparently his mother had been persistent, and persistence when he was not in a mood for it angered the father worse than anything else. Their talk came vaguely through his concentration, but he shut his ears on it. If that spot on the fence post was a coyote now, and he held the sight steady, right on it, and pulled the trigger, that old coyote would jump about eighty feet in the air and come down dead as a mackerel, and he could tack his hide on the barn the way Mr. Larsen had one, only the dogs had jumped and torn the tail and hind legs off Mr. Larsen's pelt, and he wouldn't get more than the three-dollar bounty out of it. But then Mr. Larsen had shot his with a shotgun anyway, and the hide wasn't worth much even before the dogs tore it. . . .

"I can't for the life of me see why not," his mother said inside. "We could do it now. We're not doing anything else."

"I tell you they wouldn't grow!" said his father with emphasis on every word. "Why should we run our tongues out doing everything that mealy-mouthed fool does?"

"I don't want anything but the willows. They're easy."

He made his special sound of contempt, half snort, half grunt.

After a silence she tried again. "They might even have pussies on them in the spring. Mr. Garfield thinks they'd grow, and he used to work in a greenhouse, his wife told me."

"This isn't a greenhouse, for Chrissake."

"Oh, let it go," she said. "I've stood it this long without any green things around. I guess I can stand it some more."

The boy, aiming now toward the gate where the butcher bird, coming back to his prey, would in just a minute fly right into Dead-eye's unerring bullet, heard his father stand up suddenly.

"Abused, aren't you?" he said.

The mother's voice rose. "No, I'm not abused! Only I can't see why it would be so awful to get some willows. Just because Mr. Garfield gave me the idea, and you didn't like him. . . ."

"You're right I didn't like Mr. Garfield," the father said. "He gave me a pain right under the crupper."

"Because," the mother's voice said bitterly, "he calls his wife 'dear' and puts his arm around her and likes trees. It wouldn't occur to you to put your arm around your wife, would it?"

The boy aimed and held his breath. His mother ought to keep still, because if she didn't she'd get him real mad and then they'd both have to tiptoe around the rest of the day. He heard his father's breath whistle through his teeth, and his voice, mincing, nasty. "Would you like me to kiss you now, *dear?*"

"I wouldn't let you touch me with a ten-foot pole," his mother said. She sounded just as mad as he did, and it wasn't often she let herself get that way. The boy squirmed over when he heard the quick hard steps come up behind him and pause. Then his father's big hand, brown and meaty and felted with fine black hair, reached down over his shoulder and took the .22.

"Let's see this cannon old Scissor-bill gave you," he said.

It was a single-shot, bolt-action Savage, a little rusty on the barrel, the bolt sticky with hardened grease when the father removed it. Sighting up through the barrel, he grunted. "Takes care of a gun like he takes care of his farm. Probably used it to cultivate his luv-ly trees."

He went out into the sleeping porch, and after a minute came back with a rag and a can of machine oil. Hunching the boy over on the step, he sat down and began rubbing the bolt with the oil-soaked rag.

"I just can't bear to shoot anything any more," he said, and laughed suddenly. "I just cawn't stick it, little man." He leered at the boy, who grinned back uncertainly. Squinting through the barrel again, the father breathed through his nose and clamped his lips together, shaking his head.

The sun lay heavy on the baked yard. Out over the corner of the pasture a soaring hawk caught wind and sun at the same time, so that his light breast feathers flashed as he banked and rose. Just wait, the boy thought. Wait till I get my gun working and I'll fix you, you hen-robber. He thought of the three chicks a hawk had struck earlier in the summer, the three balls of yellow with the barred mature plumage just coming through. Two of them dead when he got there and chased the hawk away, the other gasping with its crop slashed wide open and the wheat spilling from it on the ground. His mother had sewed up the crop, and the chicken had lived, but it always looked droopy, like a plant in drought time, and sometimes it would stand and work its bill as if it were choking.

By golly, he thought, I'll shoot every hawk and butcher bird in twenty miles. I'll . . .

"Rustle around and find me a piece of baling wire," his father said. "This barrel looks like a henroost."

Behind the house he found a piece of rusty wire, brought it back and watched his father straighten it, wind a bit of rag round the end, ram it up and down through the barrel, and peer through again. "He's leaded her so you can hardly see the grooves," he said. "But maybe she'll shoot. We'll fill her with vinegar and cork her up tonight."

The mother was behind them, leaning against the jamb and watching. She reached down and rumpled the father's black hair. "The minute you get a gun in your hand you start feeling better," she said. "It's just a shame you weren't born fifty years sooner."

"A gun's a good tool," he said. "It hadn't ought to be misused. Gun like this is enough to make a guy cry."

"Well, you've got to admit it was nice of Mr. Garfield to give it to Sonny," she said. It was the wrong thing to say. The boy had a feeling somehow that she knew it was the wrong thing to say, that she said it just to have one tiny triumph over him. He knew it would make him boiling mad again, even before he heard his father's answer.

"Oh, sure, Mr. Garfield's a fine man. He can preach a better sermon than any homesteader in Saskatchewan. God Almighty! everything he does is better than what I do. All right. All right, *all right!* Why the hell don't you move over there if you like it so well?"

"If you weren't so blind . . . !"

He rose with the .22 in his hand and pushed past her into the house. "I'm not so blind," he said heavily in passing. "You've been throwing that bastard up to me for two hours. It don't take very good eyes to see what that means."

His mother started to say, "All because I want a few little . . ." but the boy cut in on her, anxious to help the situation somehow. "Will it shoot now?" he said.

His father said nothing. His mother looked down at him, shrugged, sighed, smiled bleakly with a tight mouth. She moved aside when the father came back with a box of cartridges in his hand. He ignored his wife, speaking to the boy alone in the particular half-jocular tone he always used with him or the dog when he wasn't mad or exasperated.

"Thought I had these around," he said. "Now we'll see what this smoke-pole will do."

He slipped a cartridge in and locked the bolt, looking round for something to shoot at. Behind him the mother's feet moved on the floor, and her voice came purposefully. "I can't see why you have to act this way," she said. "I'm going over and get some slips myself."

There was a long silence. The angled shade lay sharp as a knife across the baked front yard. The father's cheek was pressed against the stock of the gun, his arms and hands as steady as stone.

"How'll you get there?" he said, whispering down the barrel.

"I'll walk."

"Five miles and back."

"Yes, five miles and back. Or fifty miles and back. If there was any earthly reason why you should mind . . ."

"I don't mind," he said, and his voice was soft as silk. "Go ahead."

Close to his mother's long skirts in the doorway, the boy felt her stiffen as if she had been slapped. He squirmed anxiously, but his desperation could find only the question he had asked before. His voice squeaked on it: "Will it shoot now?"

"See that sparrow out there?" his father said, still whispering. "Right out by that cactus?"

"Harry!" the mother said. "If you shoot that harmless little bird!"

Fascinated, the boy watched his father's dark face against the rifle stock, the locked, immovable left arm, the thick finger crooked inside the trigger guard almost too small to hold it. He saw the sparrow, gray, white-breasted, hopping obliviously in search of bugs, fifty feet out on the gray earth. "I just . . . can't . . . bear . . . to . . . shoot . . . anything," the father said, his face like dark stone, his lips hardly moving. "I just . . . can't . . . stick it!"

"Harry!" his wife screamed.

The boy's mouth opened, a dark wash of terror shadowed his vision of the baked yard cut by its sharp angle of shade.

"Don't, Pa!"

The rocklike figure of his father never moved. The thick finger squeezed slowly down on the trigger, there was a thin, sharp report, and the sparrow jerked and collapsed into a shapeless wad on the ground. It was as if, in the instant of the shot, all its clean outlines vanished. Head, feet, the white breast, the perceptible outlines of the folded wings, disappeared all at once, were crumpled together and lost, and the boy sat beside his father on the step with the echo of the shot still in his ears.

He did not look at either of his parents. He looked only at the crumpled sparrow. Step by step, unable to keep away, he went to it, stooped, and picked it up. Blood stained his fingers, and he held the bird by the tail while he wiped the smeared hand on his overalls. He heard the click as the bolt was shot and the empty cartridge ejected, and he saw his mother come swiftly out of the house past his father, who sat still on the step. Her hands were clenched, and she walked with her head down, as if fighting tears.

"Ma!" the boy said dully. "Ma, what'll I do with it?"

She stopped and turned, and for a moment they faced each other. He saw the dead pallor of her face, the burning eyes, the not-quite-controllable quiver of her lips. But her words, when they came, were flat and level, almost casual.

"Leave it right there," she said. "After a while your father will want to hang it on the barbed wire."

QUESTIONS

1. Wallace Stegner spent the years between five and ten in a small frontier town in Saskatchewan—years he called more important to him than any other five years of his life. From them he gets the setting for this story. How important is the setting?

2. What is the point of view, and how does it add intensity to the story?

3. Are the father and mother types or individuals?

4. What are the main characteristics of the father?

5. The author makes no direct statement about the cause of the negative, domineering attitude of the father. Do any hints in the story suggest its cause?

6. How is the mother characterized? Why does the author portray her as answering back rather than ignoring her husband's rudeness?

7. What is the effect of the parents' disagreements on the boy?

8. What is the conflict, and how is it resolved?

9. Why does the father shoot "that harmless little bird"?

10. Could the story have ended by having the husband take his wife to find the willow trees?

11. Is the boy's final plea, "Ma, what'll I do with it?" asking something more than merely what to do with the bird?

12. What is the meaning of the last sentence?

13. Various symbols are used throughout the story—the gun, the sparrow, the barren farmyard, the willow trees, the butcher bird. What do they stand for?

14. What is the theme of the story?

ROPE
KATHERINE ANNE PORTER

On the third day after they moved to the country he came walking back from the village carrying a basket of groceries and a twenty-four-yard coil of rope. She came out to meet him, wiping her hands on her green smock. Her hair was tumbled, her nose was scarlet with sunburn; he told her that already she looked like a born country woman. His gray flannel shirt stuck to him, his heavy shoes were dusty. She assured him he looked like a rural character in a play.

Had he brought the coffee? She had been waiting all day long for coffee. They had forgot it when they ordered at the store the first day.

Gosh, no, he hadn't. Lord, now he'd have to go back. Yes, he would if it killed him. He thought, though, he had everything else. She reminded him it was only because he didn't drink coffee himself. If he did he would remember it quick enough. Suppose they ran out of cigarettes? Then she saw the rope. What was that for? Well, he thought it might do to hang clothes on, or something. Naturally she asked him if he thought they were going to run a laundry? They already had a fifty-foot line hanging right before his eyes? Why, hadn't he noticed it, really? It was a blot on the landscape to her.

He thought there were a lot of things a rope might come in handy for. She wanted to know what, for instance. He thought a few seconds, but nothing occurred. They could wait and see, couldn't they? You need all sorts of strange odds and ends around a place in the country. She said, yes, that was so; but she thought just at that time when every penny counted, it seemed funny to buy more rope. That was all. She hadn't meant anything else. She hadn't just seen, not at first, why he felt it was necessary.

Well, thunder, he had bought it because he wanted to, and that was all there was to it. She thought that was reason enough, and couldn't understand why he hadn't said so, at first. Undoubtedly it would be useful, twenty-four yards of rope, there were hundreds of things, she couldn't think of any at the moment, but it would come in. Of course. As he had said, things always did in the country.

But she was a little disappointed about the coffee, and oh, look, look, look at the eggs! Oh, my, they're all running! What had he put on top of them? Hadn't he known eggs mustn't be squeezed? Squeezed, who had squeezed them, he wanted to know. What a silly thing to say. He had simply brought them along in the basket with the other things. If they got broke it was the grocer's fault. He should know better than to put heavy things on top of eggs.

She believed it was the rope. That was the heaviest thing in the pack, she saw him plainly when he came in from the road, the rope was a big package on top of everything. He desired the whole wide world to witness that this was not a fact. He had carried the rope in one hand and the basket in the other, and what was the use of her having eyes if that was the best they could do for her?

Well, anyhow, she could see one thing plain: no eggs for breakfast. They'd have to scramble them now, for supper. It was too damned bad. She had planned to have steak for supper. No ice, meat wouldn't keep. He wanted to know why she couldn't finish breaking the eggs in a bowl and set them in a cool place.

Cool place! if he could find one for her, she'd be glad to set them there. Well, then, it seemed to him they might very well cook the meat at the same time they cooked the eggs and then warm up the meat for tomorrow. The idea simply choked her. Warmed-over meat, when they might as well have had it fresh. Second best and scraps and makeshifts, even to the meat! He rubbed her shoulder a little. It doesn't really matter so much, does it, darling? Sometimes when they were playful, he would rub her shoulder and she would arch and purr. This time she hissed and almost clawed. He was getting ready to say that they could surely manage somehow when she turned on him and said, if he told her they could manage somehow she would certainly slap his face.

He swallowed the words red hot, his face burned. He picked up the rope and started to put it on the top shelf. She would not have it on the top shelf, the jars and tins belonged there; positively she would not have the top shelf cluttered up with a lot of rope. She had borne all the clutter she meant to bear in the flat in town, there was space here at least and she meant to keep things in order.

Well, in that case, he wanted to know what the hammer and nails were doing up there? And why had she put them there when she knew very well he needed that hammer and those nails upstairs to fix the window sashes? She simply slowed down everything and made double work on the place with her insane habit of changing things around and hiding them.

She was sure she begged his pardon, and if she had had any reason to believe he was going to fix the sashes this summer she would have left the hammer and nails right where he put them; in the middle of the bedroom floor where they could step on them in the dark. And now if he didn't clear the whole mess out of there she would throw them down the well.

Oh, all right, all right—could he put them in the closet? Naturally not, there were brooms and mops and dustpans in the closet, and why couldn't he find a place for his rope outside her kitchen? Had he stopped to consider there were seven God-forsaken rooms in the house, and only one kitchen?

He wanted to know what of it? And did she realize she was making a complete fool of herself? And what did she take him for, a three-year-old idiot? The whole trouble with her was she needed something weaker than she was to heckle and tyrannize over. He wished to God now they had a couple of children she could take it out on. Maybe he'd get some rest.

Her face changed at this, she reminded him he had forgot the coffee and had bought a worthless piece of rope. And when she thought of all the things they actually needed to make the place even decently fit to live in, well, she could cry, that was all. She looked so forlorn, so lost and despairing he couldn't believe it was only a piece of rope that was causing all the racket. What *was* the matter, for God's sake?

Oh, would he please hush and go away, and *stay* away, if he could, for five minutes? By all means, yes, he would. He'd stay away indefinitely if she wished. Lord, yes, there was nothing he'd like better than to clear out and never come back. She couldn't for the life of her see what was holding him, then. It was a swell time. Here she was, stuck, miles from a railroad, with a half-empty house on her hands, and not a penny in her pocket, and everything on earth to do; it seemed the God-sent moment for him to get out from under. She was surprised he hadn't stayed in town as it was until she had come out and done the work and got things straightened out. It was his usual trick.

It appeared to him that this was going a little far. Just a touch out of bounds, if she didn't mind his saying so. Why the hell had he stayed in town the summer before? To do a half-dozen extra jobs to get the money he had sent her. That was it. She knew perfectly well they couldn't have done it otherwise. She had agreed with him at the time. And that was the only time so help him he had ever left her to do anything by herself.

Oh, he could tell that to his great-grandmother. She had her notion of what had kept him in town. Considerably more than a notion, if he wanted to know. So, she was going to bring all that up again, was she? Well, she could just think what she pleased. He was tired of explaining. It may have looked funny but he had simply got hooked in, and what could he do? It was impossible to believe that she was going to take it seriously. Yes, yes, she knew how it was with a man: if he was left by himself a minute, some woman was certain to kidnap him. And naturally he couldn't hurt her feelings by refusing!

Well, what was she raving about? Did she forget she had told him those two weeks alone in the country were the happiest she had known for four years? And how long had they been married when she said that? All right, shut up! If she thought that hadn't stuck in his craw.

She hadn't meant she was happy because she was away from him. She meant she was happy getting the devilish house nice and ready for him. That was what she had meant, and now look! Bringing up something she had said a year ago simply to justify himself for forgetting her coffee and breaking the eggs and buying a wretched piece of rope they couldn't afford. She really thought it was time to drop the subject, and now she wanted only two things in the world. She wanted him to get that rope from underfoot, and go back to the village and get her coffee, and if he could remember it, he might bring a metal mitt for the skillets, and two more curtain rods, and if there were any rubber gloves in the village, her hands were simply raw, and a bottle of milk of magnesia from the drugstore.

He looked out at the dark blue afternoon sweltering on the slopes, and mopped his forehead and sighed heavily and said, if only she could wait a minute for *anything,* he was going back. He had said so, hadn't he, the very instant they found he had overlooked it?

Oh, yes, well . . . run along. She was going to wash windows. The country was so beautiful! She doubted they'd have a moment to enjoy it. He meant to go, but he could not until he had said that if she wasn't such a hopeless melancholiac she might see that this was only for a few days. Couldn't she remember anything pleasant about the other summers? Hadn't they ever had any fun? She hadn't time to talk about it, and now would he please not leave that rope lying around for her to trip on? He picked it up, somehow it had toppled off the table, and walked out with it under his arm.

Was he going this minute? He certainly was. She thought so. Sometimes it seemed to her he had second sight about the precisely perfect moment to leave her ditched. She had meant to put the mattresses out to sun, if they put them out this minute they would get at least three hours, he must have heard her say that morning she meant to put them out. So of course he would walk off and leave her to it. She supposed he thought the exercise would do her good.

Well, he was merely going to get her coffee. A four-mile walk for two pounds of coffee was ridiculous, but he was perfectly willing to do it. The habit was making a wreck of her, but if she wanted to wreck herself there was nothing he could do about it. If he thought it was coffee that was making a wreck of her, she congratulated him: he must have a damned easy conscience.

Conscience or no conscience, he didn't see why the mattresses couldn't very well wait until tomorrow. And anyhow, for God's sake, were they living *in* the house, or were they going to let the house ride them to death? She paled at this, her face grew livid about the mouth, she looked quite dangerous, and reminded him that housekeeping was no more her work than it was his: she had other work to do as well, and when did he think she was going to find time to do it at this rate?

Was she going to start on that again? She knew as well as he did that his work brought in the regular money, hers was only occasional, if they depended on what *she* made—and she might as well get straight on this question once for all!

That was positively not the point. The question was, when both of them were working on their own time, was there going to be a division of the housework, or wasn't there? She merely wanted to know, she had to make her plans. Why, he thought that was all arranged. It was understood that he was to help. Hadn't he always, in summers?

Hadn't he, though? Oh, just hadn't he? And when, and where, and doing what? Lord, what an uproarious joke!

It was such a very uproarious joke that her face turned slightly purple, and she screamed with laughter. She laughed so hard she had to sit down, and finally a rush of tears spurted from her eyes and poured down into the lifted corners of her mouth. He dashed towards her and dragged her up to her feet and tried to pour water on her head. The dipper hung by a string on a nail and he broke it loose. Then he tried to pump water with one hand while she struggled in the other. So he gave it up and shook her instead.

She wrenched away, crying out for him to take his rope and go to hell, she had simply given him up: and ran. He heard her high-heeled bedroom slippers clattering and stumbling on the stairs.

He went out around the house and into the lane; he suddenly realized he had a blister on his heel and his shirt felt as if it were on fire. Things broke so suddenly you didn't know where you were. She could work herself into a fury about simply nothing. She was terrible, damn it: not an ounce of reason. You might as well talk to a sieve as that woman when she got going. Damned if he'd spend his life humoring her! Well, what to do now? He would take back the rope and exchange it for something else. Things accumulated, things were mountainous, you couldn't move them or sort them out or get rid of them. They just lay and rotted around. He'd take it back. Hell, why should he? He wanted it. What was it anyhow? A piece of rope. Imagine anybody caring more about a piece of rope than about a man's feelings. What earthly right had she to say a word about it? He remembered all the useless, meaningless things she bought for herself: Why? because I wanted it, that's why! He stopped and selected a large stone by the road. He would put the rope behind it. He would put it in the tool-box when he got back. He'd heard enough about it to last him a life-time.

When he came back she was leaning against the post box beside the road waiting. It was pretty late, the smell of broiled steak floated nose high in the cooling air. Her face was young and smooth and fresh-looking. Her unmanageable funny black hair was all on end. She waved to him from a distance, and he speeded up. She called out that supper was ready and waiting, was he starved?

You bet he was starved. Here was the coffee. He waved it at her. She looked at his other hand. What was that he had there?

Well, it was the rope again. He stopped short. He had meant to exchange it but forgot. She wanted to know why he should exchange it, if it was something he really wanted. Wasn't the air sweet now, and wasn't it fine to be here?

She walked beside him with one hand hooked into his leather belt. She pulled and jostled him a little as he walked, and leaned against him. He put his arm clear around her and patted her stomach. They exchanged wary smiles. Coffee, coffee for the Ootsum-Wootsums! He felt as if he were bringing her a beautiful present.

He was a love, she firmly believed, and if she had had her coffee in the morning, she wouldn't have behaved so funny. . . . There was a whippoorwill still coming back, imagine, clear out of season, sitting in the crab-apple tree calling all by himself. Maybe his girl stood him up. Maybe she did. She hoped to hear him once more, she loved whippoorwills. . . . He knew how she was, didn't he?

Sure, he knew how she was.

QUESTIONS

1. Why are the characters called merely "he" and "she"?
2. From what point of view is the story told, and why is it effective?
3. What is the setting, and how important is it to the story?
4. The style of writing is the most striking aspect of this story, with a movement as swift as a quarrel itself. Ordinarily conversation is written in one of two ways:

"Did you bring the coffee?" she asked.
"Gosh, no, I didn't. Lord, now I'll have to go back," he replied.

or

She asked whether he had brought the coffee. He replied that he hadn't and now would have to go back.

Now note Katherine Anne Porter's method, which omits the "she asked" and "he replied" phrases:

Had he brought the coffee? . . .
Gosh, no, he hadn't. Lord, now he'd have to go back.

Why is this method effective?

5. The conflict is between two emotionally immature people—the petulant, contradictory wife and the exasperated, unsympathetic husband. What does the rope symbolize to her? To him?

6. What insinuations on pp. 156–57 indicate that this is something more than a petty quarrel between two basically compatible people?

7. What brings about a reconciliation? Will it last?

8. Have the characters received any new insight or changed in any way at the end of the story?

9. What observations is the author making about quarrels in general?

10. What is the theme?

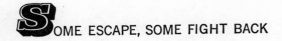

SOME ESCAPE, SOME FIGHT BACK

THE SECRET LIFE OF WALTER MITTY
JAMES THURBER

We're going through!" The Commander's voice was like thin ice breaking. He wore his full-dress uniform, with the heavily braided white cap pulled down rakishly over one cold gray eye. "We can't make it, sir. It's spoiling for a hurricane, if you ask me." "I'm not asking you, Lieutenant Berg," said the Commander. "Throw on the power lights! Rev her up to 8,500! We're going through!" The pounding of the cylinders increased: ta-pocketa-pocketa-pocketa-*pocketa-pocketa*. The Commander stared at the ice forming on the pilot window. He walked over and twisted a row of complicated dials. "Switch on No. 8 auxiliary!" he shouted. "Switch on No. 8 auxiliary!" repeated Lieutenant Berg. "Full strength in No. 3 turret!" shouted the Commander. "Full strength in No. 3 turret!" The crew, bending to their various tasks in the huge, hurtling eight-engined Navy hydroplane, looked at each other and grinned. "The Old Man'll get us through," they said to one another. "The Old Man ain't afraid of Hell!". . .

"Not so fast! You're driving too fast!" said Mrs. Mitty. "What are you driving so fast for?"

"Hmm?" said Walter Mitty. He looked at his wife, in the seat beside him, with shocked astonishment. She seemed grossly unfamiliar, like a strange woman who had yelled at him in a crowd. "You were up to fifty-five," she said. "You know I don't like to go more than forty. You were up to fifty-five." Walter Mitty drove on toward Waterbury in silence, the roaring of the SN202 through the worst storm in twenty years of Navy flying fading in the remote, intimate airways of his mind. "You're tensed up again," said Mrs. Mitty. "It's one of your days. I wish you'd let Dr. Renshaw look you over."

Walter Mitty stopped the car in front of the building where his wife went to have her hair done. "Remember to get those overshoes while I'm having my hair done," she said. "I don't need overshoes," said Mitty. She put her mirror back into her bag. "We've been all through that," she said, getting out of the car. "You're not a young man any longer." He raced the engine a little. "Why don't you wear your gloves? Have you lost your gloves?" Walter Mitty reached in a pocket and brought out the gloves. He put them on, but after she had turned and gone into the building and he had driven on to a red light, he took them off again. "Pick it up, brother!" snapped a cop as the light changed, and Mitty hastily pulled on his gloves and lurched ahead. He drove around the streets aimlessly for a time, and then he drove past the hospital on his way to the parking lot.

. . . "It's the millionaire banker, Wellington McMillan," said the pretty nurse. "Yes?" said Walter Mitty, removing his gloves slowly. "Who has the case?" "Dr. Renshaw and Dr. Benbow, but there are two specialists here, Dr. Remington from New York and Mr. Pritchard-Mitford from London. He flew over." A door opened down a long, cool corridor and Dr. Renshaw came out. He looked distraught and haggard. "Hello, Mitty," he said. "We're having the devil's own time with McMillan, the millionaire banker and close personal friend of Roosevelt. Obstreosis of the ductal tract. Tertiary. Wish you'd take a look at him." "Glad to," said Mitty.

In the operating room there were whispered introductions: "Dr. Remington, Dr. Mitty. Mr. Pritchard-Mitford, Dr. Mitty." "I've read your book on streptothricosis," said Pritchard-Mitford, shaking hands. "A brilliant performance, sir." "Thank you," said Walter Mitty. "Didn't know you were in the States, Mitty," grumbled Remington. "Coals to Newcastle, bringing Mitford and me up here for a tertiary." "You are very kind," said Mitty. A huge, complicated machine, connected to the operating table, with many tubes and wires, began at this moment to go pocketa-pocketa-pocketa. "The new anesthetizer is giving way!" shouted an interne. "There is no one in the East who knows how to fix it!" "Quiet, man!" said Mitty, in a low, cool voice. He sprang to the machine, which was now going pocketa-pocketa-queep-pocketa-queep. He began fingering delicately a row of glistening dials. "Give me a fountain pen!" he snapped. Someone handed him a fountain pen. He pulled a faulty piston out of the machine and inserted the pen in its place. "That will hold for ten minutes," he said. "Get on with the operation." A nurse hurried over and whispered to Renshaw, and Mitty saw the man turn pale. "Coreopsis has set in," said Renshaw nervously. "If you would take over, Mitty?" Mitty looked at him and at the craven figure of Benbow, who drank, and at the grave, uncertain faces of the two great specialists. "If you wish," he said. They slipped a white gown on him; he adjusted a mask and drew on thin gloves; nurses handed him shining . . .

"Back it up, Mac! Look out for that Buick!" Walter Mitty jammed on the brakes. "Wrong lane, Mac," said the parking-lot attendant, looking at Mitty closely. "Gee. Yeh," muttered Mitty. He began cautiously to back out of the lane marked "Exit Only." "Leave her sit there," said the attendant. "I'll put her away." Mitty got out of the car. "Hey, better leave the key." "Oh," said Mitty, handing the man the ignition key. The attendant vaulted into the car, backed it up with insolent skill, and put it where it belonged.

They're so damn cocky, thought Walter Mitty, walking along Main Street; they think they know everything. Once he had tried to take his chains off, outside New Milford, and he had got them wound around the axles. A man had had to come out in a wrecking car and unwind them, a young, grinning garageman. Since then Mrs. Mitty always made him drive to a garage to have the chains taken off. The next time, he thought, I'll wear my right arm in a sling; they won't grin at me then. I'll have my right arm in a sling and they'll see I couldn't possibly take the chains off myself. He kicked at the slush on the sidewalk. "Overshoes," he said to himself, and he began looking for a shoe store.

When he came out into the street again, with the overshoes in a box under his arm, Walter Mitty began to wonder what the other thing was his wife had told him to get. She had told him, twice, before they set out from their house for Waterbury. In a way he hated these weekly trips to town—he was always getting something wrong. Kleenex, he thought, Squibb's, razor blades? No. Toothpaste, toothbrush, bicarbonate, carborundum, initiative and referendum? He gave it up. But she would remember it. "Where's the what's-its-name?" she would ask. "Don't tell me you forgot the what's-its-name." A newsboy went by shouting something about the Waterbury trial.

. . . "Perhaps this will refresh your memory." The District Attorney suddenly thrust a heavy automatic at the quiet figure on the witness stand. "Have you ever seen this before?" Walter Mitty took the gun and examined it expertly. "This is my Webley-Vickers 50.80," he said calmly. An excited buzz ran around the courtroom. The Judge rapped for order. "You are a crack shot with any sort of firearms, I believe?" said the District Attorney, insinuatingly. "Objection!" shouted Mitty's attorney. "We have shown that the defendant could not have fired the shot. We have shown that he wore his right arm in a sling on the night of the fourteenth of July." Walter Mitty raised his hand briefly and the bickering attorneys were stilled. "With any known make of gun," he said evenly, "I could have killed Gregory Fitzhurst at three hundred feet *with my left hand*." Pandemonium broke loose in the courtroom. A woman's scream rose above the bedlam and suddenly a lovely, dark-haired girl was in Walter Mitty's arms. The District Attorney struck at her savagely. Without rising from his chair, Mitty let the man have it on the point of the chin. "You miserable cur!" . . .

"Puppy biscuit," said Walter Mitty. He stopped walking and the buildings of Waterbury rose up out of the misty courtroom and surrounded him again. A woman who was passing laughed. "He said 'Puppy biscuit,' " she said to her companion. "That man said 'Puppy biscuit' to himself." Walter Mitty hurried on. He went into an A. & P., not the first one he came to but a smaller one farther up the street. "I want some biscuit for small, young dogs," he said to the clerk. "Any special brand, sir?" The greatest pistol shot in the world thought a moment. "It says 'Puppies Bark for It' on the box," said Walter Mitty.

His wife would be through at the hairdresser's in fifteen minutes, Mitty saw in looking at his watch, unless they had trouble drying it; sometimes they had trouble drying it. She didn't like to get to the hotel first; she would want him to be there waiting for her as usual. He found a big leather chair in the lobby, facing a window, and he put the overshoes and the puppy biscuit on the floor beside it. He picked up an old copy of *Liberty* and sank down into the chair. "Can Germany Conquer the World Through the Air?" Walter Mitty looked at the pictures of bombing planes and of ruined streets.

. . . "The cannonading has got the wind up in young Raleigh, sir," said the sergeant. Captain Mitty looked up at him through tousled hair. "Get him to bed," he said wearily. "With the others. I'll fly alone." "But you can't, sir," said the sergeant anxiously. "It takes two men to handle that bomber and the Archies are pounding hell out of the air. Von Richtman's circus is between here and Saulier." "Somebody's got to get that ammunition dump," said Mitty. "I'm going over. Spot of brandy?" He poured a drink for the sergeant and one for himself. War thundered and whined around the dugout and battered at the door. There was a rending of wood and splinters flew through the room. "A bit of a near thing," said Captain Mitty carelessly. "The box barrage is closing in," said the sergeant. "We only live once, Sergeant," said Mitty, with his faint, fleeting smile. "Or do we?" He poured another brandy and tossed it off. "I never see a man could hold his brandy like you, sir," said the sergeant. "Begging your pardon, sir." Captain Mitty stood up and strapped on his huge Webley-Vickers automatic. "It's forty kilometers through hell, sir," said the sergeant. Mitty finished one last brandy. "After all," he said softly, "what isn't?" The pounding of the cannon increased; there was the rat-tat-tatting of machine guns, and from somewhere came the menacing pocketa-pocketa-pocketa of the new flame-throwers. Walter Mitty walked to the door of the dugout humming "Auprès de Ma Blonde." He turned and waved to the sergeant. "Cheerio!" he said. . . .

Something struck his shoulder. "I've been looking all over this hotel for you," said Mrs. Mitty. "Why do you have to hide in this old chair? How did you expect me to find you?" "Things close in," said Walter Mitty vaguely. "What?" Mrs. Mitty said. "Did you get the what's-its-name? The puppy biscuit? What's in that box?" "Overshoes," said Mitty. "Couldn't you have put them on in the store?" "I was thinking," said Walter Mitty. "Does it ever occur to you that I am sometimes thinking?" She looked at him. "I'm going to take your temperature when I get you home," she said.

They went out through the revolving doors that made a faintly derisive whistling sound when you pushed them. It was two blocks to the parking lot. At the drugstore on the corner she said, "Wait here for me. I forgot something. I won't be a minute." She was more than a minute. Walter Mitty lighted a cigarette. It began to rain, rain with sleet in it. He stood up against the wall of the drugstore, smoking. . . . He put his shoulders back and his heels together. "To hell with the handkerchief," said Walter Mitty scornfully. He took one last drag on his cigarette and snapped it away. Then, with that faint, fleeting smile playing about his lips, he faced the firing squad; erect and motionless, proud and disdainful, Walter Mitty the Undefeated, inscrutable to the last.

QUESTIONS

1. The story starts out as an ordinary air adventure story, and not until the second paragraph does the reader discover that the action is taking place "in the remote, intimate airways" of Walter Mitty's mind. Why does Mr. Mitty have a need to escape through daydreaming?
2. Why is so much more space given to Mitty's daydreams than to his real life?
3. From what point of view is the story told?
4. What external events prompt the daydreams?
5. Do any of the daydreams ever startle Mitty back into reality?
6. At the end of the story what is the meaning of "To hell with the handkerchief"?
7. What similarity is there in all the daydreams?
8. Are the characters types or individuals, and have they changed at all by the end of the story?
9. Is the tone of the story one of amusement or sympathy?
10. What is the conflict and how is it resolved?
11. What is the theme?

THE CATBIRD SEAT

JAMES THURBER

Mr. Martin bought the pack of Camels on Monday night in the most crowded cigar store on Broadway. It was theater time and seven or eight men were buying cigarettes. The clerk didn't even glance at Mr. Martin, who put the pack in his overcoat pocket and went out. If any of the staff at F & S had seen him buy the cigarettes, they would have been astonished, for it was generally known that Mr. Martin did not smoke, and never had. No one saw him.

It was just a week to the day since Mr. Martin had decided to rub out Mrs. Ulgine Barrows. The term "rub out" pleased him because it suggested nothing more than the correction of an error—in this case an error of Mr. Fitweiler. Mr. Martin had spent each night of the past week working out his plan and examining it. As he walked home now he went over it again. For the hundredth time he resented the element of imprecision, the margin of guesswork that entered into the business. The project as he had worked it out was casual and bold, the risks were considerable. Something might go wrong anywhere along the line. And therein lay the cunning of his scheme. No one would ever see in it the cautious, painstaking hand of Erwin Martin, head of the filing department at F & S, of whom Mr. Fitweiler had once said, "Man is fallible but Martin isn't." No one would see his hand, that is, unless it were caught in the act.

Sitting in his apartment, drinking a glass of milk, Mr. Martin reviewed his case against Mrs. Ulgine Barrows, as he had every night for seven nights. He began at the beginning. Her quacking voice and braying laugh had first profaned the halls of F & S on March 7, 1941 (Mr. Martin had a head for dates). Old Roberts, the personnel chief, had introduced her as the newly appointed special adviser to the president of the firm, Mr. Fitweiler. The woman had appalled Mr. Martin instantly, but he hadn't shown it. He had given her his dry hand, a look of studious concentration, and a faint smile. "Well," she had said, looking at the papers on his desk, "are you lifting the oxcart out of the ditch?" As Mr. Martin recalled that moment, over his milk, he squirmed slightly. He must keep his mind on her crimes as a special adviser, not on her peccadillos as a personality. This he found difficult to do, in spite of entering an objection and sustaining it. The faults of the woman as a woman kept chattering on in his mind like an unruly witness. She had, for almost two years now, baited him. In the halls, in the elevator, even in his own office, into which she romped now and then like a circus horse, she was constantly shouting these silly questions at him. "Are you lifting the oxcart out of the ditch? Are you tearing up the pea patch? Are you hollering down the rain barrel? Are you scraping around the bottom of the pickle barrel? Are you sitting in the catbird seat?"

It was Joey Hart, one of Mr. Martin's two assistants, who had explained what the gibberish meant. "She must be a Dodger fan," he had said. "Red Barber announces the Dodger games over the radio and he uses those expressions—picked 'em up down South." Joey had gone on to explain one or two. "Tearing up the pea patch" meant going on a rampage; "sitting in the catbird seat" meant sitting pretty, like a batter with three balls and no strikes on him. Mr. Martin dismissed all this with an effort. It had been annoying, it had driven him near to distraction, but he was too solid a man to be moved to murder by anything so childish. It was fortunate, he reflected as he passed on to the important charges against Mrs. Barrows, that he had stood up under it so well. He had maintained always an outward appearance of polite tolerance. "Why, I even believe you like the woman," Miss Paird, his other assistant, had once said to him. He had simply smiled.

A gavel rapped in Mr. Martin's mind and the case proper was resumed. Mrs. Ulgine Barrows stood charged with willful, blatant, and persistent attempts to destroy the efficiency and system of F & S. It was competent, material, and relevant to review her advent and rise to power. Mr. Martin had got the story from Miss Paird, who seemed always able to find things out. According to her, Mrs. Barrows had met Mr. Fitweiler at a party, where she had rescued him from the embraces of a powerfully built drunken man who had mistaken the president of F & S for a famous retired Middle Western football coach. She had led him to a sofa and somehow worked upon him a monstrous magic. The aging gentleman had jumped to the conclusion there and then that this was a woman of singular attainments, equipped to bring out the best in him and in the firm. A week later he had introduced her into F & S as his special adviser. On that day confusion got its foot in the door. After Miss Tyson, Mr. Brundage, and Mr. Bartlett had been fired and Mr. Munson had taken his hat and stalked out, mailing in his resignation later, old Roberts had been emboldened to speak to Mr. Fitweiler. He mentioned that Mr. Munson's department had been "a little disrupted" and hadn't they perhaps better resume the old system there? Mr. Fitweiler had said certainly not. He had the greatest faith in Mrs. Barrows' ideas. "They require a little seasoning, a little seasoning, is all," he had added. Mr. Roberts had given it up. Mr. Martin reviewed in detail all the changes wrought by Mrs. Barrows. She had begun chipping at the cornices of the firm's edifice and now she was swinging at the foundation stones with a pickaxe.

Mr. Martin came now, in his summing up, to the afternoon of Monday, November 2, 1942—just one week ago. On that day, at 3 P.M., Mrs. Barrows had bounced into his office. "Boo!" she had yelled. "Are you scraping around the bottom of the pickle barrel?" Mr. Martin had looked at her from under his green eyeshade, saying nothing. She had begun to wander about the office, taking it in with her great, popping eyes. "Do you really need *all* these filing cabinets?" she had demanded suddenly. Mr. Martin's heart had jumped. "Each of these files," he had said, keeping his voice even, "plays an indispensable part in the system of F & S." She had brayed at him, "Well, don't tear up the pea patch!" and gone to the door. From there she had bawled, "But you sure have got a lot of fine scrap in here!" Mr. Martin could no longer doubt that the finger was on his beloved department. Her pickaxe was on the upswing, poised for the first blow. It had not come yet; he had received no blue memo from the enchanted Mr. Fitweiler bearing nonsensical instructions deriving from the obscene woman. But there was no doubt in Mr. Martin's mind that one would be forthcoming. He must act quickly. Already a precious week had gone by. Mr. Martin stood up in his living room, still holding his milk glass. "Gentlemen of the jury," he said to himself, "I demand the death penalty for this horrible person."

The next day Mr. Martin followed his routine, as usual. He polished his glasses more often and once sharpened an already sharp pencil, but not even Miss Paird noticed. Only once did he catch sight of his victim; she swept past him in the hall with a patronizing "Hi!" At five-thirty he walked home, as usual, and had a glass of milk, as usual. He had never drunk anything stronger in his life—unless you could count ginger ale. The late Sam Schlosser, the S of F & S, had praised Mr. Martin at a staff meeting several years before for his temperate habits. "Our most efficient worker neither drinks nor smokes," he had said. "The results speak for themselves." Mr. Fitweiler had sat by, nodding approval.

Mr. Martin was still thinking about that red-letter day as he walked over to the Schrafft's on Fifth Avenue near Forty-sixth Street. He got there, as he always did, at eight o'clock. He finished his dinner and the financial page of the *Sun* at a quarter to nine, as he always did. It was his custom after dinner to take a walk. This time he walked down Fifth Avenue at a casual pace. His gloved hands felt moist and warm, his forehead cold. He transferred the Camels from his overcoat to a jacket pocket. He wondered, as he did so, if they did not represent an unnecessary note of strain. Mrs. Barrows smoked only Luckies. It was his idea to puff a few puffs on a Camel (after the rubbing-out), stub it out in the ashtray holding her lipstick-stained Luckies, and thus drag a small red herring across the trail. Perhaps it was not a good idea. It would take time. He might even choke, too loudly.

Mr. Martin had never seen the house on West Twelfth Street where Mrs. Barrows lived, but he had a clear enough picture of it. Fortunately, she had bragged to everybody about her ducky first-floor apartment in the perfectly darling three-story red-brick. There would be no doorman or other attendants; just the tenants of the second and third floors. As he walked along, Mr. Martin realized that he would get there before nine-thirty. He had considered walking north on Fifth Avenue from Schrafft's to a point from which it would take him until ten o'clock to reach the house. At that hour people were less likely to be coming in or going out. But the procedure would have made an awkward loop in the straight thread of his casualness, and he had abandoned it. It was impossible to figure when people would be entering or leaving the house, anyway. There was a great risk at any hour. If he ran into anybody, he would simply have to place the rubbing-out of Ulgine Barrows in the inactive file forever. The same thing would hold true if there were someone in her apartment. In that case he would just say that he had been passing by, recognized her charming house and thought to drop in.

It was eighteen minutes after nine when Mr. Martin turned into Twelfth Street. A man passed him, and a man and a woman, talking. There was no one within fifty paces when he came to the house, halfway down the block. He was up the steps and in the small vestibule in no time, pressing the bell under the card that said "Mrs. Ulgine Barrows." When the clicking in the lock started, he jumped forward against the door. He got inside fast, closing the door behind him. A bulb in a lantern hung from the hall ceiling on a chain seemed to give a monstrously bright light. There was nobody on the stair, which went up ahead of him along the left wall. A door opened down the hall in the wall on the right. He went toward it swiftly, on tip-toe.

"Well, for God's sake, look who's here!" bawled Mrs. Barrows, and her braying laugh rang out like the report of a shotgun. He rushed past her like a football tackle, bumping her. "Hey, quit shoving!" she said, closing the door behind them. They were in her living room, which seemed to Mr. Martin to be lighted by a hundred lamps. "What's after you?" she said. "You're as jumpy as a goat." He found he was unable to speak. His heart was wheezing in his throat. "I—yes," he finally brought out. She was jabbering and laughing as she started to help him off with his coat. "No, no," he said. "I'll put it here." He took it off and put it on a chair near the door. "Your hat and gloves, too," she said. "You're in a lady's house." He put his hat on top of the coat. Mrs. Barrows seemed larger than he had thought. He kept his gloves on. "I was passing by," he said. "I recognized—is there anyone here?" She laughed louder than ever. "No," she said, "we're all alone. You're as white as a sheet, you funny man. Whatever *has* come over you? I'll mix you a toddy." She started toward a door across the room. "Scotch-and-soda be all right? But say, you don't drink, do you?" She turned and gave him her amused look. Mr. Martin pulled himself together. "Scotch-and-soda will be all right," he heard himself say. He could hear her laughing in the kitchen.

Mr. Martin looked quickly around the living room for the weapon. He had counted on finding one there. There were andirons and a poker and something in a corner that looked like an Indian club. None of them would do. It couldn't be that way. He began to pace around. He came to a desk. On it lay a metal paper knife with an ornate handle. Would it be sharp enough? He reached for it and knocked over a small brass jar. Stamps spilled out of it and it fell to the floor with a clatter. "Hey," Mrs. Barrows yelled from the kitchen, "are you tearing up the pea patch?" Mr. Martin gave a strange laugh. Picking up the knife, he tried its point against his left wrist. It was blunt. It wouldn't do.

When Mrs. Barrows reappeared, carrying two highballs, Mr. Martin, standing there with his gloves on, became acutely conscious of the fantasy he had wrought. Cigarettes in his pocket, a drink prepared for him—it was all too grossly improbable. It was more than that; it was impossible. Somewhere in the back of his mind a vague idea stirred, sprouted. "For heaven's sake, take off those gloves," said Mrs. Barrows. "I always wear them in the house," said Mr. Martin. The idea began to bloom, strange and wonderful. She put the glasses on a coffee table in front of a sofa and sat on the sofa. "Come over here, you odd little man," she said. Mr. Martin went over and sat beside her. It was difficult getting a cigarette out of the pack of Camels, but he managed it. She held a match for him, laughing. "Well," she said, handing him his drink, "this is perfectly marvelous. You with a drink and a cigarette."

Mr. Martin puffed, not too awkwardly, and took a gulp of the highball. "I drink and smoke all the time," he said. He clinked his glass against hers. "Here's nuts to that old windbag, Fitweiler," he said, and gulped again. The stuff tasted awful, but he made no grimace. "Really, Mr. Martin," she said, her voice and posture changing, "you are insulting our employer." Mrs. Barrows was now all special adviser to the president. "I am preparing a bomb," said Mr. Martin, "which will blow the old goat higher than hell." He had only had a little of the drink, which was not strong. It couldn't be that. "Do you take dope or something?" Mrs. Barrows asked coldly. "Heroin," said Mr. Martin. "I'll be coked to the gills when I bump that old buzzard off." "Mr. Martin!" she shouted, getting to her feet. "That will be all of that. You must go at once." Mr. Martin took another swallow of his drink. He tapped his cigarette out in the ashtray and put the pack of Camels on the coffee table. Then he got up. She stood glaring at him. He walked over and put on his hat and coat. "Not a word about this," he said, and laid an index finger against his lips. All Mrs. Barrows could bring out was "Really!" Mr. Martin put his hand on the doorknob. "I'm sitting in the catbird seat," he said. He stuck his tongue out at her and left. Nobody saw him go.

Mr. Martin got to his apartment, walking, well before eleven. No one saw him go in. He had two glasses of milk after brushing his teeth, and he felt elated. It wasn't tipsiness, because he hadn't been tipsy. Anyway, the walk had worn off all effects of the whisky. He got in bed and read a magazine for a while. He was asleep before midnight.

Mr. Martin got to the office at eight-thirty the next morning, as usual. At a quarter to nine, Ulgine Barrows, who had never before arrived at work before ten, swept into his office. "I'm reporting to Mr. Fitweiler now!" she shouted. "If he turns you over to the police, it's no more than you deserve!" Mr. Martin gave her a look of shocked surprise. "I beg your pardon?" he said. Mrs. Barrows snorted and bounced out of the room, leaving Miss Paird and Joey Hart staring after her. "What's the matter with that old devil now?" asked Miss Paird. "I have no idea," said Mr. Martin, resuming his work. The other two looked at him and then at each other. Miss Paird got up and went out. She walked slowly past the closed door of Mr. Fitweiler's office. Mrs. Barrows was yelling inside, but she was not braying. Miss Paird could not hear what the woman was saying. She went back to her desk.

Forty-five minutes later, Mrs. Barrows left the president's office and went into her own, shutting the door. It wasn't until half an hour later that Mr. Fitweiler sent for Mr. Martin. The head of the filing department, neat, quiet, attentive, stood in front of the old man's desk. Mr. Fitweiler was pale and nervous. He took his glasses off and twiddled them. He made a small, bruffing sound in his throat. "Martin," he said, "you have been with us more than twenty years." "Twenty-two, sir," said Mr. Martin. "In that time," pursued the president, "your work and your—uh—manner have been exemplary." "I trust so, sir," said Mr. Martin. "I have understood, Martin," said Mr. Fitweiler, "that you have never taken a drink or smoked." "That is correct, sir," said Mr. Martin. "Ah, yes." Mr. Fitweiler polished his glasses. "You may describe what you did after leaving the office yesterday, Martin," he said. Mr. Martin allowed less than a second for his bewildered pause. "Certainly, sir," he said. "I walked home. Then I went to Schrafft's for dinner. Afterward I walked home again. I went to bed early, sir, and read a magazine for a while. I was asleep before eleven." "Ah, yes," said Mr. Fitweiler again. He was silent for a moment, searching for the proper words to say to the head of the filing department. "Mrs. Barrows," he said finally, "Mrs. Barrows has worked hard, Martin, very hard. It grieves me to report that she has suffered a severe breakdown. It has taken the form of a persecution complex accompanied by distressing hallucinations." "I am very sorry, sir," said Mr. Martin. "Mrs. Barrows is under the delusion," continued Mr. Fitweiler, "that you visited her last evening and behaved yourself in an—uh—unseemly manner." He raised his hand to silence Mr. Martin's little pained outcry. "It is the nature of these psychological diseases," Mr. Fitweiler said, "to fix upon the least likely and most innocent party as the—uh—source of persecution. These matters are not for the lay mind to grasp, Martin. I've just had my psychiatrist, Dr. Fitch, on the phone. He would not, of course, commit himself, but he made enough generalizations to substantiate my suspicions. I suggested to Mrs. Barrows when she had completed her—uh—story to me this morning, that she visit Dr. Fitch, for I suspected a condition at once. She flew, I regret to say, into a rage, and demanded—uh—requested that I call you on the carpet. You may not know, Martin, but Mrs. Barrows had planned a reorganization of your department—subject to my approval, of course, subject to my approval. This brought you, rather than anyone else, to her mind—but again that is a phenomenon for Dr. Fitch and not for us. So, Martin, I am afraid Mrs. Barrows' usefulness here is at an end." "I am dreadfully sorry, sir," said Mr. Martin.

It was at this point that the door to the office blew open with the suddenness of a gas-main explosion and Mrs. Barrows catapulted through it. "Is the little rat denying it?" she screamed. "He can't get away with that!" Mr. Martin got up and moved discreetly to a point beside Mr. Fitweiler's chair. "You drank and smoked at my apartment," she bawled at Mr. Martin, "and you know it! You called Mr. Fitweiler an old windbag and said you were going to blow him up when you got coked to the gills on your heroin!" She stopped yelling to catch her breath and a new glint came into her popping eyes. "If you weren't such a drab, ordinary little man," she said, "I'd think you'd planned it all. Sticking your tongue out, saying you were sitting in the catbird seat, because you thought no one would believe me when I told it! My God, it's really too perfect!" She brayed loudly and hysterically, and the fury was on her again. She glared at Mr. Fitweiler. "Can't you see how he has tricked us, you old fool? Can't you see his little game?" But Mr. Fitweiler had been surreptitiously pressing all the buttons under the top of his desk and employees of F & S began pouring into the room. "Stockton," said Mr. Fitweiler, "you and Fishbein will take Mrs. Barrows to her home. Mrs. Powell, you will go with them." Stockton, who had played a little football in high school, blocked Mrs. Barrows as she made for Mr. Martin. It took him and Fishbein together to force her out of the door into the hall, crowded with stenographers and office boys. She was still screaming imprecations at Mr. Martin, tangled and contradictory imprecations. The hubbub finally died out down the corridor.

"I regret that this has happened," said Mr. Fitweiler. "I shall ask you to dismiss it from your mind, Martin." "Yes, sir," said Mr. Martin, anticipating his chief's "That will be all" by moving to the door. "I will dismiss it." He went out and shut the door, and his step was light and quick in the hall. When he entered his department he had slowed down to his customary gait, and he walked quietly across the room to the W20 file, wearing a look of studious concentration.

QUESTIONS

1. What adjectives are used to describe Mr. Martin? In what ways is he like Walter Mitty? In what ways is he unlike him?

2. List some of the verbs used to characterize Mrs. Barrows. Why does one think of adjectives to describe Mr. Martin and verbs to describe Mrs. Barrows?

3. Are the characters types or individuals?

4. What is the purpose of the trial of Mrs. Barrows that Mr. Martin conducts in his mind? What bits of legal jargon make it realistic?

5. What indication is there that Mr. Martin intends to murder Mrs. Barrows? Why does he change his plan, and when does his new plan take shape?

6. Are the repetitions in the following passage intentional? If so, what is their purpose?

> . . . Mr. Martin followed his routine, as usual. . . . At five-thirty he walked home, as usual, and had a glass of milk, as usual. . . . He got there [to Schrafft's], as he always did, at eight o'clock. He finished his dinner and the financial page of the *Sun* at a quarter to nine, as he always did.

7. What are some of the particularly effective metaphors?

8. What use is made of irony?

9. Why is "The Catbird Seat" a good title?

10. What is the conflict?

11. As in the best humorous stories, the author is writing not only to amuse but to make a serious point as well. What is his theme?

12. Thurber once said, "The things we laugh at are awful while they are going on, but get funny when we look back. And other people laugh because they've been through it too." What gives this story its universal appeal?

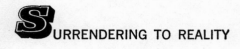URRENDERING TO REALITY

THE CODE

RICHARD T. GILL

I remember, almost to the hour, when I first began to question my religion. I don't mean that my ideas changed radically just at that time. I was only twelve, and I continued to go to church faithfully and to say something that could pass for prayers each night before I went to sleep. But I never again felt quite the same. For the first time in my life, it had occurred to me that when I grew up I might actually leave the Methodist faith.

It all happened just a few days after my brother died. He was five years old, and his illness was so brief and his death so unexpected that my whole family was almost crazed with grief. My three aunts, each of whom lived within a few blocks of our house, and my mother were all firm believers in religion, and they turned in unison, and without reservation, to this last support. For about a week, a kind of religious frenzy seized our household. We would all sit in the living room—my mother, my aunts, my two sisters, and I, and sometimes Mr. Dodds, the Methodist minister, too—saying prayers in low voices, comforting one another, staying together for hours at a time, until someone remembered that we had not had dinner or that it was time for my sisters and me to be in bed.

I was quite swept up by the mood that had come over the house. When I went to bed, I would say the most elaborate, intricate prayers. In the past, when I had finished my "Now I lay me down to sleep," I would bless individually all the members of my immediate family and then my aunts, and let it go at that. Now, however, I felt that I had to bless everyone in the world whose name I could remember. I would go through all my friends at school, including the teachers, the principal, and the janitor, and then through the names of people I had heard my mother and father mention, some of whom I had never even met. I did not quite know what to do about my brother, whom

I wanted to pray for more than for anyone else. I hesitated to take his name out of its regular order, for fear I would be committed to believing that he had really died. But then I *knew* that he had died, so at the end of my prayers, having just barely mentioned his name as I went along, I would start blessing him over and over again, until I finally fell asleep.

The only one of us who was unmoved by this religious fervor was my father. Oddly enough, considering what a close family we were and how strongly my mother and aunts felt about religion, my father had never shown the least interest in it. In fact, I do not think that he had ever gone to church. Partly for this reason, partly because he was a rather brusque, impatient man, I always felt that he was something of a stranger in our home. He spent a great deal of time with us children, but through it all he seemed curiously unapproachable. I think we all felt constrained when he played with us and relieved when, at last, we were left to ourselves.

At the time of my brother's death, he was more of a stranger than ever. Except for one occasion, he took no part in the almost constant gatherings of the family in the living room. He was not going to his office that week—we lived in a small town outside Boston—and he was always around the house, but no one ever seemed to know exactly where. One of my aunts—Sarah, my mother's eldest sister—felt very definitely that my father should not be left to himself, and she was continually saying to me, "Jack, go upstairs and see if you can find him and talk to him." I remember going timidly along the hallway of the second floor and peeking into the bedrooms, not knowing what I should say if I found him and half afraid that he would scold me for going around looking into other people's rooms. One afternoon, not finding him in any of the bedrooms, I went up into the attic, where we had a sort of playroom. I remember discovering him there by the window. He was sitting absolutely motionless in an old wicker chair, an empty pipe in his hands, staring out fixedly over the treetops. I stood in the doorway for several minutes before he was aware of me. He turned as if to say something, but then, looking at me or just above my head—I was not sure which—he seemed to lose himself in his thoughts. Finally, he gave me a strangely awkward salute with his right hand and turned again to the window.

About the only times my father was with the rest of us were when we had meals or when, in the days immediately following the funeral, we all went out to the cemetery, taking fresh flowers or wreaths. But even at the cemetery he always stood slightly apart—a tall, lonely figure. Once, when we were at the grave and I was nearest him, he reached over and squeezed me around the shoulders. It made me feel almost embarrassed, as though he were breaking through some inviolable barrier between us. He must have felt as I did, because he at once removed his arm and looked away, as though he had never actually embraced me at all.

It was the one occasion when my father was sitting in the living room with us that started me to wondering about my religion. We had just returned from the cemetery—two carloads of us. It was three or four days after the funeral and just at the time when, the shock having worn off, we were all experiencing our first clear realization of what had happened. Even I, young as I was, sensed that there was a new air of desolation in our home.

For a long time, we all sat there in silence. Then my aunts, their eyes moist, began talking about my brother, and soon my mother joined in. They started off softly, telling of little things he had done in the days before his illness. Then they fell silent and dried their eyes, and then quickly remembered some other incident and began speaking again. Slowly the emotion mounted, and before long the words were flooding out. "God will take care of him!" my Aunt Sarah cried, almost ecstatically. "Oh, yes, He will! He will!" Presently, they were all talking in chorus—saying that my brother was happy at last and that they would all be with him again one day.

I believed what they were saying and I could barely hold back my tears. But swept up as I was, I had the feeling that they should not be talking that way while my father was there. The feeling was one that I did not understand at all at the moment. It was just that when I looked over to the corner where he was sitting and saw the deep, rigid lines of his face, saw him sitting there silently, all alone, I felt guilty. I wanted everyone to stop for a while—at least until he had gone upstairs. But there was no stopping the torrent once it had started.

"Oh, he was too perfect to live!" Aunt Agnes, my mother's youngest sister, cried. "He was never a bad boy. I've never seen a boy like that. I mean he was never even naughty. He was just too perfect."

"Oh, yes. Oh, yes," my mother sighed.

"It's true," Aunt Sarah said. "Even when he was a baby, he never really cried. There was never a baby like him. He was a saint."

"He *was* a saint!" Aunt Agnes cried. "That's why he was taken from us!"

"He was a perfect baby," my mother said.

"He was taken from us," Aunt Agnes went on, "because he was too perfect to live."

All through this conversation, my father's expression had been growing more and more tense. At last, while Aunt Agnes was speaking, he rose from his chair. His face was very pale, and his eyes flashed almost feverishly. "Don't talk like that, Agnes!" he exclaimed, with a strange violence that was not anger but something much deeper. "I won't have you talking like that any more. I don't want anybody talking like that!" His whole body seemed to tremble. I had never seen him so worked up before. "Of course he was a bad boy at times!" he cried. "Every boy's bad once in a while. What do you have to change him for? Why don't you leave him as he was?"

"But he was such a perfect baby," Aunt Sarah said.

"He *wasn't* perfect!" my father almost shouted, clenching his fist. "He was no more perfect than Jack here or Betty or Ellen. He was just an ordinary little boy. He wasn't perfect. And he wasn't a saint. He was just a little boy, and I won't have you making him over into something he wasn't!"

He looked as though he were going to go on talking like this, but just then he closed his eyes and ran his hand up over his forehead and through his hair. When he spoke again, his voice was subdued. "I just wish you wouldn't talk that way," he said. "That's all I mean." And then, after standing there silently for a minute, he left the living room and walked upstairs.

I sat watching the doorway through which he had gone. Suddenly, I had no feeling for what my mother and my aunts had been saying. It was all a mist, a dream. Out of the many words that had been spoken that day, it was those few sentences of my father's that explained to me how I felt about my brother. I wanted to be with my father to tell him so.

I went upstairs and found him once again in the playroom in the attic. As before, he was silent and staring out the window when I entered, and we sat without speaking for what seemed to me like half an hour or more. But I felt that he knew why I was there, and I was not uncomfortable with him.

Finally, he turned to me and shook his head. "I don't know what I can tell you, Jack," he said, raising his hands and letting them drop into his lap. "That's the worst part of it. There's just nothing I can say that will make it any better."

Though I only half understood him then, I see now that he was telling me of a drawback—that he had no refuge, no comfort, no support. He was telling me that you were all alone if you took the path that he had taken. Listening to him, I did not care about the drawback. I had begun to see what a noble thing it was for a man to bear the full loss of someone he had loved.

II

By the time I was thirteen or fourteen I was so thoroughly committed to my father's way of thinking that I considered it a great weakness in a man to believe in religion. I wanted to grow up to face life as he did—truthfully, without comfort, without support.

My attitude was never one of rebellion. Despite the early regimen of Sunday school and church that my mother had encouraged, she was wonderfully gentle with me, particularly when I began to express my doubts. She would come into my room each night after the light was out and ask me to say my prayers. Determined to be honest with her, I would explain that I could not say them sincerely, and therefore should not say them at all. "Now, Jack," she would reply, very quietly and calmly, "you mustn't talk like that. You'll really feel much better if you say them." I could tell from the tone of her voice that she was hurt, but she never tried to force me in any way. Indeed, it might have been easier for me if she *had* tried to oppose my decision strenuously. As it was, I felt so bad at having wounded her that I was continually trying to make things up—running errands, surprising her by doing the dishes when she went out shopping—behaving, in short, in the most conscientious, considerate fashion. But all this never brought me any closer to her religion. On the contrary, it only served to free me for my decision *not* to believe. And for that decision, as I say, my father was responsible.

Part of his influence, I suppose, was in his physical quality. Even at that time—when he was in his late forties and in only moderately good health—he was a most impressive figure. He was tall and heavy-chested, with leathery, rough-cast features and with an easy, relaxed rhythm in his walk. He had been an athlete in his youth, and, needless to say, I was enormously proud of his various feats and told about them, with due exaggeration, all over our neighborhood. Still, the physical thing had relatively little to do with the matter. My father, by that time, regarded athletes and athletics with contempt. Now and again, he would take me into the back yard to fool around with boxing gloves, but when it came to something serious, such as my going out for football in high school, he invariably put his foot down. "It takes too much time," he would tell me. "You ought to be thinking of college and your studies. It's nonsense what they make of sports nowadays!" I always wanted to remind him of *his* school days, but I knew it was no use. He had often told me what an unforgivable waste of time he considered his youth to have been.

Thus, although the physical thing was there, it was very much in the background—little more, really, than the simple assumption that a man ought to know how to take care of himself. The real bond between us was spiritual, in the sense that courage, as opposed to strength, is spiritual. It was this intangible quality of courage that I wanted desperately to possess and that, it seemed to me, captured everything that was essential about my father.

We never talked of this quality directly. The nearest we came to it was on certain occasions during the early part of the Second World War, just before I went off to college. We would sit in the living room listening to a speech by Winston Churchill, and my father would suddenly clap his fist against his palm. "My God!" he would exclaim, fairly beaming with admiration. "That man's got the heart of a tiger!" And I would listen to the rest of the speech, thrilling to every word, and then, thinking of my father, really, I would say aloud that, of all men in the world, the one I would most like to be was Churchill.

Nor did we often talk about religion. Yet our religion—our rejection of religion—was the deepest statement of the bond between us. My father, perhaps out of deference to my mother and my sisters and aunts, always put his own case very mildly. "It's certainly a great philosophy," he would say of Christianity. "No one could question that. But for the rest . . ." Here he would throw up his hands and cock his head to one side, as if to say that he had tried, but simply could not manage the hurdle of divinity. This view, however mildly it may have been expressed, became mine with absolute clarity and certainty. I concluded that religion was a refuge, without the least foundation in fact. More than that, I positively objected to those— I should say those *men*, for to me it was a peculiarly masculine matter —who turned to religion for support. As I saw it, a man ought to face life as it really is, on his own two feet, without a crutch, as my father did. That was the heart of the matter. By the time I left home for college, I was so deeply committed to this view that I would have considered it a disloyalty to him, to myself, to the code we had lived by, to alter my position in the least.

I did not see much of my father during the next four years or so. I was home during the summer vacation after my freshman year, but then, in the middle of the next year, I went into the Army. I was shipped to the Far East for the tail end of the war, and was in Japan at the start of the Occupation. I saw my father only once or twice during my entire training period, and, naturally, during the time I was overseas I did not see him at all.

While I was away, his health failed badly. In 1940, before I went off to college, he had taken a job at a defense plant. The plant was only forty miles from our home, but he was working on the night shift, and commuting was extremely complicated and tiresome. And, of course, he was always willing to overexert himself out of a sense of pride. The result was that late in 1942 he had a heart attack. He came through it quite well, but he made no effort to cut down on his work and, as a consequence, suffered a second, and more serious, attack, two years later. From that time on, he was almost completely bedridden.

I was on my way overseas at the time of the second attack, and I learned of it in a letter from my mother. I think she was trying to spare me, or perhaps it was simply that I could not imagine so robust a man as my father being seriously ill. In any event, I had only the haziest notion of what his real condition was, so when, many months later,

I finally did realize what had been going on, I was terribly surprised and shaken. One day, some time after my arrival at an American Army post in Japan, I was called to the orderly room and told that my father was critically ill and that I was to be sent home immediately. Within forty-eight hours, I was standing in the early-morning light outside my father's bedroom, with my mother and sisters at my side. They had told me, as gently as they could, that he was not very well, that he had had another attack. But it was impossible to shield me then. I no sooner stepped into the room and saw him than I realized that he would not live more than a day or two longer.

From that moment on, I did not want to leave him for a second. Even that night, during the periods when he was sleeping and I was of no help being there, I could not get myself to go out of the room for more than a few minutes. A practical nurse had come to sit up with him, but since I was at the bedside, she finally spent the night in the hallway. I was really quite tired, and late that night my mother and my aunts begged me to go to my room and rest for a while, but I barely heard them. I was sure he would wake up soon, and when he did, I wanted to be there to talk to him.

We did talk a great deal that first day and night. It was difficult for both of us. Every once in a while, my father would shift position in the bed, and I would catch a glimpse of his wasted body. It was a knife in my heart. Even worse were the times when he would reach out for my hand, his eyes misted, and begin to tell me how he felt about me. I tried to look at him, but in the end I always looked down. And, knowing that he was dying, and feeling desperately guilty, I would keep repeating to myself that he knew how I felt, that he would understand why I looked away.

There was another thing, too. While we talked that day, I had a vague feeling that my father was on the verge of making some sort of confession to me. It was, as I say, only the vaguest impression, and I thought very little about it. The next morning, however, I began to sense what was in the air. Apparently, Mr. Dodds, the minister, whom I barely knew, had been coming to the house lately to talk to my father. My father had not said anything about this, and I learned it only indirectly, from something my mother said to my eldest sister at the breakfast table. At the moment, I brushed the matter aside. I told myself it was natural that Mother would want my father to see the minister at the last. Nevertheless, the very mention of the minister's name caused something to tighten inside me.

Later that day, the matter was further complicated. After lunch, I finally did go to my room for a nap, and when I returned to my father's room, I found him and my mother talking about Mr. Dodds. The conversation ended almost as soon as I entered, but I was left with the distinct impression that they were expecting the minister to pay a visit that day, whether very shortly or at suppertime or later in the evening, I could not tell. I did not ask. In fact, I made a great effort not to think of the matter at all.

Then, early that evening, my father spoke to me. I knew before he said a word that the minister *was* coming. My mother had straightened up the bedroom, and fluffed up my father's pillows so that he was half sitting in the bed. No one had told me anything, but I was sure what the preparations meant. "I guess you probably know," my father said to me when we were alone, "we're having a visitor tonight. It's—ah—Mr. Dodds. You know, the minister from your mother's church."

I nodded, half shrugging, as if I saw nothing the least unusual in the news.

"He's come here before once or twice," my father said. "Have I mentioned that? I can't remember if I've mentioned that."

"Yes, I know. I think Mother said something, or perhaps you did. I don't remember."

"I just thought I'd let you know. You see, your mother wanted me to talk to him. I—— I've talked to him more for her sake than anything else."

"Sure. I can understand that."

"I think it makes her feel a little better. I think——" Here he broke off, seemingly dissatisfied with what he was saying. His eyes turned to the ceiling, and he shook his head slightly, as if to erase the memory of his words. He studied the ceiling for a long time before he spoke again. "I don't mean it was all your mother exactly," he said. "Well, what I mean is he's really quite an interesting man. I think you'd probably like him a good deal."

"I know Mother has always liked him," I replied. "From what I gather, most people seem to like him very much."

"Well, he's that sort," my father went on, with quickening interest. "I mean, he isn't what you'd imagine at all. To tell the truth, I wish you'd talk to him a little. I wish you'd talk things over with him right from scratch." My father was looking directly at me now, his eyes flashing.

"I'd be happy to talk with him sometime," I said. "As I say, everybody seems to think very well of him."

"Well, I wish you would. You see, when you're lying here day after day, you get to thinking about things. I mean, it's good to have someone to talk to." He paused for a moment. "Tell me," he said, "have you ever . . . have you ever wondered if there wasn't some truth in it? Have you ever thought about it that way at all?"

I made a faint gesture with my hand. "Of course, it's always possible to wonder," I replied. "I don't suppose you can ever be completely certain one way or the other."

"I know, I know," he said, almost impatiently. "But have you ever felt—well, all in a sort of flash—that it *was* true? I mean, have you ever had that feeling?"

He was half raised up from the pillow now, his eyes staring into me with a feverish concentration. Suddenly, I could not look at him any longer. I lowered my head.

"I don't mean permanently or anything like that," he went on. "But just for a few seconds. The feeling that you've been wrong all along. Have you had that feeling—ever?"

I could not look up. I could not move. I felt that every muscle in my body had suddenly frozen. Finally, after what seemed an eternity, I heard him sink back into the pillows. When I glanced up a moment later, he was lying there silent, his eyes closed, his lips parted, conveying somehow the image of the death that awaited him.

Presently, my mother came to the door. She called me into the hall to tell me that Mr. Dodds had arrived. I said that I thought my father had fallen asleep but that I would go back and see.

It was strangely disheartening to me to discover that he was awake. He was sitting there, his eyes open, staring grimly into the gathering shadows of the evening.

"Mr. Dodds is downstairs," I said matter-of-factly. "Mother wanted to know if you felt up to seeing him tonight."

For a moment, I thought he had not heard me; he gave no sign of recognition whatever. I went to the foot of the bed and repeated myself. He nodded, not answering the question but simply indicating that he had heard me. At length, he shook his head. "Tell your mother I'm a little tired tonight," he said. "Perhaps—well, perhaps some other time."

"I could ask him to come back later, if you'd like."

"No, no, don't bother. I—I could probably use the rest."

I waited a few seconds. "Are you sure?" I asked. "I'm certain he could come back in an hour or so."

Then, suddenly, my father was looking at me. I shall never forget his face at that moment and the expression burning in his eyes. He was pleading with me to speak. And all I could say was that I would be happy to ask Mr. Dodds to come back later, if he wanted it that way. It was not enough. I knew, instinctively, at that moment that it was not enough. But I could not say anything more.

As quickly as it had come, the burning flickered and went out. He sank back into the pillows again. "No, you can tell him I won't be needing him tonight," he said, without interest. "Tell him not to bother waiting around." Then he turned on his side, away from me, and said no more.

So my father did not see Mr. Dodds that night. Nor did he ever see him again. Shortly after midnight, just after my mother and sisters had gone to bed, he died. I was at his side then, but I could not have said exactly when it occurred. He must have gone off in his sleep, painlessly, while I sat there awake beside him.

In the days that followed, our family was together almost constantly. Curiously enough, I did not think much about my father just then. For some reason, I felt the strongest sense of responsibility toward the family. I found myself making the arrangements for the funeral, protecting Mother from the stream of people who came to the house, speaking words of consolation to my sisters and even to my aunts. I was never alone except at night, when a kind of oblivion seized me almost as soon as my head touched the pillow. My sleep was dreamless, numb.

Then, two weeks after the funeral, I left for Fort Devens, where I was to be discharged from the Army. I had been there three days when I was told that my terminal leave would begin immediately and that I was free to return home. I had half expected that when I was at the Fort, separated from the family, something would break inside me. But still no emotion came. I thought of my father often during that time, but, search as I would, I could find no sign of feeling.

Then, when I had boarded the train for home, it happened. Suddenly, for no reason whatever, I was thinking of the expression on my father's face that last night in the bedroom. I saw him as he lay there pleading with me to speak. And I knew then what he had wanted me to say to him—that it was really all right with me, that it wouldn't change anything between us if he gave way. And then I was thinking of myself and what I had said and what I had *not* said. Not a word to help! Not a word!

I wanted to beg his forgiveness. I wanted to cry out aloud to him. But I was in a crowded train, sitting with three elderly women just returning from a shopping tour. I turned my face to the window. There, silent, unnoticed, I thought of what I might have said.

QUESTIONS

1. At first glance the conflict in this story may seem to be the religious attitude of the mother and sisters versus the nonreligious views of the father and son. But this can hardly be the main conflict, since there is little struggle between the two sides. Another possibility is the conflict at the end between the father's new interest in religion and his son's adherence to the code, but neither admits it is a conflict, and it makes no great emotional impact on the reader. What then is the real conflict of the story?

2. What is the code?

3. What indication is there early in the story of Jack's unbending adherence to the code?

4. Is there any indication that the father might at some time feel a need of support?

5. At the end when the father tries to tell Jack how he feels about him, Jack always looks down. Can this lack of warmth in Jack be traced to the father?

6. The father asks, "But have you ever felt—well, all in a sort of flash—that it *was* true? I mean, have you ever had that feeling?" What is he pleading with his son to say?

7. Jack says, "I could not look up. I could not move. I felt that every muscle in my body had suddenly frozen." Is the father at all responsible for this rigid attitude in his son?

8. More than two weeks pass after his father's death before Jack, in a moment of insight, is suddenly struck with remorse over his failure to give the approval his father sought. Why has it taken so long?

9. Has Jack changed his own views at the end of the story?

10. What is the theme?

HOULIHAN'S SURRENDER
JAMES McCONKEY

Houlihan, a white-haired old giant with a slight stoop, came to live at Mrs. Goetz's rooming house the day after his wife was buried. His face was a dark tan from a lifetime of peering from the cab of a freight locomotive, and there were little squint-wrinkles around his red-veined eyes, and he had a big blunt Irish nose and his hair was long and curly and fell down over his forehead in a defiant sort of way.

Mrs. Goetz, looking curiously out at him through a hole in her faded chintz curtains while he paid the Yellow Cab driver from a big wad of bills tied together with an old piece of string, was angry with him for his size. He was even taller than she was, and she was a good six feet; and he probably outweighed her by at least twenty pounds. He stumbled against the curb, and then pulled himself up on the sidewalk with the absurd clumsiness of an elderly lion. He was not at all like that little prune of a man, Mr. Kramper, who slept in 4A, right under the attic, and had mouse eyes and a mouse squeak for a voice.

She had expected her new roomer to be another sentimental little man like Mr. Kramper, a sickly old gentleman she could first feed and then order about, and she felt a great irritation with Mr. Kramper that Houlihan shouldn't be so; for Mr. Kramper had been the one who arranged that Houlihan should get the room. Mr. Kramper had been Houlihan's fireman on the New York to Pittsburgh freight run for ten years, and had told her (his voice trembling with pride and excitement) what a good man Houlihan was, that he had been devoted to his wife and spent all his leisure reading books; but Mr. Kramper slyly had not mentioned how *massive* Houlihan was.

The seventeen years since the death of her husband, in which period she had been sole master of fifteen roomfuls of people, had imparted to Mrs. Goetz a sense of dictatorial supremacy which was strengthened not only by her height but by her hard-muscled and heavy arms and legs, and by the wisp of blond hair under her nose. The *look* of Houlihan alone, standing on the doorstep and insistently ringing the bell, was a challenge to her. She let the bell ring for a couple of minutes, becoming angrier all the while, and then walked slowly out the front hall to the door, opening it halfway. "You don't need to wear out the bell, Mr. Houlihan," she said with all the irony of her soul. "I've been waiting all afternoon for you to show up, and couldn't get my shopping done."

There were recent food stains spattered on his baggy brown trousers, and he was wearing a faded green smoking jacket with holes burned in the sleeves and on the lapel. Mr. Kramper's clothes were always neat and clean and he kept a deodorant on the shelf above his washbasin. Mr. Houlihan smelled of tobacco. He acted as if he hadn't heard her remark, and looked right past her, squinting in the gloom as if he didn't see her at all. She had intended to lead him up to the fourth floor and show him his room, but instead she pressed the key into his hand. "Room 4B," she said sharply. "I change sheets every two weeks and no sooner, and if you wipe your shoes with the hand towel it'll be a dollar extra. I don't allow smoking in bed, and your rent's payable in advance, six-fifty for the week."

Only then did he look at her, and the look he gave her was a contemptuous one. He pulled a roll of bills from his pocket and pushed twenty-six dollars at her. "Here's a month's rent," he said, and his voice was gruff and deep. He had a gold tooth in front that gleamed when he talked, even in the faint light of the single bulb that glowed behind the dust of the glass chandelier above. "And I'll be pleased to you, Mrs. Goetz, if you don't bother coming into my room at all. I'll buy my own sheets, and have them washed, too, and I don't want any *woman* sniffing around and putting *my* room in order."

His voice was somewhat like that of the Irish cop who shouted at the traffic outside, and there was something in the sound of it that commanded respect; but Mrs. Goetz was angry at the way he pronounced the word *woman*: it was sacrilege, what with his wife just dead and buried. She didn't say anything, however, while he picked up his suitcase and started up the wide stairway. He stumbled on the third step from the second floor landing, where the carpeting had a hole in it, and she shouted after him in fine satisfaction: "Watch your step, old man!" And after he had silently made the turn at the second floor and started up the creaking third flight of stairs, she leaned over the banister and shouted up the stair well: "I reserve the right to look into the rooms I rent whenever I want to, *Mister* Houlihan!"

Old Kramper was still in bed; at six o'clock she usually brought him his supper if she didn't hear him moving about, but this day she waited until seven-thirty.

II

After Mrs. Goetz, silently and hostilely, had carried away his supper dishes, frail little Mr. Kramper lay long in bed, quivering both with anticipation and with the fever which his cold had brought. He had heard the sounds Houlihan had made, climbing the stairway, and heard him cuss a little as he tried to unlock his door in the dim light of the hallway; and then Mr. Kramper heard bangs from the room next door as Houlihan apparently changed the position of the bed and desk.

Mr. Kramper thought Mrs. Goetz might come up when she heard the noise, and demand that the furniture be put back where *she* wanted it; for, when Mr. Kramper first moved into his room, he changed the position of his desk, and threw into the wastebasket a picture that had been tacked on the back of his door. It was a color picture from the Sunday *Mirror* which displayed Deanna Durbin in a sweater; not the kind of picture for an old man's room at all. On Saturday, Mrs. Goetz cleaned up the room while he was out for supper, and put the desk back where it had been, marking the spot with chalk on the floor where it belonged; and she straightened out the crumpled picture and tacked it back on the door. Sunday morning, she accosted Mr. Kramper in the downstairs hallway as he was stepping unobtrusively out to attend the early Methodist service, and told him not to tamper with *her* pictures. "Besides," she said, "it's good for an old man to look at a young girl with big breasts once in a while." And then, to his dismay, she brayed loud and long, and the sound followed him as he ran out the door and ducked around the corner by the drugstore. He had never been able to invite his cronies in the Brotherhood or the Borrowed Time Club up to his room because of that picture. It was shameful, but there was nothing he could do.

Tonight, he kept expecting a rap on the door from Houlihan,

after he got himself settled in his room; but Houlihan never came. For a while, Mr. Kramper enjoyed his sorrow and made the tears come to his eyes; but then he remembered that Houlihan had always been like this. You always had to go to Houlihan, for Houlihan never came to you: he was too noble and proud a soul for that. Probably Houlihan was waiting in his room now for *him* to call. Mr. Kramper hastily pulled his trousers over his pajama pants, and trotted over to knock on Houlihan's door.

Houlihan opened the door part way, squinting at Kramper. "I thought it was the old hag," he muttered, but never showed any gladness that it was Mr. Kramper instead. He left the door open, and Mr. Kramper hesitantly entered, and sat himself down on the edge of the single chair in the room, like a nervous young life insurance salesman, while Houlihan fell down heavily upon the bed. Houlihan's coat was slung across the foot of the bed, and his suitcase, lying open, was in the far corner of the room, and in it were some soiled shirts. The rest of the suitcase must have contained books, for he had books lined up across the back of the desk, and other books spread out over the bed. He had apparently been lying on the bed with his shoes on without first removing the bedspread. Mr. Kramper noticed, shocked, that he had no picture of Mrs. Houlihan in the room.

"I thought you might be lonely," Mr. Kramper said awkwardly.

Houlihan relaxed on the bed, lit his pipe, and picked up one of his books, leafing through to find his place. It was *Stories of Red Hanrahan* by Yeats, W. B. Mr. Kramper coughed against his sleeve, and then offered: "I know how it is, Houlihan, when you first lose your wife. I remember how lonely *I* was, after my wife had gone." He always had been self-conscious with the word "death," and usually would find a means of circumventing its use.

Houlihan had started to frown, but went on with his reading.

"You're looking well, Houlihan, for a man that's just lost his wife."

Houlihan's lips moved as he tried to concentrate on his reading. Mr. Kramper noted once more the jumbled condition of the room, and felt a sudden surge of pity for his old engineer. "Houlihan," he said softly, "poor Houlihan, you're a lost soul now like all the rest of us."

Houlihan threw the book down savagely and jumped to his feet, towering over Mr. Kramper, who promptly sank far back into his chair and lowered his head. "I'll be greatly indebted to you, Mr. Kramper, not to offer me any of your dewy-eyed condolences," he said coldly.

Mr. Kramper, though embarrassed, still was impressed by the way Houlihan could *talk*. It was the Irish in him, he supposed. Houlihan always had been able to use beautiful language whenever he was angry. Mr. Kramper sighed to himself, thinking how splendid it would be to have Houlihan in the Club. Once Houlihan became a member, it would be only a matter of time before he became president. The thought of it so excited Mr. Kramper that he spoke up immediately, though Houlihan was still glowering down at him. "Houlihan," he said, "now that you're alone, you'll want to join us in the Club. Lots of the retired Brotherhood, like Kirkpatrick and Phillips and Jorgenson, belong to the Club, Houlihan."

"What club?" Houlihan was staring at him, his eyes narrowed. "I never was one for joining clubs and wasting my time with silly chatter, Kramper."

"You had your wife *before*," said Mr. Kramper with proper sorrow. "We call ourselves the Borrowed Time Club, Houlihan. There's clubs all over the United States, and we limit ourselves to members over sixty-five who've retired." Mr. Kramper hadn't noticed the glint in Houlihan's eyes, and he went on at a great rate: "Oh, you'll have yourself a wonderful time, Houlihan. We meet Tuesdays regular, and several other times a week too. There's a hundred of us in the city, and we meet for dinner and then talk."

"And pray tell, what do you talk about?" Houlihan's voice was strangely courteous, but Mr. Kramper did not take warning.

"We have a lot in common," he said, waving his arms vaguely.

"Like your ages and your ailments, I presume?"

"Now look here, Houlihan!" In his zeal, Mr. Kramper clambered suddenly from his chair and stared upward into Houlihan's massive nostrils. "You might as well get used to the fact that you ain't a boy no longer. Young people don't care much for the old ones. My boy lives in San Francisco, and writes me a letter maybe once a month. The Borrowed Time Club keeps old folks like us from being lonely, and sees to it that we get a good turnout when we flee this mortal coil."

"This mortal coil, eh?" Houlihan said viciously. "So you spend your measly metered time sniveling from funeral to funeral, do you, old man?" In his wrath, his nostrils contracted and dilated, and Mr. Kramper's gaze was frozen involuntarily upon them. "You spend your time looking at stiff white corpses and congratulating yourselves that you outlived *that* one, I suppose? I'll be pleased to you, Mr. Kramper, not to bother me with such cowardly notions." He strode angrily back and forth across the room, and with each step the floor boards creaked; and in his fury he stumbled against Mr. Kramper's feet.

"You'll find time hangs heavy on your shoulders now, Houlihan," Mr. Kramper prophesied meekly, pulling his feet into the chair. "You won't be knowing what to do with yourself."

"Won't, eh?" Houlihan was coldly superior, and he pointed at his books. "Do you and your rheumy old friends think that Yeats belonged to a Borrowed Time Club? Or George Bernard Shaw, maybe? Or Jesus O'Christ Himself?"

"*He* died young," Mr. Kramper protested weakly, dismayed by the sacrilege.

" 'Tis of no matter," Houlihan said savagely. "Had he lived to a ripe old seventy, do you think *He* ever would have succumbed to such a mental affliction? Any Englishman might fall to such an evil state, but never Shaw nor Jesus Christ."

"You've read a lot of books, Houlihan," said Mr. Kramper, his eyes shining with worship. "That's one of the things I always looked up to you for. Whenever they used to ask me who I was fireman for, I'd say, 'Houlihan—you know, the one that reads the books.' "

Houlihan softened at the tone in Mr. Kramper's voice, and stood over him again, his voice trumpeting: "Keep your intellect alert, Mr. Kramper. 'Tis the only way. Read about the heroes of classical antiquity, and try to be like them. Be like Caesar. Be like Ulysses."

Mr. Kramper was overpowered by this literary knowledge. "But didn't Caesar and this other fellow have wives and families?" he inquired respectfully. "In them days, folks had more kinfolk, and their children stayed to home. It was the auto that brought the curse to old men, Houlihan."

Houlihan impatiently waved aside the remark. " 'Tis no wonder that the Irish have written about the great heroes, Mr. Kramper," he thundered. "Shaw wrote about Caesar, and Joyce about Ulysses, though he weakened and gave him a Jew name. The Irish don't cry out their loneliness."

Mr. Kramper persisted in following his own peculiar logic. "But didn't Shaw have a family and friends?" he asked.

"Shaw's still alive, Kramper," Houlihan said grandiloquently. "Still alive at ninety, and younger'n you at twenty. Been living on herbs and grass like a cow, and thriving on 'em. Sure, he had a wife, and he married her so that she could clean up his room *quietly*, and never bother him. It was none of this deary-deary attachment, and 'Do you have your rubbers on, Georgie?' There's a man for you, Kramper: he knows a woman's just out to tie herself around the male like a spider, but he never let himself be drawn into the web."

Mr. Kramper's face lost color. He clenched his fingers together. "For shame," he said with passion. "You're forgetting your own wife's passing, Houlihan."

"Certainly I am," replied Houlihan coolly. "The only way to be a man is to live for the future, and don't you ever forget that, Mr. Kramper. Keep hope in your heart, and be damned to the past, even if it means chasing moonbeams through the mist, like Red Hanrahan following the hounds. I presume, Mr. Kramper, that you never heard of that great symbol of Ireland, Red Hanrahan?" Houlihan's voice had gathered so much in loudness that it reverberated throughout the room. Fortunately, Mr. Kramper had no opportunity to admit of his ignorance, for downstairs Mrs. Goetz began to hit vigorously on the water pipe with a hammer.

"That slut!" cried Houlihan; but Kramper was horrified. "Be quiet, Houlihan, she'll be up here with the hammer next," he breathed, and decided, for the present, to give up his plan to bring Houlihan into the Club.

Houlihan lay back on the bed, rubbing his shoes on the bedspread and smiling. He picked up his book once more, opening it at the middle. Mr. Kramper, slinking toward the door, noticed how red and bleary Houlihan's eyes were. "You ought to be getting yourself some glasses, Houlihan," he said, but Houlihan only snorted derisively. As the door closed between himself and Houlihan, Mr. Kramper gathered a bit more courage. "We're meeting this Tuesday, Houlihan," he said. "I'll stop by on my way, to see if you've changed your mind."

Houlihan made a vulgar sound, and Mr. Kramper shuddered, remembered his cold, and coughed loudly.

III

The next day Houlihan bought himself a hot plate and a tremendous bag of groceries, and carried them to his room, brushing right past Mrs. Goetz although she shouted at him that she wasn't going to allow him to smell up *her* house with his cooking. He locked himself in his room, and left the key in the lock; and never came out that day, or the next, or so far as anyone could tell, any days thereafter. Mrs. Goetz pounded on his door whenever she smelled the food, and the occupant of room 4C put in a complaint; but Houlihan never replied to Mrs. Goetz's noisy threats.

Mr. Kramper knocked on Houlihan's door Tuesday as he had promised, and the following Tuesday as well, but Houlihan refused to go to the Club. Once, however, he did favor Mr. Kramper with admittance, and Mr. Kramper saw the rows of canned goods stacked on the floor, the empty cans in the wastebasket, and the slab of ham tied to the window handle and dangling outside. "You must be like a bear," he said in astonishment, "holing up for the winter!"

"Certainly 'hole' is a fine way of describing this room which you were so kind to find for me, Mr. Kramper," Houlihan said; and it was the only reference he had ever made to Mr. Kramper's efforts in his behalf. Rooms for six-fifty were hard to find downtown, but Mr. Kramper bore Houlihan no ill will. "Don't you *never* go outside?" Mr. Kramper asked incredulously.

"Only when the clock strikes midnight," Houlihan answered poetically; "and then but to sally forth to replenish my cans of pork and beans."

"You should go outside, and sit in the park," Mr. Kramper said. "The air is fine these cold evenings." He was beginning to worry about the welfare of his old engineer: the room was dusty, and had begun to smell of dirty clothes and perspiration; and the bed had never been made, nor a sheet changed. Houlihan himself was unshaven and dirty, and his clothes looked as if he never took them off when he went to bed. There was a tear on Houlihan's trousers by the knee, and a bruise on his cheek. He looked thinner, but his voice was robust as ever. His eyes were strange and bulging, like the eyes of a suffering old monk.

"What do you do all day long?" asked Mr. Kramper in wonderment.

"Cook my meals and read my books and chase the moonbeams of my youth," Houlihan retorted promptly. "I'm living as a *pure* essence, Mr. Kramper, as I've always dreamed of doing; and I'll never compromise myself, now that I know the meaning of *all* existence, with the chatter of dulled and wizened old men."

But Mr. Kramper had not mentioned the Borrowed Time Club at all, having given up Houlihan as a lost cause. This remark aroused his hope once more. "I've told them about you, Houlihan," he said. "They were all disappointed you haven't come. There's Kirkpatrick, who used to take your Pittsburg run on your day off: *he'd* like to see you again."

"I'll see Kirkpatrick in hell first," Houlihan replied, the glint back in his eye. "He never was as good an engineer as me, and his intelligence was a disgrace to his race."

"That's true enough," Mr. Kramper loyally admitted; but his concern for Houlihan's welfare made him speak further. "*He's* looking fine and healthy, though, and you're beginning to resemble one of them moonbeams you talk about."

This drove Houlihan into a high rage. "I'm a better man than any of your doddering old idiots," he shouted. He grabbed Mr. Kramper by the shoulder and shook him so that his bones clattered together. "You tell them so, do you hear?"

But Mrs. Goetz was pounding at the door again, and shouting, "Shut up your noise, Mr. Houlihan! I've never had police disgrace my house, but they'll come after you, Houlihan, if you don't behave!"

Houlihan let go of Mr. Kramper's shoulder, and Mr. Kramper shrank back into the chair, wiping his forehead nervously, wondering if Houlihan had gone insane. "Oh, God in Heaven," cried Houlihan in despair, "won't the world ever allow man to fight his struggle without the voice of woman? She's my own dead wife, Mr. Kramper, come back to haunt and scold: 'Clean your room,' 'Keep your feet off the bed,' and 'Don't *you* shout at me, you wicked old man!' "

"Houlihan!" shouted Mr. Kramper in dismay. "Don't never talk like that no more." And then and there, Mr. Kramper closed his eyes, bowed his head, and said a silent prayer.

Houlihan was a man out of his senses. "You blithering fool!" he shouted. "You expect God to help *you* or *me*? We're gone, Kramper, past all hope or care. God loves the spring and growing things, and lets the old wither and die." He threw himself back on his bed with such force that one of the slats gave way with a loud crack, and he moaned for a time until some saliva caught in his throat, and then he coughed and reached for his book.

Mr. Kramper, shivering, watched him, and couldn't hold back his surprise. "Why, that's the same book you were reading the first night," he cried. "And you're still in the middle!"

Houlihan wound up and threw the book. It smashed the window glass and flew out into the air, its pages flailing like a monstrous many-winged bird. And then Mr. Kramper looked into Houlihan's red-smeary eyes, and he finally *knew*. "Oh, Houlihan," he bleated, "oh, Houlihan, you're *blind!*" He scrambled out of the chair and bent over the bed. "What is it, Houlihan? Can't you see at all?"

"I can see *you* well enough," Houlihan cried, and made a lunge for Mr. Kramper as he rose from the bed, but Mr. Kramper easily side-stepped him and he fell against the wall, breathing hard. When Houlihan straightened up again, Mr. Kramper could see the tears on his cheek following the course of the wrinkles there.

"Get out of my room," said Houlihan in a voice suddenly calm, and Mr. Kramper went.

IV

With a certain fear, Mr. Kramper told Mrs. Goetz about Houlihan. "Like an elephant," she said, "he's come here to die. Or like an old lion." And in sudden anger, she turned upon Mr. Kramper: "I told you I wanted no dying men here."

"I think it's his eyes only," Mr. Kramper whispered. "His eyes were red when he first came, but they are almost burned out now. One of the men in the Club, Frank Gibbons, has cataracts in both his eyes. They never bothered him for years. Now he's blind. When he comes to the meeting, his son brings him; and we have to feed him with a spoon."

"A man like that's apt to burn down my house, cooking his meals," Mrs. Goetz said. "I won't have him cooking meals up there, or smoking, either."

So, when she prepared Mr. Kramper's supper, she made a double portion of it, and told him to leave half with Houlihan. Mr. Kramper knocked on Houlihan's door, but Houlihan made no sound. "Tell him," Mrs. Goetz shouted up the stair well, "if he doesn't unlock the door tonight, tomorrow I'll have the police."

Mr. Kramper sighed when he heard that, but Mrs. Goetz remained at the bottom of the stairs, waiting; and Mr. Kramper could do nothing but repeat what she had told him to say, his voice trembling and apologetic. Then he left the food by the crack at Houlihan's door, hoping the smell would bring him out.

Houlihan must have eaten the food, for the next morning the dishes were stacked outside his door, empty; and the marvel of it all to Mr. Kramper was that they were neatly washed and dried. When he told Mrs. Goetz of that, she nodded wisely and decided not to call the police; and it was obvious to them both that the struggle was almost over. When he tried Houlihan's door just before he left for the Club, Mr. Kramper found it unlocked. Houlihan was sitting in his chair, and he was wearing his green smoking jacket, and his face was smoothly shaven, although there was a nick under his nose from which the blood still came.

"I have decided to come with you, Mr. Kramper," Houlihan said with grave detachment. "Please give me your hand and help me down the stairs."

And so, with Houlihan leaning on his shoulder, Mr. Kramper led him down the stairs and out the door; and all the time, Mrs. Goetz was staring after them, but neither she nor Houlihan said a word, and Mr. Kramper wasn't even sure that Houlihan had seen Mrs. Goetz.

The meeting of the Club that night was short, for the men all planned to attend the funeral parlor where Kirkpatrick, who had died unexpectedly, lay waiting for his burial. Their clubroom was on the second floor of a frame building over a grocery store, and contained nothing but chairs and tables. Pictures of all the deceased members decorated two walls, and Kirkpatrick's picture stood on the chairman's table, surrounded by roses. The men were all glad to see Houlihan, both those who knew him from his railroading days, and those who only knew him from the many admiring stories which Mr. Kramper had related. Mr. Kramper led Frank Gibbons over to Houlihan, and the two men shook hands; but Houlihan refused to talk about his eyes.

Houlihan said little, but smiled at the men around him when they came close; and he went with them in one of the long black cars which the undertaker had provided. They arrived at the funeral parlor about eight o'clock; and only then, before he saw the casket, was Houlihan the man he'd been the week before. "Funerals," Houlihan declaimed loudly, "are the sign of the decadence of our age, Kramper. It's the savage returned to us that makes us gloat over a dead soul, a shriveled-up nonentity that unfortunately, like *all* of us"—waving his finger dramatically at Mr. Kramper—"survived his wits and *real* friends by ten years. That remark was made before me by a greater man than any of us, by Mr. Shaw himself; and 'tis a sign of his greatness that to him it doesn't apply."

Mr. Kramper was beginning to regret Houlihan's presence now as much as he had been hoping for it before; and he began to turn crimson, so much had he identified himself with his old engineer; but Houlihan became pale and rigid as the men, one by one, filed past him to look at Kirkpatrick, who lay surrounded by flowers in his casket, his cheeks puffed out unnaturally, and a strange tranquil expression on his face. A smell of flowers and chemicals was heavy in the air, and somewhere in the distance a cracked phonograph record played austere and heavenly organ music. Some of the men had brought little red roses with them, and after gazing upon their deceased Club member, dropped their tokens into the casket. Mr. Kramper sat next to Houlihan in one of the little folding chairs, never dreaming that he would wish to look into the casket, too; but Houlihan rose abruptly, and Mr. Kramper rose with him, and together they looked into the casket. Houlihan suddenly put his hand down and rubbed it across the face of Kirkpatrick, feeling the waxen smoothness of his cheek; and then he rubbed his own. Then, with composure, "I'd like to go home now," Houlihan said in a low voice; and Mr. Kramper instantly breathed, "Yes, yes, of course," and he scurried for the entrance of the building, holding Houlihan's hand. Mr. Kramper nodded and whispered apologetically to the men looking curiously after them:

"It's the excitement, I think. Don't worry your heads about *us*. I'll hire a taxi."

When they reached the rooming house, Mr. Kramper led Houlihan upstairs, where they met Mrs. Goetz, who had just finished cleaning up Houlihan's room. Clean, starched sheets were on the bed, the floor had been washed and a clean rug placed upon it, and all the books had been neatly piled into an old soapbox and put on the shelf in the closet. She had taken the empty cans from the wastebasket and put the still unopened ones alongside the hot plate in the hall. "Now, Mr. Houlihan," she said firmly but not without kindness, "I'm taking this food of yours downstairs, and I'll use it for your meals. I'll cook your food and have Mr. Kramper bring it up to you, and you mustn't try to do any more cooking of your own. And for the sake of everybody, you won't be able to smoke unless Mr. Kramper or I am with you; and please take off your shoes before you climb into bed, and try to be more considerate of your neighbors than you have in the past."

"All right, Mrs. Goetz," said Houlihan quietly, and he walked slowly over to his bed and felt the pillow as he had the cheek of Kirkpatrick. "All right," he said again, and then started to lie down on the bed, but sat in the chair instead. Mrs. Goetz began to smile, and she was still smiling when she closed the door, and that night she cooked T-bone steaks for both Houlihan and Mr. Kramper.

"Mr. Kramper, I think we have turned your friend into a *gentleman*," Mrs. Goetz said triumphantly, when she brought the food to him; and Mr. Kramper nodded and said that he was sure she was right.

And Mr. Kramper, who stayed awake most of the night with his ear next to the wall that separated his room from Houlihan's, never heard anything from Houlihan except when his shoes dropped on the floor, and then a muffled cough, followed by the sound of his regular, quiet breathing.

QUESTIONS

1. Here is a story built upon the irony of situation. It is ironic that Houlihan, at last free from a wife who ordered him about, gets

into a situation in which the landlady echoes all the commands for cleanliness and orderliness that he has just escaped. What other examples of irony are found in the story?

2. The surface conflict is that between Houlihan and Mrs. Goetz, but what is the real conflict?

3. What details early in the story foreshadow Houlihan's approaching blindness?

4. Houlihan, in speaking of Red Hanrahan as the great symbol of Ireland, is referring to a character in a group of stories by William Butler Yeats. Red Hanrahan was a poet, an individual, who roamed the Irish countryside alone, the victim of sorrow and persecution and enchantment; but through all his disappointments and failures he always had great courage. When he became old, however, "there came on him a great anger against old age and all it brought with it." Why does Houlihan feel a kinship with Red Hanrahan?

5. As Mrs. Goetz pounds at the door, Houlihan cries in despair, ". . . won't the world ever allow man to fight his struggle without the voice of woman?" What struggle does he mean?

6. At what point does Houlihan give up his fight?

7. How has Houlihan's character changed at the end of the story? What is his surrender?

8. What irony is there in the last statement by Mrs. Goetz?

9. What theme does the outcome of the story suggest?

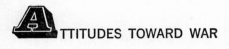ATTITUDES TOWARD WAR

THEN WE'LL SET IT RIGHT
ROBERT GORHAM DAVIS

A great many new families had come to Marbury since the war began. The little fireworks plant had been expanded, with government help, to twenty times its former size and was producing ammunition in great quantities. The incoming executives had taken all the vacant winter houses, beautiful old houses, many of them, and the summer places were filled with families of officers at Camp Peters, fifteen miles away.

Young Laurence Purvis had been having a wonderful summer. He had never had so many playmates with such interesting backgrounds. Marbury was his second home; his father, who had grown up and had his first law practice here, still made it his legal residence, although the family spent most of their year in the city.

This Saturday, a hot, still, August day, the Purvises had lunched late so that Mr. Purvis, who had come down from town, could be with them. Laurence had eaten very fast, bending low over his plate and putting in one mouthful before the preceding one had been swallowed. He said he did not want dessert.

"What's the matter with you, Laurence?" his mother asked. "You've bolted your food so, and now no dessert!"

Laurence lifted his chin eagerly. His narrow face and close-cropped, knobby head were the same shade of light brown. Only his large, dark eyes gave contrast and focus to his face. "It's the Powderhouse Point gang. We're expecting an attack. They've got an army too. We've had sentinels posted all morning." He jammed his napkin into his ring and pushed his chair back from the table.

"Can I be excused now?" He began backing toward the door, his eyes on his father's face. On the shoulders of his khaki shirt were stars cut from beer cans.

His father was a large man with smooth, soft skin and a states-man-like jaw, slightly cleft in the middle. He looked at his son. "Excused?" he asked mildly.

"Yes. They're waiting for me."

"No doubt. But aren't you forgetting something?" Mr. Purvis said.

"What?" Laurence asked in an alarmed and defensive voice.

"I think you know."

"The dishes," Laurence said grudgingly, and came slowly back to the table. "But just this once. It's our big day."

"You think your mother should do them, then?"

"No, but . . ."

"And the garden this morning. How much time did you put in?"

"But . . ." Laurence's voice trailed off, then he sat down in his chair, sprawling defiantly, watching every bite his parents took.

"Come, boy," said Mr. Purvis in his deep, rich voice. "Is this the way your troops obey orders?"

"No . . . sir," Laurence answered, sitting up straight now.

"I wonder what sort of soldier you are." Mr. Purvis paused, looking thoughtfully at Laurence. Laurence returned the gaze, not letting himself hope, moving a finger up and down one seam of his pants. "Because I'm more interested in the spirit in which it's done than in the work itself, I'm going to make a counter-proposal. I could take over your dishwashing this once—" He held up his hand as Laurence moved eagerly. "This is going to be equally hard. You don't want to just get out of something, do you?"

"No, Dad."

"If things are too easy, you don't feel good about them, do you? Well, you may go now if you will come back promptly at four-thirty and work for one full hour and a half in the garden."

Laurence blinked and looked uneasily up at the clock. It was twenty-five minutes past two.

"Without any reminding. You're on your honor, now. Remember."

"All right, Dad." With a little sigh Laurence grabbed up a belt and cap pistol from the table and rushed out the door.

Mr. Purvis smiled and turned to his wife. "He's O.K.," he said cheerfully. "We just have to deal with things as they come up, get them into the open, not let anything build up inside."

From the road, where Laurence was racing to catch up with two members of his company, came the sounds of shooting produced with tireless mechanical precision by the mouths of small boys.

Mr. Purvis put down his spoon and listened. "Anti-aircraft and Thompsons," he said. "In my day we had nothing to guide us on the sounds. We actually went around shouting 'Bang, bang,' the way it was written in books. Very crude by present standards."

"In a way it's terrible, though," his wife said. "Laury told me how to kill a man in the dark with a knife without making a sound."

Mr. Purvis laughed and pretended to cringe away from her. "You aren't going to try it?" he asked. "But really, puss, it's not terrible at all. Death is a word to them, a theatrical fall to the ground. They have all that destructive energy that they can blow off by pretending to shoot each other. It gets it out of their system."

"The terms he uses!" Mrs. Purvis laughed. "And those books in his room. I can't understand a word of them."

"He really organizes those boys," Mr. Purvis said. "Sixteen kids showing up every day, to take his orders and like it. In my day we just bickered." The sweet dessert, the warm air, and thoughts of the weekend merged tranquilly. He looked down at the table.

"Oh, God," he said. "The dishes."

"Oh, I'll do them. You've had a hard week."

"Do you really mind, puss?" he asked, patting her arm.

Laurence's company was encamped in a rarely used sand pit which made a crater in the side of a high, wooded hill. Except for one opening, where the winding truck road ran onto the floor of the pit, it was enclosed by sand walls rising for forty or fifty feet. It was a perfect place for dugouts and foxholes, although not defensible against an enemy who had gained the rim above. This was protected, however, by machine-gun and mortar emplacements.

As Laurence came along the truck road into the pit, a small boy stepped from behind a barricade and presented arms.

"Any news?" Laurence asked.

"We just sent out another scout. Chuck didn't find out anything," the small boy said.

A larger boy with tin bars on his shoulders came up and saluted.

"Order the company to fall in, Captain," Laurence said. "We can't just stand around waiting."

A group of four or five boys stood waiting across the floor of the pit. "No more close-order drill!" one of them shouted insubordinately.

Laurence frowned. "Order the company to fall in," he repeated, ignoring the shout. As the group came toward him he said, "This is different. Wait and see."

When the nine boys not on sentry or scout duty were lined up before Laurence and had quieted down, he took a scrap of newspaper from his pocket and looked at it, frowning. "This is what real training is," he said, and began to read: " 'And this program is no strength-through-joy movement. It's a grim, tough business. Weaklings, morally and physically, can't take it; they're not wanted. At Fort Bragg, the emphasis is on developing aggressiveness. There physical toughening takes place in the course of this program to' "—he stumbled over the word—" 'to inculcate the "killer" instinct. There is none of the emphasis on the niceties of the game or on sportsmanship. In some of the contests I witnessed a number of palpable fouls. "We're interested only in teaching them to go out and win," explained . . .' " Laurence broke off impatiently. "Oh, never mind all that. I'll just tell you what the rest of it says."

He took a deep breath and looked directly at his audience, which had grown restless during his reading. "Why did we have so many casualties in Africa at first? Because the men hadn't learned to keep cover, they exposed themselves. And do you know how they cure that now? By using live bullets in training." This was what he had been working toward, and it got some show of interest from the shifting line of boys. "And that's how we're going to train from now on."

Laurence looked around for a moment at the familiar geography of the pit. Then he faced the ranks. "At the command 'Fall out' go back beyond that bush, and then at the command 'Advance' start crawling straight for where I am now. Remember, keep everything down right flat to the ground. Dick, you get into that foxhole beside me with some round stones about this size"—he leaned over and selected one from the ground—"and keep throwing them just thirty inches above the ground. It has to be thirty inches." He waited until they were in their positions and then gave the commands. "Now then, get down flat and crawl. Make it fast. Keep your guns ready."

Laurence looked on with satisfaction as the line of grunting boys, wooden guns in their right hands, crept toward the foxhole across the sand and through the crab grass, while the boy in the foxhole, about twenty feet from them, threw stones happily. But it didn't work out well. The first stone was too high. The second, a piece of slate, curved down and hit the first crawler on the hand. He jumped up angrily.

"You threw that at me on purpose, Dick!"

"No, I didn't," Dick said.

"Well, you were looking right at me when you threw."

"Back to line, all of you, and keep on!" Laurence shouted. He turned to the thrower. "Don't think about them. Just keep throwing level, thirty inches above the ground."

They began to crawl again, but a stone which just missed a boy's face brought another angry protest. "Hey, that was no thirty inches!"

"Well, what is thirty inches?" Dick yelled. "Let's see you try it."

"All right, I will."

"Stop! As you were," Laurence called. "This has got to be right." He stopped a moment to consider. Then he shook his head. "A gun would be the only thing that would be right. We'd have to have a real gun."

"Nuts. You aren't shooting any old bullets at me," one boy said, shaking his head excitedly. The others were held by the idea, testing themselves in their minds.

"We could fix it so it would be safe," Laurence said.

"You could if you had a gun."

"We can get one," Laurence said impressively. He grinned at Ed Peterson for confirmation. "Hey, Ed?"

Ed frowned. "What?" he asked, as if he did not understand. He was a chunky boy with deep-set eyes and a scar showing through his cropped brown hair.

"You know," Laurence said impatiently. "The thirty-two. You said you could have it any time you wanted."

"Well, not over here I can't."

"Why not? If you can have it any time you want it, why can't you have it when we need it here?"

"Well, that isn't the same," Ed said uneasily.

The others were eager. "Come on, Ed." "Does he let you shoot it?" "Could I shoot it, Ed?"

"No, no one else can shoot it but me."

"All right, you'll be the only one to shoot it," Laurence said, "but hurry up."

"I'd have to ask my father."

"You *said* you didn't have to ask him. Anyway, your tool shed's out of sight of the house."

Ed looked around for support, but none was forthcoming. The wooden guns the boys were playing with had become absurd.

"But I have to go home early," Ed said. "We're going on a picnic out on the point."

"I have to be home early too. That's why we've got to hurry." Laurence glanced over at the captain's wristwatch. "Look, Ed, we've got to have this right and you're spoiling everything." He paused and looked firmly at Ed. "I wonder what kind of soldier you are," he said slowly.

He waited in silence, until Ed had to give in. "I hadn't ought to, but I suppose this once," Ed said reluctantly, and began trudging off.

"Be back in ten minutes and bring plenty of shells," Laurence said, glancing impatiently at the watch again. The boys were excited now, and all began talking at once with nervous boastfulness.

When Ed came back with the rifle, he was still uneasy. "My father came out to go to the garden," he said, "and I dropped it in the high grass. He didn't see it, but I nearly got caught." He blew out his breath and shook his head.

"O.K.," Laurence murmured, absorbed in what he was doing. By much winding of string and wire, he was fastening the barrel to the top of a box placed at the edge of the foxhole. It was very unsteady, but they piled sand and rocks on it until it was good and firm.

"You won't be able to see to shoot now," Ed said.

"You're not supposed to. That would spoil it." Laurence was still making adjustments. He finally got the gun fixed and placed a large cardboard carton about thirty feet away. When Ed dropped into the foxhole and tried the gun, with three shots, the bullets plopped through the cardboard at just about the right distance from the ground. "There!" Laurence said with satisfaction.

The group quieted as the shots sounded, flat and unechoing within the enclosure of the sand pit. Then their excitement burst out again. "Boy, you don't get me in front of that gun." "I'd dig right through the ground like an old mole."

"I'll show you," Laurence said. "Shoot twice when I call out," he told Ed, who was out of sight, behind the gun. The others, crawling under the barrage of rocks, had made a track through the sand. Laurence followed it, hitching forward on his elbows. As he approached the gun he called out to Ed and then put his face almost into the sand and kept on advancing. The two shots went well above his head and barely enlarged the hole in the carton. Laurence jumped up.

"See," he said. "But we can't use so many shots for each one. We can keep in single file and let him fire sort of unevenly so we won't know when it's going off. That will teach us to keep down."

He considered the faces of the boys. "Anyone afraid?" he asked. "Those who want to get in line, come forward."

"I want to, too," Ed called from the hole.

"All right. Neil, you know how to shoot it, don't you? Just every once in a while. But wait till we're ready."

The first time the file of boys wriggled forward they were obviously fearful and hesitant, flinching at the sound of the gun and struggling with the desire to raise their heads and see where the bullet struck. But once safely past the line of fire, they leaped up in ecstatic joy and ran around the gun pit to take their places again.

Laurence glanced up and saw that the sentries stationed on the rim above were watching the maneuvers in the pit. "Corporal Higgins," he said, turning to the boy at the head of the file, "go up and remind the sentries that we are expecting an attack. They've got to watch those woods for men coming up the hill. Tell them to turn around and forget we are down here."

After the file of boys had gone toward the foxhole twice, Ed halted abruptly and looked at his watch. "I have to have the gun now," he said. "I have to go home."

"Aw, Ed!" they said. "Once more. Come on, Ed. It only takes a minute."

"All right," he said. "Once more, but fast."

It was when the file of boys had started forward toward the gun for the third time, and some twenty-five shots had been fired, that the expected attack from the Powderhouse Point army came. One of the sentinels saw them in the woods at the foot of the hill and shouted a warning, raising his gun horizontally above his head. Ed, who was first in file and a squad leader, recognized the signal and excitedly started to scramble to his feet. Neil, who was down in the pit, could not see the sentinel. He fired the gun again. Ed collapsed on the ground.

"Stop, Neil, stop!" Laurence shouted. He waited a moment, then got to his knees. There were heavy steps behind him as a man in overalls hurried up. "Who's shooting that gun around here?" he bellowed. It was Joe Tobin, the contractor, who owned the pit. "You know what I've told you." He looked past Laurence and saw Ed lying face down on the ground. Blood was draining into the grass around his head.

"For the love of God in heaven!" Tobin cried out, and went over to kneel by Ed. Laurence leaned down beside him. Tobin lifted the boy by the shoulders and looked at his head. There was not much blood at the wound—it came mostly from his mouth—and Tobin could see where the bullet had entered the head and where it had come out.

Up on the rim the sentinels were engaging the enemy. The Powderhouse Point boys were calling, "You're dead," "I got you." The outnumbered sentinels, retreating, looked down to see why help was not coming. When they noticed the circle around Ed and realized someone was hurt, they began running and sliding down the sides of the pit, their attackers with them.

"He isn't *dead*, is he?" Laurence asked Tobin in a protesting voice.

"Of course he's dead!" Tobin shouted angrily. He looked at the boys who had come down from above. "Go on, get out of here!" he yelled. "What's the matter with you!" Then he groaned and sat down heavily on a rock, staring at Ed and twisting his old felt hat in his hands.

There was a hubbub of questions from the boys who had just come down. "Ed got shot," someone said. "He's dead." They fell silent.

"Shouldn't we *do* something?" Laurence said desperately.

"Of course, of course. We're not going to leave him here." Tobin got up, stopped, and went back to the rock. "I've got to stay here," he said, brushing distractedly at a green fly about his head. "Go on, get somebody, quick. Get an ambulance, get his father. I'll stay here."

Some of the boys still stood looking on, silently, at a little distance, but the rest turned and started off down the rutted road. Tobin called them back in sudden fright. "You kids can't go telling the Petersons!" He looked at Laurence. "You live next door. Your father home?" Laurence nodded. "You tell him, then," Tobin said. "And let him break the news."

Laurence whirled and ran. The other boys broke up into small, straggling groups, walking slowly and talking in soft, excited voices.

Mr. Purvis was sitting on his screened porch, alternately reading *Time* and looking at his garden; Laurence could clear out some of the stuff that was past yielding and pick corn and beans for supper. He saw Laurence coming, running hard. "The warrior returneth," he called to his wife. "Only ten minutes late. If you approach him right he really tries."

Laurence leaped over the low picket fence and came up to the porch. His father said, "I think I'll join you on the job. I was relieved of the dishes by the beneficence of your mother." Laurence came in with his face turned away, panting. From the next house down the road they could hear a man's voice calling. Laurence did not speak. Mr. Purvis frowned. "Look," he said, "remember what . . ." but Laurence pushed past him toward the hall. His father grabbed him angrily and swung him around. "I said I expected . . ."

Then he saw that Laurence was sobbing. Mr. Purvis looked down at his son in surprise. "Come, boy," he said softly, "I think we can forget these ten minutes." He tried to distract him, as one would a much younger child. "Listen to Mr. Peterson calling Ed," he said. He smiled. "He sounds like an old cow."

The sobs broke out into sound. Mrs. Purvis rushed from the kitchen, but Mr. Purvis held up his hand to silence her. Through a great many domestic crises, he had learned to take a detached and scientific attitude. It was easier on the nerves and accomplished more. Not the attitude of the judge, for Mr. Purvis was well aware of the remedial weaknesses of the law. The attitude of the doctor, the healer, rather, finding first what was wrong and then compounding the proper remedy.

"Is it something else, then?" he asked in a firm, suggestive, soothing voice. "Tell us about it. You know we'll understand. We deal with these things together, you know. Just tell us."

The sobs became still more violent, the boy's body shuddering in a kind of sickness against the man's.

"Nothing's ever so bad once you've told it," Mr. Purvis said to him, shaking his head a little as he talked. He glanced up at Mrs. Purvis, smiling gently in anticipation of early climax and release. They waited. Through the screen they could see Mr. Peterson set a picnic hamper down on his curbstone and, still calling, start up the road. He had huge, freckled arms and a very small cloth cap set squarely on his head. He made a rather absurd figure. Mr. Purvis looked down once more at his son. "Just get it outside so's we can look at it, Laury," he said confidently, "and then we'll set it right."

QUESTIONS

1. Is this merely a story about children playing war, or does it have a broader meaning?

2. Is the father or the son the more important character?

3. Mr. Purvis appears to be an ideal father, kind and understanding, yet firm. An amateur psychologist, he is confident that war play is of value, that troubles should be brought out into the open, and that by using his "detached and scientific attitude" and dealing with "things as they come up" he can set anything right. Why is so much emphasis placed on his understanding attitude and his confidence in his ability to cope with problems?

4. What similarities are there between father and son?

5. What is the conflict? Is it evident throughout the story, or is it something implied that the reader becomes fully aware of only at the very end?

6. What theme is brought out by the resolution of the conflict?

7. Might the theme apply to other areas of life besides war?

WAR
LUIGI PIRANDELLO

The passengers who had left Rome by the night express had had to stop until dawn at the small station of Fabriano in order to continue their journey by the small old-fashioned "local" joining the main line with Sulmona.

At dawn, in a stuffy and smoky second-class carriage in which five people had already spent the night, a bulky woman in deep mourning was hoisted in—almost like a shapeless bundle. Behind her—puffing and moaning, followed her husband—a tiny man, thin and weakly, his face death-white, his eyes small and bright and looking shy and uneasy.

Having at last taken a seat he politely thanked the passengers who had helped his wife and who had made room for her; then he turned round to the woman trying to pull down the collar of her coat and politely enquired:

"Are you all right, dear?"

The wife, instead of answering, pulled up her collar again to her eyes, so as to hide her face.

"Nasty world," muttered the husband with a sad smile.

And he felt it his duty to explain to his travelling companions that the poor woman was to be pitied for the war was taking away from her her only son, a boy of twenty to whom both had devoted their entire life, even breaking up their home at Sulmona to follow him to Rome where he had to go as a student, then allowing him to volunteer for war with an assurance, however, that at least for six months he would not be sent to the front and now, all of a sudden, receiving a wire saying that he was due to leave in three days' time and asking them to go and see him off.

The woman under the big coat was twisting and wriggling, at times growling like a wild animal, feeling certain that all those explanations would not have aroused even a shadow of sympathy from those people who—most likely—were in the same plight as herself. One of them, who had been listening with particular attention, said:

"You should thank God that your son is only leaving now for the front. Mine has been sent there the first day of the war. He has already come back twice wounded and been sent back again to the front."

"What about me? I have two sons and three nephews at the front," said another passenger.

"Maybe, but in our case it is our *only* son," ventured the husband.

"What difference can it make? You may spoil your only son with excessive attentions, but you cannot love him more than you would all your other children if you had any. Paternal love is not like bread that can be broken into pieces and spilt amongst the children in equal shares. A father gives *all* his love to each one of his children without discrimination, whether it be one or ten, and if I am suffering now for my two sons, I am not suffering half for each of them but double. . . ."

"True . . . true . . ." sighed the embarrassed husband, "but suppose (of course we all hope it will never be your case) a father has two sons at the front and he loses one of them, there is still one left to console him . . . while . . ."

"Yes," answered the other, getting cross, "a son left to console him but also a son left for whom he must survive, while in the case of the father of an only son if the son dies the father can die too and put an end to his distress. Which of the two positions is the worse? Don't you see how my case would be worse than yours?"

"Nonsense," interrupted another traveller, a fat, red-faced man with bloodshot eyes of the palest grey.

He was panting. From his bulging eyes seemed to spurt inner violence of an uncontrolled vitality which his weakened body could hardly contain.

"Nonsense," he repeated, trying to cover his mouth with his hand so as to hide the two missing front teeth. "Nonsense. Do we give life to our children for our own benefit?"

The other travellers stared at him in distress. The one who had

had his son at the front since the first day of the war sighed: "You are right. Our children do not belong to us, they belong to the Country. . . ."

"Bosh," retorted the fat traveller. "Do we think of the Country when we give life to our children? Our sons are born because . . . well, because they must be born and when they come to life they take our own life with them. This is the truth. We belong to them but they never belong to us. And when they reach twenty they are exactly what we were at their age. We too had a father and mother, but there were so many other things as well . . . girls, cigarettes, illusions, new ties . . . and the Country, of course, whose call we would have answered—when we were twenty—even if father and mother had said no. Now, at our age, the love of our Country is still great, of course, but stronger than it is the love for our children. Is there any one of us here who wouldn't gladly take his son's place at the front if he could?"

There was a silence all round, everybody nodding as to approve.

"Why then," continued the fat man, "shouldn't we consider the feelings of our children when they are twenty? Isn't it natural that at their age they should consider the love for their Country (I am speaking of decent boys, of course) even greater than the love for us? Isn't it natural that it should be so, as after all they must look upon us as upon old boys who cannot move any more and must stay at home? If Country exists, if Country is a natural necessity like bread, of which each of us must eat in order not to die of hunger, somebody must go to defend it. And our sons go, when they are twenty, and they don't want tears, because if they die, they die inflamed and happy (I am speaking, of course, of decent boys). Now, if one dies young and happy, without having the ugly sides of life, the boredom of it, the pettiness, the bitterness of disillusion . . . what more can we ask for him? Everyone should stop crying: everyone should laugh, as I do . . . or at least thank God—as I do—because my son, before dying, sent me a message saying that he was dying satisfied at having ended his life in the best way he could have wished. That is why, as you see, I do not even wear mourning. . . ."

He shook his light fawn coat as to show it; his livid lip over his missing teeth was trembling, his eyes were watery and motionless and soon after he ended with a shrill laugh which might well have been a sob.

"Quite so . . . quite so . . ." agreed the others.

The woman who, bundled in a corner under her coat, had been sitting and listening had—for the last three months—tried to find in the words of her husband and her friends something to console her in her deep sorrow, something that might show her how a mother should resign herself to send her son not even to death but to a probable danger of life. Yet not a word had she found amongst the many which had been said . . . and her grief had been greater in seeing that nobody—as she thought—could share her feelings.

But now the words of the traveller amazed and almost stunned her. She suddenly realized that it wasn't the others who were wrong and could not understand her but herself who could not rise up to the same height of those fathers and mothers willing to resign themselves, without crying, not only to the departure of their sons but even to their death.

She lifted her head, she bent over from her corner trying to listen with great attention to the details which the fat man was giving to his companions about the way his son had fallen as a hero, for his King and his Country, happy and without regrets. It seemed to her that she had stumbled into a world she had never dreamt of, a world so far unknown to her and she was so pleased to hear everyone joining in congratulating that brave father who could so stoically speak of his child's death.

Then suddenly, just as if she had heard nothing of what had been said and almost as if waking up from a dream, she turned to the old man, asking him:

"Then . . . is your son really dead?"

Everybody stared at her. The old man, too, turned to look at her, fixing his great, bulging, horribly watery light grey eyes, deep in her face. For some little time he tried to answer, but words failed him. He looked and looked at her, almost as if only then—at that silly, incongruous question—he had suddenly realized at last that his son was really dead . . . gone for ever . . . for ever. His face contracted, became horribly distorted, then he snatched in haste a handkerchief from his pocket and, to the amazement of everyone, broke into harrowing, heart-rending, uncontrollable sobs.

QUESTIONS

1. Unusually lacking in physical action, this brief story is composed of the conversation among the occupants of a railway carriage on the subject of sending their sons to war. Various opinions are expressed, but the main conflict is between the two extreme positions —that of the fat man whose son has just been killed and that of the woman in the big coat whose son has just been called to service. How do their opinions differ?

2. Is there any foreshadowing of the end of the story, any indication that the fat man may not be quite so sure of his arguments as he would have his fellow travelers think?

3. Greatly moved by the fat man's brave attitude, the woman in the big coat realizes that she has been at fault in failing to rise to the height of other parents who are willing to resign themselves "not only to the departure of their sons but even to their death." Amazed at the fat man's stoicism and just ready to embrace it, she asks, to reassure herself, "Then . . . is your son really dead?" Why does this unnecessary, silly question unnerve the man?

4. The last paragraph of the story is an excellent example of the author's ability to portray an emotional change—from shock to realization to uncontrollable grief. What is ironic about this outcome of the conflict?

5. What theme evolves from the outcome?

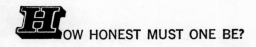

HOW HONEST MUST ONE BE?

HOW MR. HOGAN ROBBED A BANK

JOHN STEINBECK

On the Saturday before Labor Day, 1955, at 9:04½ A.M., Mr. Hogan robbed a bank. He was forty-two years old, married, and the father of a boy and a girl, named John and Joan, twelve and thirteen respectively. Mrs. Hogan's name was Joan and Mr. Hogan's was John, but since they called themselves Papa and Mama that left their names free for the children, who were considered very smart for their ages, each having jumped a grade in school. The Hogans lived at 215 East Maple Street, in a brown-shingle house with white trim—there are two. 215 is the one across from the street light and it is the one with the big tree in the yard, either oak or elm—the biggest tree in the whole street, maybe in the whole town.

John and Joan were in bed at the time of the robbery, for it was Saturday. At 9:10 A.M., Mrs. Hogan was making the cup of tea she always had. Mr. Hogan went to work early. Mrs. Hogan drank her tea slowly, scalding hot, and read her fortune in the tea leaves. There was a cloud and a five-pointed star with two short points in the bottom of the cup, but that was at 9:12 and the robbery was all over by then.

The way Mr. Hogan went about robbing the bank was very interesting. He gave it a great deal of thought and had for a long time, but he did not discuss it with anyone. He just read his newspaper and kept his own counsel. But he worked it out to his own satisfaction that people went to too much trouble robbing banks and that got them in a mess. The simpler the better, he always thought. People went in for too much hullabaloo and hanky-panky. If you didn't do that, if you left hanky-panky out, robbing a bank would be a relatively sound venture—barring accidents, of course, of an improbable kind, but then they could happen to a man crossing the street or anything. Since Mr. Hogan's method worked fine, it proved that his thinking was sound. He often considered writing a little booklet on his technique when the how-to rage was running so high. He figured out the first sentence, which went: "To successfully rob a bank, forget all about hanky-panky."

Mr. Hogan was not just a clerk at Fettucci's grocery store. He was more like the manager. Mr. Hogan was in charge, even hired and fired the boy who delivered groceries after school. He even put in orders with the salesmen, sometimes when Mr. Fettucci was right in the store too, maybe talking to a customer. "You do it, John," he would say and he would nod at the customer, "John knows the ropes. Been with me—how long you been with me, John?"

"Sixteen years."

"Sixteen years. Knows the business as good as me. John, why he even banks the money."

And so he did. Whenever he had a moment, Mr. Hogan went into the storeroom on the alley, took off his apron, put on his necktie and coat, and went back through the store to the cash register. The checks and bills would be ready for him inside the bankbook with a rubber band around it. Then he went next door and stood at the teller's window and handed the checks and bankbook through to Mr. Cup and passed the time of day with him too. Then, when the bankbook was handed back, he checked the entry, put the rubber band around it, and walked next door to Fettucci's grocery and put the bankbook in the cash register, continued on to the storeroom, removed his coat and tie, put on his apron, and went back into the store ready for business. If there was no line at the teller's window, the whole thing didn't take more than five minutes, even passing the time of day.

Mr. Hogan was a man who noticed things, and when it came to robbing the bank, this trait stood him in good stead. He had noticed, for instance, where the big bills were kept right in the drawer under the counter and he had noticed also what days there were likely to be more than other days. Thursday was payday at the American Can Company's local plant, for instance, so there would be more then. Some Fridays people drew more money to tide them over the week-end. But it was even Steven, maybe not a thousand dollars difference, between Thursdays and Fridays and Saturday mornings. Saturdays were not terribly good because people didn't come to get money that early in the morning, and the bank closed at noon. But he thought it over and came to the conclusion that the Saturday before a long weekend in the summer would be the best of all. People going on trips, vacations, people with relatives visiting, and the bank closed Monday. He thought it out and looked, and sure enough the Saturday morning before Labor Day the cash drawer had twice as much money in it—he saw it when Mr. Cup pulled out the drawer.

Mr. Hogan thought about it during all that year, not all the time, of course, but when he had some moments. It was a busy year too. That was the year John and Joan had the mumps and Mrs. Hogan got her teeth pulled and was fitted for a denture. That was the year when Mr. Hogan was Master of the Lodge, with all the time that takes. Larry Shield died that year—he was Mrs. Hogan's brother and was buried from the Hogan house at 215 East Maple. Larry was a bachelor and had a room in the Pine Tree House and he played pool nearly every night. He worked at the Silver Diner but that closed at nine and so Larry would go to Louie's and play pool for an hour. Therefore, it was a surprise when he left enough so that after funeral expenses there were twelve hundred dollars left. And even more surprising that he left a will in Mrs. Hogan's favor, but his double-barreled twelve-gauge shotgun he left to John Hogan, Jr. Mr. Hogan was pleased, although he never hunted. He put the shotgun away in the back of the closet in the bathroom, where he kept his things, to keep it for young John. He didn't want children handling guns and he never bought any shells. It was some of that twelve hundred that got Mrs. Hogan her dentures. Also, she bought a bicycle for John and a doll buggy and walking-talking doll for Joan—a doll with three changes of dresses and a little suitcase, complete with play make-up. Mr. Hogan thought it might spoil the children, but it didn't seem to. They made just as good marks in school and John even got a job delivering papers. It was a very busy year. Both John and Joan wanted to enter the W. R. Hearst National "I Love America" Contest and Mr. Hogan thought it was almost too much, but they promised to do the work during their summer vacation, so he finally agreed.

II

During that year, no one noticed any difference in Mr. Hogan. It was true, he was thinking about robbing the bank, but he only thought about it in the evening when there was neither a Lodge meeting nor a movie they wanted to go to, so it did not become an obsession and people noticed no change in him.

He had studied everything so carefully that the approach of Labor Day did not catch him unprepared or nervous. It was hot that summer and the hot spells were longer than usual. Saturday was the end of two weeks heat without a break and people were irritated with it and anxious to get out of town, although the country was just as hot. They didn't think of that. The children were excited because the "I Love America" Essay Contest was due to be concluded and the winners announced, and the first prize was an all-expense-paid two days trip to Washington, D.C., with every fixing—hotel room, three meals a day, and side trips in a limousine—not only for the winner, but for an accompanying chaperone; visit to the White House —shake hands with the President—everything. Mr. Hogan thought they were getting their hopes too high and he said so.

"You've got to be prepared to lose," he told his children. "There're probably thousands and thousands entered. You get your hopes up and it might spoil the whole autumn. Now I don't want any long faces in this house after the contest is over."

"I was against it from the start," he told Mrs. Hogan. That was the morning she saw the Washington Monument in her teacup, but she didn't tell anybody about that except Ruth Tyler, Bob Tyler's wife. Ruthie brought over her cards and read them in the Hogan kitchen, but she didn't find a journey. She did tell Mrs. Hogan that the cards were often wrong. The cards had said Mrs. Winkle was going on a trip to Europe and the next week Mrs. Winkle got a fishbone in her throat and choked to death. Ruthie, just thinking out loud, wondered if there was any connection between the fishbone and the ocean voyage to Europe. "You've got to interpret them right." Ruthie did say she saw money coming to the Hogans.

"Oh, I got that already from poor Larry," Mrs. Hogan explained.

"I must have got the past and future cards mixed," said Ruthie. "You've got to interpret them right."

Saturday dawned a blaster. The early morning weather report on the radio said "Continued hot and humid, light scattered rain Sunday night and Monday." Mrs. Hogan said, "Wouldn't you know? Labor Day." And Mr. Hogan said, "I'm sure glad we didn't plan anything." He finished his egg and mopped the plate with his toast. Mrs. Hogan said, "Did I put coffee on the list?" He took the paper from his handkerchief pocket and consulted it. "Yes, coffee, it's here."

"I had a crazy idea I forgot to write it down," said Mrs. Hogan.

"Ruth and I are going to Altar Guild this afternoon. It's at Mrs. Alfred Drake's. You know, they just came to town. I can't wait to see their furniture."

"They trade with us," said Mr. Hogan. "Opened an account last week. Are the milk bottles ready?"

"On the porch."

Mr. Hogan looked at his watch just before he picked up the bottles and it was five minutes to eight. He was about to go down the stairs, when he turned and looked back through the opened door at Mrs. Hogan. She said, "Want something, Papa?"

"No," he said. "No," and he walked down the steps.

He went down to the corner and turned right on Spooner, and Spooner runs into Main Street in two blocks, and right across from where it runs in, there is Fettucci's and the bank around the corner and the alley beside the bank. Mr. Hogan picked up a handbill in front of Fettucci's and unlocked the door. He went through to the storeroom, opened the door to the alley, and looked out. A cat tried to force its way in, but Mr. Hogan blocked it with his foot and leg and closed the door. He took off his coat and put on his long apron, tied the strings in a bowknot behind his back. Then he got the broom from behind the counter and swept out behind the counters and scooped the sweepings into a dustpan; and, going through the storeroom, he opened the door to the alley. The cat had gone away. He emptied the dustpan into the garbage can and tapped it smartly to dislodge a piece of lettuce leaf. Then he went back to the store and worked for a while on the order sheet. Mrs. Clooney came in for a half a pound of bacon. She said it was hot and Mr. Hogan agreed. "Summers are getting hotter," he said.

"I think so myself," said Mrs. Clooney. "How's Mrs. standing up?"

"Just fine," said Mr. Hogan. "She's going to Altar Guild."

"So am I. I just can't wait to see their furniture," said Mrs. Clooney, and she went out.

III

Mr. Hogan put a five-pound hunk of bacon on the slicer and stripped off the pieces and laid them on wax paper and then he put the wax-paper-covered squares in the cooler cabinet. At ten minutes to nine, Mr. Hogan went to a shelf. He pushed a spaghetti box aside and took down a cereal box, which he emptied in the little closet toilet. Then, with a banana knife, he cut out the Mickey Mouse mask that was on the back. The rest of the box he took to the toilet and tore up the cardboard and flushed it down. He went into the store then and yanked a piece of string loose and tied the ends through the side holes of the mask and then he looked at his watch—a large silver Hamilton with black hands. It was two minutes to nine.

Perhaps the next four minutes were his only time of nervousness at all. At one minute to nine, he took the broom and went out to sweep the sidewalk and he swept it very rapidly—was sweeping it, in fact, when Mr. Warner unlocked the bank door. He said good morning to Mr. Warner and a few seconds later the bank staff of four emerged from the coffee shop. Mr. Hogan saw them across the street and he waved at them and they waved back. He finished the sidewalk and went back in the store. He laid his watch on the little step of the cash register. He sighed very deeply, more like a deep breath than a sigh. He knew that Mr. Warner would have the safe open now and he would be carrying the cash trays to the teller's window. Mr. Hogan looked at the watch on the cash register step. Mr. Kenworthy paused in the store entrance, then shook his head vaguely and walked on and Mr. Hogan let out his breath gradually. His left hand went behind his back and pulled the bowknot on his apron, and then the black hand on his watch crept up on the four-minute mark and covered it.

Mr. Hogan opened the charge account drawer and took out the store pistol, a silver-colored Iver Johnson .38. He moved quickly to the storeroom, slipped off his apron, put on his coat, and stuck the revolver in his side pocket. The Mickey Mouse mask he shoved up under his coat where it didn't show. He opened the alley door and looked up and down and stepped quickly out, leaving the door slightly ajar. It is sixty feet to where the alley enters Main Street, and there he paused and looked up and down and then he turned his head toward the center of the street as he passed the bank window. At the bank's swinging door, he took out the mask from under his coat and put it on. Mr. Warner was just entering his office and his back was to the door. The top of Will Cup's head was visible through the teller's grill.

Mr. Hogan moved quickly and quietly around the end of the counter and into the teller's cage. He had the revolver in his right hand now. When Will Cup turned his head and saw the revolver, he froze. Mr. Hogan slipped his toe under the trigger of the floor alarm and he motioned Will Cup to the floor with the revolver and Will went down quick. Then Mr. Hogan opened the cash drawer and with two quick movements he piled the large bills from the tray together. He made a whipping motion to Will on the floor, to indicate that he should turn over and face the wall, and Will did. Then Mr. Hogan stepped back around the counter. At the door of the bank, he took off the mask, and as he passed the window he turned his head toward the middle of the street. He moved into the alley, walked quickly to the storeroom, and entered. The cat had got in. It watched him from a pile of canned goods cartons. Mr. Hogan went to the toilet closet and tore up the mask and flushed it. He took off his coat and put on his apron. He looked out into the store and then moved to the cash register. The revolver went back into the charge account drawer. He punched No Sale and, lifting the top drawer, distributed the stolen money underneath the top tray and then pulled the tray forward and closed the register, and only then did he look at his watch and it was 9:07½.

He was trying to get the cat out of the storeroom when the commotion boiled out of the bank. He took his broom and went out on the sidewalk. He heard all about it and offered his opinion when it was asked for. He said he didn't think the fellow could get away—where could he get to? Still, with the holiday coming up——

It was an exciting day. Mr. Fettucci was as proud as though it were his bank. The sirens sounded around town for hours. Hundreds of holiday travelers had to stop at the roadblocks set up all around the edge of town and several sneaky-looking men had their cars searched.

Mrs. Hogan heard about it over the phone and she dressed earlier than she would have ordinarily and came to the store on her way to Altar Guild. She hoped Mr. Hogan would have seen or heard something new, but he hadn't. "I don't see how the fellow can get away," he said.

Mrs. Hogan was so excited, she forgot her own news. She only remembered when she got to Mrs. Drake's house, but she asked permission and phoned the store the first moment she could. "I forgot to tell you. John's won honorable mention."

"What?"

"In the 'I Love America' Contest."

"What did he win?"

"Honorable mention."

"Fine. Fine—— Anything come with it?"

"Why, he'll get his picture and his name all over the country. Radio too. Maybe even television. They've already asked for a photograph of him."

"Fine," said Mr. Hogan. "I hope it don't spoil him." He put up the receiver and said to Mr. Fettucci, "I guess we've got a celebrity in the family."

Fettucci stayed open until nine on Saturdays. Mr. Hogan ate a few snacks from cold cuts, but not much, because Mrs. Hogan always kept his supper warming.

It was 9:05, or :06, or :07, when he got back to the brown-shingle house at 215 East Maple. He went in through the front door and out to the kitchen where the family was waiting for him.

"Got to wash up," he said, and went up to the bathroom. He turned the key in the bathroom door and then he flushed the toilet and turned on the water in the basin and tub while he counted the money. Eight thousand three hundred and twenty dollars. From the top shelf of the storage closet in the bathroom, he took down the big leather case that held his Knight Templar's uniform. The plumed hat lay there on its form. The white ostrich feather was a little yellow and needed changing. Mr. Hogan lifted out the hat and pried the form up from the bottom of the case. He put the money in the form and then he thought again and removed two bills and shoved them in his side pocket. Then he put the form back over the money and laid the hat on top and closed the case and shoved it back on the top shelf. Finally he washed his hands and turned off the water in the tub and the basin.

In the kitchen, Mrs. Hogan and the children faced him, beaming. "Guess what some young man's going on?"

"What?" asked Mr. Hogan.

"Radio," said John. "Monday night. Eight o'clock."

"I guess we got a celebrity in the family," said Mr. Hogan.

Mrs. Hogan said, "I just hope some young lady hasn't got her nose out of joint."

Mr. Hogan pulled up to the table and stretched his legs. "Mama, I guess I got a fine family," he said. He reached in his pocket and took out two five-dollar bills. He handed one to John. "That's for winning," he said. He poked the other bill at Joan. "And that's for being a good sport. One celebrity and one good sport. What a fine family!" He rubbed his hands together and lifted the lid of the covered dish. "Kidneys," he said. "Fine."

And that's how Mr. Hogan did it.

QUESTIONS

At first reading one is likely to find the ending of this story shocking. Here is a man who robs a bank, is not caught, is not going to be caught, is not sorry, and does not feel guilty. Furthermore, the author seems not to blame him or even to consider his act out of the ordinary. It is as if the author were writing about "How Mr. Hogan Painted his House" or "How Mr. Hogan Caught a Fish." The style is so matter-of-fact that it almost seems as if the author approves of the crime. A closer look may reveal what the author is saying.

1. A story may be peopled with type characters—stereotypes who can be summed up in a sentence or two—or with individual characters who are complex and many-sided. Which kind are the Hogans? And why has the author made them so?

2. From what point of view is the story told?

3. What details suggest that Mr. Hogan is not the kind of man one would expect to have criminal tendencies?

4. Is there anything unusual about the sentence on p. 231 ". . . if you left hanky-panky out, robbing a bank would be a relatively sound venture . . ."?

5. Is anything wrong with the statement on p. 231: "Since Mr. Hogan's method worked fine, it proved that his thinking was sound"? Does it suggest any popular saying?

6. Why would Steinbeck make the above statements? Is he serious, or is he using irony?

7. Since the author has used irony early in the story, the reader

might well expect that there will be more. Is there any irony of situation?

8. Why does the author have Mr. Hogan use a Mickey Mouse mask rather than some other kind? And why does he call the contest the "I Love America" contest?

9. What is Mr. Hogan's motive for committing the crime?

10. What is the first question Mr. Hogan asks when he hears that his son has won honorable mention in the "I Love America" contest? Does the question suggest anything about Mr. Hogan's character?

11. What statement by Mrs. Hogan indicates that she is a bit materialistic?

12. Is there any change in the characters by the end of the story?

13. What is the conflict?

14. What, then, is the theme of the story?

15. If, as was pointed out earlier, the Hogans are typical Americans and act as typical Americans act, how does the bank robbery fit into the picture? Is Steinbeck saying that the average American would rob a bank?

16. If Steinbeck is not saying that the average American would rob a bank, what less spectacular forms of robbing might he be thinking of?

17. A satire is writing which criticizes something by ridiculing it. How is this story a satire?

18. In accepting the Nobel Prize for literature in 1962 Mr. Steinbeck said, "The ancient commission of the writer has not changed. He is charged with exposing our many grievous faults and failures. . . ." How is this story a more effective exposure of an American fault than if Steinbeck had written an essay asserting that Americans are materialistic and are losing their sense of right and wrong?

19. Is there any similarity of purpose between this story and "The Secret Life of Walter Mitty"?

20. Do you agree with what Steinbeck is saying? How honest must one be?

THE FORKS
J. F. POWERS

That summer when Father Eudex got back from saying Mass at the orphanage in the morning, he would park Monsignor's car, which was long and black and new like a politician's, and sit down in the cool of the porch to read his office. If Monsignor was not already standing in the door, he would immediately appear there, seeing that his car had safely returned, and inquire:

"Did you have any trouble with her?"

Father Eudex knew too well the question meant, Did you mistreat my car?

"No trouble, Monsignor."

"Good," Monsignor said, with imperfect faith in his curate, who was not a car owner. For a moment Monsignor stood framed in the screen door, fumbling his watch fob as for a full-length portrait, and then he was suddenly not there.

"Monsignor," Father Eudex said, rising nervously, "I've got a chance to pick up a car."

At the door Monsignor slid into his frame again. His face expressed what was for him intense interest.

"Yes? Go on."

"I don't want to have to use yours every morning."

"It's all right."

"And there are other times." Father Eudex decided not to be maudlin and mention sick calls, nor be entirely honest and admit he was tired of busses and bumming rides from parishioners. "And now I've got a chance to get one—cheap."

Monsignor, smiling, came alert at *cheap*.

"New?"

"No, I wouldn't say it's new."

Monsignor was openly suspicious now. "What kind?"

"It's a Ford."

"And not new?"

"Not new, Monsignor—but in good condition. It was owned by a retired farmer and had good care."

Monsignor sniffed. He *knew* cars. "V-Eight, Father?"

"No," Father Eudex confessed. "It's a Model A."

Monsignor chuckled as though this were indeed the damnedest thing he had ever heard.

"But in very good condition, Monsignor."

"You said that."

"Yes. And I could take it apart if anything went wrong. My uncle had one."

"No doubt." Monsignor uttered a laugh at Father Eudex's rural origins. Then he delivered the final word, long delayed out of amusement. "It wouldn't be prudent, Father. After all, this isn't a country parish. You know the class of people we get here."

Monsignor put on his Panama hat. Then, apparently mistaking the obstinacy in his curate's face for plain ignorance, he shed a little more light. "People watch a priest, Father. *Damnant quod non intelligunt*. It would never do. You'll have to watch your tendencies."

Monsignor's eyes tripped and fell hard on the morning paper lying on the swing where he had finished it.

"Another flattering piece about that crazy fellow. . . . There's a man who might have gone places if it weren't for his mouth! A bishop doesn't have to get mixed up in all that stuff!"

Monsignor, as Father Eudex knew, meant unions, strikes, race riots—all that stuff.

"A parishioner was saying to me only yesterday it's getting so you can't tell the Catholics from the Communists, with the priests as bad as any. Yes, and this fellow is the worst. He reminds me of that bishop a few years back—at least he called himself a bishop, a Protestant— that was advocating companionate marriages. It's not that bad, maybe, but if you listened to some of them you'd think that Catholicity and capitalism were incompatible!"

"The Holy Father——"

"The Holy Father's in Europe, Father. Mr. Memmers lives in this parish. I'm his priest. What can I tell him?"

"Is it Mr. Memmers of the First National, Monsignor?"

"It is, Father. And there's damned little cheer I can give a man like Memmers. Catholics, priests, and laity alike—yes, and princes of the Church, all talking atheistic communism!"

This was the substance of their conversation, always, the deadly routine in which Father Eudex played straight man. Each time it happened he seemed to participate, and though he should have known better he justified his participation by hoping that it would not happen again, or in quite the same way. But it did, it always did, the same way, and Monsignor, for all his alarums, had nothing to say really and meant one thing only, the thing he never said—that he dearly wanted to be, and was not, a bishop.

Father Eudex could imagine just what kind of bishop Monsignor would be. His reign would be a wise one, excessively so. His mind was made up on everything, excessively so. He would know how to avoid the snares set in the path of the just man, avoid them, too, in good taste and good conscience. He would not be trapped as so many good shepherds before him had been trapped, poor souls—caught in fair-seeming dilemmas of justice that were best left alone, like the first apple. It grieved him, he said, to think of those great hearts broken in silence and solitude. It was the worst kind of exile, alas! But just give him the chance and he would know what to do, what to say, and, more important, what not to do, not to say—neither yea nor nay for him. He had not gone to Rome for nothing. For him the dark forest of decisions would not exist; for him, thanks to hours spent in prayer and meditation, the forest would vanish as dry grass before fire, his fire. He knew the mask of evil already—birth control, indecent movies, salacious books—and would call these things by their right names and dare to deal with them for what they were, these new occasions for the old sins of the cities of the plains.

But in the meantime—oh, to have a particle of the faith that God had in humanity! Dear, trusting God forever trying them beyond their feeble powers, ordering terrible tests, fatal trials by nonsense (the crazy bishop). And keeping Monsignor steadily warming up on the side lines, ready to rush in, primed for the day that would perhaps never dawn.

At one time, so the talk went, there had been reason to think that Monsignor was headed for a bishopric. Now it was too late; Monsignor's intercessors were all dead; the cupboard was bare; he knew it at heart, and it galled him to see another man, this *crazy* man, given the opportunity, and making such a mess of it.

Father Eudex searched for and found a little salt for Monsignor's wound. "The word's going around he'll be the next archbishop," he said.

"I won't believe it," Monsignor countered hoarsely. He glanced at the newspaper on the swing and renewed his horror. "If that fellow's right, Father, I'm"—his voice cracked at the idea—"*wrong!*"

Father Eudex waited until Monsignor had started down the steps to the car before he said, "It could be."

"I'll be back for lunch, Father. I'm taking her for a little spin."

Monsignor stopped in admiration a few feet from the car—her. He was as helpless before her beauty as a boy with a birthday bicycle. He could not leave her alone. He had her out every morning and afternoon and evening. He was indiscriminate about picking people up for a ride in her. He kept her on a special diet—only the best of gas and oil and grease, with daily rubdowns. He would run her only on the smoothest roads and at so many miles an hour. That was to have stopped at the first five hundred, but only now, nearing the thousand mark, was he able to bring himself to increase her speed, and it seemed to hurt him more than it did her.

Now he was walking around behind her to inspect the tires. Apparently O.K. He gave the left rear fender an amorous chuck and eased into the front seat. Then they drove off, the car and he, to see the world, to explore each other further on the honeymoon.

Father Eudex watched the car slide into the traffic, and waited, on edge. The corner cop, fulfilling Father Eudex's fears, blew his whistle and waved his arms up in all four directions, bringing traffic to a standstill. Monsignor pulled expertly out of line and drove down Clover Boulevard in a one-car parade; all others stalled respectfully. The cop, as Monsignor passed, tipped his cap, showing a bald head. Monsignor, in the circumstances, could not acknowledge him, though he knew the man well—a parishioner. He was occupied with keeping his countenance kindly, grim, and exalted, that the cop's faith remain whole, for it was evidently inconceivable to him that Monsignor should ever venture abroad unless to bear the Holy Viaticum, always racing with death.

Father Eudex, eyes baleful but following the progress of the big black car, saw a hand dart out of the driver's window in a wave. Monsignor would combine a lot of business with pleasure that morning, creating what he called "good will for the Church"—all morning in the driver's seat toasting passers-by with a wave that was better than a blessing. How he loved waving to people!

Father Eudex overcame his inclination to sit and stew about things by going down the steps to meet the mailman. He got the usual handful for the Monsignor—advertisements and amazing offers, the unfailing crop of chaff from dealers in church goods, organs, collection schemes, insurance, and sacramental wines. There were two envelopes addressed to Father Eudex, one a mimeographed plea from a missionary society which he might or might not acknowledge with a contribution, depending upon what he thought of the cause—if it was really lost enough to justify a levy on his poverty—and the other a check for a hundred dollars.

The check came in an eggshell envelope with no explanation except a tiny card, "Compliments of the Rival Tractor Company," but even that was needless. All over town clergymen had known for days that the checks were on the way again. Some, rejoicing, could hardly wait. Father Eudex, however, was one of those who could.

With the passing of hard times and the coming of the fruitful war years, the Rival Company, which was a great one for public relations, had found the best solution to the excess-profits problem to be giving. Ministers and even rabbis shared in the annual jack pot, but Rival employees were largely Catholic and it was the checks to the priests that paid off. Again, some thought it was a wonderful idea, and others thought that Rival, plagued by strikes and justly so, had put their alms to work.

There was another eggshell envelope, Father Eudex saw, among the letters for Monsignor, and knew his check would be for two hundred, the premium for pastors.

Father Eudex left Monsignor's mail on the porch table by his cigars. His own he stuck in his back pocket, wanting to forget it, and went down the steps into the yard. Walking back and forth on the shady side of the rectory where the lilies of the valley grew and reading his office, he gradually drifted into the back yard, lured by a noise.

He came upon Whalen, the janitor, pounding pegs into the ground.

Father Eudex closed the breviary on a finger. "What's it all about, Joe?"

Joe Whalen snatched a piece of paper from his shirt and handed it to Father Eudex. "He gave it to me this morning."

He—it was the word for Monsignor among them. A docile pronoun only, and yet when it meant the Monsignor it said, and concealed, nameless things.

The paper was a plan for a garden drawn up by the Monsignor in his fine hand. It called for a huge fleur-de-lis bounded by smaller crosses—and these Maltese—a fountain, a sundial, and a cloister walk running from the rectory to the garage. Later there would be birdhouses and a ten-foot wall of thick gray stones, acting as a moat against the eyes of the world. The whole scheme struck Father Eudex as expensive and, in this country, Presbyterian.

When Monsignor drew the plan, however, he must have been in his medieval mood. A spouting whale jostled with Neptune in the choppy waters of the fountain. North was indicated in the legend by a winged cherub huffing and puffing.

Father Eudex held the plan up against the sun to see the watermark. The stationery was new to him, heavy, simulated parchment, with the Church of the Holy Redeemer and Monsignor's name embossed, three initials, W. F. X., William Francis Xavier. With all those initials the man could pass for a radio station, a chancery wit had observed, or if his last name had not been Sweeney, Father Eudex added now, for high Anglican.

Father Eudex returned the plan to Whalen, feeling sorry for him and to an extent guilty before him—if only because he was a priest like Monsignor (now turned architect) whose dream of a monastery garden included the overworked janitor under the head of "labor."

Father Eudex asked Whalen to bring another shovel. Together, almost without words, they worked all morning spading up crosses, leaving the big fleur-de-lis to the last. Father Eudex removed his coat first, then his collar, and finally was down to his undershirt.

Toward noon Monsignor rolled into the driveway.

He stayed in the car, getting red in the face, recovering from the pleasure of seeing so much accomplished as he slowly recognized his curate in Whalen's helper. In a still, appalled voice he called across the lawn, "Father," and waited as for a beast that might or might not have sense enough to come.

Father Eudex dropped his shovel and went over to the car, shirtless.

Monsignor waited a moment before he spoke, as though annoyed by the everlasting necessity, where this person was concerned, to explain. "Father," he said quietly at last, "I wouldn't do any more of that—if I were you. Rather, in any event, I wouldn't."

"All right, Monsignor."

"To say the least, it's not prudent. If necessary"—he paused as Whalen came over to dig a cross within earshot—"I'll explain later. It's time for lunch now."

The car, black, beautiful, fierce with chromium, was quiet as Monsignor dismounted, knowing her master. Monsignor went around to the rear, felt a tire, and probed a nasty cinder in the tread.

"Look at that," he said, removing the cinder.

Father Eudex thought he saw the car lift a hoof, gaze around, and thank Monsignor with her headlights.

Monsignor proceeded at a precise pace to the back door of the rectory. There he held the screen open momentarily, as if remembering something or reluctant to enter before himself—such was his humility—but then called to Whalen with an intimacy that could never exist between them.

"Better knock off now, Joe."

Whalen turned in on himself. "*Joe*—is it!"

Father Eudex removed his clothes from the grass. His hands were all blisters, but in them he found a little absolution. He apologized to Joe for having to take the afternoon off. "I can't make it, Joe. Something turned up."

"Sure, Father."

Father Eudex could hear Joe telling his wife about it that night —yeah, the young one got in wrong with the old one again. Yeah, the old one, he don't believe in it, work, for them.

Father Eudex paused in the kitchen to remember he knew not what. It was in his head, asking to be let in, but he did not place it until he heard Monsignor in the next room complaining about the salad to the housekeeper. It was the voice of dear, dead Aunt Hazel, coming from the summer he was ten. He translated the past into the present: I can't come out and play this afternoon, Joe, on account of my monsignor won't let me.

In the dining room Father Eudex sat down at the table and said grace. He helped himself to a chop, creamed new potatoes, pickled beets, jelly, and bread. He liked jelly. Monsignor passed the butter.

"That's supposed to be a tutti-frutti salad," Monsignor said, grimacing at his. "But she used green olives."

Father Eudex said nothing.

"I said she used green olives."

"I like green olives all right."

"I like green olives, but *not* in tutti-frutti salad."

Father Eudex replied by eating a green olive, but he knew it could not end there.

"Father," Monsignor said in a new tone. "How would you like to go away and study for a year?"

"Don't think I'd care for it, Monsignor. I'm not the type."

"You're no canonist, you mean?"

"That's one thing."

"Yes. Well, there are other things it might not hurt you to know. To be quite frank with you, Father, I think you need broadening."

"I guess so," Father Eudex said thickly.

"And still, with your tendencies . . . and with the universities honeycombed with Communists. No, that would never do. I think I meant seasoning, not broadening."

"Oh."

"No offense?"

"No offense."

Who would have thought a little thing like an olive could lead to all this, Father Eudex mused—who but himself, that is, for his association with Monsignor had shown him that anything could lead to everything. Monsignor was a master at making points. Nothing had changed since the day Father Eudex walked into the rectory saying he was the new assistant. Monsignor had evaded Father Eudex's hand in greeting, and a few days later, after he began to get the range, he delivered a lecture on the whole subject of handshaking. It was Middle West to shake hands, or South West, or West in any case, and it was not done where he came from, and—why had he ever come from where he came from? Not to be reduced to shaking hands, you could bet! Handshaking was worse than foot washing and unlike that pious practice there was nothing to support it. And from handshaking Monsignor might go into a general discussion of Father Eudex's failings. He used the open forum method, but he was the only speaker and there was never time enough for questions from the audience. Monsignor seized his examples at random from life. He saw Father Eudex coming out of his bedroom in pajama bottoms only and so told him about the dressing gown, its purpose, something of its history. He advised Father Eudex to barber his armpits, for it was being done all over now. He let Father Eudex see his bottle of cologne, "Steeple," special for clergymen, and said he should not be afraid of it. He suggested that Father Eudex shave his face oftener, too. He loaned him his Rogers Peet catalogue, which had sketches of clerical blades togged out in the latest, and prayed that he would stop going around looking like a rabbinical student.

He found Father Eudex reading *The Catholic Worker* one day and had not trusted him since. Father Eudex's conception of the priesthood was evangelical in the worst sense, barbaric, gross, foreign to the mind of the Church, which was one of two terms he used as sticks to beat him with. The other was taste. The air of the rectory was often heavy with The Mind of the Church and Taste.

Another thing. Father Eudex could not conduct a civil conversation. Monsignor doubted that Father Eudex could even think to himself with anything like agreement. Certainly any discussion with Father Eudex ended inevitably in argument or sighing. Sighing! Why didn't people talk up if they had anything to say? No, they'd rather sigh! Father, don't ever, ever sigh at me again!

Finally, Monsignor did not like Father Eudex's table manners. This came to a head one night when Monsignor, seeing his curate's plate empty and all the silverware at his place unused except for a single knife, fork, and spoon, exploded altogether, saying it had been on his mind for weeks, and then descending into the vernacular he declared that Father Eudex did not know the forks—now perhaps he could understand that! Meals, unless Monsignor had guests or other things to struggle with, were always occasions of instruction for father Eudex, and sometimes of chastisement.

And now he knew the worst—if Monsignor was thinking

of recommending him for a year of study, in a Sulpician seminary probably, to learn the forks. So this was what it meant to be a priest. *Come, follow me. Going forth, teach ye all nations. Heal the sick, raise the dead, cleanse the lepers, cast out devils.* Teach the class of people we get here? Teach Mr. Memmers? Teach Communists? Teach Monsignors? And where were the poor? The lepers of old? The lepers were in their colonies with nuns to nurse them. The poor were in their holes and would not come out. Mr. Memmers was in his bank, without cheer. The Communists were in their universities, awaiting a sign. And he was at table with Monsignor, and it was enough for the disciple to be as his master, but the housekeeper had used green olives.

Monsignor inquired, "Did you get your check today?"

Father Eudex, looking up, considered. "I got *a* check," he said.

"From the Rival people, I mean?"

"Yes."

"Good. Well, I think you might apply it on the car you're wanting. A decent car. That's a worthy cause." Monsignor noticed that he was not taking it well. "Not that I mean to dictate what you shall do with your little windfall, Father. It's just that I don't like to see you mortifying yourself with a Model A—and disgracing the Church."

"Yes," Father Eudex said, suffering.

"Yes. I dare say you don't see the danger, just as you didn't a while ago when I found you making a spectacle of yourself with Whalen. You just don't see the danger because you just don't think. Not to dwell on it, but I seem to remember some overshoes."

The overshoes! Monsignor referred to them as to the Fall. Last winter Father Eudex had given his overshoes to a freezing picket. It had got back to Monsignor and—good Lord, a man could have his sympathies, but he had no right clad in the cloth to endanger the prestige of the Church by siding in these wretched squabbles. Monsignor said he hated to think of all the evil done by people doing good! Had Father Eudex ever heard of the Albigensian heresy, or didn't the seminary teach that any more?

Father Eudex declined dessert. It was strawberry mousse.

"Delicious," Monsignor said. "I think I'll let her stay."

At that moment Father Eudex decided that he had nothing to

lose. He placed his knife next to his fork on the plate, adjusted them this way and that until they seemed to work a combination in his mind, to spring a lock which in turn enabled him to speak out.

"Monsignor," he said. "I think I ought to tell you I don't intend to make use of that money. In fact—to show you how my mind works —I have even considered endorsing the check to the strikers' relief fund."

"So," Monsignor said calmly—years in the confessional had prepared him for anything.

"I'll admit I don't know whether I can in justice. And even if I could I don't know that I would. I don't know why . . . I guess hush money, no matter what you do with it, is lousy."

Monsignor regarded him with piercing baby blue eyes. "You'd find it pretty hard to prove, Father, that *any* money *in se* is . . . what you say it is. I would quarrel further with the definition 'hush money.' It seems to me nothing if not rash that you would presume to impugn the motive of the Rival company in sending out these checks. You would seem to challenge the whole concept of good works—not that I am ignorant of the misuses to which money can be put." Monsignor, changing tack, tucked it all into a sigh. "Perhaps I'm just a simple soul, and it's enough for me to know personally some of the people in the Rival company and to know them good people. Many of them Catholic. . . ." A throb had crept into Monsignor's voice. He shut it off.

"I don't mean anything that subtle, Monsignor," Father Eudex said. "I'm just telling you, as my pastor, what I'm going to do with the check. Or what I'm not going to do with it. I don't know what I'm going to do with it. Maybe send it back."

Monsignor rose from the table, slightly smiling. "Very well, Father. But there's always the poor."

Monsignor took leave of Father Eudex with a laugh. Father Eudex felt it was supposed to fool him into thinking that nothing he had said would be used against him. It showed, rather, that Monsignor was not winded, that he had broken wild curates before, plenty of them, and that he would ride again.

Father Eudex sought the shade of the porch. He tried to read his office, but was drowsy. He got up for a glass of water. The saints in Ireland used to stand up to their necks in cold water, but not for drowsiness. When he came back to the porch a woman was ringing the doorbell. She looked like a customer for rosary beads.

"Hello," he said.

"I'm Mrs. Klein, Father, and I was wondering if you could help me out."

Father Eudex straightened a porch chair for her. "Please sit down."

"It's a German name, Father. Klein was German descent," she said, and added with a silly grin, "It ain't what you think, Father."

"I beg your pardon."

"Klein. Some think it's a Jew name. But they stole it from Klein."

Father Eudex decided to come back to that later. "You were wondering if I could help you?"

"Yes, Father. It's personal."

"Is it matter for confession?"

"Oh no, Father." He had made her blush.

"Then go ahead."

Mrs. Klein peered into the honeysuckle vines on either side of the porch for alien ears.

"No one can hear you, Mrs. Klein."

"Father—I'm just a poor widow," she said, and continued as though Father Eudex had just slandered the man. "Klein was awful good to me, Father."

"I'm sure he was."

"So good . . . and he went and left me all he had." She had begun to cry a little.

Father Eudex nodded gently. She was after something, probably not money, always the best bet—either that or a drunk in the family —but this one was not Irish. Perhaps just sympathy.

"I come to get your advice, Father. Klein always said, 'If you got a problem, Freda, see the priest.' "

"Do you need money?"

"I got more than I can use from the bakery."

"You have a bakery?"

Mrs. Klein nodded down the street. "That's my bakery. It was Klein's. The Purity."

"I go by there all the time," Father Eudex said, abandoning himself to her. He must stop trying to shape the conversation and let her work it out.

"Will you give me your advice, Father?" He felt that she sensed his indifference and interpreted it as his way of rejecting her. She either had no idea how little sense she made or else supreme faith in him, as a priest, to see into her heart.

"Just what is it you're after, Mrs. Klein?"

"He left me all he had, Father, but it's just laying in the bank."

"And you want me to tell you what to do with it?"

"Yes, Father."

Father Eudex thought this might be interesting, certainly a change. He went back in his mind to the seminary and the class in which they had considered the problem of inheritances. Do we have any unfulfilled obligations? Are we sure? . . . Are there any impedimenta? . . .

"Do you have any dependents, Mrs. Klein—any children?"

"One boy, Father. I got him running the bakery. I pay him good —too much, Father."

"Is 'too much' a living wage?"

"Yes, Father. He ain't got a family."

"A living wage is not too much," Father Eudex handed down, sailing into the encyclical style without knowing it.

Mrs. Klein was smiling over having done something good without knowing precisely what it was.

"How old is your son?"

"He's thirty-six, Father."

"Not married?"

"No, Father, but he's got him a girl." She giggled, and Father Eudex, embarrassed, retied his shoe.

"But you don't care to make a will and leave this money to your son in the usual way?"

"I guess I'll have to . . . if I die." Mrs. Klein was suddenly crushed and haunted, but whether by death or charity, Father Eudex did not know.

"You don't have to, Mrs. Klein. There are many worthy causes. And the worthiest is the cause of the poor. My advice to you, if I understand your problem, is to give what you have to someone who needs it."

Mrs. Klein just stared at him.

"You could even leave it to the archdiocese," he said, completing the sentence to himself: but I don't recommend it in your case . . . with your tendencies. You look like an Indian giver to me.

But Mrs. Klein had got enough. "Huh!" she said, rising. "Well! You *are* a funny one!"

And then Father Eudex realized that she had come to him for a broker's tip. It was in the eyes. The hat. The dress. The shoes. "If you'd like to speak to the pastor," he said, "come back in the evening."

"You're a nice young man," Mrs. Klein said, rather bitter now and bent on getting away from him. "But I got to say this—you ain't much of a priest. And Klein said if I got a problem, see the priest— huh! You ain't much of a priest! What time's your boss come in?"

"In the evening," Father Eudex said. "Come any time in the evening."

Mrs. Klein was already down the steps and making for the street.

"You might try Mr. Memmers at the First National," Father Eudex called, actually trying to help her, but she must have thought it was just some more of his nonsense and did not reply.

After Mrs. Klein had disappeared Father Eudex went to his room. In the hallway upstairs Monsignor's voice, coming from the depths of the clerical nap, halted him.

"Who was it?"

"A woman," Father Eudex said. "A woman seeking good counsel."

He waited a moment to be questioned, but Monsignor was not awake enough to see anything wrong with that, and there came only a sigh and a shifting of weight that told Father Eudex he was simply turning over in bed.

Father Eudex walked into the bathroom. He took the Rival check from his pocket. He tore it into little squares. He let them flutter into the toilet. He pulled the chain—hard.

He went to his room and stood looking out the window at nothing. He could hear the others already giving an account of their stewardship, but could not judge them. I bought baseball uniforms for the school. I bought the nuns a new washing machine. I purchased a Mass kit for a Chinese missionary. I bought a set of matched irons. Mine helped pay for keeping my mother in a rest home upstate. I gave mine to the poor.

And you, Father?

QUESTIONS

1. In this story about two Catholic priests, one of them is presented in an unsympathetic light. Does the author intend the story to be a criticism of priests in general and of the Catholic Church at large? That is, which of the two priests does the author make representative of the Church?

2. Why, since the story seems to belong to Father Eudex, is most of the description of Monsignor?

3. The characterization of the two priests is accomplished through a series of contrasts, a piling up of examples, each further widening the breach between the two. Can the examples be grouped into fairly large subjects upon which the two disagree, such as their sense of values, their social beliefs, their guiding motives?

4. Point out some of the metaphors from the sports world that are used in connection with Monsignor. In choosing them, is the author suggesting anything about Monsignor's character?

5. What are the two conflicts—one between characters and the other within the mind of a character?

6. After Father Eudex has helped Joe in the garden, his "hands were all blisters, but in them he found a little absolution." Absolution for what?

7. What is the meaning of the sentence "He translated the past into the present: I can't come out and play this afternoon, Joe, on account of my monsignor won't let me"?

8. The paragraph beginning on p. 249 "And now he knew the worst . . . ." brings out the conflict in the mind of Father Eudex between the life according to Biblical commands (in italics) that he had thought he would be able to follow as a priest, and the actual situation in which he finds himself under Monsignor. With what expression does he sum up his disillusionment?

9. In what instances does Father Eudex assert himself, thus foreshadowing the final outcome of the story?

10. How does the scene with Mrs. Klein add to the disillusionment of Father Eudex?

11. Why does Father Eudex say "A woman seeking good counsel" rather than "A woman asking for good advice"?

12. What symbolism is found in the names—Father Eudex, Mrs. Klein, the Purity, the Rival company? Looking up the roots *eu* and *dex* will suggest the meaning of Eudex.

13. Might the story have been called "Green Olives" just as well as "The Forks"?

14. Why does Father Eudex finally destroy the check instead of sending it to the striker's relief fund, giving it to the poor, or sending it back?

15. Has either of the two priests grown or gained a new insight by the end of the story?

16. When Father Eudex is thinking of how the others will use their checks, is he doubting whether he did the right thing?

17. What theme is brought out by the resolution of the conflict?

18. The story happens to be about two priests. Could it have been about two individuals in some other field as well?

19. Do you agree with the stand taken by Father Eudex? What similar problems about "tainted" money face individuals and institutions today?

 QUESTION OF VALUES

THE OTHER SIDE OF THE HEDGE

E. M. FORSTER

My pedometer told me that I was twenty-five; and, though it is a shocking thing to stop walking, I was so tired that I sat down on a milestone to rest. People outstripped me, jeering as they did so, but I was too apathetic to feel resentful, and even when Miss Eliza Dimbleby, the great educationist, swept past, exhorting me to persevere, I only smiled and raised my hat.

At first I thought I was going to be like my brother, whom I had had to leave by the roadside a year or two round the corner. He had wasted his breath on singing, and his strength on helping others. But I had travelled more wisely, and now it was only the monotony of the highway that oppressed me—dust under foot and brown crackling hedges on either side, ever since I could remember.

And I had already dropped several things—indeed, the road behind was strewn with the things we all had dropped; and the white dust was settling down on them, so that already they looked no better than stones. My muscles were so weary that I could not even bear the weight of those things I still carried. I slid off the milestone into the road, and lay there prostrate, with my face to the great parched hedge, praying that I might give up.

A little puff of air revived me. It seemed to come from the hedge; and, when I opened my eyes, there was a glint of light through the tangle of boughs and dead leaves. The hedge could not be as thick as usual. In my weak, morbid state, I longed to force my way in, and see what was on the other side. No one was in sight, or I should not have dared to try. For we of the road do not admit in conversation that there is another side at all.

I yielded to the temptation, saying to myself that I would come back in a minute. The thorns scratched my face, and I had to use my arms as a shield, depending on my feet alone to push me forward.

Halfway through I would have gone back, for in the passage all the things I was carrying were scraped off me, and my clothes were torn. But I was so wedged that return was impossible, and I had to wriggle blindly forward, expecting every moment that my strength would fail me, and that I should perish in the undergrowth.

Suddenly cold water closed round my head, and I seemed sinking down for ever. I had fallen out of the hedge into a deep pool. I rose to the surface at last, crying for help, and I heard someone on the opposite bank laugh and say: "Another!" And then I was twitched out and laid panting on the dry ground.

Even when the water was out of my eyes, I was still dazed, for I had never been in so large a space, nor seen such grass and sunshine. The blue sky was no longer a strip, and beneath it the earth had risen grandly into hills—clean, bare buttresses, with beech trees in their folds, and meadows and clear pools at their feet. But the hills were not high, and there was in the landscape a sense of human occupation—so that one might have called it a park, or garden, if the words did not imply a certain triviality and constraint.

As soon as I got my breath, I turned to my rescuer and said: "Where does this place lead to?"

"Nowhere, thank the Lord!" said he, and laughed. He was a man of fifty or sixty—just the kind of age we mistrust on the road—but there was no anxiety in his manner, and his voice was that of a boy of eighteen.

"But it must lead somewhere!" I cried, too much surprised at his answer to thank him for saving my life.

"He wants to know where it leads!" he shouted to some men on the hill side, and they laughed back, and waved their caps.

I noticed then that the pool into which I had fallen was really a moat which bent round to the left and to the right, and that the hedge followed it continually. The hedge was green on this side—its roots showed through the clear water, and fish swam about in them—and it was wreathed over with dog-roses and Traveller's Joy. But it was a barrier, and in a moment I lost all pleasure in the grass, the sky, the trees, the happy men and women, and realized that the place was but a prison, for all its beauty and extent.

We moved away from the boundary, and then followed a path

almost parallel to it, across the meadows. I found it difficult walking, for I was always trying to out-distance my companion, and there was no advantage in doing this if the place led nowhere. I had never kept step with anyone since I left my brother.

I amused him by stopping suddenly and saying disconsolately, "This is perfectly terrible. One cannot advance: one cannot progress. Now we of the road——"

"Yes. I know."

"I was going to say, we advance continually."

"I know."

"We are always learning, expanding, developing. Why, even in my short life I have seen a great deal of advance—the Transvaal War, the Fiscal Question, Christian Science, Radium. Here for example——"

I took out my pedometer, but it still marked twenty-five, not a degree more.

"Oh, it's stopped! I meant to show you. It should have registered all the time I was walking with you. But it makes me only twenty-five."

"Many things don't work in here," he said. "One day a man brought in a Lee-Metford, and that wouldn't work."

"The laws of science are universal in their application. It must be the water in the moat that has injured the machinery. In normal conditions everything works. Science and the spirit of emulation—those are the forces that have made us what we are."

I had to break off and acknowledge the pleasant greetings of people whom we passed. Some of them were singing, some talking, some engaged in gardening, hay-making, or other rudimentary industries. They all seemed happy; and I might have been happy too, if I could have forgotten that the place led nowhere.

I was startled by a young man who came sprinting across our path, took a little fence in fine style, and went tearing over a ploughed field till he plunged into a lake, across which he began to swim. Here was true energy, and I exclaimed: "A cross-country race! Where are the others?"

"There are no others," my companion replied; and, later on, when we passed some long grass from which came the voice of a girl singing exquisitely to herself, he said again: "There are no others." I was bewildered at the waste in production, and murmured to myself, "What does it all mean?"

He said: "It means nothing but itself"—and he repeated the words slowly, as if I were a child.

"I understand," I said quietly, "but I do not agree. Every achievement is worthless unless it is a link in the chain of development. And I must not trespass on your kindness any longer. I must get back somehow to the road, and have my pedometer mended."

"First, you must see the gates," he replied, "for we have gates, though we never use them."

I yielded politely, and before long we reached the moat again, at a point where it was spanned by a bridge. Over the bridge was a big gate, as white as ivory, which was fitted into a gap in the boundary hedge. The gate opened outwards, and I exclaimed in amazement, for from it ran a road—just such a road as I had left—dusty under foot, with brown crackling hedges on either side as far as the eye could reach.

"That's my road!" I cried.

He shut the gate and said: "But not your part of the road. It is through this gate that humanity went out countless ages ago, when it was first seized with the desire to walk."

I denied this, observing that the part of the road I myself had left was not more than two miles off. But with the obstinacy of his years he repeated: "It is the same road. This is the beginning, and though it seems to run straight away from us, it doubles so often, that it is never far from our boundary and sometimes touches it." He stooped down by the moat, and traced on its moist margin an absurd figure like a maze. As we walked back through the meadows, I tried to convince him of his mistake.

"The road sometimes doubles, to be sure, but that is part of our discipline. Who can doubt that its general tendency is onward? To what goal we know not—it may be to some mountain where we shall touch the sky, it may be over precipices into the sea. But that it goes forward—who can doubt that? It is the thought of that that makes us strive to excel, each in his own way, and gives us an impetus which is lacking with you. Now that man who passed us—it's true that he ran well, and jumped well, and swam well; but we have men who can run better, and men who can jump better, and who can swim better. Specialization has produced results which would surprise you. Similarly, that girl——"

Here I interrupted myself to exclaim: "Good gracious me! I could have sworn it was Miss Eliza Dimbleby over there, with her feet in the fountain!"

He believed that it was.

"Impossible! I left her on the road, and she is due to lecture this evening at Tunbridge Wells. Why, her train leaves Cannon Street in—of course my watch has stopped like everything else. She is the last person to be here."

"People always are astonished at meeting each other. All kinds come through the hedge, and come at all times—when they are drawing ahead in the race, when they are lagging behind, when they are left for dead. I often stand near the boundary listening to the sounds of the road—you know what they are—and wonder if anyone will turn aside. It is my great happiness to help someone out of the moat, as I helped you. For our country fills up slowly, though it was meant for all mankind."

"Mankind have other aims," I said gently, for I thought him well-meaning; "and I must join them." I bade him good evening, for the sun was declining, and I wished to be on the road by nightfall. To my alarm, he caught hold of me, crying: "You are not to go yet!" I tried to shake him off, for we had no interests in common, and his civility was becoming irksome to me. But for all my struggles the tiresome old man would not let go; and, as wrestling is not my speciality, I was obliged to follow him.

It was true that I could have never found alone the place where I came in, and I hoped that, when I had seen the other sights about which he was worrying, he would take me back to it. But I was determined not to sleep in the country, for I mistrusted it, and the people too, for all their friendliness. Hungry though I was, I would not join them in their evening meals of milk and fruit, and, when they gave me flowers, I flung them away as soon as I could do so unobserved. Already they were lying down for the night like cattle—some out on the bare hillside, others in groups under the beeches. In the light of an orange sunset I hurried on with my unwelcome guide, dead tired, faint for want of food, but murmuring indomitably: "Give me life, with its struggles and victories, with its failures and hatreds, with its deep moral meaning and its unknown goal!"

At last we came to a place where the encircling moat was spanned by another bridge, and where another gate interrupted the line of the boundary hedge. It was different from the first gate; for it was half transparent like horn, and opened inwards. But through it, in the waning light, I saw again just such a road as I had left—monotonous, dusty, with brown crackling hedges on either side, as far as the eye could reach.

I was strangely disquieted at the sight, which seemed to deprive me of all self-control. A man was passing us, returning for the night to the hills, with a scythe over his shoulder and a can of some liquid in his hand. I forgot the destiny of our race. I forgot the road that lay before my eyes, and I sprang at him, wrenched the can out of his hand, and began to drink.

It was nothing stronger than beer, but in my exhausted state it overcame me in a moment. As in a dream, I saw the old man shut the gate, and heard him say: "This is where your road ends, and through this gate humanity—all that is left of it—will come in to us."

Though my senses were sinking into oblivion, they seemed to expand ere they reached it. They perceived the magic song of nightingales, and the odour of invisible hay, and stars piercing the fading sky. The man whose beer I had stolen lowered me down gently to sleep off its effects, and, as he did so, I saw that he was my brother.

QUESTIONS

E. M. Forster made long visits to India in 1912 and again in 1921 and was impressed with the calm, contemplative life he found there in contrast to the hurried, struggling life he was used to in England. This fact may throw some light on the meaning of this story.

1. What effect is achieved by mixing *time* and *place* words as in "My pedometer told me that I was twenty-five" and "a year or two round the corner"?

2. After the traveler goes through the hedge he says, ". . . I had never been in so large a space, nor seen such grass and sunshine." Might this indicate that he is getting a different view of life, one not so narrow as the one he has been used to?

3. Why does the rescuer, a man of fifty or sixty, have the voice of a boy of eighteen?

4. The first thing the traveler wants to know about the other side of the hedge is where it leads. What does this indicate about his previous life on the road?

5. Why does he find it hard to walk with his rescuer?

6. What is a pedometer, and why has it stopped registering?

7. Compare life on the road and life on the other side of the hedge as to view, beauty, leisure, purpose, brotherhood, competition, pace, sense of duty. Why does the traveler find it impossible to be happy on the other side of the hedge?

8. What does walking symbolize? When was humanity first seized with the desire to walk?

9. What is a maze (p. 262), and why is the old man unable to convince the traveler that his road is a maze which does not really lead anywhere?

10. When the traveler finds Miss Eliza Dimbleby on the other side of the hedge with her feet in the fountain, why does he say, "She is the last person to be here"?

11. What is the meaning of the lines "People always are astonished at meeting each other. All kinds come through the hedge, and come at all times—when they are drawing ahead in the race, when they are lagging behind, when they are left for dead"?

12. Explain the line "For our country fills up slowly, though it was meant for all mankind."

13. Why does the traveler refuse to eat the meal of milk and fruit, and why does he throw away the flowers that were given him?

14. How do the two gates differ, and what does the old man say about each?

15. In describing the gates, Forster is alluding to a story in Homer's *Odyssey* in which Penelope tells about two gates through which dreams come. She says the dreams that come through the ivory gate cheat the dreamer with promises that will never be fulfilled, but those that come through the gate of horn tell the dreamer what will

really happen. How does this allusion clarify the meaning of the two gates in this story?

16. Why is the traveler "strangely disquieted" when he sees his road again?

17. Why does he wrench the can of beer out of the man's hand when he could have had it for the asking?

18. How might the following sentence be interpreted: "This is where your road ends, and through this gate humanity—all that is left of it—will come in to us"? Remembering the kind of life that most elderly people lead may give a clue.

19. Are there two meanings for the statement in the last paragraph "I saw that he was my brother"?

20. Point out some of the symbols and give their meanings.

21. What is the conflict and how is it resolved?

22. Forster once wrote: "There seems to be something else in life besides time, something which may conveniently be called 'value,' something which is measured not by minutes or hours, but by intensity." And again he said, "Tolerance, good temper, and sympathy—well, they are what matter really, and if the human race is not to collapse they must come to the front before long." Do these statements help clarify the meaning of the story?

23. What is the theme?

24. Do you agree with Forster? What may be said for the opposite view?

THE HEYDAY OF THE BLOOD
DOROTHY CANFIELD FISHER

The older professor looked up at the assistant, fumbling fretfully with a pile of papers. "Farrar, what's the *matter* with you lately?" he said sharply.

The younger man started, "Why . . . why . . ." the brusqueness of the other's manner shocked him suddenly into confession. "I've lost my nerve, Professor Mallory, that's what the matter with me. I'm frightened to death," he said melodramatically.

"What *of?*" asked Mallory, with a little challenge in his tone.

The flood-gates were open. The younger man burst out in exclamations, waving his thin, nervous, knotted fingers, his face twitching as he spoke. "Of myself . . . no, not myself, but my body! I'm not well . . . I'm getting worse all the time. The doctors don't make out what is the matter . . . I don't sleep . . . I worry . . . I forget things, I take no interest in life . . . the doctors intimate a nervous breakdown ahead of me . . . and yet I rest . . . I rest . . . more than I can afford to! I never go out. Every evening I'm in bed by nine o'clock. I take no part in college life beyond my work, for fear of the nervous strain. I've refused to take charge of that summer-school in New York, you know, that would be such an opportunity for me . . . if I could only sleep! But though I never do anything exciting in the evening . . . heavens! what nights I have. Black hours of seeing myself in a sanitarium, dependent on my brother! I never . . . why, I'm in hell . . . that's what the matter with me, a perfect hell of ignoble terror!"

He sat silent, his drawn face turned to the window. The older man looked at him speculatively. When he spoke it was with a cheerful, casual quality in his voice which made the other look up at him surprised.

"You don't suppose those great friends of yours, the nerve

specialists, would object to my telling you a story, do you? It's very quiet and unexciting. You're not too busy?"

"Busy! I've forgotten the meaning of the word! I don't dare to be!"

"Very well, then; I mean to carry you back to the stony little farm in the Green Mountains, where I had the extreme good luck to be born and raised. You've heard me speak of Hillsboro; and the story is all about my great-grandfather, who came to live with us when I was a little boy."

"Your great-grandfather?" said the other incredulously. "People don't remember their great-grandfathers!"

"Oh, yes, they do, in Vermont. There was my father on one farm, and my grandfather on another, without a thought that he was no longer young, and there was 'gran'ther' as we called him, eighty-eight years old and just persuaded to settle back, let his descendants take care of him, and consent to be an old man. He had been in the War of 1812—think of that, you mushroom!—and had lost an arm and a good deal of his health there. He had lately begun to get a pension of twelve dollars a month, so that for an old man he was quite independent financially, as poor Vermont farmers look at things; and he was a most extraordinary character, so that his arrival in our family was quite an event.

"He took precedence at once of the oldest man in the township, who was only eighty-four and not very bright. I can remember bragging at school about Gran'ther Pendleton, who'd be eighty-nine come next Woodchuck day, and could see to read without glasses. He had been ailing all his life, ever since the fever he took in the war. He used to remark triumphantly that he had now outlived six doctors who had each given him but a year to live; 'and the seventh is going downhill fast, so I hear!' This last was his never-failing answer to the attempts of my conscientious mother and anxious, dutiful father to check the old man's reckless indifference to any of the rules of hygiene.

"They were good disciplinarians with their children, and this naughty old man, who would give his weak stomach frightful attacks of indigestion by stealing out to the pantry and devouring a whole mince pie because he had been refused two pieces at the table—this rebellious, unreasonable, whimsical old madcap was an electric element in our quiet, orderly life. He insisted on going to every picnic and church sociable, where he ate recklessly of all the indigestible dainties he could lay his hands on, stood in drafts, tired himself to the verge of fainting away by playing games with the children, and returned home, exhausted, animated, and quite ready to pay the price of a day in bed, groaning and screaming out with pain as heartily and unaffectedly as he had laughed with the pretty girls the evening before.

"The climax came, however, in the middle of August, when he announced his desire to go to the county fair, held some fourteen miles down the valley from our farm. Father never dared let gran'ther go anywhere without himself accompanying the old man, but he was perfectly sincere in saying that it was not because he could not spare a day from the haying that he refused pointblank to consider it. The doctor who had been taking care of gran'ther since he came to live with us said that it would be crazy to think of such a thing. He added that the wonder was that gran'ther lived at all, for his heart was all wrong, his asthma was enough to kill a young man, and he had no digestion; in short, if father wished to kill his old grandfather, there was no surer way than to drive fourteen miles in the heat of August to the noisy excitement of a county fair.

"So father for once said 'No,' in the tone that we children had come to recognize as final. Gran'ther grimly tied a knot in his empty sleeve—a curious, enigmatic mode of his to express strong emotion —put his one hand on his cane, and his chin on his hand, and withdrew himself into that incalculable distance from the life about him where very old people spend so many hours.

"He did not emerge from this until one morning toward the middle of fair-week, when all the rest of the family were away—father and the bigger boys on the far-off upland meadows haying, and mother and the girls off blackberrying. I was too little to be of any help, so I had been left to wait on gran'ther, and to set out our lunch of bread and milk and huckleberries. We had not been alone half an hour when gran'ther sent me to extract, from under the mattress of his bed, the wallet in which he kept his pension money. There was six dollars and forty-three cents—he counted it over carefully, sticking out his tongue like a schoolboy doing a sum, and when he had finished he began to laugh and snap his fingers and sing out in his high, cracked old voice:

" 'We're goin' to go a skylarkin'! Little Jo Mallory is going to the county fair with his Gran'ther Pendleton, an' he's goin' to have more fun than ever was in the world, and he——'

" 'But, gran'ther, father said we mustn't!' I protested, horrified.

" 'But I say we *shall!* I was your gre't-gran'ther long before he was your feyther, and anyway I'm here and he's not—so, *march!* Out to the barn!'

"He took me by the collar, and, executing a shuffling fandango of triumph, he pushed me ahead of him to the stable, where old white Peggy, the only horse left at home, looked at us amazed.

" 'But it'll be twenty-eight miles, and Peg's never driven over eight!' I cried, my old-established world of rules and orders reeling before my eyes.

> " 'Eight—and—twenty-eight!
> But I—am—*eighty*-eight!'

"Gran'ther improvised a sort of whooping chant of scorn as he pulled the harness from the peg. 'It'll do her good to drink some pink lemonade—old Peggy! An' if she gits tired comin' home, I'll git out and carry her part way myself!'

"His adventurous spirit was irresistible. I made no further objection, and we hitched up together, I standing on a chair to fix the check-rein, and gran'ther doing wonders with his one hand. Then, just as we were—gran'ther in a hickory shirt, and with an old hat flapping over his wizened face, I bare-legged, in ragged old clothes—so we drove out of the grassy yard, down the steep, stony hill that led to the main valley road, and along the hot, white turnpike, deep with the dust which had been stirred up by the teams on their way to the fair. Gran'ther sniffed the air jubilantly, and exchanged hilarious greetings with the people who constantly overtook old Peg's jogging trot. Between times he regaled me with spicy stories of the hundreds of thousands—they seemed no less numerous to me then— of county fairs he had attended in his youth. He was horrified to find that I had never been even to one.

" 'Why, Joey, how old be ye? 'Most eight, ain't it? When I was your age I had run away and been to two fairs an' a hangin'.'

" 'But didn't they lick you when you got home?' I asked shudderingly.

" 'You *bet* they did!' cried gran'ther with gusto.

"I felt the world changing into an infinitely larger place with every word he said.

" 'Now, this is somethin' *like!*' he exclaimed, as we drew near to Granville and fell into a procession of wagons all filled with country people in their best clothes, who looked with friendly curiosity at the little, shriveled cripple, his face shining with perspiring animation, and at the little boy beside him, his bare feet dangling high above the floor of the battered buckboard, overcome with the responsibility of driving a horse for the first time in his life, and filled with such a flood of new emotions and ideas that he must have been quite pale."

Professor Mallory leaned back and laughed aloud at the vision he had been evoking—laughed with so joyous a relish in his reminiscences that the drawn, impatient face of his listener relaxed a little. He drew a long breath, he even smiled a little absently.

"Oh, that was a day!" went on the professor, still laughing and wiping his eyes. "Never will I have such another! At the entrance to the grounds gran'ther stopped me while he solemnly untied the knot in his empty sleeve. I don't know what kind of hairbrained vow he had tied up in it, but with the little ceremony disappeared every trace of restraint, and we plunged head over ears into the saturnalia of delights that was an old-time county fair.

"People had little cash in those days, and gran'ther's six dollars and forty-three cents lasted like the widow's cruse of oil. We went to see the fat lady, who, if she was really as big as she looked to me then, must have weighed at least a ton. My admiration for gran'ther's daredevil qualities rose to infinity when he entered into free-and-easy talk with her, about how much she ate, and could she raise her arms enough to do up her own hair, and how many yards of velvet it took to make her gorgeous, gold-trimmed robe. She laughed a great deal at us, but she was evidently touched by his human interest, for she confided to him that it was not velvet at all, but furniture covering; and when we went away she pressed on us a bag of peanuts. She said she had more peanuts than she could eat—a state of unbridled opulence which fitted in for me with all the other superlatives of that day.

"We saw the dog-faced boy, whom we did not like at all; gran'-ther expressing, with a candidly outspoken cynicism, his belief that 'them whiskers was glued to him.' We wandered about the stock exhibit, gazing at the monstrous oxen, and hanging over the railings where the prize pigs lived to scratch their backs. In order to miss nothing, we even conscientiously passed through the Woman's Building, where we were very much bored by the serried ranks of preserve jars.

" 'Sufferin' Hezekiah!' cried gran'ther irritably. 'Who cares how gooseberry jel *looks*. If they'd give a felly a taste, now——'

"This reminded him that we were hungry, and we went to a restaurant under a tent, where, after taking stock of the wealth that yet remained of gran'ther's hoard, he ordered the most expensive things on the bill of fare."

Professor Mallory suddenly laughed out again. "Perhaps in heaven, but certainly not until then, shall I ever taste anything so ambrosial as that fried chicken and coffee ice-cream! I have not lived in vain that I have such a memory back of me!"

This time the younger man laughed with the narrator, settling back in his chair as the professor went on:

"After lunch we rode on the merry-go-round, both of us, gran'-ther clinging desperately with his one hand to his red camel's wooden hump, and crying out shrilly to me to be sure and not lose his cane. The merry-go-round had just come in at that time, and gran'ther had never experienced it before. After the first giddy flight we retired to a lemonade-stand to exchange impressions, and finding that we both alike had fallen completely under the spell of the new sensation, gran'-ther said that we 'sh'd keep on a-ridin' till we'd had enough! King Solomon couldn't tell when we'd ever git a chance again!' So we returned to the charge, and rode and rode and rode, through blinding clouds of happy excitement, so it seems to me now, such as I was never to know again. The sweat was pouring off from us, and we had tried all the different animals on the machine before we could tear ourselves away to follow the crowd to the race-track.

"We took reserved seats, which cost a quarter apiece, instead of the unshaded ten-cent benches, and gran'ther began at once to pour out to me a flood of horse-talk and knowing race-track aphorisms, which finally made a young fellow sitting next to us laugh superciliously. Gran'ther turned on him heatedly.

" 'I bet-che fifty cents I pick the winner in the next race!' he said sportily.

" 'Done!' said the other, still laughing.

"Gran'ther picked a big black mare, who came in almost last, but he did not flinch. As he paid over the half-dollar he said: 'Everybody's likely to make mistakes about *some* things; King Solomon was a fool in the head about women-folks! I bet-che a dollar I pick the winner in *this* race!' and 'Done!' said the disagreeable young man, still laughing. I gasped, for I knew we had only eighty-seven cents left, but gran'ther shot me a command to silence out of the corner of his eyes, and announced that he bet on the sorrel gelding.

"If I live to be a hundred and break the bank at Monte Carlo three times a week," said Mallory, shaking his head reminiscently, "I could not know a tenth part of the frantic excitement of that race or of the mad triumph when our horse won. Gran'ther cast his hat upon the ground, screaming like a steam-calliope with exultation as the sorrel swept past the judges' stand ahead of all the others, and I jumped up and down in an agony of delight which was almost more than my little body could hold.

"After that we went away, feeling that the world could hold nothing more glorious. It was five o'clock, and we decided to start back. We paid for Peggy's dinner out of the dollar we had won on the race—I say 'we,' for by that time we were welded into one organism —and we still had a dollar and a quarter left. 'While ye're about it, always go the whole hog!' said gran'ther, and we spent twenty minutes in laying out that money in trinkets for all the folks at home. Then, dusty, penniless, laden with bundles, we bestowed our exhausted bodies and our uplifted hearts in the old buckboard, and turned Peg's head toward the mountains. We did not talk much during that drive, and though I thought at the time only of the carnival of joy we had left, I can now recall every detail of the trip—how the sun sank behind Indian Mountain, a peak I had known before only through distant views; then, as we journeyed on, how the stars came out above Hemlock Mountain—our own home mountain behind our house, and later, how the fireflies filled the darkening meadows along the river below us, so that we seemed to be floating between the steady stars of heaven and their dancing, twinkling reflection in the valley.

"Gran'ther's dauntless spirit still surrounded me. I put out of mind doubts of our reception at home, and lost myself in delightful ruminatings on the splendors of the day. At first, every once in a while, gran'ther made a brief remark, such as, ' 'Twas the hind-quarters of the sorrel I bet on. He was the only one in the hull kit and bilin' of 'em that his quarters didn't fall away'; or, 'You needn't tell *me* that them Siamese twins ain't unpinned every night as separate as you and me!' But later on, as the damp evening air began to bring on his asthma, he subsided into silence, only broken by great gasping coughs.

"These were heard by the anxious, heart-sick watchers at home, and, as old Peg stumbled wearily up the hill, father came running down to meet us. 'Where you be'n?' he demanded, his face pale and stern in the light of his lantern. 'We be'n to the county fair!' croaked gran'ther with a last flare of triumph, and fell over sideways against me. Old Peg stopped short, hanging her head as if she, too, were at the limit of her strength. I was frightfully tired myself, and frozen with terror of what father would say. Gran'ther's collapse was the last straw. I began to cry loudly, but father ignored my distress with an indifference which cut me to the heart. He lifted gran'ther out of the buckboard, carrying the unconscious little old body into the house without a glance backward at me. But when I crawled down to the ground, sobbing and digging my fists into my eyes, I felt mother's arms close around me.

" 'Oh, poor, naughty little Joey!' she said. 'Mother's bad, dear little boy!' "

Professor Mallory stopped short.

"Perhaps that's something else I'll know again in heaven," he said soberly, and waited a moment before he went on: "Well, that was the end of our day. I was so worn out that I fell asleep over my supper, in spite of the excitement in the house about sending for a doctor for gran'ther, who was, so one of my awe-struck sisters told me, having some kind of 'fits.' Mother must have put me to bed, for the next thing I remember, she was shaking me by the shoulder and saying, 'Wake up, Joey. Your great-grandfather wants to speak to you.

He's been suffering terribly all night, and the doctor think's he's dying.'

"I followed her into gran'ther's room, where the family was assembled about the bed. Gran'ther lay drawn up in a ball, groaning so dreadfully that I felt a chill like cold water at the roots of my hair; but a moment or two after I came in, all at once he gave a great sigh and relaxed, stretching out his legs and laying his arms down on the coverlid. He looked at me and attempted a smile.

"'Well, it was wuth it, warn't it, Joey?' he said gallantly, and closed his eyes peacefully to sleep."

"Did he die?" asked the younger professor, leaning forward eagerly.

"Die? Gran'ther Pendleton? Not much! He came tottering down to breakfast the next morning, as white as an old ghost, with no voice left, his legs trembling under him, but he kept the whole family an hour and a half at the table, telling them in a loud whisper all about the fair, until father said really he would have to take us to the one next year. Afterward he sat out on the porch watching old Peg graze around the yard. I thought he was in one of his absent-minded fits, but when I came out, he called me to him, and, setting his lips to my ear, he whispered:

"'An' the seventh is a-goin' down-hill fast, so I hear!' He chuckled to himself over this for some time, wagging his head feebly, and then he said: 'I tell ye, Joey, I've lived a long time, and I've larned a lot about the way folks is made. The trouble with most of 'em is, they're 'fraid-cats! As Jeroboam Warner used to say—he was in the same rigiment with me in 1812—the only way to manage this business of livin' is to give a whoop and let her rip! If ye just about half-live, ye just the same as half-die; and if ye spend yer time half-dyin', some day ye turn in and die all over, without rightly meanin' to at all—just a kind o' bad habit ye've got yerself inter.' Gran'ther fell into a meditative silence for a moment. 'Jeroboam, he said that the evenin' before the battle of Lundy's Lane, and he got killed the next day. Some live, and some die; but folks that live all over die happy, anyhow! Now I tell you what's my motto, an' what I've lived to be eighty-eight on——' "

Professor Mallory stood up and, towering over the younger man, struck one hand into the other as he cried: "This was the motto he told me: 'Live while you live, and then die and be done with it!' "

QUESTIONS

1. Here is a story in a frame. The main story, about Gran'ther and Joey, is told within the framework of the conversation between Professor Mallory and the young assistant. The frame conversation is presented in the first nine paragraphs, then in brief paragraphs inserted in the main story, and finally in the last paragraph. Why would the Gran'ther-Joey story be less effective if it were told without the frame?

2. The title of the story comes from a statement Hamlet makes to his mother, the Queen, when he is blaming her for marrying his uncle:

> . . . for at your age
> The hey-day in the blood is tame.

Heyday means "the time of greatest health or vigor." Why does the author choose this expression from *Hamlet* as the title of the story?

3. What is the answer—almost a theme song—that Gran'ther gives to all those who worry about his health?

4. What does tying a knot in his empty sleeve symbolize for Gran'ther?

5. Why does Joey feel that the world is "changing into an infinitely larger place" with every word that Gran'ther says?

6. When Professor Mallory says on p. 271, ". . . gran'ther's six dollars and forty-three cents lasted like the widow's cruse of oil," he is referring to an Old Testament story in which a widow made for Elijah a little cake from the last of her provisions—a handful of meal in a barrel and a little oil in a cruse—and was told that for her good deed her reward would be that "the barrel of meal shall not waste, neither shall the cruse of oil fail." How does this allusion make clear the statement about Gran'ther's money?

7. Professor Mallory says, "Perhaps in heaven, but certainly not until then, shall I ever taste anything so ambrosial as that fried chicken and coffee ice-cream!" What is "ambrosial"?

8. What is the second thing that Professor Mallory says perhaps he will know again in heaven (p. 274)?

9. Is Gran'ther a type or an individual character?

10. What is the conflict in the Gran'ther-Joey story? Is there any similarity between this conflict and that in "The Elephant's Child"?

11. What is the theme?

THE STRUGGLE FOR FREEDOM

EVELINE
JAMES JOYCE

She sat at the window watching the evening invade the avenue. Her head was leaned against the window curtains and in her nostrils was the odour of dusty cretonne. She was tired.

Few people passed. The man out of the last house passed on his way home; she heard his footsteps clacking along the concrete pavement and afterwards crunching on the cinder path before the new red houses. One time there used to be a field there in which they used to play every evening with other people's children. Then a man from Belfast bought the field and built houses in it—not like their little brown houses but bright brick houses with shining roofs. The children of the avenue used to play together in that field—the Devines, the Waters, the Dunns, little Keogh the cripple, she and her brothers and sisters. Ernest, however, never played: he was toc grown up. Her father used often to hunt them in out of the field with his blackthorn stick; but usually little Keogh used to keep *nix* and call out when he saw her father coming. Still they seemed to have been rather happy then. Her father was not so bad then; and besides, her mother was alive. That was a long time ago; she and her brothers and sisters were all grown up; her mother was dead. Tizzie Dunn was dead, too, and the Waters had gone back to England. Everything changes. Now she was going to go away like the others, to leave her home.

Home! She looked round the room, reviewing all its familiar objects which she had dusted once a week for so many years, wondering where on earth all the dust came from. Perhaps she would never see again those familiar objects from which she had never dreamed of being divided And yet during all those years she had never found out the name of the priest whose yellowing photograph hung on the wall above the broken harmonium beside the coloured print of the promises made to Blessed Margaret Mary Alacoque. He had been a school friend of her father. Whenever he showed the photograph to a visitor her father used to pass it with a casual word:

"He is in Melbourne now."

She had consented to go away, to leave her home. Was that wise? She tried to weigh each side of the question. In her home anyway she had shelter and food; she had those whom she had known all her life about her. Of course she had to work hard, both in the house and at business. What would they say of her in the Stores when they found out that she had run away with a fellow? Say she was a fool, perhaps; and her place would be filled up by advertisement. Miss Gavan would be glad. She had always had an edge on her, especially whenever there were people listening.

"Miss Hill, don't you see these ladies are waiting?"

"Look lively, Miss Hill, please."

She would not cry many tears at leaving the Stores.

But in her new home, in a distant unknown country, it would not be like that. Then she would be married—she, Eveline. People would treat her with respect then. She would not be treated as her mother had been. Even now, though she was over nineteen, she sometimes felt herself in danger of her father's violence. She knew it was that that had given her the palpitations. When they were growing up he had never gone for her, like he used to go for Harry and Ernest, because she was a girl; but latterly he had begun to threaten her and say what he would do to her only for her dead mother's sake. And now she had nobody to protect her. Ernest was dead and Harry, who was in the church decorating business, was nearly always down somewhere in the country. Besides, the invariable squabble for money on Saturday nights had begun to weary her unspeakably. She always gave her entire wages—seven shillings—and Harry always sent up what he could but the trouble was to get any money from her father. He said she used to squander the money, that she had no head, that he wasn't going to give her his hard-earned money to throw about the streets, and much more, for he was usually fairly bad on Saturday night. In the end he would give her the money and ask her had she any intention of buying Sunday's dinner. Then she had to rush out as quickly as she could and do her marketing, holding her black leather purse tightly in her hand as she elbowed her way through the crowds and returning home late under her load of provisions. She had hard work to keep the house together and to see that the two young children who had been left to her charge went to school regularly and got their meals regularly. It was hard work—a hard life—but now that she was about to leave it she did not find it a wholly undesirable life.

She was about to explore another life with Frank. Frank was very kind, manly, open-hearted. She was to go away with him by the night-boat to be his wife and to live with him in Buenos Ayres where he had a home waiting for her. How well she remembered the first time she had seen him; he was lodging in a house on the main road where she used to visit. It seemed a few weeks ago. He was standing at the gate, his peaked cap pushed back on his head and his hair tumbled forward over a face of bronze. Then they had come to know each other. He used to meet her outside the Stores every evening and see her home. He took her to see *The Bohemian Girl* and she felt elated as she sat in an unaccustomed part of the theatre with him. He was awfully fond of music and sang a little. People knew that they were courting and, when he sang about the lass that loves a sailor, she always felt pleasantly confused. He used to call her Poppens out of fun. First of all it had been an excitement for her to have a fellow and then she had begun to like him. He had tales of distant countries. He had started as a deck boy at a pound a month on a ship of the Allan Line going out to Canada. He told her the names of the ships he had been on and the names of the different services. He had sailed through the Straits of Magellan and he told her stories of the terrible Patagonians. He had fallen on his feet in Buenos Ayres, he said, and had come over to the old country just for a holiday. Of course, her father had found out the affair and had forbidden her to have anything to say to him.

"I know these sailor chaps," he said.

One day he had quarrelled with Frank and after that she had to meet her lover secretly.

The evening deepened in the avenue. The white of two letters in her lap grew indistinct. One was to Harry; the other was to her father. Ernest had been her favourite but she liked Harry too. Her father was becoming old lately, she noticed; he would miss her. Sometimes he could be very nice. Not long before, when she had been laid up for a day, he had read her out a ghost story and made toast for her at the fire. Another day, when their mother was alive, they had all gone for a picnic to the Hill of Howth. She remembered her father putting on her mother's bonnet to make the children laugh.

Her time was running out but she continued to sit by the window, leaning her head against the window curtain, inhaling the odour of dusty cretonne. Down far in the avenue she could hear a street organ playing. She knew the air. Strange that it should come that very night to remind her of the promise to her mother, her promise to keep the home together as long as she could. She remembered the last night of her mother's illness; she was again in the close dark room at the other side of the hall and outside she heard a melancholy air of Italy. The organ-player had been ordered to go away and given sixpence. She remembered her father strutting back into the sickroom saying:

"Damned Italians! coming over here!"

As she mused the pitiful vision of her mother's life laid its spell on the very quick of her being—that life of commonplace sacrifices closing in final craziness. She trembled as she heard again her mother's voice saying constantly with foolish insistence:

"Derevaun Seraun! Derevaun Seraun!"

She stood up in a sudden impulse of terror. Escape! She must escape! Frank would save her. He would give her life, perhaps love, too. But she wanted to live. Why should she be unhappy? She had a right to happiness. Frank would take her in his arms, fold her in his arms. He would save her.

She stood among the swaying crowd in the station at the North Wall. He held her hand and she knew that he was speaking to her, saying something about the passage over and over again. The station was full of soldiers with brown baggages. Through the wide doors of the sheds she caught a glimpse of the black mass of the boat, lying in beside the quay wall, with illumined portholes. She answered nothing. She felt her cheek pale and cold and, out of a maze of distress, she prayed to God to direct her, to show her what was her duty. The boat blew a long mournful whistle into the mist. If she went, tomorrow she would be on the sea with Frank, steaming towards Buenos Ayres. Their passage had been booked. Could she still draw back after all he had done for her? Her distress awoke a nausea in her body and she kept moving her lips in silent fervent prayer.

A bell clanged upon her heart. She felt him seize her hand:

"Come!"

All the seas of the world tumbled about her heart. He was drawing her into them: he would drown her. She gripped with both hands at the iron railing.

"Come!"

No! No! No! It was impossible. Her hands clutched the iron in frenzy. Amid the seas she sent a cry of anguish.

"Eveline! Evvy!"

He rushed beyond the barrier and called to her to follow. He was shouted at to go on but he still called to her. She set her white face to him, passive, like a helpless animal. Her eyes gave him no sign of love or farewell or recognition.

QUESTIONS

1. Although a Dubliner by birth and education, James Joyce spent most of his life on the Continent and wrote critically of the moral and spiritual decay of Irish society. He said that he intended the collection of stories *Dubliners* to "betray the soul of that paralysis . . . which many consider a city" and that he intended the stories to give his countrymen "one good look at themselves." In other words, Joyce considered Dublin ("dear dirty Dublin" as he once called it) not a city but a living death, with all the citizens too "paralyzed" to do anything about the corruption in their city. How does "Eveline" fit into this theme of the paralysis of the citizens of Dublin?

2. From what point of view is the story told?

3. What is the conflict?

4. Generally, the more sense impressions an author gives, the more vivid his description will be. James Joyce, almost blind, was particularly aware of the sensations of sound, touch, and smell and was adept at portraying them in his stories. In the first five sentences of this story, which details appeal to the various senses?

5. What does the "odour of dusty cretonne" symbolize?

6. Why does the author choose Buenos Ayres (Buenos Aires) as the city to which Eveline plans to escape? The meaning of the Spanish name gives a clue.

7. What details throughout the story indicate the dusty drabness and monotony of Eveline's surroundings?

8. As do many people after making a decision, Eveline wonders whether she has made a wise choice; and sitting at the window she again weighs the merits of each side of the question. She does not, however, doubt that she will go: she has agreed to go, the plans have been made, her passage has been booked, and she has written the letters to her brother and father. As she remembers what has happened to her family and to her childhood friends, she thinks, "Everything changes." Why does she dwell on this idea?

9. The author says on p. 281, "Now she was going to go away like the others, to leave her home." And three paragraphs below, "She had consented to go away, to leave her home." Would not the first half of each sentence be sufficient? Why does Joyce add "to leave her home"?

10. Eveline went with Frank to see *The Bohemian Girl*, an opera by a Dublin-born composer, containing the familiar song:

> I dreamt that I dwelt in marble halls
> With vassals and serfs at my side,
> And of all who assembled within those walls
> That I was the hope and the pride.
>
> I had riches too great to count; could boast
> Of a high ancestral name,
> But I also dreamt, which pleased me most,
> That you loved me still the same.

Aside from the fact that it was written by a Dubliner, why does the author choose to have Eveline see this opera rather than some other?

11. As with most people, Eveline's thinking about her decision is not done logically. Her mind jumps from pro to con and back again as one idea suggests another. Show how her mind vacillates between wanting to leave and wanting to stay.

12. How does she happen to recall that once, when her mother was alive, her father had put on her mother's bonnet to make the children laugh?

13. What is the turning point in Eveline's thinking, that point at which her mind, whether she is conscious of it or not, moves toward staying at home rather than going?

14. Why does the author choose an Italian organ grinder to recall to Eveline the night of her mother's death?

15. Why does the memory of her mother's crazed words turn her mind again toward escape?

16. Note the number of references to evening or night: "watching the evening invade the avenue . . . used to play every evening . . . squabble for money on Saturday nights . . . usually fairly bad on Saturday night . . . returning home late . . . night-boat . . . meet her outside the Stores every evening . . . The evening deepened in the avenue. . . . Strange that it should come that very night . . . the last night of her mother's illness. . . ."

Rarely is day mentioned: "Another day . . . they had all gone for a picnic" and "if she went, tomorrow she would be on the sea with Frank."

Why do evening and night predominate?

17. Note the number of times brown and black are used: brown houses, blackthorn stick, black leather purse, brown baggages, black mass of the boat. Only once is white mentioned: "The white of two letters in her lap grew indistinct." What might that sentence symbolize?

18. Even at the boat Eveline is still vacillating ("Could she still draw back after all he had done for her?"). Yet her mind is really made up when she prays to God "to direct her, to show her what was her duty." Is there a difference between those two phrases?

19. As Eveline sees the "black mass of the boat" and hears its "long mournful whistle," she becomes frightened. She is not used to the sea and fears it: "All the seas of the world tumbled about her heart. He was drawing her into them: he would drown her." Thus she is afraid of the very thing that would save her. She knows the sea offers her escape and life, but she also fears that it might offer death. How does the sea, then, symbolize her indecision?

20. What is the real reason Eveline is too paralyzed to leave Dublin?

21. What does the iron railing that Eveline grasps symbolize?

22. The author piles up one contrast after another to underscore Eveline's two choices. List some of these contrasts.

23. What happens to Eveline in the last two sentences?

24. What is the theme?

FREEDOM'S A HARD-BOUGHT THING

STEPHEN VINCENT BENÉT

A long time ago, in times gone by, in slavery times, there was a man named Cue. I want you to think about him. I've got a reason.

He got born like the cotton in the boll or the rabbit in the pea patch. There wasn't any fine doings when he got born, but his mammy was glad to have him. Yes. He didn't get born in the Big House, or the overseer's house, or any place where the bearing was easy or the work light. No, Lord. He came out of his mammy in a field hand's cabin one sharp winter, and about the first thing he remembered was his mammy's face and the taste of a piece of bacon rind and the light and shine of the pitch-pine fire up the chimney. Well, now, he got born and there he was.

His daddy worked in the fields and his mammy worked in the fields when she wasn't bearing. They were slaves; they chopped the cotton and hoed the corn. They heard the horn blow before the light came and the horn blow that meant the day's work was done. His daddy was a strong man—strong in his back and his arms. The white folks called him Cuffee. His mammy was a good woman, yes, Lord. The white folks called her Sarah, and she was gentle with her hands and gentle with her voice. She had a voice like the river going by in the night, and at night when she wasn't too tired she'd sing songs to little Cue. Some had foreign words in them—African words. She couldn't remember what some of them meant, but they'd come to her down out of time.

Now, how am I going to describe and explain about that time when that time's gone? The white folks lived in the Big House and they had many to tend on them. Old Marster, he lived there like Pharaoh and Solomon, mighty splendid and fine. He had his flocks and his herds, his butler and his baker; his fields ran from the river to the woods and back again. He'd ride around the fields each day

288

on his big horse, Black Billy, just like thunder and lightning, and evenings he'd sit at his table and drink his wine. Man, that was a sight to see, with all the silver knives and the silver forks, the glass decanters, and the gentlemen and ladies from all over. It was a sight to see. When Cue was young, it seemed to him that Old Marster must own the whole world, right up to the edge of the sky. You can't blame him for thinking that.

There were things that changed on the plantation, but it didn't change. There were bad times and good times. There was the time young Marse Edward got bit by the snake, and the time Big Rambo ran away and they caught him with the dogs and brought him back. There was a swivel-eyed overseer that beat folks too much, and then there was Mr. Wade, and he wasn't so bad. There was hog-killing time and Christmas and springtime and summertime. Cue didn't wonder about it or why things happened that way; he didn't expect it to be different. A bee in a hive don't ask you how there come to be a hive in the beginning. Cue grew up strong; he grew up smart with his hands. They put him in the blacksmith shop to help Daddy Jake; he didn't like it, at first, because Daddy Jake was mighty cross-tempered. Then he got to like the work; he learned to forge iron and shape it; he learned to shoe a horse and tire a wagon wheel, and everything a blacksmith does. One time they let him shoe Black Billy, and he shod him light and tight and Old Marster praised him in front of Mr. Wade. He was strong; he was black as night; he was proud of his back and his arms.

Now, he might have stayed that way—yes, he might. He heard freedom talk, now and then, but he didn't pay much mind to it. He wasn't a talker or a preacher; he was Cue and he worked in the blacksmith shop. He didn't want to be a field hand, but he didn't want to be a house servant either. He'd rather be Cue than poor white trash or owned by poor white trash. That's the way he felt; I'm obliged to tell the truth about that way.

Then there was a sickness came and his mammy and his daddy died of it. Old Miss got the doctor for them, but they died just the same. After that, Cue felt lonesome.

He felt lonesome and troubled in his mind. He'd seen his daddy and his mammy put in the ground and new slaves come to take their cabin. He didn't repine about that, because he knew things had to be that way. But when he went to bed at night, in the loft over the black-smith shop, he'd keep thinking about his mammy and his daddy—how strong his daddy was and the songs that his mammy sang. They'd worked all their lives and had children, though he was the only one left, but the only place of their own they had was the place in the burying ground. And yet they'd been good and faithful servants, be-cause Old Marster said so, with his hat off, when he buried them. The Big House stayed, and the cotton and the corn, but Cue's mammy and daddy were gone like last year's crop. It made Cue wonder and trouble.

He began to take notice of things he'd never noticed. When the horn blew in the morning for the hands to go to the fields, he'd won-der who started blowing that horn, in the first place. It wasn't like thunder and lightning; somebody had started it. When he heard Old Marster say, when he was talking to a friend, "This damned epidemic! It's cost me eight prime field hands and the best-trained butler in the state. I'd rather have lost the Flyaway colt than old Isaac," Cue put that down in his mind and pondered it. Old Marster didn't mean it mean, and he'd sat up with Old Isaac all night before he died. But Isaac and Cue and the Flyaway colt, they all belonged to Old Marster and he owned them, hide and hair. He owned them, like money in his pockets. Well, Cue had known that all his life, but because he was troubled now, it gave him a queer feeling.

Well, now, he was shoeing a horse for young Marster Shepley one day, and he shod it light and tight. And when he was through, he made a stirrup for young Marster Shepley, and young Marster Shep-ley mounted and threw him a silver bit, with a laughing word. That shouldn't have bothered Cue, because gentlemen sometimes did that. And Old Marster wasn't mean; he didn't object. But all night Cue kept feeling the print of young Marster Shepley's heel in his hands. And yet he liked young Marster Shepley. He couldn't explain it at all.

Finally, Cue decided he must be conjured. He didn't know who had done it or why they'd done it. But he knew what he had to do. He had to go see Aunt Rachel.

Aunt Rachel was an old, old woman, and she lived in a cabin by herself, with her granddaughter, Sukey. She'd seen Old Marster's father and his father, and the tale went she'd seen George Washing-ton with his hair all white, and General Lafayette in his gold-plated suit of clothes that the King of France gave him to fight in. Some folks said she was a conjure and some folks said she wasn't, but everybody on the plantation treated her mighty respectful, because, if she put her eye on you, she mightn't take it off. Well, his mammy had been friends with Aunt Rachel, so Cue went to see her.

She was sitting alone in her cabin by the low light of a fire. There was a pot on the fire, and now and then you could hear it bubble and chunk, like a bullfrog chunking in the swamp, but that was the only sound. Cue made his obleegances to her and asked her about the misery in her back. Then he gave her a chicken he happened to bring along. It was a black rooster, and she seemed pleased to get it. She took it in her thin black hands and it fluttered and clucked a minute. So she drew a chalk line from its beak along a board, and then it stayed still and frozen. Well, Cue had seen that trick done before. But it was different, seeing it done in Aunt Rachel's cabin, with the big pot chunking on the fire. It made him feel uneasy and he jingled the bit in his pocket for company.

After a while, the old woman spoke. "Well, Son Cue," said she, "that's a fine young rooster you've brought me. What else did you bring me, Son Cue?"

"I brought you trouble," said Cue, in a husky voice, because that was all he could think of to say.

She nodded her head as if she'd expected that. "They mostly brings me trouble," she said. "They mostly brings trouble to Aunt Rachel. What kind of trouble, Son Cue? Man trouble or woman trouble?"

"It's my trouble," said Cue, and he told her the best way he could. When he'd finished, the pot on the fire gave a bubble and a croak, and the old woman took a long spoon and stirred it.

"Well, Son Cue, son of Cuffee, son of Shango," she said, "you've got a big trouble, for sure."

"Is it going to kill me dead?" said Cue.

"I can't tell you right about that," said Aunt Rachel. "I could give you lies and prescriptions. Maybe I would, to some folks. But your Granddaddy Shango was a powerful man. It took three men to put the irons on him, and I saw the irons break his heart. I won't lie to you, Son Cue. You've got a sickness."

"Is it a bad sickness?" said Cue.

"It's a sickness in your blood," said Aunt Rachel. "It's a sickness in your liver and your veins. Your daddy never had it that I knows of —he took after his mammy's side. But his daddy was a Corromantee, and they is bold and free, and you takes after him. It's the freedom sickness, Son Cue."

"The freedom sickness?" said Cue.

"The freedom sickness," said the old woman, and her little eyes glittered like sparks. "Some they break and some they tame down," she said, "and some is neither to be tamed or broken. Don't I know the signs and the sorrow—me, that come through the middle passage on the slavery ship and seen my folks scattered like sand? Ain't I seen it coming, Lord—O Lord, ain't I seen it coming?"

"What's coming?" said Cue.

"A darkness in the sky and a cloud with a sword in it," said the old woman, stirring the pot, "because they hold our people and they hold our people."

Cue began to tremble. "I don't want to get whipped," he said. "I never been whipped—not hard."

"They whipped your Granddaddy Shango till the blood ran twinkling down his back," said the old woman, "but some you can't break or tame."

"I don't want to be chased by dogs," said Cue. "I don't want to hear the dogs belling and the paterollers after me."

The old woman stirred the pot.

"Old Marster, he's a good marster," said Cue. "I don't want to do him no harm. I don't want no trouble or projecting to get me into trouble."

The old woman stirred the pot and stirred the pot.

"O God, I want to be free," said Cue. "I just ache and hone to be free. How I going to be free, Aunt Rachel?"

"There's a road that runs underground," said the old woman. "I never seen it, but I knows of it. There's a railroad train that runs, sparking and snorting, underground through the earth. At least that's what they tell me. But I wouldn't know for sure," and she looked at Cue.

Cue looked back at her bold enough, for he'd heard about the Underground Railroad himself—just mentions and whispers. But he knew there wasn't any use asking the old woman what she wouldn't tell.

"How I going to find that road, Aunt Rachel?" he said.

"You look at the rabbit in the brier and you see what he do," said the old woman. "You look at the owl in the woods and you see what he do. You look at the star in the sky and you see what she do. Then you come back and talk to me. Now I'm going to eat, because I'm hungry."

That was all the words she'd say to him that night; but when Cue went back to his loft, her words kept boiling around in his mind. All night he could hear that train of railroad cars, snorting and sparking underground through the earth. So, next morning, he ran away.

He didn't run far or fast. How could he? He'd never been more than twenty miles from the plantation in his life; he didn't know the roads or the ways. He ran off before the horn, and Mr. Wade caught him before sundown. Now, wasn't he a stupid man, that Cue?

When they brought him back, Mr. Wade let him off light, because he was a good boy and never run away before. All the same, he got ten, and ten laid over the ten. Yellow Joe, the head driver, laid them on. The first time the whip cut into him, it was just like a fire on Cue's skin, and he didn't see how he could stand it. Then he got to a place where he could.

After it was over, Aunt Rachel crope up to his loft and had her granddaughter, Sukey, put salve on his back. Sukey, she was sixteen, and golden-skinned and pretty as a peach on a peach tree. She worked in the Big House and he never expected her to do a thing like that.

"I'm mighty obliged," he said, though he kept thinking it was Aunt Rachel got him into trouble and he didn't feel as obliged as he might.

"Is that all you've got to say to me, Son Cue?" said Aunt Rachel, looking down at him. "I told you to watch three things. Did you watch them?"

"No'm," said Cue. "I run off in the woods just like I was a wild turkey. I won't never do that no more."

"You're right, Son Cue," said the old woman. "Freedom's a hard-bought thing. So, now you've been whipped, I reckon you'll give it up."

"I been whipped," said Cue, "but there's a road running underground. You told me so. I been whipped, but I ain't beaten."

"Now you're learning a thing to remember," said Aunt Rachel, and went away. But Sukey stayed behind for a while and cooked Cue's supper. He never expected her to do a thing like that, but he liked it when she did.

When his back got healed, they put him with the field gang for a while. But then there was blacksmith work that needed to be done and they put him back in the blacksmith shop. And things went on for a long time just the way they had before. But there was a difference in Cue. It was like he'd lived up till now with his ears and his eyes sealed over. And now he began to open his eyes and his ears.

He looked at the rabbit in the brier and he saw it could hide. He looked at the owl in the woods and he saw it went soft through the night. He looked at the star in the sky and he saw she pointed north. Then he began to figure.

He couldn't figure things fast, so he had to figure things slow. He figure the owl and the rabbit got wisdom the white folks don't know about. But he figure the white folks got wisdom he don't know about. They got reading and writing wisdom, and it seem mighty powerful. He ask Aunt Rachel if that's so, and she say it's so.

That's how come he learned to read and write. He ain't supposed to. But Sukey, she learned some of that wisdom, along with the young misses, and she teach him out of a little book she tote from the Big House. The little book, it's all about bats and rats and cats, and Cue figure whoever wrote it must be sort of touched in the head not to write about things folks would want to know, instead of all those trifling animals. But he put himself to it and he learn. It almost bust his head, but he learn. It's a proud day for him when he write his name, "Cue," in the dust with the end of a stick and Sukey tell him that's right.

Now he began to hear the first rumblings of that train running underground—that train that's the Underground Railroad. Oh, children, remember the names of Levi Coffin and John Hansen! Remember the Quaker saints that hid the fugitive! Remember the names of all those that helped set our people free!

There's a word dropped here and a word dropped there and a word that's passed around. Nobody know where the word come from or where it goes, but it's there. There's many a word spoken in the quarters that the Big House never hears about. There's a heap said in front of the fire that never flies up the chimney. There's a name you tell to the grapevine that the grapevine don't tell back.

There was a white man, one day, came by, selling maps and pictures. The quality folks, they looked at his maps and pictures and he talked with them mighty pleasant and respectful. But while Cue was tightening a bolt on his wagon, he dropped a word and a word. The word he said made that underground train come nearer.

Cue meet that man one night, all alone, in the woods. He's a quiet man with a thin face. He hold his life in his hands every day he walk about, but he don't make nothing of that. Cue's seen bold folks and bodacious folks, but it's the first time he's seen a man bold that way. It makes him proud to be a man. The man ask Cue questions and Cue give him answers. While he's seeing that man, Cue don't just think about himself any more. He think about all his people that's in trouble.

The man say something to him; he say, "No man own the earth. It's too big for one man." He say, "No man own another man; that's too big a thing too." Cue think about those words and ponder them. But when he gets back to his loft, the courage drains out of him and he sits on his straw tick, staring at the wall. That's the time the darkness comes to him and the shadow falls on him.

He aches and he hones for freedom, but he aches and he hones for Sukey too. And Long Ti's cabin is empty, and it's a good cabin. All he's got to do is to go to Old Marster and take Sukey with him. Old Marster don't approve to mix the field hand with the house servant, but Cue's different; Cue's a blacksmith. He can see the way Sukey would look, coming back to her in the evening. He can see the way she'd be in the morning before the horn. He can see all that. It ain't freedom, but it's what he's used to. And the other way's long and hard and lonesome and strange.

"O Lord, why you put this burden on a man like me?" say Cue. Then he listen a long time for the Lord to tell him, and it seem to him, at last, that he get an answer. The answer ain't in any words, but it's a feeling in his heart.

So when the time come and the plan ripe and they get to the boat on the river and they see there's one too many for the boat, Cue know the answer. He don't have to hear the quiet white man say, "There's one too many for the boat." He just pitch Sukey into it before he can think too hard. He don't say a word or a groan. He know it's that way and there's bound to be a reason for it. He stand on the bank in the dark and see the boat pull away, like Israel's children. Then he hear the shouts and the shot. He know what he's bound to do then, and the reason for it. He know it's the paterollers, and he show himself. When he get back to the plantation, he's worn and tired. But the paterollers, they've chased him, instead of the boat.

He creep by Aunt Rachel's cabin and he see the fire at her window. So he scratch at the door and go in. And there she is, sitting by the fire, all hunched up and little.

"You looks poorly, Son Cue," she say, when he come in, though she don't take her eye off the pot.

"I'm poorly, Aunt Rachel," he say. "I'm sick and sorry and distressed."

"What's the mud on your jeans, Son Cue?" she say, and the pot, it bubble and croak.

"That's the mud of the swamp where I hid from the paterollers," he say.

"What's the hole in your leg, Son Cue?" she say, and the pot, it croak and bubble.

"That's the hole from the shot they shot at me," say Cue. "The blood most nearly dried, but it make me lame. But Israel's children, they's safe."

"They's across the river?" say the old woman.

"They's across the river," say Cue. "They ain't room for no more in the boat. But Sukey, she's across."

"And what will you do now, Son Cue?" say the old woman. "For that was your chance and your time, and you give it up for another. And tomorrow morning, Mr. Wade, he'll see that hole in your leg and he'll ask questions. It's a heavy burden you've laid on yourself, Son Cue."

"It's a heavy burden," say Cue, "and I wish I was shut of it. I never asked to take no such burden. But freedom's a hard-bought thing."

The old woman stand up sudden, and for once she look straight and tall. "Now bless the Lord!" she say. "Bless the Lord and praise him! I come with my mammy in the slavery ship—I come through the middle passage. There ain't many that remember that, these days, or care about it. There ain't many that remember the red flag that witched us on board or how we used to be free. Many thousands gone, and the thousands of many thousands that lived and died in slavery. But I remember. I remember them all. Then they took me into the Big House—me that was a Mandingo and a witch woman—and the way I live in the Big House, that's between me and my Lord. If I done wrong, I done paid for it—I paid for it with weeping and sorrow. That's before Old Miss' time and I help raise up Old Miss. They sell my daughter to the South and my son to the West, but I raise up Old Miss and tend on her. I ain't going to repine of that. I count the hairs on Old Miss' head when she's young, and she turn to me, weak and helpless. And for that there'll be a kindness between me and the Big House—a kindness that folks will remember. But my children's children shall be free."

"You do this to me," say Cue, and he look at her, and he look dangerous. "You do this to me, old woman," he say, and his breath come harsh in his throat, and his hands twitch.

"Yes," she say, and look him straight in the eyes. "I do to you what I never even do for my own. I do it for your Granddaddy Shango, that never turn to me in the light of the fire. He turn to that soft Eboe woman, and I have to see it. He roar like a lion in the chains, and I have to see that. So, when you come, I try you and I test you, to see if you fit to follow after him. And because you fit to follow after him, I put freedom in your heart, Son Cue."

"I never going to be free," say Cue, and look at his hands. "I done broke all the rules. They bound to sell me now."

"You'll be sold and sold again," say the old woman. "You'll know the chains and the whip. I can't help that. You'll suffer for your people and with your people. But while one man's got freedom in his heart, his children bound to know the tale."

She put the lid on the pot and it stop bubbling.

"Now I come to the end of my road," she say, "but the tale don't stop there. The tale go backward to Africa and it go forward, like clouds and fire. It go, laughing and grieving forever, through the earth and the air and the waters—my people's tale."

Then she drop her hands in her lap and Cue creep out of the

cabin. He know then he's bound to be a witness, and it make him feel cold and hot. He know then he's bound to be a witness and tell that tale. O Lord, it's hard to be a witness, and Cue know that. But it help him in the days to come.

Now, when he get sold, that's when Cue feel the iron in his heart. Before that, and all his life, he despise bad servants and bad marsters. He live where the marster's good; he don't take much mind of other places. He's a slave, but he's Cue, the blacksmith, and Old Marster and Old Miss, they tend to him. Now he know the iron in his heart and what it's like to be a slave.

He know that on the rice fields in the hot sun. He know that, working all day for a handful of corn. He know the bad marsters and the cruel overseers. He know the bite of the whip and the gall of the iron on the ankle. Yes, Lord, he know tribulation. He know his own tribulation and the tribulation of his people. But all the time, somehow, he keep freedom in his heart. Freedom mighty hard to root out when it's in the heart.

He don't know the day or the year, and he forget, half the time, there ever was a gal named Sukey. All he don't forget is the noise of the train in his ears, the train snorting and sparking underground. He think about it at nights till he dream it carry him away. Then he wake up with the horn. He feel ready to die then, but he don't die. He live through the whip and the chain; he live through the iron and the fire. And finally he get away.

When he get away, he ain't like the Cue he used to be—not even back at Old Marster's place. He hide in the woods like a rabbit; he slip through the night like an owl. He go cold and hungry, but the star keep shining over him and he keep his eyes on the star. They set the dogs after him and he hear the dogs belling and yipping through the woods.

He's scared when he hear the dogs, but he ain't scared like he used to be. He ain't more scared than any man. He kill the big dog in the clearing—the big dog with the big voice—and he do it with his naked hands. He cross water three times after that to kill the scent, and he go on.

He got nothing to help him—no, Lord—but he got a star. The star shine in the sky and the star shine—the star point north with its shining. You put that star in the sky, O Lord; you put it for the prisoned and the humble. You put it there—you ain't never going to blink it out.

He hungry and he eat green corn and cowpeas. He thirsty and he drink swamp water. One time he lie two days in the swamp, too puny to get up on his feet, and he know they hunting around him. He think that's the end of Cue. But after two days he lift his head and his hand. He kill a snake with a stone, and after he's cut out the poison bag, he eat the snake to strengthen him, and go on.

He don't know what the day is when he come to the wide, cold river. The river yellow and foaming, and Cue can't swim. But he hide like a crawdad on the bank; he make himself a little raft with two logs. He know this time's the last time and he's obliged to drown. But he put out on the raft and it drift him to the freedom side. He mighty weak by then.

He mighty weak, but he careful. He know tales of Billy Shea, the slave catcher; he remember those tales. He slide into the town by night, like a shadow, like a ghost. He beg broken victuals at a door; the woman give them to him, but she look at him suspicious. He make up a tale to tell her, but he don't think she believe the tale. In the gutter he find a newspaper; he pick it up and look at the notices. There's a notice about a runaway man named Cue. He look at it and it make the heart beat in his breast.

He patient; he mighty careful. He leave that town behind. He got the name of another town, Cincinnati, and a man's name in that town. He don't know where it is; he have to ask his way, but he do it mighty careful. One time he ask a yellow man directions; he don't like the look on the yellow man's face. He remember Aunt Rachel; he tell the yellow man he conjure his liver out if the yellow man tell him wrong. Then the yellow man scared and tell him right. He don't hurt the yellow man; he don't blame him for not wanting trouble. But he make the yellow man change pants with him, because his pants mighty ragged.

He patient; he very careful. When he get to the place he been told about, he look all about that place. It's a big house; it don't look right. He creep around to the back—he creep and he crawl. He look in a window; he see white folks eating their supper. They just look like any white folks. He expect them to look different. He feel mighty bad. All the same, he rap at the window the way he been told.

They don't nobody pay attention and he just about to go away. Then the white man get up from the table and open the back door a crack. Cue breathe in the darkness.

"God bless the stranger the Lord sends us," say the white man in a low, clear voice, and Cue run to him and stumble, and the white man catch him. He look up and it's a white man, but he ain't like thunder and lightning.

He take Cue and wash his wounds and bind them up. He feed him and hide him under the floor of the house. He ask him his name and where he's from. Then he send him on. O Lord, remember thy tried servant, Asaph Brown! Remember his name!

They send him from there in a wagon, and he's hidden in the straw at the bottom. They send him from the next place in a closed cart with six others, and they can't say a word all night. One time a tollkeeper ask them what's in the wagon, and the driver say, "Southern calico," and the tollkeeper laugh. Cue always recollect that.

One time they get to big water—so big it look like the ocean. They cross that water in a boat; they get to the other side. When they get to the other side, they sing and pray, and white folks look on, curious. But Cue don't even feel happy; he just feel he want to sleep.

He sleep like he never sleep before—not for days and years. When he wake up, he wonder; he hardly recollect where he is. He lying in the loft of a barn. Ain't nobody around him. He get up and go out in the air. It's a fine sunny day.

He get up and go out. He say to himself, *I'm free,* but it don't take hold yet. He say to himself, *This is Canada and I'm free,* but it don't take hold. Then he start to walk down the street.

The first white man he meet on the street, he scrunch up in himself and start to run across the street. But the white man don't pay him any mind. Then he know.

He say to himself in his mind, *I'm free. My name's Cue—John H. Cue. I got a strong back and strong arms. I got freedom in my heart. I got a first name and a last name and a middle name. I never had them all before.*

He say to himself, *My name's Cue—John H. Cue. I got a name and a tale to tell. I got a hammer to swing. I got a tale to tell my peo-*

ple. I got recollection. I call my first son 'John Freedom Cue.' I call my first daughter 'Come-Out-of-the-Lion's-Mouth.'

Then he walk down the street, and he pass a blacksmith shop. The blacksmith, he's an old man and he lift the hammer heavy. Cue look in that shop and smile.

He pass on; he go his way. And soon enough he see a girl like a peach tree—a girl named Sukey—walking free down the street.

QUESTIONS

1. From the dialect it may be assumed that the narrator of this story is an elderly Negro. Is it possible to be more specific?

2. What is the conflict?

3. What causes Cue to begin thinking about freedom?

4. The style of writing brings this story very close to poetry; the soft, melodious rhythm and the beauty of the language are even more apparent when the story is read aloud. As in poetry, there are many figures of speech. Point out some particularly effective metaphors.

5. Another figure of speech is the analogy—a comparison used to make something clear. Find an analogy on p. 289 used to explain Cue's early attitude toward slavery.

6. An allusion is a reference to some historical or literary figure or event, frequently to something in mythology or the Bible. Point out two allusions to Bible stories.

7. Benét uses symbolism extensively in this story. The most important symbol is the pot that "bubbles and croaks" on Aunt Rachel's fire, symbolizing the boiling unrest of the slaves and their desire for freedom. When Cue first goes to Aunt Rachel's cabin and tells her about his wish to be free, "the pot on the fire gave a bubble and a croak, and the old woman took a long spoon and stirred it." As they talk, the old woman repeatedly stirs the pot, symbolizing her stirring up in Cue the desire for freedom. Later, after he has given up his chance for freedom by putting Sukey on the boat in his place, he again goes to Aunt Rachel and finds her "all hunched up and little," a symbol of despair. But as he comes in "she don't take her eye off the pot," and finally when Cue says, ". . . freedom's a hard-bought thing,"

indicating that he intends to struggle until he is free, Aunt Rachel stands up and "for once she look straight and tall," a symbol of assurance. At the end of that conversation she puts "the lid on the pot and it stop bubbling" because she knows that now she no longer needs to urge Cue on to freedom; her work is done.

What do the following symbols stand for?

. . . the horn blow before the light came and the horn blow that meant the day's work was done.

. . . the print of young Marster Shepley's heel in his hands.

It took three men to put the irons on him, and I saw the irons break his heart.

A darkness in the sky and a cloud with a sword in it. . . .

There's a railroad train that runs, sparking and snorting, underground through the earth.

. . . he got a star.

. . . and Cue run to him and stumble, and the white man catch him. . . . He take Cue and wash his wounds and bind them up.

The blacksmith, he's an old man and he lift the hammer heavy.

8. What statement of Cue's on p. 294 is a good characterization of him?

9. What is the theme of the story?

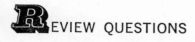# REVIEW QUESTIONS
THE EIGHT ELEMENTS OF THE SHORT STORY

1. List the conflicts in the various stories, indicating which ones are physical, which mental, and which stories have almost no conflict at all.

2. Which stories are told by an *all-knowing narrator*, by a *limited all-knowing narrator*, by a *character*, by an *observer*?

3. Which settings have an effect upon the characters and the actions?

4. Which characters are types and which individuals? Which characters change or gain a new insight by the end of the story?

5. Briefly state the themes of the stories.

6. Which stories have styles so distinctive that the author's writing would be easy to recognize elsewhere?

7. Which stories make especial use of irony?

8. Which stories use symbols extensively? How do they enrich the meaning of the stories?

1. List the conflicts in the various stories, indicating which ones are physical, which mental, and which stories have almost no conflict at all.

2. Which stories are told by an all-knowing narrator, by a limited all-knowing narrator, by a character, by an observer?

3. Which settings have an effect upon the characters and the action?

4. Which characters are round and which individual? Which characters change or gain a new insight by the end of the story?

5. Restate the themes of the stories.

6. Which stories have styles so distinctive that the author's writing could be easily recognized elsewhere?

7. Which stories show the skill of foreshadowing?

8. Which stories are subtle or exclusive? How do they enrich the meaning of the story?

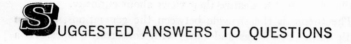# SUGGESTED ANSWERS TO QUESTIONS

THE ELEPHANT'S CHILD
RUDYARD KIPLING

1. The conflict is a simple one, with the Elephant's Child and his friends the Kolokolo Bird and the Bi-Coloured-Python-Rock-Snake on the one side, and the Crocodile and all the dear families on the other. It is the simplest pattern on which a story can be built—two sides pitted against each other, the hero's side at first threatened with defeat and then winning out in the end.

In trying to define the conflict in other stories, it may be helpful to recall this simplest conflict of all. Many of the others will be variations of it.

2. The story is told by an adult *all-knowing narrator,* who reports not only what happens but also what goes on in the minds of the characters (". . . till he trod on what he thought was a log of wood . . ."; "They were very glad to see him . . ."). The listener is a young child, as can be inferred from the many repetitions that appeal to children, from the explanations thrown in ("And by this he meant the Crocodile"), from the words mispronounced as the child might mispronounce them ("dretful," "hijjus," and " 'satiable curtiosity"), and of course from the frequent use of "O Best Beloved" in addressing the child. In this story more than in most, the reader is conscious of the listener (the child hearing a tale of how the elephant got its trunk) as well as of the teller (the adult having a good time playing with words and thinking of a broader meaning for the story).

3. The setting in Africa is an essential part of the story because the characters and action are so closely involved with the scene.

4. The characters are types. The Elephant's Child is just like most curious children, and the dear families are like most people in authority. No individual characteristics are given to make them differ-

ent from the rest of their kind. The Elephant's Child has not changed as a result of his conflict—except that he has a new nose—but his dear families have had to change their views about curiosity.

5. The theme is the struggle between the generations, between those with daring new ideas and those with conservative ones. To a child Kipling is saying that children sometimes know better than their parents, or that curiosity is a good rather than a bad thing. To an adult he is saying that people with new ideas and a bit of curiosity are often wiser than conservative people.

6. It is ironic that in the end the dear families profit from the curiosity of the Elephant's Child.

7. Several of Kipling's stylistic devices are readily seen:

(a) his repetition of words, phrases, and sentences for effect. The expression "great grey-green, greasy Limpopo River, all set about with fever trees" is repeated over and over almost like the refrain of a song.

(b) his choice of words for their sound effect ("mere-smear nose" and "schlooped up a schloop of mud").

(c) his use of alliteration (words starting with the same sound). He says "great grey-green" and then for no reason at all except to have another word beginning with a "gr" he adds "greasy." Sometimes the word he puts in simply for alliteration does not even make sense ("promiscuous parts"), but that is part of the fun he is having with words.

(d) his choice of words for humorous effect. He uses big words that a child would not understand but would not need to understand (". . . there was nothing left of the Equinoxes because the Precession had preceded according to precedent . . .").

(e) his particular kind of humor ("The rest of the time he picked up the melon rinds that he had dropped on his way to the Limpopo—for he was a Tidy Pachyderm").

THE LAMENT
ANTON CHEKHOV

1. Chekhov's description of Iona and his surroundings—quiet, motionless, blanketed with layers of snow—suggests isolation from other human beings and creates a mood of loneliness.

2. Iona is trying to make himself agreeable and hoping to start a conversation.

3. Perhaps it is not surprising that the first fare, an officer, is gruff and unresponsive. The second fares include a "humpback," who might be expected to have sympathy for another unfortunate, but no. The hall porter, unlike the fares, is going nowhere and has plenty of time to talk but tells Iona to move on. Finally, in the building beside the stables a cabdriver—a fellow worker with nothing to do but listen —hides his face and goes to sleep.

4. Iona's incompetence adds to the pathos of the situation. He says, "I am too old to drive—my son could have, not I. He was a first-rate cabdriver." A more competent or popular cabdriver might have had friends, might have found someone to listen.

5. When Iona is with people, his grief is less poignant; when he is alone, it is more than he can bear.

6. The conflict is between Iona's desperate need to unburden himself of his grief and the callous indifference of everyone toward his suffering. The conflict remains essentially unresolved because Iona can find no one to turn to for sympathy except his little horse, who cannot understand.

7. By telling the story in a matter-of-fact way without comment, the author keeps it from becoming too sentimental.

8. Chekhov is dealing here with one of his common themes— the individual isolated in a cold society. He is saying that man has a desperate need to communicate, to find someone who will listen to him, especially in time of grief, but that since human beings are generally indifferent to the sufferings of others, man seldom finds anyone to share his deepest emotions.

HOW BEAUTIFUL WITH SHOES
WILBUR DANIEL STEELE

1. Mare's yellow hair worn in a braid is important later in the story.

2. If the young man knew her, he would call her Mare instead of

Amarantha, as he has heard her mother call her. Also no one she knows talks about poetry.

3. She has dealt with enough ailing animals that she recognizes an ailing creature almost by instinct and knows that this must be the "loony" the men are hunting.

4. Her name and her braid of yellow hair remind him of the Lovelace poem.

5. Jewett had gone to college and taught in an academy.

6. This instability of mood prepares the reader for Jewett's later flitting from one scene to another of his past life and of his imaginary world. Each shift is made "in a wink's time."

7. Mare says, "Aw, no, don't talk so!" and Jewett is immediately reminded of Dr. Ryeworth's forbidding him to read the poem to his literature classes.

8. He thinks Mare is "Mary, Mother of God" and that he is Christ.

9. If the story had ended with the death of Jewett, it would then have been a simple adventure story, well told and interesting but hardly memorable. The theme of the story—what the author wants to say—is brought out not in what happens but in Mare's reflection on what happens.

10. Sometimes a frightening experience is more vivid in retrospect than it was when it actually took place.

11. Mare has had a glimpse of a way of life which she had not known existed, a glimpse of a world "more immense than she had ever known the world could be, and more beautiful."

12. She has never before known anyone who recites poetry nor anyone who finds pleasure in running. In her limited environment she would have no way of finding out whether it is only crazy folks who act that way.

13. To her the shoes have now become a symbol of poetry, gentleness, beauty.

14. It is ironic that the person who awakens Mare to a more sensitive view of life and love should be a lunatic.

15. The obvious conflict is between Mare and the madman, but the more meaningful conflict takes place later in Mare's mind as she weighs the uncouth behavior of Ruby Herter against the sensitive and tender manner of Humble Jewett. The conflict goes still further as she

struggles to decide whether others or only madmen speak and act as Jewett does. Neither conflict in her mind is solved.

16. Mare has been awakened to the beautiful in love; she is not the same person she was at the beginning of the story nor will she ever be again. It would be unrealistic, however, to imagine that she will marry anyone except Ruby or someone like him, but she will always retain an awareness of a world of beauty which has touched her briefly.

17. The theme might be stated in several ways: Sometimes a single incident will bring one an awareness of another way of life. Or, a most unlikely incident may lift a person out of a prosaic way of life. Or, even an insensitive person may have the capacity to appreciate beauty once he becomes aware of it.

THE KILLERS
ERNEST HEMINGWAY

1. Hemingway tells the story almost entirely through clipped, colloquial dialogue, using short concrete words and making every word count. The few sentences he uses to connect the bits of dialogue are short and simple and often strung together with "and's" as they might be in speech, rather than being carefully constructed with subordinate parts as they usually are in writing.

Such a simple, spare style points up the bare horror of the action and makes it as realistic and immediate as a newspaper report. Though simple, the style has a distinctive verbal and rhythmic pattern, which will be evident if the story is read aloud.

2. The story, told from an *observer* point of view as if it were a play, is a masterpiece of this kind of narration. The entire story takes place in three scenes—a long one in the lunchroom, a short one at Ole's (including the conversation with Mrs. Bell), and a final short one again in the lunchroom—with only a few sentences of transition. Hemingway once said that he wrote "the way it was." That is, he reports objectively what happens and makes no interpretation or explanation, thus putting the burden of moral judgment upon the reader. It is as if he is saying, "Here are the facts. Judge for yourself."

3. The clothes and the language of the two men suggest that they are from the underworld, and no doubt is left about it as they eat with their gloves on to avoid fingerprints and keep their eyes on the mirror to see who is coming through the door.

4. Since Henry's has been made over from a saloon into a lunch-room, the time is the prohibition era of the 1920's, when lawlessness was at a high.

5. Having the killers eat in the lunchroom suggests that this is just an ordinary day and that their job is nothing special but merely something to be done after dinner.

6. The killers' insolent insistence about the food suggests that they are aggressive, their low humor and abusive comments show their contempt for others, and the prolonged wrangling forebodes some impending conflict.

7. Max's bold casualness indicates such a prevalence of crime that he has no fear of being prevented from committing the murder or even of being punished for it afterward. Society seems somehow to be ignoring such deeds.

8. Nick has just had a horrifying experience in Ole's room, and Mrs. Bell's little speech brings him back suddenly to the ordinary world. The triviality of the statement, used as a contrast to the intense emotional dialogue in Ole's room, suggests that the rest of the world moves along in its normal humdrum fashion as if crime did not exist.

9. Sam represents those who are not concerned about evil so long as it does not touch their own lives: "I don't want any more of that" and "I don't even listen to it."

George represents those who assume that there will always be evil in the world and that not much can be done about it; he accepts it and is able to dismiss it from his mind: "It's a hell of a thing. . . . You better not think about it."

Nick is the one upon whom the impression is made, the one who discovers the terror of lawlessness and violence. For the first time he comes face to face with evil and is horrified not only by its presence in the world but by the world's acceptance of it. He is amazed that Ole accepts the code of the killers and will not try to do anything about it, but he is even more disturbed that Sam and George accept what has happened in a matter-of-fact way.

10. Although the story is partly Ole's—and Hemingway is saying something when Ole turns his face to the wall—the story is mainly about Nick and the impact upon him of his personal discovery of evil in the world. It is the final scene in the lunchroom that brings out the theme of the story.

11. The first conflict that comes to mind is that between the killers and Ole, and yet that is hardly the real conflict because both accept the same code of the underworld, and Ole does not try to escape the killers. Another conflict is that between good (represented by Sam, George, and Nick) and evil (represented by the killers and Ole). But again there is no real struggle between the two. The real conflict, which becomes apparent only in the last scene, is Nick's struggle between rejecting evil—as his principles tell him he must—and accepting it as part of life—the way Sam and George are doing. His moral principles make him feel a personal responsibility to fight against evil, but he also feels a disillusionment and a helplessness when he discovers how readily Sam and George accept evil as commonplace. The struggle in his mind is so upsetting that he would like to run away and forget it.

12. A minor theme is that there are certain things in life one can do nothing about, certain things one simply must accept (as Ole accepts his fate). The major theme is that a young person, brought face to face with evil for the first time, must decide whether to fight it as his principles demand or to accept it the way much of society seems to do.

A WORN PATH
EUDORA WELTY

1. What little conflict there is in this story is between Old Phoenix and the hazards of her journey. To her it is hardly a conflict at all. An ordinary traveler would have had a mental conflict about the wisdom of making the journey in the first place and a physical

conflict with the obstacles encountered. But Phoenix is so full of love for her grandson that she has no problem in deciding to go, and she is so at one with nature and so full of good will toward other human beings that nothing for her is a struggle. She can joyously make a journey that for anyone else would be a hardship; instead of fighting against the obstacles she lightheartedly overcomes them, her indomitable spirit triumphing over her aged body. It is this attitude toward life, this refusal to see anything as a struggle that the author is writing about and that leads to the meaning of the story.

2. The author calls the old woman Phoenix because, like the legendary bird, she is fabulously old and returns periodically to the same place. She has the red and gold coloring of the phoenix bird (". . . her head tied in a red rag . . . Her skin had a pattern all its own . . . but a golden color ran underneath, and the two knobs of her cheeks were illumined by a yellow burning under the dark"); and her cane "made a grave and persistent noise in the still air, that seemed meditative like the chirping of a solitary little bird." Also like the legendary bird that went back to the golden sun, Phoenix goes back to the doctor's office where she sees "the document that had been stamped with the gold seal and framed in the gold frame." This parallel with the Egyptian legend gives more depth of meaning to the story, suggesting that the periodic return of Phoenix to Natchez is like a ceremonial journey which brings her renewed life. At least the reader gets the impression that the serene and indomitable Phoenix is, as she said about her grandson, "going to last," and that she will take the worn path triumphantly again one day.

3. The setting and the action are inseparable, each small scene becoming an important part in the characterization of Old Phoenix. Also, the time of the year—the Christmas season—underscores the spirit of unselfish giving that Phoenix displays toward her grandchild.

4. Every incident on the journey adds something to the portrait of Old Phoenix: she is perfectly in harmony with nature, talking to the animals and to the bushes as if they were people ("Thorns, you doing your appointed work. Never want to let folks pass, no sir"); she has fantasies ("a little boy brought her a plate with a slice of marble-cake on it"); she can laugh at herself ("I ought to be shut up for good. My senses is gone"); she still has a great deal of life in her

("Dance, old scarecrow, while I dancing with you"); she is devoted to her grandson ("I bound to go to town, mister. The time come around"); she is clever enough to send the hunter away while she picks up the nickel ("Look! Look at that dog!"); she believes in God but does not let it deter her from picking up the coin ("God watching me the whole time"); she is not afraid of a gun ("I seen plenty go off closer by"); she recognizes no class or race distinctions ("I doesn't mind asking a nice lady to tie up my shoe"); her memory lapses at times ("It was my memory had left me. There I sat and forgot why I made my long trip"); she has never gone to school (". . . I was too old at the Surrender"); she has no selfish thoughts ("I going to the store and buy my child a little windmill they sells . . .").

5. Some of the most striking metaphors are the following:

> . . . moving a little from side to side in her steps, with the balanced heaviness and lightness of a pendulum in a grandfather clock.
> Her skin had a pattern all its own of numberless branching wrinkles and as though a whole little tree stood in the middle of her forehead . . . .
> Big dead trees, like black men with one arm . . .
> . . . the moss hung as white as lace from every limb.
> Over she went in the ditch, like a little puff of milkweed.
> Lying on my back like a June-bug waiting to be turned over . . .
> Her fingers slid down and along the ground under the piece of money with the grace and care they would have in lifting an egg from under a setting hen.

6. Setting, style of writing, and character can hardly be separated in this story. The vivid scenes of the countryside, the metaphorical language, and the simple but dignified character of Old Phoenix combine to give the story its warm appeal.

7. The author avoids pathos simply by making Old Phoenix a person who feels no self pity, a person who is so at peace with life that she needs no sympathy. And the humorous details prevent the story from becoming somber.

8. Perhaps the author is saying that it is possible for a person to be so full of love, so in tune with nature and man, so free of fear, that he is able to overcome obstacles that for others would be insurmountable.

BUTCHER BIRD
WALLACE STEGNER

1. The story takes place on the treeless, coulee-cut, wheat-growing prairie of Saskatchewan. The setting is important because the barren farmyard "without any green things around" leads to the conflict between the boy's parents. The weather too is important because the still, breathless, hot afternoon following two weeks of drought has an air of "tense and teeth-gritting expectancy" setting the stage for something to happen. The father, always affected by the weather, is grumpy as he awaits rain for his crop.

The homesteaders, the gramophone, and cranking the Ford set the time around 1915, although—except for these details—the story could take place today.

2. The events are presented by a *limited all-knowing narrator*—through the eyes, ears, and thoughts of the boy. This point of view adds intensity to the story by showing the parents' conflict through its disturbing effect upon the boy.

3. The father and mother are individuals with both good and bad qualities, as complicated as are people in real life.

4. The father is a practical, determined, hard-working homesteader, more skilled in farming and in taking care of a gun than his neighbor Mr. Garfield. But he is a negative person, saying "yes" only once in the story, and then rather grudgingly as he allows the boy to accept the gun. He repulses the Garfields' friendship, sneers at the lemonade, resents the others enjoying the gramophone, is contemptuous of Mr. Garfield's efforts to grow trees, feels jealous of his wife's liking the Garfields, criticizes Garfield for the tenderness and sensitivity that he himself lacks, reveals his provincialism by making fun of the English accent, refuses to let grass grow near the house, refuses to plow a wider fireguard (although he had spent two weeks digging his icehouse), refuses to take his wife on a trip for willows, and finally refuses her plea not to kill the small bird. In other words, he is unable

to say yes to the suggestions of others and "kills" their ideas, seemingly for no better reason than the fun of killing them. He always dominates and does not allow his wife to have her way in even so small a matter as having grass around the house.

5. The father's reticence about going to visit the Garfields, who are trying to make "the desert blossom like the rose," suggests that he resents his wife's aesthetic longings and fears their being strengthened. The visit confirms his fears, with his son being entranced by the gramophone and his wife by the willow trees. The Garfields have ideas and values that he does not possess and cannot even understand, and seeing his wife and son enthralled by them intensifies his feeling of inadequacy. To combat this feeling he must show his power—as he does throughout the story, especially in the last scene.

6. The mother is friendly, a bit provincial like her husband ("He can't help being English"), but willing to accept others as they are. Her longing for beauty ("I'd give almost anything to have some [trees] on our place") and for human qualities ("They're trying to make a home, not just a wheat crop") are a contrast to her husband's practicality and materialism; her eagerness to try to grow trees is a contrast to his negativism. She is an individual, however, with faults as well as good qualities: she cannot refrain at times from pressing a point, and she fails to understand the reason for her husband's negative nature—though she comes near to it when she rumples his hair and says, "The minute you get a gun in your hand you start feeling better." Perhaps she senses that the gun, a symbol of power, gives him a feeling of security that he does not ordinarily have. And when she says, "It's just a shame you weren't born fifty years sooner," she is recognizing his good frontiersman qualities. But instead of continuing to bolster his ego, she brings the conversation back to the one person he does not want to hear about—Mr. Garfield.

If she had been portrayed as never answering back or adding her bit to the quarrel, the reader might be led to pity her too much, and the story might have become too sentimental. As it is, her final barb lends realism and obviates any sentimentality.

7. The boy has learned to watch out for the moods of his father, tries not to listen to the quarreling, and makes an attempt to divert his parents' attention when quarrels occur. Not until the end of the story is he fully aware that their two views of life are diametrically opposite.

8. The surface conflict is between the father's insensitivity to beauty and the mother's aesthetic longings. More fundamentally, it is the desperate feeling of inadequacy of the father in the face of the confident idealism of the mother. The conflict is not resolved, the final scene serving only to establish more firmly the father's negative, domineering role and to strengthen the mother's idealism and longing for beauty.

9. Aware of his own insensitivity to beauty, the father is impelled to destroy beauty wherever he finds it, whether it be grass around the house or a sparrow on the ground. Just as he dismisses the Garfields' ideas with laughter and tells his wife to shut up about the willow trees, so he shoots the sparrow, a symbol of beauty. Also his feeling of inadequacy makes him sullenly reject anyone else's suggestions, and shooting the sparrow is his answer to Mr. Garfield and to his wife, both of whom speak against shooting harmless creatures.

10. With the characteristics the father has been given, it would be impossible for him to act otherwise than as he does. Any other ending would not be true to his character.

11. The boy is perhaps asking what he can do with the upsetting situation in which he finds himself, a situation in which beauty is being "killed."

12. In the moment when the sparrow is shot, the mother becomes aware, perhaps for the first time, that the father will never change, that he will always be domineering and "kill" her ideas. In this moment of insight she speaks the words which sum up her frustration, the cutting words which call her husband a butcher bird.

13. As has been pointed out, the gun is a symbol of the power the father covets, and the sparrow a symbol of beauty. The barren farmyard is symbolic of the life the mother leads, devoid of beauty, and the willow trees symbolize her aesthetic longings. The butcher bird, who kills for the fun of killing and impales his victims on thorns or on barbed wire, is a symbol of the father, who "kills" all beauty and sentiment.

14. Several themes are woven into this story. The author is saying that it is almost impossible for the materialist and the idealist to come to terms. He is also saying that a person who feels inadequate often compensates by being domineering. And finally he is saying that some-

times a single event may bring to a focus all the aspects of a conflict and give rise to an awareness of the enormity and finality of a situation.

THE SECRET LIFE OF WALTER MITTY
JAMES THURBER

1. Walter Mitty is frustrated by a domineering wife, bored with the trivial details of an unexciting existence, and made to feel inferior by traffic cops, parking-lot attendants, and grinning garagemen. It is not surprising that he dreams himself into exciting situations in which he is masterful and efficient.

2. For Mitty his daydreams *are* his real life. He has simply reversed the usual pattern and made his dream life dominant and his ordinary life unimportant.

3. The story is told through Mitty's eyes and daydreams. The conversations and dreams are so skillfully presented that the reader understands the characters without any comment from the narrator.

4. Passing the hospital turns Mitty into a doctor, hearing a newsboy shouting about a trial puts him in the witness stand, seeing a magazine article about bombing planes makes him the captain of one, and standing against the drugstore wall causes him to face a firing squad.

5. When in his daydream he says to the District Attorney, "You miserable cur!" he is suddenly reminded of the puppy biscuit his wife had told him to buy.

6. Offered a handkerchief to cover his eyes before his execution, he says with characteristic bravery, "To hell with the handkerchief."

7. The situation is always one of tense excitement with death in the offing, and Walter Mitty is always the hero—a commander who flies an eight-engined Navy hydroplane through a hurricane, a surgeon of international repute who performs a spectacular operation, a crack shot who can kill at three hundred feet with his left hand, a captain who flies a bomber alone into enemy territory, a man who bravely faces

a firing squad. Each time Mitty fearlessly takes command of the situation and displays his expertise.

8. The characters are types—Mr. Mitty is Everyman. They have not changed at the end of the story, and the reader is convinced that the next day Mr. Mitty will continue his daring exploits.

9. The author is poking fun at Mitty's inefficiency and his method of escape into grandiose and ludicrously impossible situations, but he is also sympathetic with him in his browbeaten role. The reader laughs at Mitty but loves him at the same time because in Mitty he sees himself.

10. The conflict between Mitty's prosaic, wife-dominated everyday life and his exciting life of daydreams is not solved—although the daydreaming has the last word, with the implication that it will continue to afford escape.

11. Thurber here presents a common human foible. He is saying that most people—and particularly people who feel frustrated, bored, inferior—find release from the unsatisfactory present by escaping into the land of daydreams.

THE CODE
RICHARD T. GILL

1. The real conflict is in the boy's mind—between his adherence to the code and the necessity of forsaking it to ease his dying father's mind. At the time, however, the boy does not even recognize the conflict, and not until two weeks later does he realize, in a moment of insight, what he might have said. Since the conflict can now never be resolved, the result is remorse.

2. The code is an understanding between the father and son that they are not dependent upon religion, that they can face life with courage and without comfort or support. Jack says on p. 188, ". . . our religion—our rejection of religion—was the deepest statement of the bond between us."

3. Jack expresses his unbending adherence to the code when he says:

As I saw it, a man ought to face life as it really is, on his own two feet, without a crutch, as my father did. . . . By the time I left home for college, I was so deeply committed to this view that I would have considered it a disloyalty to him, to myself, to the code we had lived by, to alter my position in the least.

4. The father is a lonely person (". . . at the cemetery he always stood slightly apart—a tall, lonely figure," and in the living room he is "sitting there silently, all alone . . ."); but more than that, when he says to Jack, "That's the worst part of it. There is just nothing I can say that will make it any better," he is confessing that there is a drawback to the path he has taken, that he has "no refuge, no comfort, no support."

5. The father has avoided emotion all his life. At the cemetery he once squeezed Jack around the shoulders and then immediately removed his arm and looked away. Therefore it is not surprising that Jack does not respond to his father's avowal of affection.

6. The father is pleading for his son's approval of his interest in religion, for some assurance that if he weakens in his adherence to their code it will not change anything between them.

7. All his life Jack has modeled himself after his father, who has been inflexibly committed to the code, and he now reacts as they both have reacted all their lives toward any suggestion of religion—with rigid disapproval. Although he knows that what he has said is not enough, yet he cannot on the spur of the moment bring himself to show the slightest deviation from his stand.

8. Since the importance of the code is so ingrained in Jack's character, it takes a long time before a moment of insight shows him that following the code rigidly was not the best thing to do.

9. There is no indication that Jack has changed his views; he is merely filled with remorse that he should have been so unfeeling as to put adherence to the code above his father's plea, that he could not unbend enough to meet a human need.

10. The author is saying that breaking a code of behavior to meet a human need may sometimes take greater wisdom and courage than rigidly adhering to it. Also, a knowledge of what one might have said or done often comes too late and brings with it only remorse.

THEN WE'LL SET IT RIGHT
ROBERT GORHAM DAVIS

1. If the story were merely about children playing war, then it would have no great impact except upon the parents of young children. The author, however, is telling a story about children in order to say something about adults and their attitudes toward war.

2. Both are important. The father is the one who is more fully characterized, the one upon whom the attention is focused both in the first and the last scene, the one to whom the title refers, and the one who will have to rethink his values because of the outcome of the story. The son, a little shadow of his father, is the center of the action.

3. The father's confidence that he can handle any problem and "set it right" makes the ending of the story more dramatic.

4. Just as the father confidently controls his son and gives reasons to justify his actions, so Laury confidently commands his little army and gives them reasons for everything he demands of them; just as the father says he can set things right, so Laury assures his soldiers, "We could fix it so it would be safe"; and just as the father uses the expression "I wonder what sort of soldier you are" to get his son to conform, so Laury uses the same words to make Ed get the gun.

5. Although there are slight struggles throughout the story— between father and son, between Laurence and Ed, between Ed and his conscience—none of these is the main conflict. Only at the end does it become evident that the conflict is between the romantic view of war and the reality. The father rationalizes war play by saying, "They have all that destructive energy that they can blow off by pretending to shoot each other. It gets it out of their system"; and he is proud that his son "organizes those boys. Sixteen kids showing up every day, to take his orders and like it." The mother too— although she is shocked by Laury's talk of "how to kill a man in the dark with a knife without making a sound"—laughs about the terms

her son uses and the books he reads. It is all psychologically sound play—until an accident forces reality upon them.

6. The resolution of the conflict—realism winning out over the romantic, rationalized view of war—brings out the theme: no amount of romanticizing or rationalizing, even in child's play, can obviate the realism of war.

But the theme goes beyond child's play. The author is really talking about adults and war. Just as good reasons are advanced for children playing at war, so adults advance good reasons for their wars. Just as Ed, the conscience of the little army, cannot stand up against majority pressure, so the conscience of mankind capitulates to popular opinion. And just as the play war is turned into reality by an accident, so adults "playing with war" might produce an accident that could annihilate mankind. In other words, man is playing a dangerous game that could have a tragic result beyond anyone's power to "set it right."

7. The theme might have a broader application also. In any area it is dangerous to assume that nothing could happen that could not be set to rights by those in command. Some things are irrevocable.

HOW MR. HOGAN ROBBED A BANK
JOHN STEINBECK

1. The Hogans are definitely type characters, with no particular characteristics which distinguish them from their neighbors. Except that Mr. Hogan robs a bank, he is just like hundreds of ordinary middleclass Americans—a trusted employee, a good husband and father, a good provider, a lodge member, the owner of an ordinary house on an ordinary street. Mrs. Hogan too is like hundreds of good American housewives, and the children are the ordinary nice children one would expect to find in a happy home. As type characters, the Hogans are typical of Americans in general. Perhaps Steinbeck wants to make the point that they act much the way all middleclass Americans act.

2. An *all-knowing narrator* tells the story almost entirely through the eyes and mind of Mr. Hogan, but he makes no judgments whatsoever about the action, thus putting the burden of moral judgment upon the reader.

3. Mr. Hogan has been a faithful employee for sixteen years; he is Master of the Lodge; he has at least a nodding acquaintance with the church since his wife goes to the Altar Guild; he believes in education, enterprise, and the solid middleclass virtues in general.

4. The term "sound venture" is one ordinarily associated with honest business investments rather than with robbing a bank.

5. The fact that something works does not necessarily mean that the thinking behind it is sound. It is reminiscent of the popular saying, "It's o.k. if you can get by with it."

6. Steinbeck, speaking through Mr. Hogan, is using verbal irony, saying just the opposite of what he thinks is true. Obviously, Steinbeck does not think robbing a bank is a sound venture nor that anything that "works" is necessarily all right.

7. It is ironic that such a "good" man as Mr. Hogan should commit such a gross crime and furthermore that he should fail to see anything morally wrong about it. Hiding the stolen money in the box with the Knight Templar's uniform is ironic because the lodge stands for the highest moral values. Similarly it is ironic that Mr. Hogan gives his son some of the stolen money as a reward for winning honorable mention in the "I Love America" contest, which praises American virtues.

8. Perhaps Mr. Hogan intends to show that robbing a bank is as simple as the exploits of Mickey Mouse. It is ironic that he uses the mask of such a good, wholesome, children's character, and it is also ironic that his robbery denies all the values his children are defending in the "I Love America" contest.

9. No motive is stated. It is just something Mr. Hogan plans to do as he might plan to take a trip to Bermuda, something he sees no reason for not doing if he wishes. Although he obviously wants the money, he is not in need of it since his wife has just received a small legacy that was used for luxuries for the children.

10. His "Anything come with it?" indicates a rather materialistic view.

11. Mrs. Hogan's saying "I can't wait to see their furniture" suggests a materialistic attitude toward a newcomer to the town.

12. The characters are in no way changed. His criminal act has had no effect whatsoever upon Mr. Hogan.

13. A slight suspense about the outcome of Mr. Hogan's plan keeps the reader interested, but there is no real conflict. Certainly Mr. Hogan had no struggle in deciding whether to commit the robbery, he has no real struggle in carrying out his plan, and there is no indication of any future struggle with the law. The real conflict which *should* have taken place—between Mr. Hogan and his conscience—does not exist. Perhaps this very lack of conflict leads to the theme of the story.

14. Steinbeck seems to be saying that Americans no longer recognize a conflict between right and wrong but think that anything is all right if they can get away with it. They have become materialistic and lost their sense of integrity.

15. Perhaps he is not saying that the average American would rob a bank, but he is suggesting something fairly close to it.

16. He may be thinking of such things as expense account padding, price fixing, income tax evasion—in other words, less open forms of robbing.

17. Steinbeck is ridiculing middleclass morality, which he thinks condones many forms of dishonesty.

18. The author gets his point across by shocking and amusing his readers; the story will be remembered longer than a sermon.

19. In each story the author has exaggerated a human fault or foible to bring it to the attention of the reader—the loss of the sense of right and wrong in this story, and the tendency to escape into daydreams in "The Secret Life of Walter Mitty."

THE OTHER SIDE OF THE HEDGE
E. M. FORSTER

1. Mixing time and place words indicates immediately that this is not a realistic story but a fantasy, probably with a symbolic meaning. The road seems to be measured not in miles but in years. The

travelers therefore are hurrying, without realizing it, toward the end of their years, the end of their lives.

2. The traveler's new, broader view of life includes beauty and vision.

3. Perhaps the rescuer's voice is a symbol of the ideas he "voices" —young and fresh ideas, unlike the striving ideas of the road.

4. Progress, getting somewhere, is of paramount importance on the road.

5. He has become so used to competing, trying to pass any companion, that he finds it difficult to walk normally.

6. A pedometer ordinarily measures the miles one walks, but on the road it measures years. At any rate, machines do not work on the other side of the hedge. Perhaps the author is questioning the necessity and importance of machines.

7. On the road there is no view, no beauty, no leisure, no brotherhood, but there is great purpose, competition, a fast pace, and a sense of duty in getting ahead as fast as possible. On the other side of the hedge everything is completely the opposite.

So imbued is the traveler with the importance of progress that he cannot accept the leisurely life on the other side of the hedge. He cannot understand, for example, how a runner could be running for the sheer joy of running and not for competition.

8. Walking symbolizes ambition, the desire for progress. Humanity was first seized with the desire to walk when men began to strive for progress instead of quietly enjoying life.

9. A maze is an intricate network of winding pathways that may end close to where it started. The traveler will not believe his road is a maze because he has spent his life believing that it leads somewhere, although he is not sure where.

10. When he had stopped to rest on the road, Miss Dimbleby had swept past him, exhorting him to persevere; therefore she is the last person he would expect to leave the competition of the road.

11. People may at any time give up the competitive life for a peaceful life of happiness. They may change when they are making great progress in the world, when they are failing, or when they are afraid of dying.

12. Most people live the strenuous life; only a few at a time

discover the values of living on the other side of the hedge—although all mankind was meant to enjoy life and live in brotherhood.

13. He fears that eating food might somehow cast the spell of the other side of the hedge upon him. And the flowers he discards as of no value in getting ahead.

14. The first gate "as white as ivory" opens outward. "It is through this gate that humanity went out countless ages ago, when it was first seized with the desire to walk." The second gate, half transparent like horn, opens inward, and ". . . through this gate humanity—all that is left of it—will come in to us."

15. Those who go out through the ivory gate onto the road find that their dreams of progress lead nowhere and are not fulfilled, while those coming into the other side of the hedge through the gate of horn find that their dreams of happiness come true.

16. He has learned enough of the life on the other side of the hedge to begin to doubt the value of "progress" on the road.

17. He has for so long lived a life of competition and grabbing that he cannot realize such actions are not necessary.

18. If people have not learned to come through to the other side of the hedge and live a life of peace before they get old, they are bound to do so then because they can no longer compete.

19. The traveler recognizes his own brother whom he had left "by the roadside a year or two round the corner," but he also recognizes that every man is his brother. One of the recurring themes in Forster's writings is the importance of the brotherhood of man.

20. Some of the symbols with their possible meanings are:

the traveler—mankind journeying through life
the road—the competitive life
walking—ambition
the pedometer—machines in general
the things scraped off in the hedge—worries, possessions
falling into the moat—baptism into a new life, regeneration
the old man—that portion of mankind who know true values
the runner—the enjoyment of living
Miss Eliza Dimbleby—useless pursuit of scientific knowledge and progress
the other side of the hedge—the life of simplicity, happiness, brotherhood

21. The conflict is between the competitive life of progress on the road and the leisurely life of brotherhood on the other side of the

hedge. The traveler is won over to the life on the other side of the hedge.

22. The life on the road is measured by time, whereas life on the other side of the hedge is measured by value. The latter, says Forster, is the life that will save the human race.

23. The author is saying that mankind is too much concerned with machines, competition, and progress, and has forgotten about the real values—the enjoyment of simple living and the happiness of brotherhood. Forster would probably agree with Professor Carl L. Becker, who says: "If we look back a hundred years, it is obvious that there has been progress in the mastery of physical forces. If we look back two thousand years, it is uncertain whether there has been much if any progress in intelligence and the art of living." *

EVELINE
JAMES JOYCE

1. Eveline is too emotionally paralyzed to move from her dusty home in Dublin to the freedom and freshness of a foreign land.

2. The story is told by a *limited all-knowing narrator*, with all the incidents seen through the eyes of Eveline. Except for the few sentences which tell that she is sitting by the window, that she stands up in a sudden impulse of terror, that she stands among the crowd in the station, and that she does not go with Frank, the entire story is an account of what goes on in Eveline's mind.

3. The conflict is entirely within Eveline's mind, between the forces drawing her toward escape to Buenos Aires and the forces compelling her to stay at home.

4. The author appeals to the sense of sight ("watching the evening invade the avenue" and "the new red houses"); the sense of touch ("Her head was leaned against the window curtains"); the sense of smell ("the odour of dusty cretonne"); and the sense of

* "Progress," in *Encyclopedia of the Social Sciences*, ed. E. R. A. Seligman (New York: Macmillan, 1938).

hearing ("his footsteps clacking along the concrete pavement and afterwards crunching on the cinder path").

5. The "odour of dusty cretonne" is a symbol of the kind of life Eveline leads—drab, colorless, unpleasant, deathlike. Dust is often a symbol of death, as in the phrase "dust to dust" in funeral services.

6. Buenos Aires is Spanish for "good air," exactly the opposite of the dusty air of Eveline's present life.

7. All the details of her surroundings speak of dusty drabness and monotony: ". . . the odour of dusty cretonne . . . Few people passed. . . . wondering where on earth all the dust came from . . . yellowing photograph . . . broken harmonium . . . close dark room . . ."

8. She is trying to convince herself that change is acceptable, that her going away is part of the normal pattern of life, but actually it is the idea of change that she cannot face.

9. "Going away" and "leaving her home" are two different things to Eveline. The idea of going away to Buenos Aires is not difficult for her to face; the idea of leaving her home is.

10. The marble halls of *The Bohemian Girl* are in sharp contrast with the dusty brown house that Eveline lives in and are a symbol of the life she hopes to find in Buenos Aires.

11. Her mind vacillates between wanting to leave and wanting to stay: she had been rather happy in childhood . . . in her home she has shelter and food, familiar objects, and "those whom she had known all her life about her" . . . she does not mind leaving her job . . . she will be respected in her new home . . . she fears her father and is weary of the squabble over money . . . her life is hard and yet not "wholly undesirable" . . . Frank is kind and open-hearted . . . her father is becoming old and will miss her . . . once he read to her and made toast for her.

12. The occasions when her father had been pleasant were so few that the incident of the bonnet has stayed in Eveline's memory.

13. The turning point in Eveline's thinking comes when she hears a street organ playing a familiar air and she is reminded of the time she had heard it before, the night of her mother's death when she had promised to keep the home together.

14. Italy suggests a foreign land of happiness, the opposite of the life of desperation she is living with her father. The song of the

organ grinder is a call to escape to a happier life and at the same time a reminder of her promise to her mother.

15. One editor suggests that the meaning of the words "Derevaun Seraun! Derevaun Seraun!" which the mother repeats before her death, may be corrupt Gaelic for "the end of pleasure is pain." Whatever the meaning of the words, the memory of them and of her mother's life of sacrifice ending in final insanity causes Eveline to have a sudden impulse of terror, a desire to escape—her promise to her mother for the moment forgotten.

16. The emphasis on evening and night foreshadows the outcome of the story—Eveline's choosing dark Dublin rather than a bright future in a foreign land.

17. Just as the white letters in her lap announcing her leaving Dublin are growing indistinct, so her determination to leave is growing less certain.

18. The phrase "to direct her" asks for direction; the second phrase, "to show her what was her duty," merely asks for reinforcement of her decision to stay with her duty.

19. The sea, standing for both life and death, is a symbol of her dilemma—life in Buenos Aires or death in Dublin.

20. She has been so conditioned by her past life, so warped by her mean surroundings, that she is unable to choose voluntarily. The choice seems already to have been made for her by all the experiences that have made her the person she is, a forlorn soul rooted to her surroundings.

21. The iron railing symbolizes a cage, a trap that will not let her escape Dublin. Trapped and immobilized by her past experiences, she grasps the bars and cannot move.

22. Some of the contrasts are:

good air of Buenos Aires—dusty Dublin
happy marriage—dreary spinster life
marble halls of *Bohemian Girl*—dusty brown house in Dublin
kind, manly, open-hearted Frank—brutal father
organ grinder calling her to a happier land—organ grinder reminding her
                                            of her promise to her mother
sea offering her escape and life—sea making her fear death

23. She has become paralyzed with fear and indecision and is as unable to move as a terrorized animal. The author is saying that Irish paralysis has frustrated her bold plan.

24. James Joyce has given here a little segment of life, a glimpse of a soul torn by indecision. He seems to be saying that no matter how much one wants to escape an impossible situation, the actual leaving is often too difficult to bear. He is also saying that often a person's previous life has so conditioned him that he is unable to make a free choice—his decision is determined by his past.

*B*IOGRAPHICAL NOTES

SHERWOOD ANDERSON was born in 1876 in Camden, Ohio. The son of a saddle and harness dealer, he finished his formal education before he was fourteen, and after serving in the Spanish-American War became the manager of a paint factory and then an advertising copywriter. Not until he was nearly forty did he devote himself entirely to writing. His first novels were not successful, but in 1919 *Winesburg, Ohio,* a collection of stories about people in a small town, brought him public recognition. Although he published twelve novels and various other writings, it is for the short stories in *Winesburg, Ohio* and *The Triumph of the Egg* that he is best known. He died in 1941.

STEPHEN VINCENT BENÉT was born in 1898 in Bethlehem, Pennsylvania, and began writing when he was twelve years old. He is best known for his long poem about the Civil War, *John Brown's Body,* which won in 1929 the first of his two Pulitzer Prizes for poetry. The second was awarded posthumously in 1944 for *Western Star.* His most popular story, "The Devil and Daniel Webster," for which he received the O. Henry Memorial Award, has been made into a movie and an opera. He died in 1943.

ANTON CHEKHOV was born in Russia in 1860, the son of a grocer who had been a serf. Although he took a degree in medicine at the University of Moscow, he practiced only a year and spent the rest of his life writing. He is recognized as perhaps the greatest Russian short story writer. His actionless plots and impressionistic style have had great influence on the form of the modern short story. His themes of isolation, lack of communication, and ineffectiveness of action have also influenced Existentialist writers. He became associated with the Moscow Art Theater and contributed a number of plays, the best known being *Uncle Vanya* and *The Cherry Orchard.* He died of tuberculosis at the age of forty-four.

ROBERT GORHAM DAVIS was born in Cambridge, Massachusetts, in 1908 and was educated at Harvard. He has taught at Harvard, Smith, and various foreign universities, and has been Professor of English at Columbia University since 1958. In 1942 one of his short stories appeared in the O. Henry prize collection, and his essays have been published in *Partisan Review, Commentary,* and *American Scholar.* He is also the editor of a book on the short story, *Ten Modern Masters.*

DOROTHY CANFIELD FISHER was born in Kansas in 1879. At the age of ten she attended school in Paris for a year and later received her Ph.D. in French from Columbia. She was married in 1907, and she and her husband spent three years in France during the first world war. After 1923 most of her life was spent in Vermont, where her Canfield ancestors had pioneered. There she wrote about New Englanders as she had previously written about French peasants and Middlewesterners. The best known of her books are a novel, *The Bent Twig,* and a collection of short stories, *Hillsboro People.* She died in 1958.

E. M. FORSTER was born in 1879 in England and was educated at Cambridge. He is known primarily as a novelist and is regarded as one of the major writers of the twentieth century. Two trips to India provided him with material for his most famous novel, *A Passage to India* —a story of British and Indian character—which was published in 1924. He has also written essays, biography, criticism, and two collections of short stories, *The Celestial Omnibus* and *The Eternal Moment.*

RICHARD T. GILL was born in 1927 in Long Branch, New Jersey. He received his A.B. from Harvard and did further work at Oxford. He first became interested in writing while working for his Ph.D. in Economics at Harvard and published several stories in *The Atlantic* and *The New Yorker.* He is now master of Leverett House and a Lecturer in Economics at Harvard.

ERNEST HEMINGWAY was born in 1899 in Oak Park, Illinois. During World War I he served in an American ambulance unit in the Italian army and was seriously wounded. After the war he became a newspaper correspondent in Paris, and later covered the Spanish Civil War. His experiences provided material for his novels *A Farewell to Arms, The Sun Also Rises,* and *For Whom the Bell Tolls.* In World War II he volunteered for anti-submarine patrol duty in Cuban waters and then served as a correspondent in France and Germany. In 1954 he was awarded the Nobel Prize in literature, with a citation reading, "For his powerful, style-forming mastery of the art of modern narration . . . ." He died in 1961.

JAMES JOYCE was born in 1882 in Dublin, and although he left Ireland in 1904 to spend the rest of his life on the Continent, Ireland is the setting for almost all of his works. During his first year away from Dublin he wrote most of the fifteen stories in *Dubliners,* stories lacking in action but portraying human emotions with great intensity. Although impending blindness and difficulty in getting his work published made his literary life a constant struggle, he continued writing and is today rated by some critics as one of the greatest writers of his age. His best known works are the autobiographical sketch *A Portrait of the Artist as a Young Man* and the stream of consciousness novel *Ulysses,* which describes a single day in Dublin. He died in 1941 in Zurich.

RUDYARD KIPLING was born in 1865 in Bombay, India. At six he was sent to England, returning to India in 1883 to begin a career in journalism. He returned to England in 1889. In 1892 he married an American girl and came with her to Vermont, where they lived for four years. The rest of his life was spent primarily in England. Some of his best known works are *Plain Tales from the Hills, The Jungle Book, Captains Courageous, Kim,* and *Just So Stories.* In 1907 he received the Nobel Prize in literature. He died in 1936.

JAMES MCCONKEY was born in Lakewood, Ohio, in 1921. After serving in World War II he took his Ph.D. at the University of Iowa. Since 1961 he has been an Associate Professor of English at Cornell University and has done critical writing in the field of literature, *The Novels of E. M. Forster* being his best known work. His short stories have appeared in *The Atlantic, Yale Review, Perspective, The New Yorker,* and *Western Review.*

LOUISA NEWLIN was born in Philadelphia in 1936. She was graduated in 1960 from Radcliffe College, where she studied creative writing under Archibald MacLeish. In 1965 her story "Our Last Day in Venice" won second place in the annual Atlantic Firsts awards for stories by unestablished writers making their first appearance in *The*

Atlantic. Mrs. Newlin has traveled extensively and lived for a time in Hawaii and Paris. Currently, she, her husband—who is in the U.S. Foreign Service—and their three children live in Guatemala.

LUIGI PIRANDELLO was born in 1867 in Sicily but lived most of his life in Rome, where he was a professor of Italian literature in a girls' school. Finding his career as a teacher uncongenial, he turned to writing and produced forty plays, some 300 stories, several collections of poetry, and seven novels. He is best known for his play *Six Characters in Search of an Author,* published in 1921. In 1934 he was awarded the Nobel Prize in literature. He died in 1936.

KATHERINE ANNE PORTER, a descendant of Daniel Boone, was born at Indian Creek, Texas, in 1890. She wrote stories for many years before her first collection *Flowering Judas,* published in 1930, brought her recognition. Two other books of short fiction, *Pale Horse, Pale Rider* and *The Leaning Tower,* were published before her long-awaited novel *Ship of Fools* appeared in 1962. She has taught at a number of universities including Stanford, Virginia, and Michigan.

J. F. POWERS was born in Jacksonville, Illinois, in 1917 and received his high school education under Franciscan friars. From his observation of them he has created a number of stories concerning the private lives and consciences of the clergy. His collection *Prince of Darkness, and Other Stories,* published in 1947, is the book for which he is best known. In 1962 he published his first novel, *Morte d'Urban,* concerning a priest's struggle with the world. He has taught writing courses at several universities and was writer-in-residence at Smith College in 1965-66.

MARJORIE KINNAN RAWLINGS was born in Washington, D.C., in 1896. After graduating from the University of Wisconsin she did newspaper work for ten years, then left the north and went to live in isolated Cross Creek, Florida. This back country of Florida furnished the setting for many of her writings, the best known being *The Yearling,* which won the Pulitzer Prize for fiction in 1939. She died in 1953.

WILBUR DANIEL STEELE was born at Greensboro, North Carolina, in 1886 and grew up in Denver. After graduation from the University of

Denver, he decided to become a painter and first began writing while a member of the artists' colony in Provincetown, Massachusetts. He wrote eight novels but is best known for his short stories, four of which received the O. Henry Memorial Award. The story in this collection, "How Beautiful with Shoes," has also been made into a play.

WALLACE STEGNER was born near Lake Mills, Iowa, in 1909. His family traveled widely in the Great Plains States and the Pacific Northwest. He graduated from high school and college in Salt Lake City, Utah. After graduate work at California and Iowa, he taught at a number of universities and since 1947 has been Director of the Creative Writing Center at Stanford University. His writings include *Remembering Laughter, The Big Rock Candy Mountain, The Women on the Wall,* and *Wolf Willow.*

JOHN STEINBECK was born in 1902 in Salinas, California, and has made Monterey County the scene of much of his writing. He studied at Stanford University but left in 1925 without a degree. He worked as a reporter, hod carrier, painter, laboratory assistant, ranch hand, and fruit picker while he wrote his first novels. In 1940 his *Grapes of Wrath,* a novel about itinerant farm laborers, won the Pulitzer Prize. Other works include *Tortilla Flat, Of Mice and Men,* and *Travels with Charley.* In 1962 he was awarded the Nobel Prize in literature, special mention being made of his novel *The Winter of our Discontent,* an indictment of declining American values. It is an elaboration of the story in this collection, "How Mr. Hogan Robbed a Bank."

JAMES THURBER, humorist and satirist, was born in 1894 in Columbus, Ohio, and was educated at Ohio State University. For thirty-five years he was associated with *The New Yorker,* to which he contributed cartoons, sketches, and stories, satirizing various aspects of American life. Among his best known books are *My Life and Hard Times, Fables for Our Times, My World—and Welcome to It!* and *The Thurber Carnival,* a collection of his best work, which has been dramatized. He died in 1961.

EUDORA WELTY was born in 1909 in Jackson, Mississippi, where she still lives. One of the most distinguished Southern writers, she has been called "perhaps the most notable regionalist today." She has published four volumes of short stories—*A Curtain of Green, The Wide Net,*

The Golden Apples, and *The Bride of Innisfallen.* In 1955 her novel *The Ponder Heart* was awarded the Howells Medal, given every five years by the American Academy of Arts and Letters, for "the most distinguished work of American fiction."

JESSAMYN WEST was born in 1907 in Indiana and grew up in California, where she graduated from Whittier College. She began writing while bedridden as a result of tuberculosis. She is best known for *The Friendly Persuasion,* a novel about an Indiana Quaker family during the Civil War. Among her other writings are *Cress Delahanty,* a series of stories about a sensitive teen-age girl, and *Love, Death and the Ladies' Drill Team,* a collection of short stories. She has taught writing at a number of universities.

P
G
H
I
J
4
5